No Further Questions

C. W. Arnold

No Further Questions

Published by Kindle Direct Publishing

Printed in the United States of America

ISBN-13: 9781090257895

PROLOGUE

The television was still on and both doors to the second floor balcony were swung full open. Styx, his big black cat, sat on the wooden bowl that lay upturned on the coffee table. Popcorn was strewn on the floor between the couch and the coffee table. Billy tried to fluff up the volume of *Moore's Federal Practice* that he had used for a pillow. When he reached behind his head to adjust the book, his bare back stuck to the leather couch. He squinted in an effort to see the clock on the bookshelf of the walnut paneled library. No luck. Without getting up he couldn't tell what time it was. Styx caterwauled. The unfamiliar sound of morning birds filled the room and the pale washed-out morning light crept through the cracks in the Venetian blinds that covered the glass wall. *It had to be early. Saturday.* Or, at least he hoped it was. Each heartbeat produced a dull pain. Each thump of pulse ricocheted in his head like a golf ball bouncing in a tin pail.

"God damn it," he whispered. "That's it. Never again."

Styx stepped onto Billy's chest and nuzzled his nose against Billy's mouth. He sniffed at the foul smell of stale beer and popcorn. He started to purr and then gently put his paw on Billy's lips. Billy brushed him aside and sat up. Nothing in the room came into focus. Not the television, not the fireplace, not the volumes of books, not the furniture, not his paper-strewn desk, not his open briefcase on the floor, not his computer screen that displayed a partially complete court pleading, not the lead glass gun cabinet next to the fireplace, not the double doors to the wet bar, not anything. Billy swung his feet onto the floor and kicked over a half-full bottle of beer.

"Shit."

Styx flagged his full black tail and walked out of the library, down the stairs on his way to his empty food dish and the rest of the seared ahi tuna left on the dining room table down on the first floor.

CHAPTER ONE

"Look here man, I didn' hire no dam' lawyer. Plus you shaw 'nuf don' look like no dam' lawyer that I ever seen." The inmate gathered his six-foot-four-inch frame from the steel bench as the jailer locked the door to the holdover cell behind Billy.

The Montgomery County jail holdover cell is where lawyers consult with their clients who haven't been released on bail bond. It's located on the same floor as the main reception room. More as a reason to keep the inmates occupied than a need for maintenance, the holdover cell had been painted and repainted so many times that a chipped spot looked like the growth rings of an old tree, a record of the occupants who had nothing more in common than crime and incarceration. The most recent coat left the floor and walls a shiny battleship grey and the cell bars a deceptively placid pastel blue.

"That's right. You didn't have to. The court appointed me to—"

"Court! What 'chu mean court? That was a judge. Ain't no dam' court. Only one talkin' to me was that judge." Johnson sat back down on the bench.

"Well, that's right. The judge is actually the one who appoints an attorney to represent the—"

1

"Attorney. What 'chu talkin' 'bout? I didn' hire no dam' attorney neither. Shit. They got me jammed up here. I don' know nothin 'bout no insurance co-operation. No dam' court neither. What they got me up here for?"

"You've been charged with robbing a bank. You've been indicted by the Federal grand jury under Chapter 28, Section 1802 of the United States Code, for bank robbery. Here's the indictment. According to this indictment, last year on December twenty-three, you robbed the Farmer's and Mechanic's Bank at gun point."

"There might have been some kind of robbery, but I didn' do nothin' to no insurance co-operation. What the fuck are they talkin' 'bout anyway? I ain't never heard of no insurance co-operation. You gonna get me outta this dam' place? I just want to do my state time and get out of this place. Federal time. I ain't got no time for no Federal time. Jammed up in here. Shit, man."

"Let's start from the beginning. If you're doing state time, you must know something about the system. If you can't afford a lawyer—"

"Afford. Fuck, I'm in jail. I can't afford nothin'."

"... if you can't afford a lawyer or don't have enough money, or any money, I guess, the court will—"

"Court. What the hell do you mean court?"

"... alright. I mean the judge. Court. The judge ... that's what the judge is, he's the court. That's what he's called."

"Just call the court the judge then, not the judge the court. You got that backwards, man. Ha, ha. Ain't no court. It's just the dam' judge. Court ain't got shit to do with it. I mean shit, that's what I mean."

"Well, in any case, call it what you want. If you can't afford a lawyer the court ... or the judge ... will appoint one. And, that's what I am; I'm the lawyer that the court appointed for you."

"Maybe you that lawyer, but I don' know nothin' 'bout no insurance co-operation. What's that judge talkin' 'bout?"

"Oh. I see what you mean. You're talking about the

Federal Savings and Loan Insurance Corporation. That's why robbing a bank is a federal crime. That's what gives the Federal Government jurisdiction in a bank robbery case. They have jurisdiction because the bank deposits are insured by the federal government. FSLIC. Federal Savings and Loan Insurance Corporation."

"That may be, but I didn' do nothin' to no insurance co-operation. Shit. I never even had insurance. I always figured if you gonna die, ain't no sense leaving a bunch of insurance money for somebody else who never gave a shit about your ass, no-how."

"Well, I guess that's a point. It just gives the FBI the authority to get in the case. You know what I mean?" Billy asked.

"I don' know if I knows what you mean or not."

"Okay. We can talk about that later. The point is, I've been appointed to represent you and you don't have to pay for it. If you don't want me, the court will probably appoint another lawyer. You're entitled to have an attorney and you can't be forced to go to trial without one, that's your constitutional right."

Thackeray Frederick Johnson pressed his head against the pastel blue bars and smiled. He was missing one top front tooth, but the tooth next to the blank space had a perfectly inlaid six pointed gold star. "Gotcha man." He pulled a pack of Kool cigarettes from his left stocking. With a prodigious fingernail on his right little finger, he carefully removed a cigarette from a neat hole he had bored into the bottom of the pack. "Got any matches? What's your name? Think you can get me out of this indictment?"

Billy looked up from the indictment. "I checked with the U.S. attorney. They're required to tell us what evidence they've got. He gave me the investigation report and some photographs taken by the security camera in the bank." Billy took three photographs out of his briefcase and handed them to Johnson. "You can see at the bottom. It shows the day and time when they were taken. He also gave me this signed confession and a waiver of your right to an attorney during questioning. Is this your signature?"

"That picture don' look nothin' like me. I ain't ever owned no coat that looks like that. Whose coat is that? That coat ain't mine. I never owned a coat that looks like that. Look here." Johnson pointed. "Dude in that picture's got a mask on. I ain't got no mask that looks like that. You can ask Annie Joe, she's who I was livin' with when them Feds rousted my ass. She'd tell you that I ain't ever, long as she's been knowin' me, ever had no—"

"They also gave me this signed confession." Billy held up the confession so Johnson could read it. "Did you tell them this? Is this your signature?"

Johnson glanced at the confession and nonchalantly took a deep drag of the Kool. He pushed the smoke from his mouth and inhaled it into his nose and after a pause and an audible sigh, he simultaneously blew smoke through his nose and mouth.

"Well," he said. "I don' remember waiving no rights to no lawyer or no attorney neither. Nobody said nothin' to me about rights. One way or the other. That's for shaw. And I don' remember signin' no confession. If that's what you call it."

"Are you telling me you didn't give this confession?" Billy said. "Is this your signature?"

Johnson crossed his arms and belligerently jutted his goateed chin at the confession and rubbed the amber of his cigarette off on the cell bar. He replaced the three quarter length cigarette butt in the bottom of the pack as carefully as he had removed it.

"Did you tell them that you wanted an attorney present?" Billy pressed. "When were you arrested?"

"Like I jus' told you, *asshole*. I was at Annie Joe's when they come bustin' in and grab me, yelling, 'Are you Thackeray Frederick Johnson?'. I say, 'who wants to know?' And, the next thing I know, they've got me handcuffed and draggin' down to this fuckin' jailhouse. I know they need some kind of a warrant or something. What about my constitutional rights or something?"

"I don't see it here," Billy said, "but I'm sure they had an arrest warrant, they must have."

"They just handcuffed me and dragged my ass down to this here jailhouse. I could have been anybody. I told them that maybe I was Mr. Thackeray Frederick Johnson and maybe I wasn't. And they pushed me down an' two big ol' fat bastards put their knees in my back, twisted my arms up behind my ass, and put handcuffs on me so tight my hands got numb. Then they dragged my po' ass off to this here jailhouse. In front of Annie Joe and her kids and everything. Looks to me like they violated my civil rights."

"Are you telling me that you didn't rob this bank? Do you have some kind of defense that I can't see? I can't tell by looking at this photograph, strictly speaking, if this is you. I'd have to agree, you can't tell a whole lot by the face. Your goatee is covered up ... and well, you just can't tell for sure. The United States needs to prove their case beyond a reasonable doubt, and there could be reasonable doubt from this picture of you ... if that's all they had ... which it isn't. Where were you last year on December twenty-three?"

"Shit. Who knows? Not robbin' no bank, that's for show. Don't they need to prove beyond a reasonable doubt where I was? If they can't prove I was in that bank, how can they say I robbed it?"

Billy flipped through the information that the United States Attorney had given him. It was a typical FBI report with a list of physical evidence that included, amongst other things, photographs of a navy pea coat and a wool ski mask, exactly like the suspect in the three photographs.

"Johnson," Billy said, "the FBI recovered a coat and mask just like the ones in the pictures."

"Sure they did," he said, "but that stuff was in the trunk of Annie Joe's car and them cops didn' have no search warrant. That shit ain't no evidence. Even I know that."

"You might be right, but they've got a coat that looks like

the one in the pictures; a mask that looks like the one in the pictures; gloves that sure look like the ones in the pictures; and I would guess that—"

"Guess. Shit, what 'chu talkin' 'bout? They've got to prove it beyond a reasonable doubt. Them ain' my clothes."

"They've got lots of pretty good evidence. You don't have an alibi, do you? You can't tell me where you were when the robbery was committed. They've got three pictures of someone in a navy pea coat, a ski mask, and white gloves ... all of which were found in your girlfriend's car—"

"That don' prove nothin' beyond a reasonable doubt."

"... and they've got a signed confession. What am I supposed to do with the signed confession?"

Johnson bristled and stepped toward Billy and sneered. "You callin' me a liar, Mr. Lawyer?" He knocked the file out of Billy's hand. "You look smarter than that." He poked his large index finger in Billy's chest and grinned.

Before Johnson could react, in one motion Billy grabbed the finger, twisted it back into Johnson's face and smashed a perfectly placed forearm into Johnson's chest.

Johnson careened off the cell bars before catching his balance next to the steel bench. He stood for a moment looking at his dislocated finger. He twisted the finger back into place and flexed it like he was trying on a rubber glove. Just as he started back toward Billy, a deputy jailer appeared.

"Everything alright here?"

"No problem," Billy said.

Johnson uncoiled and retrieved the cigarette butt from his pack of Kools, lit it, and sat down on the bench. Smoke billowed around his petulant grin. He folded his arms and smiled.

"What you supposed to do? I don' know. You the lawyer. You figure that out."

CHAPTER TWO

He was slightly over six feet tall and weighed one hundred and ninety-seven pounds, just seven pounds over his college football playing days and two pounds more than when he was discharged from the Navy. Despite the regular consumption of empty calories from alcohol, his rigorous physical exercise regiment kept his weight and general health intact. Since leaving the "Big Firm," as he called it, he wore a coat and tie to his office only if he had an appointment or a court appearance. And sometimes, not even then. He kept a blue blazer, a dark suit, two white shirts, two neckties, a pair of shoes and socks, and a black belt in his office closet. If something popped up and he'd come to the office in shorts and a polo shirt or some other un-lawyer-like attire, in five minutes he could morph into a perfectly presentable attorney at law.

William C. Tapp's law office was on the fifth floor of 190 Market Street, two blocks east of Constitution Avenue. If there had been a window on the west side, he'd have had a perfect view of the United States Capitol. As it was, he could see part of the Federal Mall, the Potomac River, and the north end of Ronald Reagan Washington National Airport. His small suite contained a reception area, a combination conference room and library, a vacant room, a small kitchenette, and a large office with an elaborate bathroom that included a closet, a vanity, a fancy over sized toilet, and a shower big enough for two people.

"The landlord will remove this bathroom," the leasing agent told Billy. "I don't know why anybody would want such a monstrosity for this little office. The tenant before you paid for this thing and moved out three weeks later. The bathroom takes up perfectly good space that most tenants aren't willing to pay for."

"It's okay. I'll take it the way it is … if I don't have to pay for the water."

She seemed relieved and quickly thrust her hand toward Billy. "It's a deal then. We'll shake on it now. It's a deal. You can sign the lease whenever you want to . . . but, you'll need to sign it before you can move in."

That was seven years ago. The other tenants on the fifth floor were lawyers and lobbyists, a publisher of some kind, and a dentist who, in ten years, Billy had never seen.

* * * *

Today Billy was wearing running pants, New Balance shoes, and a royal-blue Polo sweatshirt. When he got back to his office, his secretary, paralegal, and bookkeeper had a book open, studying for a mid-term exam in a night school course at the American University.

"You look nice. Real lawyer-like. You didn't go to court looking like that, did you? How'd court go? You've got a bunch of calls. That guy from the health insurance company called; he said you could add me. He said he'd send us the cost breakdown next week."

Vickie had neatly written the messages on small pink slips that she handed to Billy as he walked past her desk.

"Here's your mail, too."

"No court. I went to the jail. Thanks. Any calls?"

"Billy!" Vickie pointed at the wad of pink messages that he held in his left hand.

"Oh yeah. Anything urgent?"

"No. Jason called. He said if you get back before noon to call. Something about the FDIC ... or something. Maybe FSLIC. But F something."

"FSLIC? Did Thackeray Johnson call here? How in the hell did he get my number? I'm court appointed. Who let him call me?"

"I don't know," Vickie said, "but don't forget to call Jason."

Billy went into his office and shuffled through the mail. Except for the usual advertisements, a flyer for a seminar called Winning the Jury Trial Through Effective Psychology, and other junk mail there was one check; it was for twenty dollars, partial payment on a twenty-five hundred dollar divorce fee. A hand written note on the invoice said, "I'll pay the balance in nine equal installments—if that's okay with you. We're having a little financial difficulty. I hope you don't mind."

Billy looked up when Vickie walked into his office. "Who in the shit is we?" he said.

"What?"

"Nothing. Never mind. Here." He stuffed the check back in its envelope and handed it to her. "Deposit this."

Vickie took the check out of the envelope and looked at it. "Great. I was afraid we weren't going to collect any money this week. Is it okay if I go to lunch a little early? I want to drop some stuff at the post office and run over to American U to pick up a book. I'll come back a little bit early."

"Sure, put the phone on answering mode or whatever you call it."

"Don't forget to call Jason." She said as she walked out of his office.

Billy glanced through the pile of messages. "Vickie, I can't find the message from Johnson. What's the number down at the county jail?"

"Who?" She yelled back.

"Johnson. I thought you said Thackeray Frederick

Johnson called."

"Billy! Look at your messages. They're the only calls you got. Who's Thackeray Frederick Johnson? Also, Ann called. Let's see; it's past noon, so you can't call her back. She wanted you to call before noon. Your mother called too. See you later."

The phone rang and Billy picked it up. "Tapp."

"Billy. This is Jason. What's going on?"

"Not much. Vickie said you called."

"Yeah. I've got a client with a problem that's probably a conflict of interest for me. You had lunch yet?"

"No. I have to return a couple of calls, but most of them can wait."

"Meet me at Clyde's; you buy beer and I'll buy lunch," Jason said.

"It's a deal. The other line is ringing. Let me get it. I'll see you in a few minutes." Billy picked up the other line.

"William. This is your mother. How are you doing? I'm at your brother's house. It is hot isn't it? How are you doing? I mean, really how are you doing? I walked outside today and I knew it was going to be hot. It's hot now. It's going to get hotter. Lucy's birthday is Saturday. Are you going to see her? I bought her a little card and a gift. I don't know if I should send it to her or bring it over to your ... ah ... place. Do you think you will see her on Saturday? I don't—"

"That's right! It is her birthday. God, I almost forgot. No, this weekend is not my . . . "

". . . think it is supposed to be quite so hot this weekend, I think we are supposed to get a little rain, but—"

"Mom!"

"Yes?"

"I don't have the children this weekend. But, I'm sure Ann won't mind if you stop by and see her or drop off a present for Lucy. I'm going to try to get by to see her sometime this weekend, but I'm not sure when."

"It is such a shame that your father's not here. He loved

10

our children and your children too. It is just a shame that—"

"Mom. My other phone is ringing. Let me get it. I'll call you back in a while. I've got to meet Jason for lunch."

"Alright. I love you. Give those children a big hug for me. I will get—"

"Okay. Good-bye."

"Good-bye."

* * * *

Billy's mother and father met in Bremen, Germany in spring 1939. His mother was the niece of Gerrhardt Miedelbaum, a leather merchant. Billy's father was the third son of Karl Gotlieb, a cobbler, whose shop the Nazis appropriated to make boots for Hitler's army. For several generations, the two families had had a perfect business relationship: the Miedelbaums sold the leather that the Gotliebs bought to make shoes.

Three weeks after Billy's parents met, they secretly married and, on August 31, 1939, came to the United States. After an endless wait and what seemed to the young expatriates like an eternity filled alternately with boredom and a barrage of questions from the authorities, the Immigration and Naturalization Service issued them green cards and released them from Ellis Island to find their way in a land as remote to them as the moon. They migrated to Cincinnati where, on a stranger's advice while at Ellis Island, they expected to find a gracious and receptive German community. What they found in southern Ohio wasn't quite what they expected. They found a community that suspected all Germans of sedition or some other undefined treachery. The Gotliebs changed their name to Tapp and retreated to Washington D.C., believing the nation's capital, if anywhere in the world, would embrace them for what Mrs. Gotlieb, now Mrs. Tapp, referred to as a huddled mass of two, yearning to breathe free.

Their experiences in pre-war Nazi Germany, compounded

by the frightening disappointment of their first encounter in the United States, persuaded Billy's parents to bury any lingering national pride for the Fatherland, disavow their origin, deny their history, and expunge their German family and friends from their lives forever. For inexplicable reasons and without warning, they moved to Birmingham, Alabama, and started life in their new country, determined to neither expose nor disclose the truth of their past -- a life that each member of Billy's family would pay for, in one way or another, for the rest of their lives.

The Gotliebs spoke no English when they arrived in the United States and the Tapps spoke no German after they settled in Birmingham. To this day, Billy didn't know more than a dozen German words. He hadn't even known that his father's name was Gotlieb until five years after graduation from law school, while at his mother's best and only friend's funeral, in a flood of tears his mother told him that it was a shame she had hidden his heritage.

With tears streaming down her cheeks, through a chorus of staccato sobs she told him: "You are the oldest son, *my* oldest son. I have lived a lie my entire life, for all you know ... you could be Russian or Polish or Latvian or Jewish. How do you know? We never told you. Your last name should be Gotlieb! We changed our name to Tapp when we came to the United States. You must never tell your father what I just told you because he will deny it and use it as an excuse to lay drunk for a week. He is a drunk," she said with a startling conviction that Billy had never seen. "You should be proud that you're not a weak and self-indulgent drunk German. God bless you," she said as her eyes welled with tears.

Ruth Tapp swore to God that she would right the wrong that she somehow felt she had done to her family and the friends she left in Germany. She vowed to avenge the atrocities of World War II. The redress and the scapegoat for her retribution were Billy's father and anyone who sided with him. Billy had always known his parents were from Germany, but they had staunchly demurred to any specific

12

description or explanation of the circumstances for coming to the United States. This outburst was the first actual evidence that Billy had of his mother's secret and personal war and fruitless battle for some kind of ancestral hegemony. In retrospect, however, he realized that she had waged this conflict since August 31, 1939. The only difference was that now, he feared, she had conscripted him into her personal battle against a repressed and elusive foe.

* * * *

Billy tossed most of the mail in the waste basket and walked out of his office. He was surprised to see Vickie sitting at her desk.

"I thought you were going to lunch early?"

"I was. But I guess I kinda lost track of time. Are you going to have lunch with Jason? I guess you'll be gone for a while. Where are you going?"

"I'm meeting him at Clyde's."

"Well, I guess Thursday is over for you. I'll know where to get you."

"I'll be back. I'm just going for lunch."

"Sure. See you later."

The door to Billy's office had a cracked dark brown coat of shellac and a ridged opaque glass window with his name painted in black letters over a gold border above "Attorney at Law." The door rattled so hard when it slammed that he feared the glass would shatter and the whole damn door would fall off its hinges.

"Damn it," he said to Vickie through the closed door, "this thing is going to fall off one of these days, right here in the hallway. We've got to get this God damned door fixed," Billy yelled.

"It's not broke," Vickie yelled back, "let's not fix it."

"Good advice," he mumbled and walked down the hall to the elevators.

Billy pushed the down button. He waited about thirty

seconds. When an elevator didn't come, he walked down the five flights of stairs to the lobby, out the building, and onto Market Street. It was only June 12 and already hot. It was a typical Washington D.C. late spring day; the only thing higher than the temperature was the humidity. Heat from the sidewalk blasted up his pant legs.

Billy's office building was slightly unkempt and sometimes the utilities didn't work, but it was cheap and well located. The landlord was the last holdout in a two block land assemblage for a hotel, office building, and shopping mall development. As long as the landlord held out and Billy paid the rent, he could walk most anywhere he needed to go in the District—and that included Clyde's. Despite the heat, he decided to walk to M Street and to the alluring air-conditioning and the elixir of a soothing cold beer.

CHAPTER THREE

Billy met Jason Roberts in a torts class on their first day in law school at Georgetown University. Both were older than most of the other students because after college, Jason got a Ph.D. from New York University in international finance, and Billy did a stint in the United States Navy. Jason had a distinguished academic record and a first rate legal mind. Few lawyers in the D.C. bar had his knowledge and insight into both the practical and academic aspects of the law. Most of the major firms in D.C., Boston, and New York City had courted Jason, but he selected a midsized, prestigious law firm in Georgetown, following the footsteps of his father, who was one of the first black lawyers to achieve senior partner status in a "white-glove" D.C. law firm. Jason was slightly under six feet tall and slightly built. Although not frail, his only athletic involvement had been running cross-country in high school. His physical appearance was in obvious contrast to Billy.

Billy was often surprised by Jason's remarkable tolerance and his insight into Washington's political and social underpinnings. And, despite Billy's unpredictable and often bad behavior, to the frequent dismay of the other guests, Jason invited Billy to a surprising number of parties, brunches, cruises on the Potomac, dinners, and other official political and social functions.

* * * *

Billy walked into Clyde's Bar, a Georgetown institution since 1935. Jason introduced Billy to Clyde's soon after their first day in law school. Since that epiphany, with the exception of brief absences for vacations, weddings, funerals, and other less compelling events, one might argue that Clyde's became Billy's second home. The long wooden bar ran perpendicular to M Street and the back-bar was cluttered with items of junk that ranged from boxing gloves to post cards to dried flowers to cans of chili to street signs to Red Skins banners and to God knows what else.

Billy looked down the bar and offered an exaggerated military salute to the bartender.

"At ease Robert Bob," Billy said.

"Good morning ... ah ... good afternoon, Mr. Tapp. Busy day in court?"

"Yeah, right."

Robert Bob looked like a sumo wrestler. He was slightly less than medium height, but his burly stature gave the appearance of a much larger man. Although his girth exceeded forty-eight inches, his large hairless forearms and huge neck left the impression of muscle and not fat. He always wore a white apron, with the bib folded down and rolled around the waist and a white shirt with a black tie tucked into the space between the second and third buttons. He had a bulbous nose that had grown thick and red and large feet and an expressionless gruff bass voice. He kept his sleeves rolled up and almost always had a cigar in his mouth or lying on the back bar. Billy could never remember seeing the cigar lit. His real name was Robert Scharman, but Billy called him Robert Bob.

* * * *

Jason Roberts was sitting at a front table next to the window with a view of M Street. A pitcher of beer and two glasses set in the middle of the table.

"Mr. Tapp. How are you? The vicissitudes of the law, how do they treat you? Winning or losing? What's up?"

"Not much," Billy said. "What's up with you?"

Jason motioned toward a chair next to the wall and pointed at a glass. He casually pulled out his French-cuffs to barely show each expensive gold cuff-link. "Here. I ordered a glass, just for you. It's hot, isn't it?"

Billy slid under the table and maneuvered his chair to position his back to the corner with a clear view of the barroom.

"Yeah. It's hotter than hell. What was Vickie telling me about Johnson? How did you get involved in that case?"

"What case?" Jason took a large black cigar from his inside breast coat pocket. He unwrapped it and deftly clipped off the end with a device that looked like a miniature guillotine. "Sorry I only have one of these. A client who's putting together a low income housing project in Mexico brings these back for me. They're Cuban. I'll bring you one tomorrow. What are you talking about?"

"Let me see that thing." Billy took the guillotine and cut the eraser off a pencil that someone left on the window sill.

"Billy. Give me that. It's not a pencil sharpener." Jason reached over and snatched the clipper from Billy.

"That didn't hurt it. Vickie said you called and you said something about Johnson."

"I asked about Johnson? Who's Johnson? I called. But, I said I wanted to talk to you about a client that I met with the other day."

"Why do you order this horse piss draft beer? It's flat. Here, let's get another pitcher. Hey. Robert Bob. Is this beer flat, do you think?" Billy looked at Jason. "Was it a court appointed case?"

The bartender drew some draft beer into a whiskey glass and drank it. "Nope. Tastes good to me. You want another pitcher?"

"Absolutely."

"A what? A court appointed case! Are you kidding? You know me better than that. I wouldn't take a court appointed case if I were appointed by the court!"

"Right. You uptown white glove pricks don't take a shit unless you've got somebody to charge for it. No. I should say that you don't even take a shit unless you've got somebody to charge who you know, beyond a shadow of a doubt, will pay."

"Billy. These tailored suits are very expensive. Envy is such an unattractive trait, frequently displayed by and characteristic of the poor." Jason smiled and blew smoke toward Billy.

"Bullshit. Well, maybe so." Billy and Jason laughed. "Alright, who did you call about?"

"I haven't seen you for a while and I wanted to buy you a beer."

"Okay," Billy said, "so buy me a beer."

Jason pointed at the pitcher of beer. "Help yourself."

"Thanks a load. It's half gone. There are more damn loonies out there than you can imagine. Vickie gave me a letter that some guy over in Georgetown sent me. He wanted to know if I could get a copy of the International Domestic Wire Tap Statute. He says he's asked the Attorney General for it and they've refused to give him a copy. They're using the wire tap statute to spy on him. He knows it because he keeps picking up their signal on his scanner. How much do you think I ought to charge that guy?"

"What in the hell are you talking about?" Jason asked.

"This guy that sent me a letter. He wants me to file suit in the U.S. District Court to get a copy of the International Domestic Wire Tap Statute."

"What's the International Domestic Wire Tap Law Statute?"

"Jason, I thought you'd know that," Billy said sarcastically, "with all your international contacts. There's probably no such thing. If there were, you'd know, wouldn't you?" Billy paused and smiled at Jason. "There's no such thing. At least, not that I know of. And, if there is, anybody could get it. It would be public record. Here. I've got the letter with me. Look at this. '... *the Washington police is using wiring tape on me and told me on my scanner that I am wired ...*' Look here. He wants to hire me. Maybe you can be co-counsel with me. He says ... look here. '*I would like to know how much do you all charge for a civil law suit againts them in U. S. Dist Court for vilation of my civil rights.*' It's signed by David Nooton. What do you think?"

"Let me see that letter."

Jason took the letter and laid it on the table. He smoothed it with both hands and took his Ralph Lauren glasses from his shirt pocket. "Let's see here ... yep, you're right. This guy needs an attorney. And, you might just be the right guy. I'd like to help you in this case, but I've got more pressing commitments." Jason shoved the letter back to Billy.

"How do these people get my name?"

"It isn't because opposites attract."

"Do you ever get stuff like this?"

"No. Well, I might. But I'm sure my paralegal tosses it in the trash. Can't you get Vickie to screen this kind of stuff?"

"I guess I could. But, Vickie thinks everybody's entitled to have legal representation. She thinks that all these fruit cakes are just uneducated or poor or underprivileged ... or something, and really need help. She has the strangest notion that everyone is entitled to a lawyer. Can you imagine that?"

"Isn't that Judge Stewart's clerk sitting at the table near the end of the bar?" Jason asked.

"Yeah. I think it is. God she's great looking. Is she married? Look. Don't look up. She's looking over here at us."

Billy waved at her and offered his brightest come-let-me-fuck-you smile. She waved again. Just then, Judge Stewart's other law clerk walked past the table. He waved back and hurried over to her.

"God damn it."

"What?" Jason said.

"I said God damn it. I thought what's her face was waving at me. Apparently she was waving at Mr. Fancy Pants in his three-piece suit ... the guy who's now sitting with her."

"Oh. That's Ken Haynes. He's coming to work for us after Christmas. He's a real bright guy. He's a great guy. He played football at Duke. He's a Harvard graduate, Rhodes Scholar, and all that shit."

"Right. Blah, blah, blah."

"Wait a minute. You guys have something in common. You both are lawyers, both played football in college, both smart guys ... but he's better looking than—"

"Fuck you."

"... you. No thank you. I will tell you this though: I don't think we'll let Ken handle any of these international domestic wire tap cases when he joins the firm."

"Very funny. If he's such a great guy, why didn't he come over here and sit with you ... and me?"

"I'm sure he didn't see me when he came in."

* * * *

Robert Bob brought the pitcher of beer down to the end of the bar nearest to the door. Billy got up and walked over to the bar.

"Billy. Can I ask you a question?"

"Sure. Fire away."

"Do you have to have a name on an arrest warrant?"

"A name? You mean a name?" Billy took his eyes off Judge Stewart's pretty law clerk. "Does the warrant have to have a name on it? Yeah. Of course. Most of the time. I guess you could have a John Doe warrant. Why?"

"Some guy came in here. Some cop. He said he had a warrant, but he needed an address."

"For what? What was it for? Specifically what was the warrant for?"

"This cop came in last night about nine o'clock. We were just starting to get real busy. Anyway, he comes up to the bar, with all my customers there, and says he has a warrant for my arrest. He says that he needs to see my driver's license to get my social security number. Then he says the warrant is for me selling drinks to a minor."

"Did he see you sell a drink to a minor?"

"He didn't say. He just said he had a warrant and he needed to verify some information, my social security number and some other stuff."

"That doesn't make a lot of sense ..."

"I had all these customers at the bar and it was starting to get busy and everybody was giving me these looks. So, I asked him to come back into the office so we could discuss it. If you know what I mean."

"... that if he had a warrant, he wouldn't—"

"So we go back to the office and he tells me that he has a warrant for me selling drinks to a minor, and he needs my social security number and my address. He asks me if I've ever been arrested and how long I've worked at Clyde's. I show him my license and tell him I've worked here for almost twenty years."

"How much was your bond? Did you get recognized? Did someone put up your bond?"

"I don't know what my bond was."

"How did you get out?"

"Out of where?"

"Jail."

"Jail?"

"Yeah. Jail."

"I wasn't in jail. He didn't take me to jail."

"But I thought you said he had a warrant."

"That's what he told me. He came in and waved a piece of paper in my face, in front of all my customers, and said he had a warrant for my arrest for selling drinks to a minor. He didn't arrest me. He didn't take me to jail."

"That's fucked up. If he has a warrant, he's supposed to

arrest you. Did he say he saw you selling drinks to a minor?"

"No he didn't say anything about that."

"Did he leave anything with you? Any paper? A summons? The warrant—or anything?"

"Nope. Nothing. Can I sue somebody for this? He embarrassed me in front of a bunch of good customers. It really scared the hell out of me. Isn't that slander or libel or something?"

"Maybe. You didn't get served with any papers, right?"

"Right."

"Well, just sit tight. Let me call down to the police department and see what I can find out. In the mean time, if anybody comes in with a warrant or a summons or whatever, call me."

"Do you have a card?"

"Ah," Billy fumbled through his wallet. "No. Here give me a piece of paper, and I'll write it down for you. My secretary keeps giving me shit for not having cards. She passes more out than I do." Billy wrote his name and telephone number on the back of a food order ticket and handed it to the bartender.

"Thanks. I'll call you if I hear something."

"The United States Supreme Court has said more than once that cops can lie to you to get information. You know that don't you?"

"But can that guy come in here and tell me that he has a warrant for me. In front of my customers? That son of a bitch. I'd like to get hold of his God damned skinny little pencil neck." Robert Bob's face flushed and a vein about the size of a ball point pen throbbed in the middle of his forehead, registering the stress of the moment and the wear caused by twenty-five years of tending bar.

"Just relax. It won't help to get upset. Same thing's going to happen if you're pissed off or not pissed off. So, why worry? It's probably no big deal. Don't talk to anybody before you call me. Have you ever been arrested or charged with selling to a minor?"

"Yeah. About eight—no, five years ago. But I think it got dismissed."

"I'll call down to the police department. Don't worry. I'll get back with you."

"Okay. Thanks, Billy."

Billy took the pitcher of beer and walked back to the table. Ken Haynes was sitting with Jason. Both were laughing. Billy put the beer in the middle of the table.

"Billy," Jason said, "meet Ken Haynes. He's one of Judge Stewart's clerks. Ken, Billy Tapp."

Haynes stood up and extended his hand to Billy. "Nice to meet you. I've heard about you."

"You have? Really? Do you want a glass or something?"

"No thank you. I just saw Jason sitting here and thought I would come over and say hello."

"I've heard good things about you, Mr. Tapp. Aren't you the one who just got Judge Poopvitch reversed on the *Daubert* hearing for a tractor expert?"

"Mr. Tapp? It's Billy—or Mr. Billy. Ha! Ha! Yeah, that was me. After the hearing, opposing counsel was strutting around and saying 'I told you so.' So I bet him that I'd win on appeal and we'd be right back in Poopvitch's court again. All you can eat at The Old Ebbit Grille … any wine, any entrée, any anything. I can't wait. Poopvitch is such a dope. He doesn't know shit about the law. Never did; never will."

"Poopvitch will never leave the bench," Jason said.

"Do you want a glass?"

"No thank you. I'm going back over to sit with Robin. It was nice meeting you." Haynes stood up, smoothed his pin-striped vest and made the slightest bow.

"I'll give you a call next week. I'll buy you lunch," Jason said.

"Great." Haynes walked back to the table near the opposite end of the bar where Robin sat.

"He seems like a pretty nice guy," Billy said.

"I told you that you would like him."

"What's not to like? He apparently shares the widely held

belief that I'm Williams James Fucking Bryant. Smart kid."
"That's because he doesn't know you."

* * * *

Ken Haynes and Robin Grigsby, Judge Stewart's pretty law clerk, left. They stopped briefly at the table where Billy and Jason sat and after Robin Grigsby's brief, awkward introduction, went back to the Federal building to finish an opinion on a summary judgment motion in a sexual harassment case that was scheduled for trial in two weeks. The summary judgment had been pending for almost three weeks, and earlier in the day Judge Stewart called both Haynes and Grigsby into his elaborate office, *in camera*, and told them that he decided to overrule the motion. He told them his reason and told them to find the supporting law and write the opinion. He hoped to have it by week's end.

As they left, Hayes and Grigsby feigned servitude. "Duty calls. We must get back. Judge Stewart demands only the best. That's why he has us. He hates to look stupid. We've never let that happen." Robin smiled at Billy and walked out the door.

"Okay, Tapp. Put your tongue back in your mouth. I think she's living with somebody."

"Well, she smiled at me."

"So did the bartender."

Jason looked at his watch. He poured another glass of beer and removed a sheet of folded up yellow legal paper from his inside breast coat pocket. He carefully unfolded it and placed it on the table in the same deliberate way that he had done with David Nooton's implore for Billy's help with the Domestic Wire Tap Law. He reached in his outside jacket pocket and pulled out a business card. He carefully placed the business card next to the yellow sheet.

"I have a friend who I went to prep school with. He went to Vanderbilt undergraduate and law school at the University of Kentucky; he practices law with a real good firm in

Lexington. His name is John Morgan … John H. Morgan. The same name as the Confederate Calvary General John Hunt Morgan who was slightly famous for the Morgan's Raiders in the Civil War. I'm sure he's not related. Anyway. A few weeks ago, John called me and said that, for years, he has represented a real estate developer who's built some shopping centers and office buildings in Texas and Kentucky, and working on one up here in Frederick, Maryland. His name is Seymour Grey. He's apparently made and lost a bunch of money, like most real estate developers. This is kind of a long story, so I'm going to try to make it as short as possible. It's interesting."

"What does General Morgan have to do with it?"

"That's just coincidence. John Morgan is my friend. General Morgan has nothing to do with it."

"That's what I thought. I wouldn't expect you to side with some Confederate General. Keep going."

"Grey apparently built or is in the process of building a shopping center of some kind in Frederick. According to John, it's a mix of new construction and the rehabilitation of an old historic manufacturing facility. It was financed with a combination of private money and federal funds. UDAG – Urban Development Action Grant money. It's something that HUD does. I didn't get into all the details, but that's generally it."

"What kind of shopping center was it?"

"I don't know, exactly."

"Is it done, or opened, or what?"

"I don't know that either. But apparently Grey had some joint venture or something with his lender . . . a bank or savings and loan in Houston … that went into receivership. The FDIC or FSLIC came in and took over the Houston lender and called the loan. One thing led to the other and the next thing you know, Grey's development stops, the loans are called, lawsuits are filed, and now there are lawsuits in Texas and in Washington."

Jason paused and took a long drink of beer. He handed

John Morgan's card to Billy and wadded up the yellow sheet.

"We looked at the case, but decided not to take it because we weren't sure Grey could pay our fees. John said that Grey was about out of money. But he's apparently an honest guy with what might be a good claim, but no money."

"Can I look at that paper?"

"Sure. But it's just my scribbled notes from my discussion with John this morning. We did a little legal research and it is in the file at the office. Honestly, I think it's a pretty interesting case, and I think there's a statutory provision for attorney's fees if you win. John can't do the D.C. litigation from Lexington. He seemed to think the bulk of the it should be in Washington."

Jason straightened out the yellow sheet again and handed it to Billy.

"Do you want to take a look at it? I think there are some pending motions, so something needs to be done pretty soon. I told John that we needed a one hundred thousand dollar retainer. He said that Grey didn't have that kind of money. I told him I knew a few guys that might be interested in taking the case. I gave him your name first. If you're interested, call Morgan. I told him we were going to talk today."

Billy looked at the card and Jason's notes. He knew something about HUD projects and the Urban Development Action Grant, or UDAG, funding scheme. He had successfully defended a savings and loan officer who had been both criminally charged with fraud and sued by HUD. HUD filed the civil suit to recover money that it suspected the loan officer had pilfered to finance a vacation in Las Cabos. After five years of investigations, interrogatories, depositions, hearings, motions, production of documents, and an undetermined amount of copying costs, expenses, and legal fees, HUD admitted there was no fraud and voluntarily dismissed both the criminal charges and the civil suit. In the end, Billy's client was grateful but broke.

"Sure. You're right. I think there is a statute that provides for attorney's fees, but even if you're wrong, like you said, real estate developers have a way of finding money when they need it. It's worth looking at. Plus, I hate the fucking FSLIC. Maybe I can get this one up their ass. Money? Who needs money?"

* * * *

Billy learned to fly airplanes in the Navy. For the most part, college had been an excuse to play football, drink beer, and get laid. He was pretty good at the first two and hit or miss at the third. He realized that he wouldn't be either committed or good enough to play professional football so, when he graduated—not ready to actually go to work—he decided that flying airplanes off aircraft carriers would be the next best thing to getting a job. It couldn't hurt his *bona fides* for carousing and womanizing. After an exceptional flying record and a spotty conduct record, he managed to earn the rank of Commander, but as the result of dropping a fake bomb on a Mexican tanker—just for the hell of it—he received an honorable discharge at the rank of Lieutenant. His last assignment in the Navy took him briefly to Washington, D.C., and while there, he applied to and was accepted to Georgetown University's School of Law. Learning came easy and he possessed a particular bent for legal academia. During the first two and a half years of law school, without much effort, he climbed to the top of his class. He was elected editor of the law journal, selected to the legal honorary Order of the Coif, wrote and published three significant law journal articles, one in the Harvard Law Review, and he generally received praise and admiration from student and faculty alike. He coasted his last semester, and on graduating *magna cum laude*, he captured a highly prized clerkship for the chief justice of the U.S. Supreme Court.

He either authored and co-authored several significant Supreme Court opinions and distinguished himself not only amongst his fellow clerks, but also amongst the other members of the court. This status and simply the credential of clerking for the Supreme Court placed Billy in an exclusive class of highly desired first year associates for the select group of white glove law firms scattered across the country. Because Washington, D.C. is the largest small town in the United States and because the elite legal establishment is the smallest large family of gossip mongers, opportunists, greed merchants, and influence peddlers, with his military background and education record, he was exactly the first year associate that every law firm in D.C. was looking for. Several months before leaving the majestic halls of the Supreme Court of the United States of America, Bracken and Wells offered him a prestigious associate's position, at a salary of more than four times what the Supreme Court paid, with the promise, if everything went well, of junior partnership in three years and full partner in five.

Billy's legal ability was never the issue. After three years of exceptional work he was promoted to junior partner. Two weeks later, a senior partner and one of the firm's major clients caught Billy seducing a first year associate on the conference room table. He was given the option of being fired, with all the public hoopla and humiliation, or resigning in anonymity. He chose the latter. Less than three weeks later, everyone in D.C. knew he'd been shit-canned for screwing a first year associate in a conference room. However, the rumors of his transgression ranged from raping a senior partner's eighteen-year-old daughter to having a *ménage a trois* with the mail clerk and the night security guard—the mail clerk was another senior partner's grandson and the night guard was an odd acting black man who had a habit of walking unannounced into the women's bathroom.

Billy took it all in stride. His chagrin was exceeded only by his apparent amusement. He was single, highly regarded intellectually, and sick and tired of the political nonsense that pervades the Washington, D.C. legal establishment. His transition from the big law firm to single practitioner was seamless. He had hardly opened the door before calls came in asking him to be co-counsel or local counsel; referrals from members of the D.C. bar who had conflicts of interest or junior partners or associates looking for a referral fee off the books, it seemed, came once a week.

Shortly after opening his law office, he was asked to be co-counsel in a class action lawsuit against a major drug company. His share of the fee was enough to pay off the loan on his townhouse in Georgetown, buy his first Porsche, and buy a pressurized Beech Barron—tail number N9528R— a high-end twin piston engine airplane that competes with the, so-called, entry level turbine powered airplanes like the 90 series King Air and the Piper Cheyenne. *An airplane, a car, and a townhouse in Georgetown. This law stuff is going to be a piece of cake.* When Friday afternoon came, he was off in his airplane with some judge's clerk, some secretary, or anyone else that was willing to put up with his hard drinking and general impertinence. Off to Ft. Lauderdale, Key West, Charleston, New Orleans, or other locations that suited his whim. As time passed, when it came down to it, lots of lawyers wanted him in court with them, just not in their office.

CHAPTER FOUR

Before a civil case—as distinguished from a criminal case—goes to trial the lawyers engage in a sparing process, ostensibly, seeking both factual and legal information about each other's case. The lawyers bring issues to the court's attention through court papers called "motions." Sometimes the motions end the case, and sometimes the motion is a veiled excuse for lawyers to rack up time spent on the case and run up their client's bill.

* * * *

Billy arrived at his office the next morning with the fuzz of last night's beer still impeding any chance of clear thought. Vickie wasn't there yet, but she'd stuck his messages in one of the slots in the metal file holder on the front of her desk. He grabbed the messages on the way to the file room to make coffee. He pulled the wadded yellow sheet out of his pocket and put John Morgan's card in front of his telephone. He looked at his calendar to see what he had to do today. *Friday. Thank God it's Friday.* He had a nine-thirty morning motion for a pre-trial conference in U.S. District Court and a two o'clock afternoon arraignment and motion to compel in Prince George's Circuit Court. He looked at his watch, forty-five minutes to get over to District Court. It was only two blocks to the court building, so there was time to wait for the coffee and to look at the newspaper that had been thrown near his office door.

As Billy slipped the rubber band off the folded newspaper, Vickie came in. She poked her head into Billy's office. "Good morning Mr. Tapp. Did you get your phone calls?"

"Yeah. I picked—"

"An attorney from Lexington, Kentucky, called you at about five-fifteen last night. He said he was a friend of Jason. Morrison or something like that. His name is … I wrote it on the message." Vickie picked up the pink telephone messages that Billy had tossed on his desk. "Here." She handed it to Billy. "He wanted you to call him back this morning if you can. It sounded kind of urgent. He wanted to know if he could get hold of you last night. I was going to give him your cell number, but I didn't. He's going to be out of his office and he needs to talk to you about some hearing this morning, or today, or something. Did you make coffee? How many scoops did you put in? How strong is it this morning?"

"Morgan," Billy said. "This is the guy that Jason was telling me about last night."

"You got two motions today. One this morning in Federal Court and one in Prince George's Circuit Court."

"I know. Do I have time to call before I go?"

"You better make it quick."

Billy picked up the telephone and dialed the number on John Morgan's card. He looked at his watch, *9:05 a.m.; enough time for a quick introduction and an agreement to call back after court.* The telephone rang. Billy looked at his watch again. The telephone continued to ring.

"I don't think anyone's there."

"What?"

"I said I don't think anyone is there. I'm going to have to get going."

The telephone continued to ring. Billy started to hang up. "Morgan and Knott," a male voice answered.

"Can I talk to John Morgan?"

"Let me see if he's here. Ah. Who's calling? Can I tell him who's calling?"

"This is Billy Tapp. I'm a lawyer in Washington. I'm returning his call. He called me last night."

"Oh yeah. Wait just a minute. Sorry about the confusion, our receptionist ran across the street. Hold on just a minute. Let me tell him that you're on the line."

"I need to be in court in—" Music filled the line.

"Hello. Mr. Tapp. This is John Morgan. How are you? I talked with Jason Roberts yesterday. Thanks for calling me back."

"Good, good. I don't mean to be short, but I have to be in Federal Court in about ten minutes."

"Okay, real quick then. Did Jason talk to you about Seymour Grey? He's a fellow that I've represented over the years. He's a real estate developer who's—"

"Yeah, Jason told me a little bit, but—"

"... in a couple of law suits, both relating to a shopping center development in Frederick, Maryland. The problem is that I think that there's a motion for summary judgment scheduled for hearing today ... this morning ... in D. C. I didn't actually get notice. My secretary saw it on the court's on-line docket sheet. I just called Seymour and told him that I couldn't get up there. He said that he'd gotten another attorney. But yesterday I called the clerk's office, and Seymour hadn't gotten new counsel yet. So, I guess I'm still in the case. Obviously, I can't get there this morning."

"Is it a motion to dismiss the lawsuit?" Billy asked.

"It's the government's ... FSLIC's ... motion for summary judgment. I haven't had time to look at it or the law, but it doesn't seem like the court should grant it. But if no one appears for Seymour, the court will probably enter a judgment against him. I don't think he has much chance if a lawyer doesn't show up for him."

"I don't know anything about the case. How can I—?"

"Maybe you can just go over to the court and try to get a

little extra time for someone to file a response to oppose the government's motion ... or ask the judge to give us more time for Seymour to get another attorney."

"Who's the judge? If the shopping center is in Frederick, why is the case in Federal Court here in D.C.?"

"That's kind of a long story. We'll have to get into that when there's more time. I know this is short notice. What do you think?"

It was 9:30 a. m. and Billy was already late for court in Judge B. T. Mitchell's court room.

"Who's the judge in Grey's case? What time is it? I've got to get going, I'm late for court right now."

"Poopvich."

"Poopvich! He's the ... what time is it?"

"It's nine-thirty," Morgan said. "It's nine-thirty five."

"No. I mean, when is the motion in Poopvich's court?"

"Oh. That's at ten."

"Okay. Let me see what I can do. Are you going to be in your office later today?"

"Yes. I'll be back around four-thirty or so."

Billy slammed the telephone down and ran out of his office. "I'll see you in a bit."

"Do you need the file?"

"No, it's just a motion for a pre-trial conference."

"Don't forget your calendar!" Vickie dashed into Billy's office and grabbed his calendar. She handed it to him as he hurried out the door.

* * * *

The Federal Court building is a monolithic four-story stone structure. The classical Greek building has two grand entrances on each end of the block-long front. Above each, VNITED STATES FEDERAL BVILDING is carved in the frieze that spans the fluted columns.

"What's the deal with the 'V' instead of a 'U'? Vickie had asked.

"In the old Latin, 'U' and 'V' were used interchangeably," Billy explained. "The letter 'U' wasn't invented until the ninth century. The 'u' was interchangeably used for lowercase 'v' and 'V' for the uppercase."

But today Billy was more concerned with getting to court than the architectural and labeling nuances of the building. He sprinted up the stone steps and jerked open the large brass doors that led into a vestibule and another set of large brass doors and the metal detector and the three United States marshals guarding the entrance. Billy scurried through the metal detector and the buzzer sounded. He turned around to go back through; stuck his hands in both pockets to turn over any keys, coins, and anything else that might set off the metal detector.

"Shit!"

"Billy." Marshal Joe Straighter said. "How're you doing this morning? Whose court you in?"

"Which courtroom is Mitchell in this morning?"

"He's in courtroom A, on the second floor. His courtroom. Come on through." Marshal Joe Straighter waved for Billy to come in. "You're alright; come on. You're a little late aren't you? B. T.'s going to lock your ass up if you don't get up there. They've already started court. Ha, ha."

Billy grimaced and rushed over to the elevator lobby and pushed the call button. He looked over at Joe Straighter and said nervously, "It'd be a relief. No phones, no calls, no judges, no children, no ex-wives, no appointments, and most of all, no God damned clients. You'd come to see me wouldn't you, Joe?"

"If you don't get up there, I may have to."

Courtroom A was an imposing room with thirty-five foot ceilings covered in wood paneling and gold leaf plaster. The walls were dark wood paneling that ran up to within fifteen feet of the ornate ceiling. There were three sections of oak pews in the gallery, which was separated from the jury box, counsel table, and the judge's bench by an elaborate cast iron rail. Several leather captain's chairs lined the inside of the rail, intended for attorneys waiting for their cases to be called. The witness box was to the judge's right, next to the jury box, and the judge's bench was perched two full steps above the courtroom floor. Courtroom A permitted the presiding official to hold court—in every sense of the word. Two sets of large wooden doors, the first solid eight panel doors, and the second swinging doors with cut glass panes guarded the entrance.

Billy pushed open one of the big wooden doors and carefully looked into the courtroom. He pushed through the swinging doors. Except for two attorneys standing in front of the bench, a marshal near the door and another one standing next to the witness box holding a gavel in one of his folded hands, and the judge and his secretary, the courtroom was empty. United States District Judge B. T. Mitchell peered over the top of his reading glasses at Billy and, with a contrived grimace, looked at the clock hanging high on the back wall.

"Is there anything else?"

"No, Your Honor," said each attorney.

"Alright then, Mr. Marshal, let the court be in recess."

The marshal banged his gavel on the corner of the witness box and, although the august room was empty, announced, "Everyone please rise." The marshal paused and looked around. "Let the court be in recess."

Billy walked quickly to the front of the courtroom, crossed the cast iron rail, and approached the bench. Judge Mitchell was standing and rustling through the stuff on his desk. He turned to leave the courtroom.

"Ah. Excuse me judge," Billy said. Judge Mitchell acted like he hadn't heard; he continued to rustle through his things on the bench. "Excuse me, judge," Billy said again. He was now next to the bench.

"Yessss. Mr. Tapp." Judge Mitchell exaggerated a look at his watch. "We called your case … you have a case in this court don't you … during the docket call? What is it?"

"I represent Thackeray Frederick Johnson. It's a court

appointed case. He's charged with bank robbery. He was arraigned two weeks ago and I put on a motion for a pre-trial conference. For today—"

"Wait Mr. Marshal." The judge rolled his eyes and motioned to the marshal. "Mr. Tapp, the court called your case earlier, but you weren't here. The Assistant United States Attorney was here and said he didn't think there was any reason for a pre-trial conference."

"I'm sorry I'm late. I got held up on a phone call from—"

"But there was no one here for Mr. Johnson. The court called the case, but the only one here was the United States. The court can't work its schedule around all the attorneys in Washington D. C., can it?"

"No, Judge. But we need a pre-trial conference so that we can determine whether to—"

"Wait Mr. Tapp. Wait." The judge made an exasperated gesture again to the marshal and said, "Mr. Tapp. You're lucky the United States Attorney's office is in this building. Mr. Marshal, see if the United States Attorney is available." He sat back down in his oversized chair, took off his reading glasses, placed them on the bench, and folded his hands. He looked again at the clock on the back wall. With great ceremony, he put his glasses back on. "Let's wait for the United States Attorney. Mr. Tapp, wasn't there a pre-trial conference scheduled when Mr. Johnson was arraigned?"

"Yes. But the U. S. Attorney hadn't gotten the final FBI report back yet, so we agreed to reschedule. I haven't looked at any of the speedy-trial implications yet."

"Let's not get into that until the United States Attorney gets here. Mr. Marshal, has someone called the United States Attorney's office? You know it's just down the hall from this courtroom. Any word yet?"

"Yes, sir. Mr. Maloney is on his way right now."

"Alright. We'll wait for him."

John Maloney came into the courtroom and walked around the rail to counsel's table for the United States. He placed a file folder on the table and looked at the judge.

"Alright. Let the record reflect that court is back in session. Gentlemen, state your appearances for the record." The judge nodded at Billy.

"William Tapp, for the defendant Thackeray Frederick Johnson."

"Assistant United States Attorney John Maloney, Your Honor, for the United States."

"We have a motion here for a pre-trial conference, Mr. Maloney. Didn't the court set a pre-trial conference when the defendant was arraigned? Where is the defendant?"

"He's in custody." Billy said. "A five hundred thousand dollar bond, I think."

"That's right, Your Honor," Maloney said. "We had a pre-trial conference for last week, but the United States hadn't gotten the complete FBI report, so Mr. Tapp and I agreed to continue it for a week."

The judge took his reading glasses off, rubbed his eyes, and looked at Billy for a response.

"That's right, judge. But I didn't hear anything from John, so I decided I'd better put a motion on to avoid any speedy trial issues."

"Just so the record is clear, you agreed to the continuance … ah, I mean rescheduling, didn't you?"

"Yes."

"And, you're not making any kind of speedy trial motion today, are you?"

"No."

"Alright then. Mr. Maloney, do you have the FBI report yet?"

"Well Judge, I can't really tell. It's not in the file. But, I can't tell for sure. It seems like we should have it."

"You should have it? Is there a report somewhere? Is the defendant in custody? Mr. Maloney what did you present to the Grand Jury? Have you talked to the investigating agent? What are you waiting to get?" Judge Mitchell glared at the clock again. "Are you going to get it?"

"Yes, sir." Maloney fidgeted and bent to sit down; he

reconsidered and limply stood up.

"Why can't you get these things? You know this is a criminal case, Mr. Maloney. It's not a civil case. There are different considerations here." The judge waited for a response.

"Yes, sir."

"Alright. Let's set the pre-trial conference for two weeks from today. If there's going to be a problem, Mr. Maloney, you and Mr. Tapp call my clerk. Is there anything else?"

"No, Your Honor."

"No, judge," Billy said.

"Alright, Mr. Marshal, announce recess, the court will stand in recess."

"All rise," the marshal said. With the exception of the judge and his secretary, everyone in the empty courtroom was standing. "The United States District Court is in recess." The judge walked through the door behind his bench.

"I'll give you a call next week, John."

"Okay. Don't be late next time. It puts B. T. in a pissy mood and he takes it out on everybody."

"Yeah, I noticed. Who gives a shit?"

John Maloney looked up at the empty chair behind the bench and cringed.

* * * *

Judge Gregory O. Poopvitch's chambers and connected courtroom were on the fourth floor, the smallest district courtroom in the building. Before Judge Poopvitch received his appointment to the Federal bench, a magistrate had previously occupied the space. Magistrates are federal judicial officers who act as the District Judges' trial assistants. They have authority to hear Federal misdemeanor cases and civil matters referred to them by the District Judges. Poopvitch was the most recent appointment to the D. C. Federal bench, and, as such, inherited these modest chambers and courtroom.

Gregory O. Poopvitch possessed both an undistinguished education and paltry experience in private law practice. He barely eked through college while working at a racetrack in West Virginia, and he was a low to middling student at a night law school in Virginia. Between college and law school he worked as a runner for an accounting firm. He passed the Virginia Bar Examination after two tries and for the next eighteen months his law practice consisted of legal aide appointments and *pro bono* divorces. A friend of his father, who had been a successful concrete contractor and a significant political donor, managed to get Poopvitch appointed as a temporary traffic court judge in Virginia—his only previous judicial experience.

Unlike most state judicial systems where judges are elected for four or five or six years, Federal judges are appointed for life. The only way to get rid of a Federal judge is by impeachment, resignation, or death. Record and demeanor, for the most part, have no bearing on job security. Federal District judges set their own work hours and court dockets. The United State Administrative Office of The Courts pays for their office, overhead, staff, continuing legal education, and expenses. In addition to bloated six figure salaries, they get a full range of benefits, including medical insurance, life insurance, expense account, paid vacation, and a generous retirement plan. The President of the United States, with the sagacious approval of Congress, appoints Federal judges. There are a litany of selection standards and criteria, but at the District Court level, it is inevitable that the process produces an appointment based alone on political favoritism. Judge "G. O. Poop," as the local bar knew him, was such an appointment. G. O. Poop brought an ominous combination of character traits to the Federal bench; he was shallow, envious, and lazy. He was charitably described as barely competent and stupid.

* * * *

"Federal Savings and Loan Insurance Corporation, et al. v. Seymour Grey et al.," the marshal called. "Motion to dismiss."

"Michael Braxton for the plaintiff," said the attorney who took his position at the plaintiff's counsel table. Billy stood behind the defendant's counsel table.

Judge Poopvitch looked up and rubbed his bald head. "Seymour Grey. Is Mr. Grey here? Marshal, call in the hall for Mr. Seymour Grey."

"Judge. Ah ... I got a call this morning from John Morgan in Lexington, Kentucky. I believe he is attorney of record in this—"

"John Morgan," the judge intoned. "Is John Morgan in the courtroom? Marshal, call in the hall for Mr. Morgan." The marshal was already in the hall and didn't hear the judge's order.

"That's what I was saying, judge. John Morgan called me this morning ..."

The marshal came back into the courtroom. "No response, Your Honor."

"Is Mr. Morgan out there?"

"I'm sorry, Your Honor. Is who out there?"

"I said to call for Mr. John Morgan. He's plaintiff's ... Mr. Seymour Grey's ... attorney. I said to see if he is in the hallway." The judge slammed his pen down on the desk.

The marshal stuck his head out the door and yelled, "John Morgan. Is Mr. John Morgan here?" He closed the door and faced the judge. "No response, Your Honor."

"Mr. Braxton, this is your motion to dismiss? It doesn't appear that either the defendant or his counsel is here. Did they get notice of this motion?"

"Yes sir, Your Honor. I'm sure they did. But it's not a motion to dismiss. It's a motion for summary judgment. I'm sure they did. Let me see. I'm sure we sent them a copy of the motion. My secretary is very efficient. I'm sure she did."

"Well they're not here and it doesn't appear—"

"Judge," Billy said again. "I'm here because I got a

telephone call this morning from John—"

"... that anyone is here on behalf of the defendants. This is your motion to dismiss, Mr. Braxton?"

"It's for summary judgment. Not to dismiss."

Michael Braxton wore a dark blue suit, a white button down oxford shirt, and a red club tie. Braxton shifted his feet nervously and looked over at Billy and then back at the judge. "Yes, sir. It's our motion."

"Has there been a response filed? Did the defendants respond to your motion? Madam Clerk, is there a response in the record? I don't have one in my file, do I?" The judge looked at the District Court clerk who sat at a table to the right of the bench.

The clerk jumped to her feet. "No, sir. I haven't seen a response."

"Don't the rules require Mr. Grey to file an opposing response or something?"

Braxton weakly offered, "I don't think the rule *requires* that a—"

"Sure it does. If a party ignores this court, I can find against him ... or her. Mr. Braxton, have you submitted a proposed order?"

"Yes sir."

Billy leaned forward on the chair at counsel's table. "Judge!" He said a little louder. "Judge, I'm here because I got a call—"

"Clerk. Is there a proposed order in the record?" The judge looked at the court clerk again and noticeably avoided eye contact with Billy.

"I don't see one. But it may be in the—"

"Mr. Braxton. Do you have one?"

"... in the District Clerk's office."

"Well I just asked the clerk, here, and she didn't have it. Did you Miss Wallace?"

"I don't see it here, judge," the district clerk said.

"I'm sure we filed one, Your Honor. I can't imagine filing a motion for summary judgment without filing a proposed order too."

"I don't think it's so important, since the defendant doesn't appear to be here today."

"Judge!" Billy shouted. "*I* represent the defendant! I'm here. *I* represent Seymour Grey. Mr. John Morgan called me this morning. *He* apparently filed a motion to dismiss ... probably in response to the government's motion for summary judgment. The *defendant*, Seymour Grey, filed the motion to dismiss. Mr. Braxton ... the plaintiff ... filed a motion for *summary judgment*. Summary judgment. Not a motion to dismiss. Mr. Morgan said that he didn't think that he had gotten a copy of Mr. Braxton's motion for summary judgment. But that he couldn't—"

"Mr. Tapp. Yes, Mr. Tapp, I see you there. But *you* don't represent Mr. Grey on the record. Mr. Morgan represents Mr. Grey. Mr. Morgan is the attorney of record. He filed the answer and he signed the answer. Let me see here." Poopvitch leafed through the file. "See. Here, Mr. Tapp." Judge Poopvitch held the file for Billy to see. "It says, 'John H. Morgan, attorney for defendant.' It seems clear enough to me."

"John Morgan called me ... or, I called him ... this morning and he told me that he couldn't appear today. He ... ah ... had a conflict so he couldn't be here today. He said he didn't think that he'd gotten notice of this hearing. He asked me to stand in. I believe that I'm going to be co-counsel with Mr. Morgan."

"You believe? Co-counsel! Yes, I see. Well, Mr. Tapp, have you filed a response to Mr. Braxton's motion to dismiss? We couldn't find anything in the court record."

"Yes," Billy said, softly. "I was here."

"What's that, Mr. Tapp? What did you say."

"Oh. Nothing, Judge. I said yes, let me look here."

"Did Mr. Morgan file a response? Do you know?"

"I'm not sure, Judge. I don't think he did. He told me that he hadn't gotten notice of the summary judgment motion. So, I wouldn't think he'd have filed a response. We had only a few minutes to talk this morning. I had to get over here to court."

"And when you talked you didn't ask him if he'd filed a response?"

"I didn't know that he hadn't filed a response. Judge, I'd like to continue this motion until the next docket call and let me talk with Mr. Morgan and Mr. Grey. Give me time to get up to speed, to get familiar with everything in this case."

"Mr. Braxton. When did you file this lawsuit?"

"Six months ago, Your Honor."

"When did you file your motion to dismiss?"

"Summary judgment. We filed a motion for summary judgment. I believe Mr. Grey filed a motion to dismiss. But. Two weeks ago, Your Honor. It was a motion for summary judgment. Not a motion to dismiss. I think Mr. Grey's attorney filed the motion to dismiss." Braxton looked over at Billy. "Isn't' that right, Mr. Tapp?"

Poopvitch put his hands behind his head. He leaned back in his chair and stared at the ceiling.

"Excuse me, Judge," Billy said. "I'd like to have until the next docket call to talk with Mr. Grey and either find out if Mr. Morgan received a copy of the motion for summary judgment, and to see if he filed something. Or, if he didn't, give me a little time to file a response."

Poopvitch said nothing; he didn't move. Finally he leaned forward and looked at Braxton. "What do you say, Mr. Braxton? What does FSLIC say?"

"I guess we don't—"

"Mr. Tapp. You have until the next docket call to get some response in the record. Clerk. When is the next docket call?"

The District Clerk leafed through the court's calendar. "It looks like the next scheduled call is Wednesday. Next Wednesday. The one you want is a *week* from next Wednesday ... is that the one you want?"

A faint smile appeared on Poopvitch's face. "Next Wednesday, then; this matter is continued until next

Wednesday."

Billy looked down and shook his head. "I don't see how I can get anything done by then."

"You've got the week-end and three more days. Is there anything else?" the judge asked.

"That should be *more* than enough time," Billy said softly. Braxton recoiled in alarm. He looked at Billy, then the judge, then at Billy.

"What was that, Mr. Tapp?"

"I said, I would like a little more time."

"Wednesday, Mr. Tapp."

"Judge, I don't think Mr. Braxton has responded to Mr. Morgan's motion to dismiss." Billy looked over at Michael Braxton. Braxton was standing behind counsel's table, with his head bowed, looking at his well-shined black oxfords.

"Wednesday, Mr. Tapp."

CHAPTER FIVE

"Vickie. I'm afraid I've done it again. I think I've gotten into a case where there's no money and I can't win. How in the hell do I do this? Any calls?"

"Yeah. Here, this one looks interesting." Vickie handed Billy a telephone message from Mary Jacobs. "You represented Mary in a divorce a few years ago. I think her son is in jail for murder or something. Her number is on the message."

Billy took the message back to his office, tossed his brief case on the desk, and sorted through the other messages.

"Vickie," he yelled, "can you get Mary Jacobs on the phone for me?"

"Intercom, Billy. The intercom works. Push the button that says 'Vickie' and just start talking. It works."

"Okay. Right. Yelling just seems so much easier."

Vickie came to Billy's door. "Mary said you won't be able to get her until tonight. She said her son is in jail somewhere. I don't remember where. But she said she'd tell you about it when you call."

"When am I supposed to call her?"

"She won't be home until six o'clock tonight. Oh. And, also, call Ann."

* * * *

Billy picked up his telephone and dialed Ann's office number in College Park; her line was busy. After Lucy started preschool, Ann decided to go back to college to get her PhD in American Literature. She commuted to the University of Maryland every day for more than three years. Billy was amazed at both her determination to get her degree and her unflinching commitment to their children. Although he wasn't paying attention and didn't see it at the time, but the closer Ann got to her PhD, the farther she drifted from him. Instead of talking about the kids' school or whatever screwy case he was working on, they'd talk about her thesis or a faculty party or where she'd like to teach or the relevance of contemporary fiction to the Internet. She stopped talking about the family prattle and started talking about her academic interests. Then, one morning after the kids were off to school, she sat down at the kitchen table with both hands wrapped around a cup of hot coffee.

"Billy," she said gently. She stared into her coffee for a moment and without looking up, she said, "I'm not sure this is working."

"What's that? What's not working?"

"This."

Billy laid the newspaper on the table and took off his glasses. "Sorry I wasn't paying attention. I was just thinking about a motion I have to argue this morning. What time is it anyway? I've got to get out of here. I'm going to be late."

"Okay, Billy. We need to talk. Let's talk tonight."

"Okay. Great. We'll talk tonight."

* * * *

Vickie stuck her head in Billy's door again. "Are you expecting anyone?"

"No. Why?"

"There's some guy here. He said he didn't have an

appointment, but that he thought you might be expecting him." Vickie shrugged her shoulders, held her palms up, and looked at the ceiling. "What do you want me to tell him?"

"Who is it?"

"He said his name was Seymour Grey. Does that ring a bell?"

"Oh yes," Billy said. "That rings a bell."

Billy walked behind Vickie out to the reception room. There stood Seymour Grey, dressed in a gray suit with a white straight-collared shirt and a yellow printed tie. He held a worn Hartman briefcase and an umbrella. He was about five feet ten inches tall, slim, and looked to be in his early sixties. He had a full head of gray hair and a broad inviting smile. He looked like a million bucks.

"You must be William Tapp. I've heard good things about you." Seymour Grey extended his hand.

"Yes, I'm Billy Tapp." He gave Billy a firm handshake. "Come in and have a seat."

Seymour Grey followed him into the office and sat in a black pleated leather chair that Billy had taken in as fee for a drug case several years ago. Seymour Grey tucked his umbrella under the chair and carefully set his briefcase on the right side, precisely in line with the chair's front edge. He unbuttoned his suit coat and crossed his legs. "Sorry for just dropping in. I hope it is not too much of an inconvenience."

"No. Not really. I'm actually done in court for the day. Would you like a cup of coffee or a soft drink?"

"You know, I would love a cup of coffee, with just a little cream and sugar."

Billy stepped out of his office and asked Vickie to bring his unexpected guest a cup of coffee. "You don't mind fake cream do you?"

"Heavens no. Beggars can't be choosers."

Vickie brought two cups of coffee and handed one to Seymour Grey and one to Billy. She gave Billy a sarcastic grin and closed the door on the way out. Grey put the cup on the table next to the chair and took a deep breath. He held it for a moment and exhaled loudly. "Where do I start, Mr. Tapp?"

"Well at the beginning, I guess."

"Makes sense to me."

Before he had a chance to speak, Billy asked him, "How do you know Jason Roberts?"

"Who?"

"Jason Roberts. He's the lawyer that gave you my name."

"No. Well. The attorney that gave me your name was John Morgan. He is an attorney I have used over the years."

"That's right. Yeah, that's right. He's a friend of John Morgan. Actually, I think that Morgan asked Jason to take the case, and he couldn't for ... ah ... whatever reason."

"I cannot say that I remember Mr. Morgan mentioning the name Roberts. But, I do not think it makes any difference. Here we are."

"Right," Billy said.

"Do you know anything about my case?"

"Not much. I was in court this morning on your case, but that's it. Why don't you start at the very beginning."

Grey placed his hands in his lap.

"I am a real estate developer. Not by education, but by avocation. I am actually an old newspaperman. I have a journalism degree from Washington and Lee, and I worked for the Atlanta Constitution for fifteen years. I was the business editor and that's how I got interested in real estate development. I spent fifteen years writing about everyone else's successes, so I decided to do it myself. Had pretty good contacts and I started in a joint venture with a fellow I knew in Atlanta. We built a few duplexes, and we were off and running.

"Over the years, I have developed about fifteen hundred apartment units, five small shopping centers, two regional shopping centers, a few office buildings, and some land deals. Never had a bad deal. For the most part, always made lots of money.

"Not every real estate developer can say that," Billy said, laughing.

"Right." Grey smiled. "About five years ago, I had the good fortune to make the acquaintance of a Mr. Dozier Mound. He was the primary owner of a big savings and loan institution in Houston, Texas, called Federated Savings and Loan. I had been in the market to refinance one of my apartment deals. Without going into the details of that introduction ... which is another whole story ... I went out to Houston and met Dozier. We hit it off. Federated refinanced the apartment deal and Dozier and I actually became friends. Dozier was an interesting gentleman. He was a third or fourth generation Texan and had a law degree from Yale. Very bright. Very likable. So. Anyway. As time passed, I did not undertake any project without first talking about it with Dozier and Federated.

"You may know this ... it's a bit obscure ... at the time I did not. The national banks and some of the other lenders, I think, could not participate as joint venture partners in real estate deals. They had to be only the lender. But, like I said, Dozier was a real bright guy, and he concocted a way—and I think it became standard operating procedure in the industry—for saving and loan institutions to actually end up acting like joint venture partners, but still not violate the state and federal regulations."

Seymour paused his explanation long enough for it to sink in. He looked at Billy to make sure that Billy both understood everything and wasn't losing interest.

"Yeah," Billy said. "I know a little bit about state and Federal banking regulations. I've been involved in a few lender liability suits where the lenders violated the Federal Code. They faced huge liability, but we settled them out for almost no money because the plaintiffs' lawyers didn't know what they were doing. Plus, I'm a quick study." Billy smiled.

"Oh. You know something about this. That's good. My case has some lender liability issues too." Seymour's face brightened. "I think you are going to find this interesting."

"How did ... ah what's his name ... Mound get around the regulations that prohibit joint ventures in real estate deals?"

"Well counselor, I am glad you asked." Seymour smiled and took another sip of coffee. "As I said, this is a bit complex. But if you think about it, it makes perfect sense."

"Apparently there are all kinds of rules and procedures that the S&L's need to follow. For example, to make sure one person does not use the S&L as his own little fiefdom, all loans need to be approved by a loan committee. The idea, of course, is to add a factor of review and fiduciary perspective to the S&L's decisions. Protect the depositors and shareholders ... and all that. All this is good in theory. But, in the real world, as we all know, most of these kinds of boards are controlled by a few people, and those few people are usually controlled by one person. In this case that one person was Dozier. His word was law. He always got what he wanted. If you did not go along with him, you would find yourself on the outside looking in.

"Do not get me wrong. Dozier Mound was not unreasonable, not unfair, not unethical, not precipitous, and not unscrupulous. In fact, he was one of the most straight up, honest men I have ever known. I do not think he ever did anything for himself that ever had a negative impact on Federated.

As Billy grew more enthralled with Seymour's tale, he remembered the name Federated Savings and Loan. When he worked at Wellington and Becket, his morning ritual included reading the first pages of the Wall Street Journal, the New York Times, and the Houston Chronicle. With the exception of the comics, Dear Abby, and the sports section, the rest of the paper didn't hold much interest for him. "You know, I remember something about Federated, I think. Weren't they one of the biggest S&Ls in the county?"

"They were. You are correct."

"I don't know why I remember the name now but I do. I'll think of it in a minute."

"They were the largest S&L ever to go into receivership. But I will get into that in a bit."

"That's right. Now I remember. They were. At the time, they were the biggest savings and loan ever to go in the shitcan. Made the front page of the Wall Street Journal. I don't remember all the details. You want some more coffee?"

"No thank you. I am fine."

"Where were we? What were you saying about Federated? Sorry, didn't mean to interrupt." Billy was no longer taking notes. He folded his hands behind his head and leaned back in his chair.

"Dozier set up a company called Federated Building, Inc. He used to laugh and call it the FBI. FBI was a consultant for the real estate development industry and a joint venture partner for selected Federated borrowers. The truth of the matter was that FBI had some real capable people with a lot of knowledge in construction, finance, and marketing ... important components to a successful real estate project. FBI would take a ten percent profit participation in a real estate project and not only help the developer with the projects costs and what have you, but also keep an eye on the whole development process for Federated ... and the borrower. It was a win, win.

"As time passed, as I said, Dozier and I became friends. He was fifteen or so years older than me. He invited me to his parties and annual functions. A few months before I started the Frederick Mall, Dozier asked me to actually get involved with Federated Building as its primary ... consultant ... for lack of a better word, and to look at all of Federated's new real estate retail deals. I cannot begin to tell you what that could have meant to me ... in terms of money. Federated probably looked at twenty-five or thirty real estate deals per month, and it probably financed three or four. My job would have been to make sure the market was appropriate, the developer's costs were in line, and what have you."

Billy interrupted Grey. "Was that a full time job?"

"Oh no. It was never intended to be full time. We specifically agreed that I would keep doing my own real estate development interests. But, you know, I was in the market, following construction and development costs, seeing which retailers were doing what, so it really was not any more than doing what I was doing for myself."

"Were you paid?"

"Absolutely. Like I said, Federated Building got ten percent of the deal, and I was to get twenty percent of the ten percent."

"So, you didn't get a salary."

"Oh no. No. The idea was that I would only get paid if the project were successful. And, my job ... or function ... if you will, was to make sure that before Federated committed financing, the project would be successful. It was a fair deal. If I was worth my salt I got paid, if not, I did not. That's the way real estate development works anyway. Only difference with the Federated Building deal was that I did not have any of my own money at risk. My only risk was reputation and time."

"Why would FBI be any real benefit to Federated? Don't lenders have the same expertise in-house? Isn't that what lenders do? Couldn't somebody say FBI was nothing more than a sham to get money by some kind of pious extortion?"

"That was my first reaction. But, you know, counselor, the more I thought about, the more it made sense. Sure it may have been a loophole. But, it was legal, and it served a good purpose.

"You can say that generally real estate developments fail for one of four reasons: bad location, improper financing, cost overruns, or poor management. If a developer covers these four areas, chances are he will be fine. Most lenders use in-house people to monitor these things ... and we all know the quality of in-house people. Particularly banks. For the most part, if bank folks really knew what they were doing, they would not be working at the bank. They would be out in the private sector where all the real money is. Some lenders hire outside consulting firms to monitor construction and costs, but these guys are working for a fee. They are paid whether the project is successful or not. And, more importantly, they are normally looking at just one part of the four areas that can undo a real estate deal. Federated Building did not just look at part of the deal; it looked at the front-end market, financing, and cost, and then reviewed operation and management after the project opened."

"So, instead of hiring outside consultant's Federated created its own consultants and took an ownership interest in the project. That's interesting. But it seems to me that there's some regulation or something that restricts federally insured lenders from owning deals that they finance," Billy said.

"Very good. I think that is right. I do not know all the details, but Dozier circumvented the ownership issue by having Federated Building take fees for the consulting before the project opened and, what he called, a 'profit participation' after the project opened."

"Pretty slick. Is that all kosher?"

"As far as I know," Grey said.

Billy looked at his watch about the same time that Vickie stuck her head through the doorway. She had an arm full of notebooks and an umbrella.

"I'm leaving. I put the phones on answering and I'll leave your door open and the front door unlocked so you can hear if anybody comes in. Okay?"

"Sure. Oh, by the way, good luck on your test tonight. Is it raining? Everybody has an umbrella."

"No, Billy. You were out earlier today. I'm just taking my umbrella down to my car. My test was last night, but thanks anyway. See you tomorrow. Good night Mr. Grey." The front door slammed.

"She certainly seems like a pleasant girl."

"She's a good person," Billy said. "I hope she doesn't decide to leave after she gets her degree."

Seymour offered a wry smile and parenthetically added: "There are no guarantees. But, you ask," he continued, "what does all this have to do with the Frederick City Mall?" Before

Billy could respond, Seymour said, "Well maybe not much, but I think it is important that you understand the lay of the land with me and Federated and FSLIC."

"FSLIC," Billy said. "Have you had much experience with FSLIC?"

"None. Well, except in this case. But never before."

"I don't mean to interrupt here, but whenever I've dealt with FSLIC or FDIC, it's been a real pain in the ass."

"Mr. Tapp, tell me something that I do not know. And, I guess maybe I should get to the substance of ... how shall we say it ... my problems with the Frederick City Mall."

"I need to make a phone call around six o'clock. What time is it now?"

Seymour stretched his left arm through a well-starched French cuff and looked at his gold Rolex Oyster watch. "It is quarter past five."

"Good. Let's see, keep going. You were about to tell me about the Frederick City Mall."

"That's right. The Frederick City Mall." Seymour paused and took a ceremonious sip of coffee.

"Without going into all the details now, through a friend of a friend, I leaned about a piece of property in Frederick, Maryland that was available because of foreclosure. One of Dozier Mound's friends owned the lender that foreclosed on the land. Small world. Anyway, I flew up here and looked at the property. It was properly zoned, it seemed to be in a good location, and it was cheap. The next day we negotiated an option to purchase the property subject to a sixty-day inspection period. I called Dozier and told him about the deal. Before I got back to Houston, Dozier had talked to his Chevy Chase friend and had arranged for a loan. It was just that simple. We took the option to purchase ... and I say we, but I guess it was really me. Typical deal. Fifteen thousand down ... refundable, of course ... and a ninety day study period to make sure infrastructure was available, with the right to extend the option for six months."

Billy knew that real estate developers normally bought

property with an option period so they could make sure that the market and zoning were right and, more importantly, to make sure there were tenants interested enough to either rent or buy-in once the project was built.

"That's a pretty long option for only fifteen thousand dollars," Billy said.

"You are right. Yes, that is correct. But to get the additional six months, we had to forfeit the fifteen thousand dollars, and we had to put up an additional one hundred thousand dollars, of which twenty-five was not refundable. All the option money, of course, applied to the purchase price, which, I do not think I said was two point five million dollars. It was one hundred thousand dollars an acre for twenty-five acres. Hell of a deal. And, Federated Savings and Loan agreed to front all the money. This was my first deal with Federated since Dozier got me involved with FBI."

Billy leaned forward and fiddled with his pen. Seymour sensed a question; he pursed his lips and nodded very slightly at Billy.

"Wasn't there some kind of conflict of interest here? You being a member of FBI and Federated making the loan. I don't mean offense, but, if you'll pardon my presumptuousness, wasn't that ... ah, sort of, ah ... or couldn't somebody at least make the argument ... that the burglar was guarding the jewels?"

"I suppose one could," Seymour bristled. "But Dozier made it very clear to both me and everyone else that I could not and would not participate with FBI in any deal that either I or my company developed. Remember, there were two separated entities: Federated Savings and Loan ... the lender ... and Federated Building, Inc. ... the joint venture partner."

"The partner and the consultant. Right?" Billy interjected.

"Well, of course. The consultant too."

"Was that part of your written agreement with Mound?"

"What is that, Mr. Tapp? Was what part of my agreement with Mound?"

"Did you have an agreement that addressed the possible conflict of interest with your projects? Did you have a written agreement.?"

"Sure. It was not too formal. Dozier and I signed an outline of our agreement. It was to have been put in a more formal document. That, of course, never happened because of Federated S&L's problems. But, it was an agreement to enter into an agreement, and from what my lawyers tell me, that is enforceable."

"Could be. Might be. I'd need to see it first."

The front door opened and slammed shut. Billy heard someone timidly say, "Hello. Anybody here? Hello? Anybody home?" Seymour craned his head to look out into the reception room and Billy got up and came from behind his desk.

"Excuse me just a minute. Sorry."

"Do you need me to go in the other room? I could make some phone calls."

"No. No. Just sit tight. I don't know who that is. Let me go out and see. Just sit tight." Billy walked out and closed the door behind him.

"Mary. Vickie said you called. I was going to call you a little later tonight. What time is it anyway?"

"Mr. Tapp, I am so sorry to just drop in. But, I was in the neighborhood, so I thought I'd just come up here and see if you were still in."

"That's okay. I've got somebody in my office right now. But tell me real quickly what the problem is."

Billy leaned against Vickie's desk, and Mary Jacobs flopped into a chair in the reception room. She was about five feet tall and slightly overweight, wearing a long sleeved print shirt and a dark blue skirt. She held a rumpled manila envelope in her hand and two shopping bags and a large flowered haversack in both arms. She squeezed her articles together and rested them in her lap. Mary Jacobs was forty-three years old and divorced. She was born and raised in a little mining community in the southwestern part of Virginia. She had three children, the oldest was twenty-five and the youngest fifteen.

"They've arrested Terry. They said he killed somebody." Mary began sobbing. She pulled a tattered Kleenex out of her bag and wiped it across her nose. "I don't know what to do. They've put his bond at five hundred thousand dollars! I don't have that kind of money. He's in jail with all those criminals. My God, I just don't know what to do. What are we going to do? We can't let him sit down there in that jail." Mary looked at Billy in pitiful desperation. "There's no telling what's going to happen to him down there!"

"Has he been arraigned yet?"

"I don't know. What does that mean? Do you mean has he been to court yet?"

"No. It's arraigned. When they read the charges to him and he pleads guilty or not guilty."

"He's not guilty. He wouldn't plead guilty. Terry couldn't have killed anybody. This must be some kind of a mistake. They wouldn't let me see him. I went down there, and they treated me like I was some kind of criminal. Mr. Tapp, you know that Terry wouldn't hurt anybody. He wouldn't kill anybody."

"Well, apparently someone thinks he did. Where is he?"

"He's in jail."

"No that's not what I mean. I mean what jail is he in?"

"Oh. He's in the Montgomery County jail. It's in—"

"Yeah. I know where it is. Let me call over there and see what the deal is. Sit tight here for a second. Let me go back in my office for a minute. I'll be right back out in a few minutes."

"Okay. Thank you, Mr. Tapp."

Billy left Mary wiping her eyes and sobbing quietly, and he went back into his office and closed the door behind him. Seymour had gotten up, and he was looking out the window.

"You know, I have always enjoyed coming to Washington. I like the restaurants, the energy, and everything. Say, why not go somewhere and grab dinner, and I will finish telling you my story."

"Tonight's kind of tough for me."

"What about tomorrow night? I have to be in town for a few days. What do you say about getting together tomorrow night?"

"Sure," Billy said. "That sounds good. Where are you staying? I'll give you a call tomorrow and we'll coordinate."

"Ah. I am staying with my son. Over here in Georgetown. Ah ... why don't I just give you a call tomorrow, and we will decide then. That suit?"

"Sure. Sounds good to me. I look forward to it."

Seymour gathered his brief case and umbrella, stood up, buttoned his suit coat, and shook Billy's hand. He nodded formally to Mary and walked out.

"Mr. Tapp, I'm sorry to interrupt you."

"That's okay, Mary. Now. When do you think Terry has to be in court?"

"I don't know. Here's some stuff they gave me at the jail. I don't exactly know what it is. Here, maybe you do." She handed the envelope to Billy.

Billy pulled the contents out and sorted through a property list, a criminal complaint, a pre-trial report from the probation and parole office, and an arrest warrant for murder with bond hand written in at five hundred thousand dollars.

"He hasn't been to court yet?"

"I don't think so."

"Well, I'm sure he'll be arraigned tomorrow morning. I'll call the jail tonight, and I'll be there in the morning. Call Vickie in the morning and she'll tell you where and when."

"Thank you, Mr. Tapp. Thank you so much."

"Try not to worry. Go home. I'll see you tomorrow and we'll try to figure out what's going on here."

CHAPTER SIX

"We have a copy of the indictment and we'll waive reading it. Enter a plea of not guilty," Billy said.

Terry and Billy stood together at the podium. Terry wore a jail-issue Halloween orange jump suit that was at least two sizes too big. He was nineteen years old. His innocent blond-haired appearance was undermined by a dot, about the size of a pencil eraser, tattooed on his right cheek. From a distance, it could easily be mistaken for a birthmark. Jacobs was charged with the murder of a drug dealer, whose street name was Fatso Boy.

* * * *

Several months before the alleged killing, Fatso Boy borrowed two CDs from Terry, and, despite repeated requests, which turned into demands from Terry, Fatso refused to give them back. Every time Terry saw Fatso, he asked for the CDs. At first, Fatso just ignored Terry. But as time passed, Fatso became more annoyed and more truculent. On the occasion of Terry's next to last request, Fatso further clarified his position. He was sitting on a park picnic table with three large men who obviously spent a good deal of time in the gym. Fatso Boy wore a red Hawaiian shirt with the top three buttons undone, showing a small red rose tattoo framed in barbed wire on his neck.

"I ain't giving you no mother fuckin' CDs! I ain't got no mother fuckin' CDs of yours! And, you little fag shit, if you keep fuckin' with me you're damn well gonna' get something back. You're gonna' catch some shit back! Some *real* shit! It ain't about CDs, fool. It's about the street. What's on this street is mine. You on this street, you mine! CDs on this street. Mine. Get it, punk?" And, with that, Fatso pulled his shirt back and brandished the gunmetal gray handle of a nine-millimeter Gluck pistol that was stuffed in his trousers.

Terry's stomach cramped with fear, and he thought for a moment that he might pass out or piss himself. He stumbled backward and the corners of his mouth turned ashen. When he gained his composure, he looked around and hoped that his two cousins hadn't seen his fear. He turned and walked back to the car. With each step he became more furious. *Who in the hell does that fat bastard think he is?*

Fatso Boy's ridicule and laughter followed Terry to the car. "CDs. What the fuck you talkn' 'bout CDs. I'll show you CDs up your ass. Ha. Ha. Ha."

"T. J., you get your CDs?" his cousins asked when he got in the car.

"Nah. Fatso's actin' a prick. He's an asshole."

"Best not let him hear you say that. He ain't nobody to fuck with."

Terry slid into the car and started the engine. "I ain't afraid of that fat ass hole."

"T. J., you best just forget about those CDs. I just don't think he's anybody you want to fuck with. You know what his reputation is. He gets what he wants. What's his is his, and what's yours is his. You need to stay away from him. Honestly, he's dangerous. You're no match for him."

"What are you talking about. I ain't afraid of that fat fucker."

"You better be. He'll chew you up and spit you out. This is his turf. Anything on it belongs to him. You know that."

"Bullshit," Terry said.

"Yeah? Bullshit too."

Terry and his cousins drove away. Terry hated Fatso Boy, but he hated even more that Fatso Boy had backed him down and scared him to death, not to mention humiliated him in front of his two cousins. *I'll get even with that fat bastard, I'll show him who's afraid of who.* As they drove away Terry began concocting his plan for revenge.

* * * *

"Judge Barr," Billy said, "Mr. Jacobs' bond is set at five hundred thousand dollars. There's no way he can make that. I'd like to make a motion to reduce the bond or that the court set a bond hearing."

"This is a murder case, Your Honor. We'd oppose a bond reduction," the prosecuting attorney said.

"I don't want to change his bond until I look at this a little closer, but we're sort of running out of time this morning. We have a rather long civil docket, so why don't y'all get with my secretary after court and see if we can agree on bond or on a time for a short hearing this afternoon? Is there anything else on the criminal docket? Anybody have anything that I didn't call?" There were only four people in the courtroom, and no one responded. "I'm going to take about a ten minute break before I call the civil docket."

The jailer took Terry back to the holdover. Billy walked around the rail that separated the public seating from the front of the courtroom to where Mary was sitting.

"What happened? What was that? Is Terry going to get out of jail? Did you have time to talk to him?"

"This was the arraignment. Judge Barr didn't lower the bond. He didn't do anything other than make sure we know what the charge is. I need to call his secretary's office this afternoon and see if we can get a bond hearing." Billy looked at Mary. "Do you understand what I just said?"

"Yes I think so. Do you think we can get him out of jail

today?"

"I don't know. I'll try. But, I can't give you any guarantees. We'll have to wait and see what the judge wants to do."

With the exception of Billy and Mary, the courtroom was now empty. Mary wondered what she would do. She had to pay Billy almost fifteen hundred dollars for her divorce three years ago, and she was certain that a murder case would be more complicated and more expensive. She worried about Terry sitting in jail with a bunch of dangerous criminals and she worried about her fifteen-year-old daughter at home. She wondered how she would pay Billy, pay the rent, pay for her daughter's school supplies, for food, clothing, car, insurance, telephone, gas, electric, taxes, and everything else. Bond, she thought, if I pay the bond, I can't pay anything else. Mary squeezed her eyes shut and wished that she could die peacefully, right there in the courtroom. No fuss no muss. Just lay down on the big walnut bench and die. My God, she thought, I can't even stand up, much less leave this courtroom. What am I going to do?

"You okay?" Billy asked.

"Maybe. I think so. What do we do next?"

"Let me talk to the judge and I'll call you tonight."

* * * *

Billy walked the wrong way through the metal detector on his way out of the courthouse. The alarm sounded. "I guess it's okay to take your gun out, you just can't bring it in," Billy said to the hefty female guard.

She scowled at him. "Billy Tapp," she said, "All you do is cause trouble."

Billy walked over to a round concrete table that sat under a gingko tree, just to the right of the courthouse entrance. Pungent berries with the faint smell of vomit lay crushed and strewn around the table. Two men and a woman walked across the street, each man carried a large valise and the woman pulled a cart stacked with three banker's boxes. All three were dressed in dark blue suits, the only difference in their appearance was that the woman wore a skirt and the men wore pants. Stone faced and determined, they rushed past Billy and ceremoniously paraded into the courthouse.

A row of dark green curbside trash containers sat next to the courthouse in an alcove behind the concrete table. An old man dressed in dirty khaki pants, gym shoes, a sweatshirt, and a tattered black sport coat peered into one of the trash containers. He held the lid open with his head. He carried a blue mesh sack and he clinched the filter of a cigarette butt in his brown teeth.

"Ah, ah, ah. What's this? What do we have here? Paper, drywall, plaster, wire stuff, plastic to-go boxes—propriety confidential official court documents?" Some of the trash spilled onto the sidewalk as he made his way down the line. "Not much here. Not much worth anything coming out of this building. Nothing worth keeping. Nope. Nope. Nope," he said as he slammed down each lid.

After rummaging through the trashcans, he sat on the concrete bench across from Billy. He laid the blue bag on the table and fumbled through his pockets before he Styxed his gray beard and smiled at Billy.

"Excuse me sir. You don't have a light do you?" He took the cigarette butt out of his mouth and held it at Billy.

"No. I don't smoke." Billy looked away to avoid the old man's stare.

"That's smart. That's smart. Smoking will kill you. You know that? It will kill you. I quit once, but I thought, what the hell, I'm going to die anyway. Life's going to kill you too. So what difference does it make? Smoking's going to kill you, drinking's going to kill you, cancer's going to kill you, a car accident's going to kill you, high blood pressure's going to kill you, some damned fool's going to kill you … something's going to kill you. Even if it doesn't you're still going to die. That's why I said *life* is going to kill you. My dad didn't drink, didn't smoke, didn't cuss, didn't eat too much, didn't do anything bad. His only vice was that he loved chocolate candy ... especially *Reese Cups*. But, he'd only eat chocolate at Christmas and Thanksgiving and on his birthday. I can't ever remember him missing church on Sunday. At fifty-seven years of age, out of the clear blue sky, he got diabetes. It hit him in the head like a bucket of hammers. They amputated his right foot, then his right leg, then they cut of his left leg. They stuck him in a wheel chair and gave him insulin shots twice a day. Next thing you know, he'd gained a hundred seventy-five pounds. He puffed up like a beach ball. Setting in that wheel chair, he looked like a lawn bag stuffed with leaves. One day my mother called and said she thought there was something wrong with him. I came over and found him in a mess of *Reese Cup's* wrappers, dead from insulin shock. So, let me ask you, mister. Did he die from diabetes or from life?"

"Well. I'm sorry for your loss."

"Oh hell, that happened ten years ago. Water over the dam. Life. It's life. Like I said, we're all gonna die, one way or the other. Did I ask you for a light? Do you have a light?"

"No. I don't smoke."

"Yeah. I guess that's what you said. Time to mosey on. See ya later. Have a good day." The old man stuffed the cigarette in his coat pocket and shuffled away toward the fountain in the adjacent park.

Several pigeons landed on the sidewalk next to the trash containers and began walking in circles and making soft chortling sounds while pecking at specks on the sidewalk.

"You, too."

CHAPTER SEVEN

Seymour Grey suggested that they meet at La Rogue, a small French restaurant across the Potomac River in Old Town, Virginia. La Rogue had fifteen or so tables and a bar located all the way in the back with seven stools. It was old and worn but clean and neat. Each table was carefully covered with a white tablecloth and the wait-staff all wore black pants and formal white shirts with black bowties. La Rogue was owned and operated by a French woman named Madame Marcel Claret. She and her husband opened the restaurant almost twenty-five years ago. He was formally trained at Le Cordon Bleu in Paris and had worked as a master chef in London before coming to Old Town. Marcel, on the other hand, had no formal culinary training, but when her husband died shortly after opening La Rogue, she took up the helm and it had been smooth sailing since. The food was authentic French; it was consistent and served with pride and punctuality. Madame Claret was in the restaurant every day except two weeks during the Christmas holiday and three weeks at the end of the summer, when she closed and left town on a well-deserved and well-needed vacation.

Seymour called and made the reservations for two. When he arrived a little early by taxicab, all the tables were filled, so he left his name with the pretty woman at the door and picked his way through the customers and took a seat at the bar. He asked for the wine list and selected an expensive Bordeaux from a vineyard that he knew in the Haut-Medoc region of France. The bartender, who doubled as the sommelier, complimented Seymour's choice and asked if he should bring two glasses. Seymour waved his hand dismissively and asked why he should. The bartender agreed and presented the wine for Seymour's approval. After an unnecessarily ceremonious display, he opened the bottle and poured a small portion. Seymour picked up the glass, swirled the wine, looked through it, and tasted it. He frowned and sat it back on the bar. The bartender recoiled slightly and looked at Seymour. After an uncomfortable pause, Seymour looked up.

"Excellent."

"Excellent. Oh good. Good. Excellent. Ah ... can I get you a menu or are you waiting or are you ordering?"

"Meeting somebody. I am fine. Thank you."

"Well alright. If you need anything, just yell. Do you have reservations? Are you on the book?"

"Yes. I gave the maitre' d my name when I came in. She knows that I am here."

"Okay. Madame Claret. Why yes. She knows you're here. Okay, well then, enjoy your wine."

Seymour was staying at the Four Seasons Hotel in Georgetown. He had called his long time friend and attorney John Morgan after the meeting last night with Billy Tapp. There was something about Tapp that bothered Seymour. He couldn't exactly put his finger on it. Maybe it was the informal office or Vickie's nonchalance or Billy's demeanor, but there was something unsettling about Billy Tapp and Seymour was anxious to get Morgan's opinion.

The call didn't help much. Morgan told Seymour that Jason Roberts had referred Tapp. Morgan had never met Roberts, but he went to law school with one of the four senior partners in Roberts' firm. Roberts said that Tapp was a good attorney with a brilliant legal mind. He had graduated near the top of his law school class, but easily could have been number one if he'd made any effort at all. Tapp had been in the Navy, clerked for a United States Supreme Court judge, and made junior partner at Wellington and Bracket, a prestigious D.C. white glove law firm, after only three years. Tapp was apparently on the fast track at Wellington, when one day, for no apparent reason, he just up and quit. Or, at least that was what one of the stories was. He was there one day and gone the next. Morgan had asked if there was anything in Tapp's past that he should know, and Roberts assured him there was not. Tapp had been honorably discharged from the Navy, and Roberts said he had known him since law school.

"He's a guy that I call when I have an unusual or unique legal question. Mr. Morgan, there's only one Billy Tapp. If he likes your case, there's not a better attorney in D.C."

Seymour wasn't sure if Morgan's information was a compliment or a criticism. But, after the second glass of wine, his angst began to recede into the soft amber glow of the expensive Bordeaux.

Marcel Claret came to the little bar where Seymour sat alone with his wine. She knew his type. *Washington D.C. is a magnet for such self-indulgent dilettante with a proclivity for expensive public consumption.* She made her money off men like Seymour Grey.

Marcel Claret wore a yellow printed summer dress with short sleeves and a braided leather sash synched around her remarkably trim waste. She was 5' 4" tall with perfect physical proportions. The slight lines around her mouth gave her a countenance that took Seymour aback. Marcel's mother had been a member of the French underground in World War II and her father a British soldier. She grew up in France during the war, but she was educated in England. Marcel Claret was a stunning woman who, despite many opportunities, never remarried. She had adored her husband and dealt with her grief by plunging into the La Rogue, the only thing that she had left of him. Marcel often regretted that she had no children, but the restaurant had been her progeny and obsession and, although she could no longer remember when, long ago it took on its own *raison d'etre*. She'd had a smattering of romantic affairs over the years, but was never willing to let anyone interfere with her commitment to the restaurant or her husband's memory. For some time after her husband died, she often spent the night in the restaurant. She slept in the little office off the kitchen because she was afraid that if she left, she'd loose his memory. It was a ridiculous idea, but back then, she was afraid to let it go.

"Mr. Grey. Your table is ready. Are you ready to be seated?"

Seymour smiled effusively. "I am actually still waiting for my guest."

"You're welcome to wait here at the bar, or you may wait at your table if you like, and we'll bring your guest over to you."

Marcel walked behind the cash register and keyed in a food order on the point of sales computer setting on the end of the bar, which in turn, sent the information back to the kitchen cook line for preparation.

"You have a French accent. Are you from France?"

Marcel looked up. "Yes."

"I've spent a good bit of time in France. Where in France are you from?"

"Excuse me a moment please," Marcel said. She gave Seymour a terse smile and turned and walked into the kitchen. A few minutes later, she emerged with a plate in each hand. She gracefully maneuvered to a table near the entrance and put the plates in front of two customers. She smiled at them and looked up as Billy Tapp came into the restaurant's small vestibule. Marcel wiped her hands on the towels she had used to carry the plates and hurried over to Billy.

Her smile broadened and she cocked her head. "Do you have reservations, sir?"

"No, I don't. But I'm meeting someone here. I'm a little late."

"Well. Perhaps do you see her here? Please look around."

Billy made an exaggerated effort to look around the restaurant. "No. I don't see her. How about you? If she doesn't show up, how about you having dinner with me? Know where we can get anything good to eat?"

"Mr. Tapp. *Mon Dieu*, you are such a tease. If I was ten years younger ..."

Billy spotted Seymour at the bar. "There she is. That's my date sitting at the bar. She looks pretty exciting. Has she been here long?"

Marcel rolled her eyes and took Billy's hand and walked him back to the bar. She gave him a kiss on the cheek and disappeared into the kitchen.

"Do you know that woman?" Seymour asked.

"That is Madam Marcel Claret. I've known her for a long, long time. She owns this place. I've been coming here for years."

"She's stunning."

"Yep. She's that alright. Is our table ready?"

"Yes." Seymour motioned to the bartender. "We're ready to be seated now."

"Yes, sir. Let me get Marcel."

"Just bring this wine to our table," Seymour said. "Is that alright?"

Marcel came out of the kitchen and led Seymour and Billy to their table. "Mr. Tapp. This is your favorite table, I presume."

"Yes it is, Marcel. How did you know?"

Marcel smiled at Billy and gave them each a hand written menu; she said that their waiter would soon follow. The bartender brought the remainder of Seymour's wine and a glass for Billy.

"How did your case come out today? Was it Mary Jacobs ... I think I heard you say?"

"It was just an arraignment. It's a murder charge.

Murder. Sometimes they're easy and sometimes they're hard. Either way, murder has a way of getting special attention. Sell a bunch of crack that might kill who knows how many people, steal cars, abandon a kid, crack open an ATM machine, rob a liquor store, and commit God knows what other crimes, and you might not get noticed. Kill somebody … even if they deserve it. Then you really get to see what the criminal justice system is all about."

"What kind of cases do you normally do, Counselor?"

"All kinds. Mostly, these days, ones that don't pay."

"Let me tell you a little more about my case. Maybe we can fix that for you." Seymour poured Billy more wine from a second bottle.

"Fire," Billy said.

"As I told you the other day in your office, Dozier Mound arranged the financing for the development in Frederick. I tied up the property and hired an engineer and an architect to layout a shopping center. Again, I do not know how much you know about the process, but normally a civil engineer will do what is called a site plan, which is not much more than deciding the building sizes and location, parking requirements, drainage issues, and utilities. He also makes sure the site is properly zoned and the proposed development complies with the building code. It sounds a lot more complicated than it really is, but it is something that has to be done. After the site plan, I usually get with an architect and decide on ideas about design and what I want the development … the buildings and what not … to actually look like."

The waiter came to the table with a complimentary *hors d'oeuvre*. "Mr. Tapp, Marcel would like your opinion of these," he said.

"Why thank you. What is this?"

"Sautéed sweetbreads with a new Pinot Noir sauce that she's been working on. She wants your opinion." There were eight pieces on the plate and two small forks.

"Do you like sweetbreads?" Billy asked Seymour.

"My heavens yes. It is one of my favorites."

"Try it. See what you think. Marcel doesn't serve bad food."

Seymour took a fork and ate one of the pieces. He smiled and said, "Very good. Very good. An absolutely unique sauce, but the sweetbreads are excellent."

Seymour continued. "After we get an idea what the project is going to look like, we start talking to prospective tenants to lease the space. Generally speaking, there are two kinds of tenants. Anchor tenants and the rest.

"Anchor tenants are the large department stores, national grocery chains, movie theaters, and other, so called, 'big box' users. Anchor tenants not only give our bank the assurance that the project will be successful, but they also bring lots of customers to the center."

"Sure I understand. I'm familiar with the idea or theory or whatever you call it."

"You do not make much money ... if any money ... on the anchors until you refinance or pay off your first mortgage, but they are the back bone ... hence the name 'anchor' ... of any successful retail development."

"I understand," Billy said.

"Anchors are essential—"

"Yes." Billy interrupted. "I understand."

"Okay. Well, then. So, I went through the exercise. Got the engineers and architects and put together a regional center ... a center that would have more than a local draw. Everything went together like clockwork. It was almost too easy. I put together a construction budget and an operating pro forma. The idea, and again I am not trying to be too ... ah ... pedantic, is to collect enough rent to pay the debt service on the project loan."

Marcel came over to the table. "What did you think Billy? Did you like the sweetbreads, no?"

"They were great." Marcel gave a slight frown. "No really," Billy said, "they were great. Everything you make is great."

"*Tres magnifique*," Seymour said.

Marcel glowered at Seymour and winked at Billy and went back to the bar.

"We decided that the total project cost would be in the neighborhood of seventy-five million dollars. This would have been the biggest project I had done. So, we put all the parts together and Federated made the loan. It was just that easy."

"Now, was the FBI in the deal too?"

"Yes, Federated Building had a profit participation, but I had no part of their share. We broke ground and started construction. It was supposed to have taken twenty-eight months to build." Seymour paused and emptied his glass and, then, refilled it.

He continued. "Everything was going great. We had the anchors that we needed and the other tenants ... the small tenants. They were knocking our door down. The small tenants are pure profit; they are where we make our money. As I said, they pay a lot more rent and they are much cheaper to get in the center. The small tenants are the gravy." Seymour paused again, this time his expression became grave.

"It was going great. Could not have been better. And, that is when ... excuse me ... the shit hit the fan."

Marcel came by the table again and took up the empty plate and small forks. Seymour didn't look up.

"We were eighty-nine percent done. We were a month ahead of schedule and almost three million dollars under budget. Under budget! My loan agreement with Federated provided that after the center opened and the cash flow stabilized, I would get any amount that we were under budget. That money would have been simply funded to me. It would have been part of the loan to the center. No tax consequences. Do you know what that would have meant?"

"Sure. It's a loan. No taxes to you. The center pays it off and pays the taxes as they pay off the loan over the term. Probably twenty years or so. It would have been like almost free money to you."

"That is right. No taxes."

"I understand. So what happened?" Billy asked.

"The Feds forced Federated into receivership!" Seymour's face flushed.

"Who forced them? What do you mean the Feds?"

"FSLIC. The Federal Savings and Loan Insurance Corporation."

"How'd that happen?"

Seymour leaned forward. "Here is how. I will make a long story short. FSLIC requires that lenders like Federated have a certain 'net worth.' It is based on the ratio between loans and deposits. If the loan amounts are too high compared to deposits, the ratio is out of whack, and the savings and loan either must get more deposits or get rid of some of the loans. FSLIC has periodic inspections and audits and if the 'net worth' is out of balance, FSLIC has the power to put them in receivership. That is what happened. The quality of the loans does not matter, if the ratio is not right, there is a problem. And that is what happened."

"If the project construction was going so well, how did you end up in Federal court?"

"When FSLIC put Federated into receivership, someone decided that my loan was one of the ones that they needed to get rid of. They gave me thirty days to refinance or else. I could not get another loan because the money market had changed. Thirty-one days later, FSLIC filed suit to foreclose. We filed an answer and asked that the court dismiss the suit. That is pretty much where it stands right now."

Billy took a deep breath and exhaled loudly. "You spent the better part of three years cultivating this little garden of intrigue, and you want me to pull all the weeds in the better part of three days. Hell, no problem." Billy leaned back in his chair and stared at the ceiling. He squeezed his eyes shut and desperately tried to think of nothing.

"What is your basis ... why did you file a motion to dismiss? Why should the court dismiss the foreclosure lawsuit?"

"I was not in default of my loan. That is why. I was not in default."

"Somebody must have thought you were. What did your lawyer Morgan tell you?"

"I do not know. He was the one who filed the answer and the motion to dismiss. Have you talked to him? Maybe you need to talk to him."

"I'll call him in the morning. Listen. It's getting a little bit late, and I've got a full day tomorrow. We need to talk about costs here. This is going to take a bunch of time, and I'm afraid, it's not going to be cheap."

"I did not think it would be."

"I'm going to have to have a retainer to represent you in this case. The problem with Judge Poopvitch is that once a lawyer gets in a case, he won't let you out. This case could take a few years to sort out. I'm sure Morgan told you that."

"How much of a retainer do you need, counselor?"

Billy hadn't been prepared for Seymour's understanding and apparent willingness to pay a retainer. He quickly calculated in his head the time he'd need to prepare a response to the motion to dismiss. "I think I'll need a fifty thousand retainer that I'll bill against. When the balance gets down to five thousand dollars, you'll have to replenish it with forty-five thousand bucks."

Seymour didn't flinch. "Fair enough, counselor. I will bring a check by your office tomorrow."

The waiter brought the check and Seymour suggested that they might have a glass of an exceptional Port wine that he had seen on the wine list. "This place has a very respectable wine list ... for such a small place. I wonder where she keeps all those good wines?"

Billy excused himself to go to the bathroom, which was located at the end of the bar in the hallway to the kitchen. He passed Marcel coming out of the kitchen.

She nodded toward Seymour. "A friend or a client? A friend, I hope. You have been very generous to him. Did you enjoy?"

"Oh, yeah. Thanks. No. Well, he's buying. He's a new client."

"But, of course he is," Marcel said.

When Billy returned to the table, Seymour was looking at the check. "Say, counselor. This is a little bit embarrassing, but I left the wallet with my credit cards in my brief case back in the room. I only have a hundred and fifty dollars cash, and I need to get a cab back to the hotel. Would you mind getting this check and I will add it to the retainer tomorrow?"

"Hotel? Sure ... I guess so. No problem."

Seymour and Billy walked out into the warm summer night. "You wouldn't happen to be going by the Four Seasons would you?"

"Four Seasons? Not exactly."

"Okay. Just thought I would ask. My son's place was a bit inconvenient."

"I guess it wouldn't be too far out of the way. What the hell, come on, I'll give you a ride."

Seymour smiled and bowed slightly. "Thank you, counselor."

CHAPTER EIGHT

Billy lived in a three-story brick townhouse in Georgetown. He bought it a year or so after Wellington and Bracket hired him. It was the only asset of an estate that had languished for eight years in probate. One of the Wellington and Bracket partners in the Wills and Probate division said that it would be available at, what he called, "a very reasonable price." It was in a great location, and from the outside, Billy could barely see the impending symptoms of decay from the years of neglect. The furnace worked intermittently, the electricity short circuited, the sinks and toilets leaked, and when it rained, water came in around the chimneys and the windows. It had large rooms and a two-car garage. But, the price was as low as the investment potential was high. After a little arm twisting from a senior partner, one of the firm's financial clients made a below market loan to Billy to both buy the townhouse and make some of the necessary repairs. As it turned out, Billy hadn't borrowed enough money to pay for all the needed repairs, so, for the next three years, he worked seven days a week, ten hours a day at the law firm and the rest of the time he spent replacing, repairing, repainting, refurbishing, and otherwise reviving the deteriorating townhouse.

When he finished, it was a showcase. New windows, new

heating and air-conditioning, new plumbing and fixtures, new wiring, new tucked and pointed bricks, and a new modern kitchen. The oversized oak front door had stained glass panels on both sides and over the transom. It opened into a long wide hallway that led to a large staircase, then a bathroom on the left, then an elevator across from the bathroom, then the kitchen, and then a large dining room with a huge stone fireplace on the end opposite the hallway. A door from inside the garage opened into the kitchen that opened into the dining room. Opposite the kitchen side of the dining room was a wall of French doors and windows that looked into the courtyard.

The living room on the second floor was the size of the garage below, and it was connected to the library by a bar, complete with sink, refrigerator, and ice machine. Like the dining room below it, the library had French doors and windows that opened onto a balcony overlooking the courtyard. Years earlier, someone had painted the library, and Billy spent the better part of fourteen months coaxing the paint off with scrapers, turpentine, paint remover, and steel wool. His efforts were rewarded. The library walls, ceiling, and built-in bookshelves were solid walnut, as was the huge fireplace facade at the end near the bar. There was also a bathroom across the hallway from the elevator.

The third floor had three bedrooms: one large master with another large stone fireplace and a bathroom, and two smaller bedrooms with a bathroom between them. When all was said and done, Billy concluded that the place was worth more than four times what he owed on it. He had completed all the work on the townhouse before he met Ann.

Tom and John shared the larger of the two small bedrooms and Lucy occupied the other. Their rooms had not changed since Ann left. She felt it would be better to buy new bedroom furniture for them at their new house. She told Billy that she didn't want to break the children's connection to him. Although they'd been separated and divorced for more than two years, Billy still felt almost sick when he went into the children's rooms. He missed them most in the morning when he left for work.

"I love you daddy," they would say. "See you tonight. Give me a Hug. Hug. Hug. And, kiss. Kiss. Kiss." *What the hell, it wouldn't have lasted forever anyway. Do I really miss her or does this empty feeling come from the betrayal of her leaving.*

Although by any legal definition, the townhouse was not marital property, to his surprise, Ann never made it an issue in their divorce. Billy had the emotional advantage when it came time to split up the property that they accumulated during their four-year marriage. Ann left him and not vice versa. Ann's father had a successful insurance agency in Illinois, and he bought her a smaller, less elegant house in Georgetown for considerably more than Billy owed on his.

Guilt and remorse are high trump cards when dividing the pot in the game of marital poker. There is an inverse relationship between guilt and the amount of property a spouse demands. Billy always advised his divorce clients not to be too generous with alimony or child support or property because of guilt, and don't accept less than you're entitled to because you got caught cheating. You can always be generous, he would tell them, when you don't have a judge who has decided your share. It's a lot easier to change your mind than it is to change a judge's mind. Usually no one paid attention to him. *Do divorce clients even listen to me?* He couldn't count the number of divorcees who later complained that they should have taken his advice. But, by then, it was too late. At the beginning of the marriage, some duly authorized person chortles, "Let no man put apart what God has joined together," at the end of the marriage, the only response is, "Let no man put apart a judge's decree because some poor fool got caught with his tallywacker jammed in his neighbor's wife's ass." When it comes to divorce, absence does not make the heart grow fonder. *Thank God.*

Billy finished his morning coffee and decided to drive the five blocks to his office. Friday was motion day and he had several court appearances, and he needed his car to get to

Terry Jacobs' bond hearing in Montgomery County. Normally he didn't drive on Friday because his end-of-the-day stop for cold beer at Clyde's usually extended into the evening, and he didn't want to worry about getting arrested for drunk driving, something that wouldn't have concerned him fifteen years ago.

* * * *

It wasn't like she didn't have a perfectly good reason ... or reasons ... for leaving Billy. He was her first love and she still didn't hate him. After four years of marriage, three children, and at least two drunken sexual relationships that she knew about, it was evident that Billy Tapp would neither reform nor conform to her standard of decorum and fidelity. She often wondered why she felt for him as she did. During the last years, he spent more time at Clyde's, less time with her, and more time either drunk or nursing a hangover. She expressed her concern to his friend Jason.

"What do you expect? He's the same as he's always been. You aren't going to change Billy Tapp. Guys like him don't change. He is what he is," Jason had told her. That's when she decided to make her own way and shortly thereafter realized that that way didn't include Billy Tapp.

When Billy and Ann agreed on how they would split their marital property and the papers were finally drawn up, the runner from Ann's lawyer delivered the final draft to Billy on a Wednesday afternoon at three o'clock. Billy was sitting at Clyde's sloshing down his fourth beer and congratulating himself on a nine hundred thousand dollar verdict in an unfair settlement claims practices suit that he'd won the day before, despite the fact that he wouldn't see a dime of it or his fee for at least two years after the insurance company exhausted its last frivolous appeal.

"I kicked their ass, Robert Bob. And, I won't see a fucking penny until those shit-heads finish with the appellate courts. Okay with me. I get interest and attorney's fees. So answer me this. If the State Auto Insurance Company had paid my clients' eleven hundred dollar claim and they hadn't forced me to kick their asses in court for almost a million bucks. If they'd done that ... who's causing insurance costs to go up? Lawyers like me or insurance companies that decide not to pay a legitimate claim and end up getting stomped for a thousand times what they could have settled for?"

Robert Bob had already moved to the far end of the bar. Billy drained his beer. "No further questions. One more beer please."

The runner came in the front door and looked around the bar room. Billy was the only one sitting at the bar.

"Excuse me. Are you Billy Tapp? I called your office and your secretary said she thought you'd be a here. Said you won a trial yesterday and thought you'd be here with your client. Congratulations."

"Yeah. Thanks. What you got there?"

"Oh, I don't know. I just know it's for you." The runner handed Billy a large white envelope marked "Confidential, Hand Deliver, William H. Tapp, Esq."

The runner was out the door and gone as fast as he came in.

* * * *

"I may have been wrong," Billy said. "I had dinner with Seymour Grey at La Rouge last night."

"I'll bet that was cheap and delicious," Vickie said.

"It was delicious. But we talked about his case, and believe it or not, Grey agreed to a fifty thousand dollar retainer, and he's going to bring it in today. What do you think about that?"

"I'll believe it when I see it."

"Vickie, you're way too cynical for someone your age."

"No. Realistic. Something I've learned from being around you." She tilted her head and smirked.

"I need Michael Braxton's telephone number. He's the lawyer in Grey's case. He represents FSLIC, and I think he's with the Department of Justice. Can you find his telephone number for me? I need to be in court in forty-five minutes, and I'd like to talk to him before I leave. See if you can get him for me, please."

"Yep, hold on for just a sec."

"Michael," Billy said. "This is Billy Tapp. I'm calling about the Grey and Federated case. I was in court a few days ago. Standing in for John Morgan."

"Sure," Braxton said, "what can I do for you?"

"Well. To be honest with you, I don't know too much about the case. I don't even have a copy of the pleadings. I was wondering if you could fax over a copy of the complaint and your motion for summary judgment."

"I'd be glad to. But, you know, with the exhibits and everything, the complaint is about sixty pages long. And, hold on for a minute, I've got the file over on my credenza, let's see, the pleadings are about an inch and a half thick. Do you want me to fax all that to you?"

"Where's your office, Michael?"

"I'm in the Attorney General's office. Where are you?"

"My office is on Market Street. I'm not too far from you."

"Here. Let's do this. We've got a bunch of interns and clerks running around here with nothing to do. I'll make a copy of this stuff and have someone run it over to you. That way you'll have the whole file."

"That'd be great," said Billy. "Oh, one more thing. Do you mind if I call the receiver at FSLIC and talk to him about the case?"

"I guess technically he's my client and, as we all know, you're not supposed to talk to anyone who's represented by counsel. As far as I'm concerned ... I really don't care. But let me check with my boss and I'll call Mr. Morning ... he's the receiver ... and see what they say. If it's okay with them, it's okay with me. Sit tight, I'll call you back in ten minutes."

"One more thing. I really need more time to submit a

response to your motion. Would you mind meeting me this morning in Poopvitch's office, if I can get some time with the judge?"

"I don't have time this morning, but I don't care if you talk to him without me. Let me see here; let me put you on hold." There was a pause and Braxton came back on the line. "Tell you what I'll do. I'll call Poopvitch and tell him you have my permission to talk to him about more time, and I'll tell him that I won't oppose it. Does that work for you?"

"Sure. Great. Thanks. I'll call you this afternoon and tell you what he says."

"I'm probably not going to be in, but leave a message with my secretary. I'll get back with you on the Federated pleadings."

Billy waited fifteen minutes, and when Braxton didn't call, he stuffed some files in his brief case and hurried out the door to court.

"I have my cell phone, when Braxton calls back, ask him if I need to stop by his office after court today and pick up Seymour's pleadings. I'm going to Jacobs' bond hearing this morning. I have three motions this afternoon in town. I'll call you before lunch. See ya."

* * * *

Judge Thomas Barr grew up in rural Alabama and graduated with honors from Vanderbilt's law school where he had been editor of the Vanderbilt Law Review. He earned an L.L.M.— the legal equivalent of a post doctorate—from Harvard in Constitutional Law. For the next three years he clerked for United States Supreme Court Chief Justice Cardoza. Billy never missed a chance to tell people that Barr was everything that Poopvitch wasn't. And, as luck had it, this morning he was going to see Judge Barr first and then Judge Poopvitch. It's strange justice that a state circuit court judge, like Barr, had to run for re-election every seven years, and an incompetent shit-head, like Poopvitch, was appointed for life.

Barr had played football at the University of Alabama, and his office was filled with Alabama footballs, jerseys, team pictures, old football shoes, photographs of games, and a photograph of the legendary coach Bear Bryant with his arm around Barr. Barr was in his football uniform and he wore number 72; over the bottom, Coach Bryant had written, "Tom: Good luck at Vandy next year. Only believe half what those egg heads up there tell you." Barr had been a good football player and an excellent student. He was an academic All-American each of the three years that he was eligible.

* * * *

Billy came into the courtroom just as the bailiff was finishing the long-standing arcane call to order "… all ye who have claims, draw nigh, give attention and ye shall be heard. God save this honorable court. Be seated and come to order." Judge Barr looked over his reading glasses at the gathering of lawyers and their fidgeting clients, and then looked at the docket that his clerk had placed on the bench.

Twenty-five long oak pews, separated down the middle by a wide isle, filled the courtroom gallery. A massive banister separated the gallery from the jury box, the counsels' tables and the judge's bench. The judge's bench was elevated two steps, with the witness box on the left, a desk and seating area in the middle for the judge's clerk and the court reporter, and a place on the right for the bailiff. Behind the judge's chair was a massive oak paneled wall with a ponderous carved eagle in the middle glowering at the courtroom. The bailiff sat beside a large wooden newel at the corner. Several years ago the local sheriff, who was also the bailiff, used to rap his pistol on the newel top to call court to order. Over time the pistol wore a concave bowl in the newel, which the sheriff used as an ashtray—when you could still smoke in public.

It was Judge Barr's habit to expedite his criminal docket by first calling matters that didn't require long hearings. So, he arraigned three prisoners and five other defendants who appeared with lawyers and, apparently, had the fortune of posting bail bond or were showing up in court because of a summons and not an arrest warrant. Those unable to post bond, were held in a cell across the hall and individually marched into court by the jailer to answer for their alleged crimes.

"Are those all the arraignments?" Judge Barr asked his clerk.

"Yes, sir."

"Alright then, let's see here. Let me call the case of *Maryland v. Jacobs*."

Billy stood up and walked to the podium, which the bailiff had placed in front of the judge's bench. "Mr. Jacobs is in custody. This is on the docket today for a bond hearing, Judge."

Jacobs shuffled into the courtroom in front of the jailer. He had on the same orange jump suit that he wore when Billy saw him last. But now, the breast pocket was ripped and there was a splattering of blood down the front. Jacobs had on rubber flip-flops with the toe piece wedged between dirty white socks. The right side of his face was pink and puffy and his eyes were sunken and red and surrounded by deep dark lines. His hands were manacled to a chain that was hooked to leg irons. He rocked back and forth like a penguin. It was clear that Terry's short stay in jail had not been kind to him. He looked shorter and smaller than Billy remembered. When he got to the podium, Billy bent down and spoke quietly, almost gently.

"Terry. You all right? What happened to you?" Billy looked up at the judge. "Judge Barr, could I have a minute with my client before we ..."

"Certainly, Mr. Tapp. I think it would be all right if y'all used the jury room." Barr addressed the jailer. "Is that all right with you, Earl?"

Assistant Chief Jailer Earl Sabatini rarely worked with prisoners. He'd been a jailer for twenty-five years, and when he had to deal with prisoner transportation, he made it a point to be in Judge Barr's courtroom.

"Yes, sir. That's not a problem." He took Jacobs by the arm. "Come on son. Let's go in here."

Jacobs shuffled into the jury room in front of Earl, with Billy following. Earl guided him to a chair and walked past Billy on the way out.

"Your boy's had a little bit of trouble in jail. We had to separate him from the general population. He's okay though. Just needed a little gettin' used to, if you know what I mean. Want me to close this door?"

"Yeah. If you don't mind. Thanks Earl."

"Yes, sir. I'll be sitting right outside here if you need me. Just yell."

"Thanks. I think we'll be fine. I'll call you if I need anything." Billy sat down at the end of the long wooden conference table. "Are you all right? What in the world happened to you?"

"Aw nothin'. I'm okay. Nothin.' Just a little difference of opinion with some motherfuckers. I can take care of myself. Ain't nothin' with me. Ain't nothin' wrong."

"Okay. If you say so. I just wanted to make sure before we get into arguing about your bond."

"You gonna' get me out of here? Is my mother here?"

"No. She called and said she had to work. She said it'd be real difficult for her to get here this morning."

"She's not here? I thought said she was going to be here. She was going to tell the judge that I could come home and stay with her until the trial. She couldn't come?"

"No. But it won't make any difference. I'm going to tell the judge. Your mother can't post the bond anyway. We need to talk the judge into reducing the bond. But, Terry, don't get your hopes up. This is a serious charge, and I'd be surprised if the judge reduces it too much. Are you ready to get back out there?"

"Yeah. Make sure my mom's not here, will ya?"

Billy opened the door and walked down the aisle between

the benches to the podium. Earl brought Terry wobbling behind.

"Judge. Terry's bond is set at five hundred thousand dollars, full cash. He has no way ... not even close ... to post that much bond. I looked at the Pretrial Services report and, as you can see, he's never been convicted of a felony. They don't think he's a flight risk and neither do I. I actually know Terry's family. I've represented his mother in a divorce and some other unrelated matters that, by the way, weren't criminal. Terry's mother has always been employed, and she told me that Terry can stay with her until the trial. She also told me she'd make sure he gets to court for all of his required appearances. I believe she can do that and I believe that she will. I'd ask the court to either recognize Terry to return to court with no bond or reduce his bond and allow him to post ten percent."

Steve Bloomberg was the state's attorney. He was short and unkempt. He wore a rumpled blue suit and scruffy black tassel loafers. His rimless glasses sat slightly askew on his face and his hair was stringy and uncombed.

"Your Honor," he almost shouted," this is a murder case. The defendant gunned down another human being in cold blood. He shot him six times. This man is a danger to himself and most of all a danger to society. The State requests that the bond be increased to one million dollars, all cash. Mr. Tapp's request is absurd. It's ridiculous. I do not have any idea what he is thinking. This defendant should not be turned loose on society. He should be—"

"Thank you Mr. Bloomberg," Judge Barr said. "Let me look at the Pretrial Services report."

The judge leafed through the several pages, took his glasses off and looked up. "Mr. Jacobs has never been convicted of anything, but he had a few scrapes with the law when he was a juvenile. Of course, I can't consider his juvenile record in the criminal proceedings, but I can consider it in setting his bond. Ordinarily, I'd recognize him to return on his own recognizance, but as Mr. Bloomberg pointed out, this is a murder. But, even still, Mr. Jacobs' record and this report seem to indicate that he's not a flight risk."

"But, Your Honor," Bloomberg interrupted, "This man committed murder. Murder. He killed someone. Premeditated and in cold blood. The State strongly objects to a bond reduction, much less the court releasing him on his own recognizance."

Billy stuck his hands in his pockets and looked at Bloomberg, waiting for him to finish. "Yes, Mr. Tapp," the judge said.

"Terry is employed, he's never been convicted of a crime, his mother will make sure he comes to court, he's only nineteen years old, and, as maybe you can see, it looks like he's been beaten up in jail. I need him out to help me prepare his defense. He's lived all his life in the area, and I don't think he's going to run off."

"He wasn't too young to get a gun and pump six slugs into some poor innocent victim! This isn't petty larceny, its murder! The citizens of this state and the District of Columbia shouldn't have to worry about this ... this ... this ... predator while he's waiting for trial." The veins on Bloomberg's neck bulged and a thin white residue of spittle appeared at the corners of his mouth.

"Only three and a half." Billy said under his breath.

"Excuse me, Mr. Tapp. The judge said.

"Only if he were free, he could be half-way helpful in preparing his defense," Billy said.

"Free!" Bloomberg screeched. "Three and a half? Mr. Tapp thinks this is some kind of a joke. This is a murder case not a speeding ticket."

Judge Barr held up his hands. "Thank you, gentlemen. I think I've about got the picture. Mr. Tapp, this is a serious matter. I'm not sayin' he's innocent or guilty, but he is charged with murder. I'm concerned about his age and safety in jail. I'm going to set his bond at one hundred thousand dollars, ten percent, and ask the jailer—Earl can you do this for me—to check into his safety?"

"Your Honor," Bloomberg nearly yelled, "we object to the bond reduction and ask that Your Honor reconsider."

"Thank you, Mr. Bloomberg. Is there anything else gentlemen?"

* * * *

Billy finished with Terry Jacobs and drove back to the District. He parked in the garage under his office building and walked to the Federal court building. As usual, Joe Straighter stood by the metal detector kibitzing with two other marshals. Straighter motioned Billy through without inspection.

"Hey, Joe. No guns, knives, nunchakus, hand grenades, or surface to air rockets. Is Go Poop in?"

Straighter made an exaggerated recoil and looked from side to side. "Billy Tapp, you don't give a shit, do you. If Judge Poopvitch heard you, he'd toss your ass in jail."

"Great. My usual deal. Tell him all I want is a cell by myself, no telephone, no clients; all I want is a few books. I'll give you the list. You'd bring 'um to me, wouldn't you?"

"You keep being a smart ass, and I may have to. I'm not sure if the judge is in yet, but I saw one of his clerks a little while ago."

Billy rode the elevator up to the fourth floor and walked down the deserted marble and wood paneled hall, to Judge Poopvitch's office. The door was ajar and Billy pushed it open. The judge's office consisted of an expansive lobby with an empty receptionist's desk, followed by an equally large office for the judge's secretary, then the judge's huge office. Leading off the secretary's office was a smaller anteroom with three alcoves for law clerks, and after that a large state and federal law library. The furniture was wood and leather and looked like it had never been used. When Billy opened the door, he heard a distant chime. He stood in front of the empty reception's desk. A few moments passed, the judge's secretary came out of her office.

"Mr. Tapp. How did you get in?"

Billy turned and pointed at the door. "Through the door."

"Wasn't it locked?"

"Was it locked? No. I guess not. It was open and I just walked in."

"They were supposed to fix the security lock. I guess they didn't." She went over to the door and pulled it shut. "Judge Poopvitch isn't here right now. Did you come to see him?" She looked Billy up and down.

Billy turned away and said, "No, I came to order a cheeseburger and fries."

"What's that, Mr. Tapp? I'm sorry I didn't hear you."

Billy turned back and cleared his throat. "Yes. I wanted to try to talk him into a little more time in the Grey case. I talked with Braxton, and he said he didn't care if I talked to the judge *ex parte.*"

"Well, the judge is not available right now. I believe his schedule is full this morning ... or maybe even for the rest of the day. Let me get one of the clerks."

The secretary disappeared. A young man came out dressed in suit pants, a white shirt, and a red and black striped tie, carrying a cup of coffee and the last bite of a doughnut. He finished the doughnut and quickly wiped his hand on his pants and extended it to Billy.

"Oh. Good morning, Mr. Tapp. Does anybody know you're here?"

"The secretary just said she was going to get one of you."

"Well then, here I am. Can I help you? Has the judge seen you yet?"

"The Grey case. I was hoping to talk the judge into giving me a little more time to respond to Mike Braxton's motion for summary judgment."

"The judge isn't in yet. He doesn't have anything in court today, so he probably won't be in until after lunch. The judge assigned the Grey case to me, and to be honest with you, I don't know too much about it. I'd love to have a little more time to get up to speed. Tell you what I'll do. Let me talk to

Judge Poopvitch and see if we can extend this thing out for thirty days. Do both of us a favor. What's your number? Do you have a card? I'll talk to the judge later and call your office."

Billy left Poopvitch's office. He pulled the door behind him and, again, the latch didn't catch on the security lock.

* * * *

When Billy returned to his office there were four items waiting for him: a three inch stack of pleadings and other court papers from Michael Braxton; three banker's boxes marked "Frederick Mall"; and two checks from Seymour, one for twenty-five thousand dollars and another post-dated sixty days for twenty-five thousand, four hundred and forty-two dollars. Seymour had split the retainer in two and added the cost of the meal from LaRogue to the post-dated check.

"Look at all this stuff. And money too. Mr. Grey brought these boxes by and said this was about all he had for the Frederick project. He said he'd be at the Four Seasons again tonight if you had any questions. I looked in the boxes, and everything seems to be organized pretty well. Were you expecting all this stuff?"

"Some yes and some no. I wasn't expecting the banker's boxes, but I was expecting fifty thousand dollars and reimbursement for the meal last night. I guess close is better than nothing. Let's hope the checks don't bounce."

"Mr. Braxton's runner left a telephone number for some guy named Morning, and Judge Poopvitch's clerk called and said the judge gave you thirty days ... whatever that's supposed to mean."

"Let's hope that's an extension to file our response and not jail time."

CHAPTER NINE

Jerome Morning and his identical twin Tomas were born in Darby, England. Their father was a mid-level bank executive with the Barclay Bank. Their parents separated and divorced shortly after their father discovered that their mother was in an affair with a wealthy Iranian arms dealer. The scandal resulted in a small brouhaha at the bank and a large embarrassment to the father. When the boys turned eight, they moved with their mother to Grand Cayman Island. Although no one ever confirmed the rumor, people at the bank said that her Iranian paramour paid her upkeep in the islands.

After leaving England, the boys saw little of their father. They were precocious and ambitious. After grammar school, they attended Pennsylvania State University on scholarship and then Rice University in Houston for advanced degrees in business and finance. They had worked in Washington D.C. with the Federal Reserve Bank, the Federal Deposit Insurance Corporation, and Department of the Treasurer; in New York City for Chemical Bank; and most recently in Houston for Federated Savings and Loan and Mr. Dozier Mound.

* * * *

"Mr. Morning. My name is Billy Tapp. I'm a lawyer in Washington, D.C. I got your name and telephone number from Michael Braxton. He's with the Attorney General's office. I'm calling about the Seymour Grey case."

"Yes, Mr. Tapp," Morning said. "Mr. Braxton said that you might be calling. What can I do for you?" Morning's English accent was almost exaggerated and his tenor curt.

"I just got in this case. I'm not really up to speed yet, but I just thought it couldn't hurt to give you a call and, maybe, get your perspective."

"I see. My perspective on what?"

"Well. On the case. Maybe you could give me sort of an overview of what happened."

"Of Course. The Frederick Mall." Morning paused for a moment and then continued. "Mr. Grey had a loan with Federated Savings and Loan that was in default. When the Federal Savings and Loan Insurance Corporation chose to place Federated Savings and Loan in receivership they declared Mr. Grey's loan in default and demanded that he pay it off. He could not comply with the terms of the loan agreement and repay the loan, so they instituted foreclosure."

"In talking to Seymour and looking briefly at the loan documents and the construction progress, it's my understanding that Federated hadn't funded the entire loan. Hadn't given Seymour all the money that he borrowed. There was actually enough money left to finish the Frederick Mall ... and some left over."

"Technically, Mr. Tapp ... Billy, was it ... that is exactly correct. But you see, perhaps what you don't understand is that the loan was in default because Federated Savings and Loan had entered into a joint venture with Mr. Grey, which is contrary to applicable banking regulations."

"Joint venture? Do you mean the profit participation with Federated Building, Incorporated?"

"Profit participation. Joint venture. These are words. The Federal Savings and Loan Insurance Corporation looks at the substance, not the form. I am sure you will agree. FSLIC, if you will, has rather strict regulations concerning an institution's participation with it borrowers."

"Sure I understand all that stuff. But, I thought that Federated had figured out a way that didn't violate those regulations."

"I certainly cannot speak to that issue. All I can report to you is the current status."

"Mr. Morning, let me ask a dumb question."

"Of course."

"Has anybody talked about settling this lawsuit? It seems to me that everybody would be better off if we settled this thing. This case ought to be settled."

"Naturally, Mr. Tapp, these cases seem simple on the surface; but, I am certain there are nuances and subtleties that you have not had, shall we say, the opportunity to review."

"Yeah. I'm sure that's true. But, here's what I do know. Seymour did a pretty good job putting the project together. He had all the major anchor tenants either signed on leases or letters of intent to lease space in the center. He was damn near done with construction, and he was on time and under budget. Hell, just being under budget is nothing to sneeze at. But what's most important to me is that there was still money left in the budget to complete the project."

"Well, Mr. Tapp. That may very well all be true. But that is only part of the story. One of the problems with the loan balance is that the loan was actually increased after Federated Savings and Loan entered into the profit participation with Mr. Grey."

"It doesn't seem to me like that should make any difference," Billy said.

"Certainly it does, Mr. Tapp."

"In my simple way of analyzing this deal, it seems like FSLIC's interest ought to be making sure that Federated gets repaid and, therefore, its depositors and shareholders don't get screwed. Isn't that about it?"

"In a simple way, I suppose that is accurate."

"Why not let Federated honor the rest of its loan to Seymour, let him finish the project, and everybody's happy. Seymour gets his mall, Federated has a good loan, and the shareholder and depositors are all the better for it. Looks to me like it'd be a no harm no foul deal. Anybody talk about that approach?"

"Mr. Tapp. I really am afraid that it will not be quite that simple. There are more factors that you have not considered."

"I'm sure you're right. I'm just now getting into this case, and I don't know all the facts. Braxton sent over a copy of the court record to me this morning, and I haven't had a chance to look through it. But I can't help think that there must be some way we can settle this thing to everyone's satisfaction. It doesn't seem like this project ... and Seymour for that matter ... should go in the crapper because of some technical regulation. Especially, if there's somebody out there who can exercise some discretion."

"That may be, Mr. Tapp." Morning said.

"Well, I think that the judge up here has given me some additional time to file Seymour's response to your motion for summary judgment. In the meantime, I'll get up to speed and maybe we can talk again about some kind of settlement."

"We are always willing to talk. No harm in that. I am afraid that Mr. Grey has gotten himself into somewhat of a pickle the way he dealt with Federated Savings and Loan. And I agree, Mr. Tapp, it would be a shame to see Mr. Grey's project go, as you say, 'in the crapper.' My line is always open."

"I don't think you can lay all the blame on Seymour's door step. Federated made the loan. You can't expect Seymour to know all the banking regulations. Hell, I bet ninety percent of the lawyers in D.C. don't even know there is such a thing."

"That may be, Mr. Tapp. But ninety percent of the attorneys in the District do not do real estate development. Excuse me. I have another call here that I really must take. Thank you for calling. If I can be of further assistance, of course, call me. I enjoyed talking to you." Morning hung up without additional comment.

* * * *

Billy walked over to his window and looked out over the parking lot located across the street from his office. The wind had picked up and the sky was beginning to darken. People were scurrying around, holding hats against their heads, gripping papers and briefcases next to their bodies, and shielding their eyes from the blowing dust. On the far edge of the parking lot, a beam of sun still shined on an old sign painted on a brick wall that had been exposed by the recent demolition of an adjacent building. He read the message on the painted brick, "United Biscuit 5¢," it said. The green, yellow, and red paint were faded and washed out, but it was clear that once, a long time ago, you could buy United Biscuits for five cents.

"Is that per biscuit or per package?" Billy asked his faint reflection in the window.

"Biscuit?" Vickie said. She was standing in the doorway. "Seymour Grey is on the line. You have to be in court at four o'clock."

"Counselor, did you get the documents that I dropped by your office? Hope you do not mind two checks. This whole mess has put a crimp in my cash flow. In my business, you are only as good as your last deal. Oh well, I suppose some of this mess is already yesterday's trade. We need to move forward. Let's see what we can make out of it."

"I just talked to a fellow out in Houston with FSLIC. He name is Jerome Morning. He is FSLIC's representative. Mike Braxton gave me his name. Braxton is FSLIC's lawyer."

"Morning. He works for Federated," Seymour said.

"You sure? This guy I talked to—"

"Did he have a British accent? Was he English?"

"Yeah," Billy said.

"He and his brother, Tom, worked for Federated. Jerry

worked for Joe Franklin. Franklin was Federated's compliance officer. Franklin's department made sure that Federated was in compliance with all the banking regulations. Morning was one of his underlings. His brother Tom did something in accounting, I think. You sure Morning was the guy you talked to?"

"How many Jerome Mornings with British accents are there in Houston, Texas? Or, for that matter, in the United States. It must have been the same guy." Billy thought for a moment. "Did you ever talk to Morning about your loan?"

"Sure. More times than once. He certainly would have been aware of the loan and the deal. That was their job in compliance. Make sure Federated didn't violate the procedures and policies."

"That's interesting," said Billy, "Morning now works for FSLIC."

"I talked to Morning several times about the mall, now that I think about it. He had some connection to Washington. He had friends or family or something there. I think he worked in D.C. for a while. He even stopped by the project site a few times when he was in D.C. If I remember correctly, I saw some pictures on his desk that he had taken. He said they were progress photographs for the file. I really did not think too much about it. Progress pictures are pretty much normal procedure. Federated gave us monthly disbursements from the loan. We would make written requests that would include invoices, progress notes, an architect's certification, and sometimes we included photographs."

"What's in those boxes that you left at my office?"

"Pretty much everything that I have that relates to the Frederick Mall."

"Did you bring all that stuff with you on the airplane?"

"Heavens no. Most of it was at the project office in Frederick, and the rest I had shipped up to Fredrick last week."

"Listen, Seymour, I have to get to court. I'm probably

going to stop by Clyde's on the way home for a beer. You're welcome to join me."

"Why thank you counselor, I just might do that."

"Give me a call back here at my office around five thirty. If I don't answer, call me on my cell phone." Billy gave Seymour his cell telephone number and hurried off to court.

Court was uneventful. He scheduled a trial date for an uncontested divorce, set two cases for pretrial conference, and argued a motion to compel a truculent shit-head lawyer to supply answers for past due interrogatories.

*   *   *   *

In a civil case, the court rules permit the parties to "discover" the facts and witnesses of each other's case. Lawyers get this discovery by either sending questions to the other party or by taking depositions. The questions are called interrogatories and depositions are the sworn testimony of the witnesses or the parties to the lawsuit. "The idea is to separate the pigs from the slop," Billy told his clients. Prompt and skilled discovery is a boon to experienced litigators in both preparing for trial or coming to a fair settlement. But, like almost every other legal procedure, the discovery process provides the inexperienced, the lazy, the pedantic, and the unnecessarily cantankerous an irresistible opportunity for abuse. However, there's a built in safeguard.

If a lawyer doesn't answer the interrogatories within a certain time or fails to cooperate in a deposition, the court can not only force him to answer the questions, but also make him pay the other side for their trouble in getting the court to make the other side answer. For the most part, the process works and judges rarely award the lawyers a fee for the first effort to exact past due responses.

Billy asked for fees in the motion to compel, but the judge denied his request and gave the other side ten days to capitulate. Billy knew that he'd be back in court in ten days, once again, trying unsuccessfully to get his answers and his fees.

* * * *

Vickie carried Seymour's boxes into the conference room. She removed the files and stacked them according to the alphabetically marked categories starting from "Advertising" and ending with "Vendors." For some reason, she put the folders that were filed under "Financial" and "Tenants" in a separate pile. Billy opened the folder marked "Advertising." It contained several draft copies of mock-ups for a brochure promoting the Frederick Mall. He recognized Seymour's hand written changes and interlineations. The finished brochure contained a site plan, floor plans, and concise statement of the market and why a retailer should open a store in Seymour's mall. Billy was impressed.

The pile marked "Financial" was well over eighteen inches thick and comprised about one fourth of the material. Billy spent the next few hours looking through the files, more out of curiosity than with the detailed study necessary to prepare the case. Billy's first look into someone else's private business gave him the same tingle of allure and intrigue that he got as a little boy when he'd dig down into his father's sock drawer and pull out an old Smith and Wesson service revolver, carefully wrapped in an oily rag and a hand towel. Seymour's records roused that muffled excitement. Billy didn't take notes or earmark anything that might be important; he just looked, and then put everything back where he found it.

When he realized the time, he picked up the three empty banker's boxes and carried them into the kitchenette and stacked them on top of the refrigerator. On the way out the door, he noticed an envelope on the floor in the conference room. He picked it up and tossed it on Vickie's desk. He rode the elevator to the parking garage and drove the few blocks to Georgetown.

* * * *

By the time Billy got to Clyde's, the after work crowd had packed up and gone home. There was a couple sitting at the bar with their heads together and four young men at a table with three pitchers of beer and their ties undone and their sleeves rolled up. They were smoking cigars and arguing about sports. Billy slipped into a bar stool and gave the bartender, who was working on a crossword puzzle, his customary goofy salute.

"Evening, Mr. Tapp. You're a little late aren't you? Hey, what's a seven letter word that means woman's cloak?"

"Robert Bob, better late than never. Let's see, I think I'll have one of your vintage ice-cold beers. Woman's cloak?"

"What vintage suits you Billy?"

"Let me think. Do you have anything in, say, last week?"

"I think so. Let me look in the cellar." Robert Bob reached in the under counter cooler and pulled out a bottle of Tecate. He held it up for Billy's inspection. "Does this suit you?"

"Excellent. Excellent. Open it please and, if you don't mind, bring me a lime too."

"Would you like a glass?"

"Robert Bob, my boy, it's in a glass. Why would I put it in a different glass? That wouldn't make sense. Plus, it'd just increase the chance of spillage."

Billy squeezed the lime juice into the bottle and then stuffed the lime down the bottle neck. He held it up to Robert Bob and unceremoniously consumed the contents in three long gulps.

"Oh, bartender, it seems there's been a mistake. You've given me an empty bottle. How could that have happened? I demand a replacement. Be warned. If you don't, I know the management and I'll have your job."

Robert Bob fetched another beer. "I know the management too, and you can have my job."

"Never mind then. Give me another beer and you can

keep your job."

"Tell you what I'll do. You give me a beer, and you can have my job."

"Don't tempt me," Billy said. "Pelisse."

"Yeah?"

"Pelisse."

Robert Bob gave Billy a quizzical look. Please what?"

Not *please*. Pelisse. Pelisse is a woman's cloak."

"Now how in the hell did you know that?" Robert Bob shook his head and penciled in the missing word. "You're late today. Were you in court? Did you have a jury out or something?"

"No. I got back to the office a little late, and I got interested in some stuff a client brought by. The next thing you know, it was eight o'clock. Robert Bob, I must be getting old. Who ever heard of working on Friday until eight o'clock?"

"What are you talking about? Before you left Wellington and Bracket, you worked every night ... most of the time past eight o'clock. That's why you're sitting here right now, and you don't have a wife and kids at home."

"God damn it, Scharman, I didn't come in here to listen to the truth. Either lie to me, or keep you mouth shut."

"That ass hole ex-wife of yours, she must really be a bitch. What was she thinking about leaving a person of your character and wealth? You're one in a million. She never deserved you."

"Thank you," Billy said and finished his second beer. Without asking, Robert Bob replaced it and walked down to the couple with their heads together. When he came back he asked Billy, "You eating? Want to see a menu?"

"I don't think so. I was supposed to meet somebody, but I guess I'm too late."

"That reminds me," Robert Bob said, "there was some guy in here earlier who sat right where you are. A few minutes before he left, he asked me if I'd seen a guy who he described ... now that I think about it ... to look just like you. I asked him if this guy was an attorney, and he said yes. I got busy and before I could get back with him and ask if it was you, he left. But he did say that he might be back. Had three glasses of wine. Left a five dollar tip."

"Was this guy well dressed and in his early sixties? Good looking guy with a full head of graying hair?"

"That's him. Said he might be back."

"Say. By the way. Have you heard anything more on the selling to minors thing we were talking about the other day?" Billy asked.

"Nope. Did you have a chance to check on it for me? I can't afford to get busted. I've been a bartender for almost twenty years. I've forgotten how to do anything else. If I get busted, according to the law, I'm not supposed to tend bar. Isn't that right? You know me Billy; I wouldn't sell shit to a minor. I card everybody. I even carded those guys sitting over there. And, you know they're over twenty-one."

"I'll try to remember to check on Monday. Remind me again if I don't get back to you. If a cop or an investigator or anyone comes in here asking you questions, don't tell them anything; just tell him you card everyone and that your lawyer told you to keep your mouth shut. Call me. Here, let me give you my cell number and my home phone." Billy wrote the numbers on a bar napkin and slid it across the bar. Robert Bob put another beer in front of Billy.

"Here, this one's on me."

* * * *

The night crowd began to fill the bar. It was younger and more diverse looking than the after work drinkers. By now, Billy's tab showed eight beers and one fried mozzarella appetizer. The bar stools were nearly filled with casually dressed men looking up anxiously every time the front door opened. The only familiar face was Robert Bob who, with his assistant, had become increasingly busy.

Billy stared at his reflection in the mirror behind the back bar. Should I call and check on Lucy's birthday plans? I'll get Lucy a present in the morning and take it over to her in the afternoon. I'll go to my office in the morning and look through the documents that Seymour left and then just before lunch get Lucy something. Maybe call Ann and see what Lucy wanted. He wanted Lucy to be happy. The thought of her disappointment made his stomach wrench; it was almost more than he could bear. He remembered the confused look and the tears when he told her that they weren't going to live together anymore. But, that he still loved her.

"But Daddy, if you love me, why don't you want to live with me?"

He couldn't answer her. He just hugged her and hid his face so she couldn't see his tears. Billy's cell phone rang. He didn't recognize the number displayed on the caller identification.

"Hello?"

"Counselor? This is Grey."

"Who is it?" It was a little after ten o'clock, and the noise and alcohol had begun to anesthetize his senses.

"Grey. Seymour Grey. Sounds like you're having a little fun."

"Oh. Seymour. How are you? Yeah. Christ yeah. I'm at Clyde's. I didn't recognize your voice. Sorry I missed you earlier. I got busy at the office looking at all those documents you brought by." Billy's speech was not yet affected by the torpor that was creeping into his brain. The din from the bar covered any hint of intoxication. Briefly Billy came to his full senses. "Seymour let me call you back in the morning. I can hardly hear you in this place." Billy pushed the "end" button and looked up to see a familiar face.

"Mr. Tapp. How are you? I saw you setting over here by yourself. I thought I'd come over and say hi."

"I'm just fine, thank you. Mr. Tapp? It's Billy."

"Okay. Billy." Robin Grigsby put her hand on Billy's forearm and reached across him for a napkin. "You here by yourself?"

"Yeah. I was at the office late. Looking over a bunch of boring documents in a case. I was supposed to meet a client here tonight. But I missed him. That was him on the phone."

Three girls walked up to them and surrounded Robin Grigsby. "Are you ready to go?"

"Maybe,' she said. "I'd like you to meet Billy Tapp. One of D.C.'s legal brains. They say he's never forgotten anything."

Billy flushed and extended his hand to the closest. "Brains. Ha." He said, "I've forgotten what it's like to be your age."

"You're not that old. How old are you? I'll bet you're not more than forty."

"Bless you child," Billy said, and kissed the back of Robin Grigsby's hand.

"Lord have mercy, sir. You are so gallant."

"Shit, Robin," one of the girls said. I have to get home. My husband has the kids and the baby has been colicky. I know he's fit to be tied. Come on girls, if you're riding with me, let's go."

"I'm staying. Billy will take me home." Robin Grigsby smiled coyly at Billy. The girl who was driving interceded with a matronly glower.

"Robin. Get your ass going. I'm taking you home."

Before Billy could say a thing, they were gone. "Call me," Robin Grigsby said. "I'll buy you lunch next week."

Billy had another beer and drove home. He fell asleep in the library with a nearly full beer setting on the floor beside his shoes beside the soft leather couch that had swept him to rapture dreaming about Robin Grigsby's pulchritude.

CHAPTER TEN

As he had done for more than two decades, Seymour Grey arrived at Three Allen Center in downtown Houston at 6:30 a.m. He bought a large black coffee and the Houston Chronicle at the sundry shop in the lobby next to the elevator bank that lead to his twenty-third floor office suite. He unlocked the front door and took his coffee and newspaper back to the large corner office. He rubbed his eyes and consciously avoided any thought of the Frederick Mall.

Sometimes he missed the simple predictability that he had enjoyed as a reporter at the Atlanta Constitution, so many years ago, where a circulation deadline was his only real concern. He never had trouble finding a story and making it as accurate and as interesting as necessary. *You couldn't go broke writing one bad story. Nothing like real estate development, where your first bad deal could be your last.*

Seymour Grey's many good traits didn't include self-pity. To the irritation of his wife and children, he often overworked the old saw, "When you drill a dry hole, you don't fill it with tears." *You move your rig to another spot and start drilling again. You don't hit oil every time, nobody does.* Seymour's problem was that he'd never really drilled a dry hole and he knew that the Frederick Mall fiasco might not only be his first, but it might be his last.

He had seen other real estate developers, some of them his friends, lose everything: money, homes, cars, boats, airplanes, houses in Aspen, wives, children, business associates, friends, girlfriends, and finally some even lost the courage to keep living. But Seymour always told himself that failure came from not paying attention to your business. If you don't take stupid risks, if you stay focused, you had nothing to worry about. But here he was with maybe one of the best real estate deals of his life—under budget and almost leased up—and the whole thing about to go in the shit can. If it had been a bad deal or a stupid deal, he wouldn't have minded so much, but it wasn't. It was a damn fine real estate project with first class tenants and it was certain to be a very profitable project. Seymour had always attributed his success to his tenacity and the willingness to work harder and smarter than the next guy. You make your luck, he said. The more you work, the luckier you get.

He already had lenders and mortgage brokers poking around for the chance to make the permanent loan once the project was up and running. *God damn it, this deal should and by God will, make me five million dollars in less than three years.* He unfolded the newspaper and began reading the first page. Five lines down in the lead story, he found a grammatical error; he took a pen from his desk drawer and inserted a semicolon in place of a comma.

"That's better," he said.

The receptionist interrupted Seymour. "It's someone from a company called Southwest Financial. Do you want to take the call sir? Or should I get his number?"

Seymour rarely screened his calls, particularly those from lenders.

"No. No thank you. I'll take his call." He picked up the telephone, "Seymour Grey. Can I help you?"

"Mr. Grey. Howard Slone with Southwest Financial." There was a short pause. "You probably don't know who I am, but Southwest Financial owns Bethesda Equity ... the institution that loaned you forty-seven thousand dollars to buy a small strip of land for a utility easement on your Frederick Mall property. We've never met. Do you remember the loan? The utility easement?"

"Sure. Of course I do. If we had not been lucky enough to buy that piece of land, it would have cost more than ten times that amount to bring the utilities to the site."

The engineers and attorneys had somehow overlooked utility access for the project. For some reason, no one realized that the perfect shopping center tract had one problem. One big problem. There was no way to get water, sewer, electricity, gas, or telephone service to the property without spending almost a million dollars. It really wasn't Seymour's oversight, but blame didn't matter. Without utilities, the property couldn't be used for much more than growing corn or grazing cattle. When Seymour discovered the problem, he immediately flew to Frederick and resolved what could have been a catastrophic blunder. Fortunately, he was able to talk a local farmer out of a strip of land fifteen feet wide and two hundred feet long and pay him ten times what it was worth, and at the same time save himself more than one hundred times what it cost. At first the farmer simply refused to sell. Then, for reasons that Seymour never fully understood, the farmer called Seymour and agreed to sell. The whole deal was completed without Seymour even attending the closing.

He hadn't bothered to tell Dozier Mound. Bethesda Equity appeared at the right time and at the right price, so Seymour didn't have to tell anybody about the screw up. It seemingly resolved itself quietly, quickly, and with no fuss. The only one at Federated who knew about the little glitch was a second level compliance Vice President named Jerome Morning.

"I understand that FSLIC has called your loan. That they've filed a foreclosure action in Federal court," Slone said.

"Yes. Unfortunately, that is all true," Seymour confirmed.

"There weren't any problems with the loan, were there? I mean, you weren't in default, were you?"

"Heavens no. We were under budget and ahead of schedule. Apparently FSLIC called the loan because of a profit participation agreement that I entered into with Federated Building, Inc. They say that it violates Federal banking regulations. FSLIC called the loan, not Federated."

"I guess it doesn't matter who called it, the fact is you're in foreclosure. What do you plan to do?"

"I have hired an attorney in Washington, and he is going to get the foreclosure lawsuit tossed out," Seymour said. "He filed a motion, or whatever you call it, to dismiss the lawsuit."

"That's good. Because, as you know, a default of the Federated loan triggers a default of our loan, Bethesda Equity's loan."

"I did not know that, but it makes sense. I guess I should tell Tapp about your loan. William Tapp is my attorney in Washington," Seymour said.

"It's a shame that you have to get a bunch of attorneys involved if we don't have to. Have you talked to any other lenders about paying off the Federated loan? Wouldn't that solve the problem?"

"Sure it would. But I have not done that yet. I am putting an information package together right now to shop the project to some other lenders. I really do not think it is going to be too hard to find a lender or someone to replace Federated."

"I think that's right, Mr. Grey. Tell you what. Don't waste a lot of time on a package. In fact, Bethesda would be very interested in your project. Could you Fed Ex your leases and budget to me right now?"

"Absolutely. But I do not have much of a post-development presentation put together yet, with actual cash-flow analysis. All I have is the pre-development brochure. It will probably take a few days. I want to be sure it is done accurately and correctly," Seymour said. "You know what I mean."

"You know, Seymour, I can't give you a one hundred percent assurance, but I'm certain that either Southwest

Financial or Bethesda Equity will step into Federated's shoes, and you wouldn't even miss a beat. I hate to see you waste a lot of time shopping around for a lender and putting some package together if we can solve the problem right now. Shoot, we've already looked at the project to some extent. We liked it then, no reason we won't like it now."

"That would be great," Seymour said. "It would save me a lot of time and expense."

"Before you waste a bunch of time with a package for lenders ... putting some fancy package together ... let us take a look at it first. I know we can do this deal."

"That would be just great," Seymour said.

"Here's what I'd like to see," Howard Slone said. "Send me a copy of all your signed leases and all your signed letters of intent. Also, send me your prospect list. I need their telephone numbers, so we can call and verify the information. You don't mind if we call them do you?"

"Well, I—"

"Why don't you call them and explain what's going on, and that they can expect a call from us."

"Sure, I think that would work. I just do not want anybody to think there is a problem with the project."

"There's no problem. We'll explain to them that Federated has gone into receivership, that you're under budget and ahead of schedule, and that we're replacing the Federated loan. There shouldn't be any problem. Don't you agree?"

"I agree."

"We need to do our due diligence, just like Federated did, just like any other lender. The sooner we get the information from you, the sooner we can get started. I'll make a list of the information I need, and I'll fax it to you. Take a look at it and give me a call."

Seymour gave his fax number to Howard Slone and hung up the telephone. *Another problem, another solution.* He returned to the newspaper and, in his custom, read every line of every story, from the front to the back. When he finished, he tossed it in the waste can and decided to call Dozier Mound.

* * * *

Seymour dialed Dozier Mound's direct telephone line. "Dozier. This is Seymour Grey."

Like Seymour, Dozier Mound rarely screened his calls and frequently answered the telephone himself when it rang too long with no one answering. "This is a service business," he often said. "We need to talk to our depositors and borrowers. Tell them both the good news and the bad news. Don't be afraid to take a telephone call."

"Seymour, how are you. I've been meaning to call you. Say, I heard that those sons-of-bitches in Washington D. C. called your loan. What the hell is that all about?"

Dozier Mound and his family were Texans before Texas was a state. His forbearers lived in Texas long before Davy Crockett and Jim Bowie died at the siege of the Alamo. During the early stages of the Texas Revolution while on one of his many excursions into the land that now is Texas, Santa Anna kidnapped Mound's great grandfather, who was also named Dozier Mound, and dragged him all over Mexico. Mound's great-great grandfather, whose name was Robert, spent the better part of the next two years following Santa Anna through Mexico and back into Texas and into Mexico again before he finally caught up with him outside of Guadalajara. Robert Mound slipped into Santa Anna's camp and nabbed his son and, before anyone was the wiser, escaped across the Rio Grande, back to the family's seventy-five hundred acre ranch in the Rio Grande Valley.

Santa Anna had developed a fondness for the boy and had tutored him in the Spanish culture and language. In less than two years, the boy spoke Spanish as if it were his native tongue. Through a series of letters to Robert Mound and gifts and envoys to the Mound ranch, Santa Anna and the great-great grandfather became acquaintances and then, finally, friends. It was widely believed that Robert Mound was responsible for the authorities in Washington D.C. releasing Santa Anna after his capture by Sam Houston following Santa Anna's route of the Alamo in 1836.

For years after this unlikely friendship germinated, the kidnapped Dozier Mound spent several weeks each year with Santa Anna and his family in Mexico City. Dozier Mound the younger never knew his great grandfather. During his childhood and into his adult life, however, he maintained an insatiable appetite for stories, photographs, and anything else that connected him to his namesake. A large painting of his great grandfather and Santa Anna sitting next to each other on horseback, both with rifles in their laps and ammunition bandoliers slung across their shoulders hung in his home. He loved Texas, he loved Mexico, and he loved his unique heritage.

"I cannot figure it out. You know the project. We were ahead of schedule and under budget," Seymour said.

"I know that Seymour. Don't let them do this to you. You're going to fight them aren't you? You can figure a way out of this. You're a smart guy. You'll figure out something."

"Yes. I am working on a few things now. By the way, did you know a fellow by the name of Jerry Morning? He worked for Joe Franklin, down in compliance."

"Sure. I know him. He and his brother worked for us. Despite being God damned limeys, I always thought they were bright guys. Hell, I'm the one who hired them.

"He is working for FSLIC now. Did you know that? He apparently has an office at Federated, and he is FSLIC's representative for Federated." Seymour hesitated. "From what I gather, he is in charge of my loan. I was ... ah ... wondering if you might put in a good word or something for me?"

"Hell yes, I know that. The son-of-a-bitch has taken over my savings and loan." Mound hesitated. "Morning has turned into a big shot. Believe it or not, FSLIC put him in

Joe's office, and Joe is in Morning's old office. It's the damnedest thing. Morning is actually running Federated. Running Federated. And, there's not a damn thing I can do about it. He reviews everything. The other day I approved a draw request on a loan for a gas station down near Buffalo Bayou, and that son-of-a-bitch disapproved it. When I went to see him, his secretary said he was busy and she asked me if I wanted to make an appointment. Me. She wanted me to make an appointment to see Jerry Morning. She said he had a lunch meeting and that he might be free between three and three forty-five this afternoon. Jesus H. Christ."

CHAPTER ELEVEN

"Well, how does it work?"

"How does it work." Billy paused and took another gulp of beer. "You really want to know?"

"Sure." Robert Bob spit a fleck of tobacco at the floor and wiped his mouth on his apron.

"This is pretty boring shit."

"Give me the short version."

The government is supposed to give the defendant confessions, fingerprints, scientific data and testing, FBI reports, and anything else the prosecutor intends to use at trial.

"No kidding?"

"You really want to hear this bullshit?"

"That's part of my job. At least I'm interested ... sort of ... that's not always the case."

"I can only imagine. You do it for tips and hope your customers are fair; I do it for a ridiculous hourly fee and don't give a fuck if it's fair. The government also has to hand over any exculpatory information or the names of witnesses that might show that the defendant isn't guilty."

"That seems fair to me."

"Right. Are you actually listening to this clap-trap?"

"I am."

"Okay it's my dime but your ear. For example, at a pretrial conference today , there was plenty of the former and none of the latter. The prosecutor handed me a confession, fingerprints, scientific results from hair samples taken from my clients stocking cap, photographs from the security cameras, the gun, the money, and statements from six witnesses."

"Looks like you client is in deep do-do."

"Yeah. He's court appointed. He has to suffer the consequences, I have to suffer the procedure. The prosecutor has an airtight case and Johnson's conviction is as certain as tomorrow."

"Who?"

"Oh. Johnson. That's my client's last name."

* * * *

Prosecutors and defense lawyers used to engaged in plea bargain negotiations and frequently they'd strike a deal based on the strength or weakness of their cases, ostensibly to do substantial justice and under the pretext of not wasting the court's time. Although Billy scoffed at the notion of modulating justice with saving time for some judge being paid a six-figured salary and benefits to boot, in spite of itself, the barter for justice system worked.

Responding to pressure from law and order fanatics and the harsh reality that minorities often received more severe sentences than their white counterparts, members of the United State Congress realized that there might be a way to satisfy both sides and, maybe, in the process gain some electoral votes. In 1986, Congress enacted the United States Sentencing Guidelines and changed the way the Federal Courts meted out justice. Under this flawed system, the Federal judges were left with little or no discretion in sentencing.

A person's sentence was based on points. If the accused owned up to his crime, he got points deducted. If he lied on the stand during his trial, he got points added. If he accepted responsibility, he got points deducted. If he used a gun, he got points added, and so on and so forth. About the same time, the federal drug laws stiffened and the government became obsessed with putting drug dealers in jail. What actually happened, of course, was that the federal courts got log jammed with penny ante drug cases and the United States Sentencing Guidelines packed the prisons with thousands of street punks, leaving most of the drug kingpins to impudently ply their trade. There was one more result. More often than not, the defendants that the federal government decided to prosecute couldn't risk going to trial. Losing at trial almost always meant more points. The United States Sentencing Guidelines undercut every rational person accused of a crime the free decision to exercise his Constitutional right to a trial by jury. It simply wasn't worth the risk.

* * * *

The U.S. marshals brought Johnson into the witness room that was located in the back of Judge Mitchell's courtroom. He was shackled and carried a wadded manila envelope filled with papers that he'd collected during his travels through the state and Federal penal systems. One of the marshals unlocked the handcuffs and nudged him into a chair next to the end of the table between Maloney and Billy Tapp. The marshal stepped back and leaned against the wall.

"Billy, if you don't mind, we're going to stay in here. It's a new order from the judge. We had a little problem with a prisoner last week, and we've been ordered to keep all prisoners in direct sight when they're out of lock-up."

"Sure, that's Okay. You don't mind do you, Thackeray?" Billy asked.

"I don' need no damn' guard in here. Where they think I'm goin', anyway?" Thackeray Johnson crossed his arms and defiantly leaned back in his chair.

The marshal smiled and folded his arms. Billy looked at

Maloney who was fumbling through a large brown accordion file.

"Let's see here," Maloney started. He reviewed the list of evidence and concluded by handing Billy a packet of papers that he had prepared to comply with the court's standing discovery order. "And last, but not least," he finally said, "a transcription of Mr. Johnson's signed confession. Oh, and a video tape of the confession, which includes, let me add, the *Miranda* warning and Mr. Johnson's own statement that his confession was voluntary."

Billy leafed through the material and quickly read the confession. It was typed and signed by Johnson.

"Let me see that stuff." Johnson said. "I din' tell nobody they could make no video tape of me! I got constitutional rights, don' include no god damn' movie wifout my permission."

"Thackeray," Billy said, "I told you earlier not to say anything. Just be quiet. I'll talk to you when we get done here." Billy looked back at Maloney. "Anything else?"

"No. That's it. If you plead guilty, I'll tell the probation folks that he cooperated and I'll do what I can to get point deductions. I'll also agree not to appeal any sentence that Judge Mitchell gives him. But, you know, this stuff is pretty much out of our control." Maloney closed his file and smiled at Billy. "Let me know."

The old days of plea-bargaining were over. Now, the parties simply entered into a plea agreement, with favors and past animosities no longer as valuable as they used to be.

When Thackeray Johnson allegedly committed the bank robbery, he was on state probation from a five-year sentence for selling drugs, which was compounded by three DUIs and one conviction by guilty plea for driving without a license. He was also on probation for Federal convictions of stealing welfare checks and selling fifteen grams of counterfeit crack cocaine. After adding up the points, the United State Sentencing Guidelines netted him 151 to 188 months if he plead guilty, or 210 to 262 months if he went to trial and lost.

If Thackeray Johnson decided to exercise his constitutional right to a trial by a jury of his peers, he had absolutely nothing to gain and most likely 111 months to lose. Billy looked at Johnson and frowned. *Nine years and three months was a stiff price to pay for a trial, particularly if conviction is more certain than the coming day.*

"Any thoughts on what you want to do?" Maloney asked.

"Well," Billy said, "give me a little time to look over this stuff and we'll talk."

"I don't think you have a lot of time."

"What do you mean?"

"I'm guessing that Judge Mitchell is about at the end of his rope with Mr. Johnson. He wasn't very happy at the sentencing hearing."

"Sentencing hearing?"

"Yeah. When Mr. Johnson said he wanted to change his plea, the judge hit the ceiling."

"Change his plea?"

"Yeah."

Billy looked over at Thackeray. "Plea?"

"Not no voluntary plea. That was befo' I got me a lawyer. Not knoin'ly."

"Had you planned on telling me?"

"It's in da record. Do I have to tell you everything?"

"Mr. Johnson made an oral motion to withdraw his earlier guilty plea. I thought you knew."

Billy stuffed the papers in his brief case and shook his head. "Alright, I'll call you after Thackeray and I have a chance to discuss this."

The marshals replaced the handcuffs and led Thackeray back to the holding cell in the courthouse.

"I'll see you in a few minutes," Billy said.

"A bunch of fuckin' good that's gonna do," Thackeray said. "Say. You don' have a cigarette fo' me?" Thackeray asked the marshals, "I left mine back in the jailhouse."

"Sure, we'll find you one. Any preference?"

"Preference? I show enough got a preference. My

preference is outa' this fuckin' place, a cold beer, and three naked hoes."

Johnson and the marshals laughed as they escorted him to the holdover cell.

* * * *

"I know it's not what you want to hear, but it is what it is. Poopvitch overruled our motion to dismiss and he shortened our time to complete discovery," Billy said.

"What exactly does that mean?" Seymour asked.

"It means that Poopvitch didn't buy our argument and apparently FSLIC wants this thing over sooner rather than later. I talked to Braxton this morning, and he said that Jerry Morning instructed him to ask the court to move your case up on the docket. I got a scheduling order from the judge this afternoon and he's given us some pretty short deadlines. I must say, I can't understand the urgency. Any thoughts?"

"Hell, Billy, I have no idea."

"I guess I'll need to get my ass in gear. We've only got thirty days to get everything done. This is going to take all my time for the next few weeks."

Seymour had asked Billy not to deposit the second check, and Vickie reminded Billy that he would soon be running in the red with Seymour. She asked Billy several times to call Seymour and ask him if they could deposit the second check.

"Do what you have to do. I do not want to lose this project," Seymour told Billy.

"I will. But there's only so much I can do. There're only so many hours in the day."

"I know counselor. But there may be light at the end of the tunnel. I talked to some guy at Southwest Financial again the other day. He was going to fax me a list of information that he wanted to see on the Frederick Mall so either Southwest Financial or Bethesda Equity could step in Federated's shoes. I called to ask him if he was still interested. He said he was and apologized for not getting his list to me. But, while we were talking he offered to increase the loan on the utility strip that I told you about. I did not even ask for it. He just more or less offered. He said he was sure they were going to do the loan, and he said it was a show of his good faith and he was sorry for not getting back to me."

"No shit," Billy said.

"Yes. And, by the by, I called Vickie earlier today and told her to deposit that second check that you were holding for me."

"Great. That all sounds good. How much did you get?"

"This is too good to be true. One hundred thousand dollars," Seymour said.

"What? Did you say one hundred thousand dollars?"

"Yes sir, counselor. So let's not let this thing be sold in foreclosure before I get my deal done. I know you are going to need a little more money. Just let me know. But keep it reasonable. If we pull this off, I will make it well worth your while."

Billy knew about promised fees that clients based on a favorable outcome in cases that couldn't be won. He'd felt the sting of one third of nothing too many times. "Well, let's keep our fingers crossed," he said.

"Oh. I almost forgot. Howard Slone is going to be in Frederick tomorrow, and I wondered if you might meet with him? He said he would let me know tonight. Would you mind if I called you at home, or left a message on your answering machine at the office. I will call you later and let you know when he is going to be there."

"Who?"

"Howard Slone. The guy with Bethesda Equity or whatever it is."

"Not a problem. I should be home sometime after nine o'clock. Just call me."

* * * *

Billy didn't get a telephone call from Seymour and there was no message on his answering machine. He'd closed down Clyde's the night before and he was getting a late start. He skipped his usual morning run down through Georgetown and out the towpath for one and a half miles and then back. Instead, he quickly showered, dressed, and drove to his office. After fumbling with the buttons and the instruction book for the recently installed telephone system, he confirmed that there was no message from either Seymour or Howard Slone. It was eight fifteen and the telephone rang.

"Billy. Is that you?"

"Yeah. Seymour?"

"Yes. I am glad I caught you. Slone never called last night. I called his cell phone first thing this morning and told him you would be out in Frederick to see him. If that was a problem, to call me back and let me know. I just got a call from someone from Slone's office ... some guy ... who said that Slone definitely was going to be at the project this morning. So maybe you should try to see him. It only takes about fifty minutes from your office. You will be going against traffic."

"Sure. I guess I can run out there. I need to look at a record in the clerk's office in Frederick anyway, and I can kill two birds with one stone. What time does he want me to meet him?"

"Well, we did not actually set a time. I just felt you ought to meet him, especially since he is going to give us financing. He might have some questions about the foreclosure suit and where all that stands. He might have some questions for you. I do not think it would hurt for you to be available if he needs something."

"So I don't have any set time to meet him?"

"Not exactly, I told him I wanted you to meet him."

"What did he say about that?" Billy asked.

"Nothing, really. I left the message on his answering machine. The other day he told me he was going to be in Frederick today, and I told him I wanted the two of you to get together. We did not specify a time. We have sort of been playing phone tag."

"But he knows I'm coming out to see him?"

"Yes, counselor, I told him I wanted you two to get together, and I told him this morning that you were coming out to Frederick."

"But you didn't actually talk to him?"

"No. But, as I said, I left a message on his cell phone. He is expecting you." Seymour gave Billy Howard Slone's cell phone number. "Call me after you and Slone have a chance to talk."

Billy rode the elevator down to the lobby and jumped into his car that he'd parked in front of the building. He drove through Georgetown, past Clyde's, across the Potomac River, and onto the George Washington Memorial Parkway, out the Cabin John Parkway, and north to Frederick, Maryland. Seymour was right.

There was almost no traffic heading away from D.C. On the other side of I-270 a bumper-to-bumper snake of Federal functionaries and workers were making their daily commute into the District, coming from Rockville, Frederick, Hagerstown, Baltimore, Morgantown, and everywhere in between. Talking on cell phones, drinking coffee, reading newspapers, putting on makeup, listening to radios, daydreaming—a litany of motor vehicles edging along, gulping the gasoline made from the crude oil squeezed from the vestige of primordial life long past gone, only to be burned at fifteen miles per gallon with the residue spewed into the sky, hastening the next ice age to replenish the dwindling supply of squandered fossil fuel. Dutifully working their way to cubicles, offices, reception desks, kitchens, boardrooms, broom closets, courtrooms, libraries, and the rest of the morass of employment destinations in D.C.

Damn it. If I had to join that daily ritual, I'd kill myself.

* * * *

Frederick is Maryland's second largest city. It's a quaint town that sits between the eastern boundary of Catoctin Mountain in the Blue Ride Mountain chain and the Piedmont Plateau. Frederick has a contingent of history preservationists who harbor a ferocious pride in a few church spires that were spawned before the Civil War from the Reformed, Lutheran, and Anglican churches. Francis Scott Key was a lawyer in Frederick and Fort Detrick holds a cache of biological weapons big enough to wipe out the entire East Coast of the United States. Frederick is also a bedroom community where, to the chagrin of the natives, more than half of its residents commute into Washington D.C. for work.

Billy took the first Frederick exit, and after directions from a gas station attendant, found his way to the Frederick Mall construction site. He was surprised to see that the buildings looked completed, the parking lot was striped and sealed, and most of the stores had their signs installed. With the exception of some scattered construction equipment and a few workers, it looked like the place was ready to open for business. At the far end of one large building, there was a trailer with the name Ross Brothers Construction, Inc. printed on a huge white sign. He parked in front of the trailer next to a black Chevrolet Suburban and walked up the wooden steps into what he thought was the construction office. Inside there were several telephones, architectural plans and drawings everywhere, a line of hard hats hanging on the wall, and a man in khaki pants and a plaid shirt talking on the telephone and leafing through a set of worn architectural plans. He looked up and nodded to Billy.

"I know. I can see that. But look up at the top. Look where section A is. There's no VAV box. I don't care, God damn it. There's nothing shown on the drawing." There was a pause. "John, God damn it, I bid what the God damn architect drew, not what he meant to draw. I'm a contractor, not a God damn mind reader." There was another long pause, and the man in the trailer took the telephone away from his ear and waved to Billy. "John, we can install one thousand fucking VAV boxes, but that's a change order. Get me a change order and we'll put them in. No change order, no VAV boxes." Another pause. "I know you didn't draw these plans, but someone in your office did. It ain't my fuck-up. You get me a change order, and I'll get you the VAV boxes." He hung up the telephone and smiled at Billy.

"Problems?" Billy said with a smile. "I'm Billy Tapp. I'm Seymour Grey's lawyer." Billy extended his hand.

"Naw. Business as usual. If a detail is left off the plans, it's always a finger-pointing contest until somebody takes credit for it and coughs up the dough. We haven't had any serious problems with this job. I wish every job I bid was as good as this one. Doug Ross. How you doing? What can I do for you?"

"I'm looking for Howard Slone. Seymour said he was going to be out here today, and wanted me to come out and meet him."

"You mean Slone, right? Not Seymour."

"Yeah. Slone."

"Seymour called me a minute ago, and asked if Mr. Slone was here yet. He wanted to know if you'd gotten here. I told him I hadn't seen either one of you, but there was a black Suburban in front of the job trailer. I've been arguing with the architect since I talked to Seymour, so maybe that Suburban belongs to Slone. I saw some people in suits and ties over near the Itsell's department store. That might be them. I was going to go out and see who it was after I finished here. What does Howard Slone look like?"

"I don't have the slightest idea. I guess I'll walk out there and see if that's him."

"Here," said Ross, "put this hard hat on. OSHA requirement."

Billy and Ross walked out onto the make shift porch attached to the trailer. Ross pointed toward a large brick building that had several smaller stores clustered around it. There was a sign that was as big as some of the other stores. Itsell's Department Store, it said.

"I think I saw them go into Itsell's. Go on over there and take a look, I'll join up in few minutes."

Billy certainly recognized the name Itsell's Department Store. It was the largest department store chain in the country. Seymour was right, if the rest of the national tenants that follow Itsell's around the country come to the Frederick Mall, this place will be a huge success. Billy was impressed with the design and layout. The combination of brick, stone, and ceramic tile was exactly in balance and made the development as attractive as anything Billy had ever seen. The standing seam roofs and colorful canvas awnings were in perfect balance. The light standards along the brick sidewalks tied the landscaping and building design together. Billy understood why Seymour believed that the Frederick Mall would make lots of money and, after all, that's what it's all about, making lots of money. But, it was nice to see good taste factored into the equation.

Billy crossed the asphalt parking lot to the glass entrance. He cupped his hands around his eyes to shield the sun so he could see into the department store. He didn't see anyone. He pulled open on one of the several doors and walked into a vast open space with array of display cases, wooden partitions, wiring, shelves, racks, and all the other stuff necessary to show off and sell the exhaustive inventory of merchandise that Itsell's carried. Everywhere he looked, there were workmen putting on the finishing touches. He wandered toward the back and saw a group of men clustered around a table, hunched over a set of plans. When Billy approached, the group looked up.

"You wouldn't happen to know where I could find Howard Slone, would you?" Billy asked.

Slone stepped forward and offered a handshake to Billy. "I'm Howard Slone." He paused and waited for Billy's response.

Billy took his hand and said, "I'm Billy Tapp. Seymour's lawyer."

"Mr. Tapp. Well how are you?"

Howard Slone was about five feet four inches tall. He was almost completely bald and wore an expensive blue pinstriped suit and a very light gray shirt with a white collar and white French cuffs. His shoes where brightly shined and he had a short well-manicured beard. He had a large hook nose that had seemed to point toward his shinny little chin. Despite that curiosity, he looked healthy and rich. It was clear that he was holding sway over the gathering. Slone pulled Billy away from the group. "Listen, how long are you going to be in Frederick?"

"I came to see you. Seymour asked me to come out here this morning."

Slone looked back at the men standing around the table. "I've got a few things to go over with these fellows. I think it will take a few hours. Do you want to meet for lunch somewhere? Where are you staying?"

"Staying? Nowhere. I drove out from D.C. My office is in D.C."

"That's right. I don't know what I'm thinking about. Tell you what. I'm staying at the Willard. Why don't we meet somewhere for drinks this afternoon. I can finish here, and then we'll have enough time to talk. Sorry you had to drive all the way out here. I didn't talk to Mr. Grey, I would have told him that we could meet in your office or in town. Come by the Willard around five o'clock and I'll buy you a drink. Does that work for you?"

"Sure. I'll see you then."

Slone turned abruptly and went back to the group, where someone would point at the plans and then at some corresponding place in the department store and then at the plans and then at some other part of the store.

Billy went back to the job trailer; it was empty. He went out to his car. Billy nodded politely to a large muscular man, dressed in dark pants and a polo shirt, leaning against the front fender of the Suburban and reading a newspaper.

CHAPTER TWELVE

It was well past noon when Billy drove into downtown Frederick and parked across the street from the Frederick County Courthouse. The modern architecture of the courthouse looked out of place with the surrounding historic buildings. Since his meeting with Slone had been cut short, there was nothing pressing, so he meandered down Patrick Street to North Market Street looking for a place to have a late lunch. He passed a few curio shops and an antique store before coming to Bushweiler's Bar & Grille, which, according to the gold leaf sign on the door, had been established more than one hundred years ago. He pulled the large oak door open and stepped through a burst of cold air into the smell of food.

The ceiling was more than twenty-five feet high and a balcony surrounded the three walls opposite the massive back-bar, which had a dark wooden edifice with carved filigree and two huge lions on either end. In the middle, ensconced above the entire affair, an eagle—similar to the one in Judge Barr's courtroom—glowered down over the bar and dining area.

The place was empty. Billy pulled a rickety stool up to the bar and ordered a tuna salad sandwich on toasted wheat with Dijon mustard.

"Do you want chips or fries with that?" the bartender asked.

"What does it come with?"

"Chips or fries."

"Could I get a small green salad instead? I'd also like a draft beer. What do you have on tap?"

"You may, but I'll have to charge you ninety-five cents extra. We have Bud, Bud Light, Miller, Heineken, and Bass."

The bartender smiled and pointed at the taps behind the bar. She was wearing black spandex tights and a white knit shirt that struck her muscular rump about two inches below the curve of her ass. She had on white running shoes and a red bandanna. She was slender and looked fit.

"I guess I'll have a Heineken."

The bartender turned to fetch Billy's beer. When she reached to pull the tap, her shirt hiked up over her butt. On her lower back a small wedge of sweat soaked through the black spandex; the dark spot extended down toward the crack of her ass. When she turned to put the beer on the bar, she caught Billy staring. He looked up quickly and grinned uncomfortably. She reached around and rubbed her lower back.

"Been out running?" Billy said quickly.

"Yes. I try to get a few miles in between lunch and happy hour. I just got back."

"How far do you usually run?"

"Today I ran two and a half miles, I like to go between three and five."

"Yeah. Me too. I try to run in the morning. I run twenty-five miles a week and work out in the gym at least three days a week, just to stay fat." Billy and the bartender laughed.

"You're not fat," she said. "You're just ... big. You can't change your genes. You look good. I can tell you're in shape." She blushed slightly. "Here let me get this back into the kitchen."

"Let me have another beer while you're at it. What's your name?"

"Valerie."

"I'm Billy Tapp." He offered his hand. She awkwardly wiped her hand on the white shirt and extended her hand to Billy. It was small and warm; its dampness sent a tingle through Billy's body.

"Are you from here?" she asked.

"No. I'm from D.C. I had to come out here on business. I'm a lawyer. I represent the developers of the Frederick Mall. You know about that development?"

"Sure. I know where it is. Actually, I've driven by it a couple of times. It's pretty big. So, you're their lawyer, huh. I need to take your order back to the kitchen. I'll be right back."

A few minutes later, Valerie came back carrying a plate with the tuna salad sandwich and a fake wooden bowl with lettuce and a few tomato wedges. She put them on the bar and asked Billy if he wanted another beer.

"Where do you run in D.C.?"

"I actually live in Georgetown, and I run most of the time down on the tow-path. It's a great place to run."

"Yeah. I've heard that. I need to try it some time."

"Sure. You ought to come in some time and run with me."

Billy fumbled through his wallet and pulled out a business card. Valerie took it and laid it beside the cash register.

"I'll do that."

She gave Billy her cell phone number and told him she was leaving to shower and get ready for the happy hour rush. He paid his bill and wandered over to the courthouse to inspect the Circuit Court criminal record for a witness that he intended to call in an upcoming trial. Billy had wasted most of the afternoon, and before he knew it, it was half past four. *Damn, I'd better get back. I'm supposed to meet Howard Slone for drinks at five.*

* * * *

127

Howard Slone left a message at the front desk of the Willard Hotel saying that he would be in the Round Robin Bar.

"I'm glad you could make it. Seymour has mentioned your name. He's never had anything bad to say about you, even though you're an attorney." Slone offered a passive smile. "Just kidding, of course."

"Sorry I'm a little late. I got tied up in Frederick."

"Not a problem. I'm done for the day. Time to enjoy a few drinks and a good meal."

Howard Slone had changed from his suit to a blue double-breasted blazer, dark gray pants, a club tie, and a magenta handkerchief stuffed into his breast pocket. There was a half-filled martini glass on the table and an empty glass flask in an ice bath.

"Can I get you a drink?" Slone asked. He waved at the waitress who stood at the service station at the end of the mahogany bar.

They sat in blue leather captain's chairs around a thick square mahogany table. There was an oil lamp burning in the middle, which cast a flickering shadow over the table and Howard Slone. The dim light shown on Slone's face the same way Billy used to shine a flashlight on his own face to scare his younger brother. And, the same way he shined it on his face to scare his kids when they camped in the small back yard of his townhouse in Georgetown.

* * * *

His parents had been visiting and the children got the idea to camp in the yard from a story their grandfather told about Billy and his brother camping in the back yard.

"No such thing happened," Billy's mother said.

"Yes it did. Don't tell me that it didn't," his father barked.

"You don't know what you're talking about," she quickly retorted.

"I by God ... yes I do. It happened just like I said." Billy's father leaned over a table lamp setting on an end table, causing it to cast shadows over his face. "See," he said. "Arrr. Gurrr. Watch out. I'm a monster and I'm going to get you."

"What are you doing?" Billy's mother said. "Stop that!" she yelled. "You're going to scare these poor children."

Both children sat quietly and watched. Neither said a word and neither looked away.

"Well, it doesn't really matter," Billy said. "How would you kids like to go camping tonight?"

Both children looked first at their mother and then at their red-faced grandparents. They looked back at Billy.

"Can we? Can we?"

"I don't think so," Ann said. "You don't have any camping equipment. No tent. No sleeping bags. No camping equipment. Maybe some other time."

"Tell you what I'll do," Billy said, "we'll go to the store and buy some camping equipment. What do you think about that?"

"Billy Tapp," Ann said, "that's stupid. You're going to buy all that stuff for one night in the back yard. Plus it's too late. You wouldn't get back until midnight."

Billy and Ann argued, and the children went to bed and listened to the argument that started about camping equipment and ended about Billy staying too late at Clyde's. The next weekend, Billy took the kids to L.L. Bean and bought a tent, sleeping bags, and a camp stove. He pitched the tent in the back yard and shined a flashlight in his face. Lucy screamed and grabbed John.

"It's a monster," she yelled. "Help. It's a monster."

The kids took turns making faces at each other, and they laughed and laughed. They didn't remember the harsh words between their grandparents or the argument about Billy coming home drunk. That was the first and last time that they used the tent, the camp stove, and the sleeping bags.

* * * *

"Seymour tells me that you own Bethesda Equity.

Slone nodded. For a moment, the shadows in his face looked like he was laughing. "Yes. I'm in Washington frequently. I, more or less, keep a room here. It's convenient and I'm comfortable with the staff and the accommodations."

"This is one of my favorite places," Billy said.

The waitress came over to the table. She wore black pants with a satin stripe on the side and a formal white shirt with a black bowtie. She was overweight and her make-up exaggerated the undistinguished features of her mouth and her eyebrows and the blush of her cheeks.

"What can I get you? Are you ready for another, sir?"

"What would you like, Mr. Tapp?" Slone nodded at Billy and then gulped the last of his martini. "I'll have another martini. Bombay Sapphire. Right? Dry. Remember? Up. And you, Mr. Tapp?"

"Well, I guess I'll have a beer. Maybe a Budweiser ... no. Make that a Heineken."

Slone's cell phone rang, and he quickly answered. "Yes. Uh huh. Sure. I'll see you a little bit later. Let me call you back in a bit," he said and quickly snapped the telephone shut and stuck it back in the breast pocket of his sport coat.

The waitress brought their drinks. Billy tapped the label on the Heineken bottle and Slone adjusted his shirt collar. Billy took a long drink of his beer, and waited for the missing part of Seymour's story.

"What kind of deals does Bethesda Equity prefer? Do y'all do mostly commercial or some residential too?"

Slone pushed back slightly from the table and crossed his legs. He then leaned back and took a delicate sip of his martini.

"Bethesda Equity is actually a wholly owned subsidiary of Southeast Financial, which is located in Fort Lauderdale. Bet E, as we call it, was organized as an investment vehicle to take advantage of any project that offers an exceptional opportunity and requires a quick decision. Bet E can move on a moment's notice. That gives it a huge advantage over the commercial banks and other conventional lenders who answer to loan committees, boards of directors, and all the state and federal lending requirements. Bet-E can move faster than even the most mobile real estate investment trust. For the most part, I decide the underwriting and lending criteria. In some deals, I talk with my partners, but that's just a telephone call ... and, they always follow my advice."

"How do you find the investment opportunities?"

"Contacts. You would be surprised how small the lending community is. Everyone knows everyone else. Small world. Word gets around."

"That's right. Since most all of the S & Ls are in the shit-can, the Federal Government has tightened up on everybody. Regulations out the ass, appraisals, stiffer lending requirements, and nothing has changed for the good. In fact, I think there's a pretty good argument that the quality of deals has actually gone downhill. What do you think?"

"I try not to get too involved with the Federal Government. We don't have public shareholders and we don't rely on the Fed for funds. I don't get too much involved with it." Slone laughed sarcastically and brushed at his coat lapel.

"Tell me, Mr. Slone—"

"Howard. Call me Howard. I'm not that much older than you."

"Sure. Howard. Call me Billy. How'd you get involved in the real estate business? Do you mind me asking?"

"Ah. No. Not at all. Do you do primarily real estate law?"

"No. Not really. I actually have a pretty diverse practice. I used to be with a big firm, but I guess I wasn't cut out for that kind of ... shall we say ... environment. I do some tort law, a good bit of criminal law, employment law. I represent a few guys in the television and radio business who keep getting sued for sexual harassment. I've done a bunch of securities fraud stuff. Mostly on the criminal side."

"Criminal law. Prosecute or defend?"

"Oh, defend. I've never had much taste for prosecuting. When I say criminal law, I'm making the distinction between administrative enforcement of securities regulations and that kind of stuff and, for example, selling unregistered securities. Although they are related, one is like reading the dictionary, and the other is dealing with the person who tries to redefine the dictionary. That make any sense to you?"

"Sure it does, Mr. Tapp."

"Billy."

"Billy. We have issues with the Federal government sometimes ... ah, over the years. Sometimes problems sometimes not. You ever do any work in Arizona?"

"No. Have not."

"I have a good friend out there. He's with the firm of ... Say, ready for another drink? Looks like your beer is about gone."

"Sure. Why not? I guess I'm done for the day."

Slone motioned to the waitress and held up two fingers and made a circular motion with his hand. He smiled at the waitress and tugged on his shirt sleeves.

"Seymour tells me that you're thinking about paying off Federated in the Frederick deal and giving him enough dough to finish the project."

The waitress came with the martini and the Heineken. When she put the beer in front of Billy, he drained the one he had and handed her the empty bottle.

"Thanks." He looked over at Slone and smiled.

"I don't need to tell you how grateful and relieved that Seymour is. It kind of seemed to me that he was running out of options."

"Yes. I know that." A faint smile showed on Slone's face. "We don't know all the details yet. But either Bet E or Southeast will probably make the loan.

"Now. You said that Bethesda Equity. Who is South*west* Financial? For some reason, seems to me like Seymour said something about Southwest Financial. Didn't you just say that Bethesda Equity was owned by South*east* Financial?"

Slone fidgeted in his chair and quickly stirred his martini with the olive impaled on the tiny yellow plastic sword. The candle on the table flickered and the light shown up on Slone's shiny bald head. He pulled a pair of glasses out of his coat pocket and fitted them over his ears.

"Did I say Southeast? You see, Southeast is the holding company. It owns Bethesda Equity, and Southeast and Southwest are two different companies. One doesn't own the other or vice versa. Southwest was set up to do deals in Texas, out west for the most part. Not here, except maybe in this case. Just special cases."

"Seymour wants me to be sure all the documents are in order and make sure this deal gets closed before the foreclosure slams the door on his ass. He doesn't want to lose this project. If you know what I mean. So. Do you want me to call your lawyers for the documents, or what's our next step? So, who's actually going to make the loan?"

"Well it will either be Bet E or Southwest Financial. That's what they told Seymour, I think. Whichever it is, I don't think it should matter too much, should it? A loan is a loan. If the project works, it works. I don't think it really makes too much difference. It shouldn't matter."

"Want me to call your attorneys and start on the paperwork?"

"Absolutely. We need to get the paper work started right away."

"Great. Give me a number and I'll call him in the morning."

Slone patted his coat pockets and pulled out a small black appointment book. He looked through it quickly and took a long drink of his martini. He looked back in the little book and drank the rest of his martini.

"Well, damn. I don't see it here. I'll call you and give it to you in the morning." He brushed at the lapel of his jacket and stood up.

"Well, Mr. Tapp. I'll call you in the morning."

Slone quickly turned and walked away. He stopped and turned to the waitress. "Put these drinks on my room, if you don't mind." He handed her a folded bill.

"Do you have my number?" Billy asked. "Would you like a card?"

"Ah. Yes, well no. I don't have it, but I'll get it in the morning." Slone turned again and, as if avoiding the bulls in Pamplona, hurried off.

CHAPTER THIRTEEN

"You have three calls. One from some girl named Robin Grigsby, one from Michael Braxton, and one from Judge Barr's office. The girl said you'd know what it was; Braxton wants you to call him back; I think Barr wants to see you ... I don't know what it's about."

Billy decided to return the calls in reverse order. He'd call Judge Stewart's law clerk last. He always enjoyed talking to Judge Barr. He was sure that that Braxton's call had something to do with Judge Poopvitch, and anything to do with Poopvitch would be unpleasant, irrational, or ridiculous. He called Braxton first.

"Mike? This is Billy Tapp. I just got your message. What's up?"

Michael Braxton was in his mid-forties. He attended Harvard Law School fifteen years after receiving a PhD in mathematics from Georgia Tech. Before Harvard, he was a computer whiz for a now defunct California software company. The remote chance of stability and job security, and his general boredom prompted him to get another advanced degree and a career change. So, although most of his new colleagues had been practicing law for more or less twenty years, he was a relative neophyte, and consequently he hadn't yet developed the proper and predicable cynicism and general disdain for incompetent judges that Billy Tapp brandished with impunity.

"Mr. Tapp. I received a call from Judge Poopvitch's clerk. He said that he'd seen you and that you mentioned the possibility of getting a little extra time to respond to my motion for summary judgment. One of the timing issues involves my response to your motion to dismiss. Frankly, I don't think Judge Poopvitch really understood who had filed which motion."

"Really." Billy said. "I don't think Poopvitch knows the difference between apple sauce and cat shit."

"I can't—"

"Do you think he has any idea what this case is about?"

"Well, Mr. Tapp—"

"Billy."

"Billy. I know he has a pretty full docket, and it's probably a little hard to keep track of everything."

"Bullshit. But, I guess that's not the issue. What'd his clerk say?"

"He said that the judge was giving us an additional sixty days to submit affidavits or anything else in support of our motions, and then thirty days to file memoranda in support and ten days for responses. He didn't say anything about replies to response, so I guess that means we can't file replies. Do you think we need to file replies?"

"No."

"I guess I don't either, but if you don't mind, I'd like the chance to think about it a little before I finally decide."

"Sure."

"Let's see. That means, then, that we need to submit any additional proof on ... do you have your calendar in front of you?"

"No. Why don't you just calculate it and stick it in the order and send it over to me. I'll sign it."

"Do you think Judge Poopvitch wants an agreed order? Do you think we need to both sign it and send it to him?"

"Beats me. Want me to call him?"

"Oh no. No. I'll call his clerk. On a conference call with you. I'll call you right back. Are you going to be there for a while?"

"Maybe. If I'm not, just tell Vickie. I don't need to be in the conference call. I trust you."

"Vickie?"

"My secretary ... ah paralegal."

"Oh yes. Sure. Are you sure this works for you?"

"Yep. I planned on spending a few days in Florida, and Poopvitch's general stupidity and knee jerk ruling the other day screwed up my plans. Now I can go. Saved by the voice of reason. That doesn't happen very often in Poopvitch's court. He must not be in charge of hiring his own law clerks. Keep me posted. Thanks, Mike." Billy tossed the telephone back in its cradle and rummaged through the message slips on his desk for Judge Barr's number.

"Vickie. Do you have Barr's number? I can't seem to find the damn thing."

"He's on the line. He's been holding for you."

"Why didn't you tell me? Why didn't you interrupt me?"

"I was coming in to tell you when you yelled. Relax, Billy. He told me not to interrupt you. Who should I pay attention to? You or a judge." She pointed at Billy and then at the sky. "Are you more important than a judge?"

"Who pays you?"

"Sometimes, nobody."

"But I'll be your friend forever." Billy grinned and Vickie feigned disgust and closed the door behind her.

"Tom. What's going on? How ya doing?"

"Good. Good. Not much."

"Sorry to leave you on hold. I gave Vickie a little shit for not telling me you were on the line."

"That's okay. I told her to just leave me on hold. I had the speaker on and I was working on an opinion. Say. This isn't why I called, but do you know off the top of your head what the notice requirement is for an *ex parte* motion in a prejudgment attachment?"

"State or Federal?"

"State."

"Seven days."

"You sure?"

"Pretty sure."

"Great. Thanks. You don't need a job as a law clerk do you?"

"How much does it pay?"

"Not much, but it will look good on your resume."

"Judge. I'm afraid it's too late for that. The damage has already been done."

"Billy, I just got word from Earl, over at the jail. He said that there was another incident with that Terry Jacobs kid. Seems like he may have been beaten up and raped by a couple of inmates. Have you heard any of this yet?"

"Nope. Not a word. If his mother knew, I'm sure she'd have called me. What condition is he in? Was he hurt?"

"I don't exactly know. I really don't know why Earl called me. I guess it's because Jacobs looked pretty bad when y'all were in court the other day, and I asked Earl to kinda look after him or something. There's only so much I can do."

"Yeah. That's what you said in court. You don't run the jail. Ain't much you can do about it. I suppose I need to find out what the deal is."

"He's not at the jail. Earl said they took him over to the hospital. So, he must have been hurt. Unless it's just for precautionary reasons."

"God damn it." Billy paused and thought for a moment. "The moral is: Don't kill anybody because you're likely to land in jail, and jail has a certain unpleasant side to it."

"Counselor. Innocent until proven guilty."

"Right."

"Find out what's going on and let me know. The boys down at the jail might be a little closed-mouth about the whole thing. I'd be surprised if you get much cooperation. But let me know. Rape and a thrashing aren't the punishment for homicide ... might be appropriate in some cases, but it should wait until at least a guy's convicted ... I didn't say that."

"Let me find out. I'll get back with you if I think it will affect our schedule. Does Bloomberg know about this yet?"

"Don't know. I expect that depends on the tact the jail is taking to cover their asses. In any case, I don't think you'll get too much sympathy from Bloomberg. How are the kids?"

"Good. Good. They're getting older."

"Do you ever talk to Ann?"

"Sure. I think she's dating some doc. The head of the otolaryngology department."

"The what department?"

"Head, neck, nose, blah, blah, blah. You know, the kind of doc who re-plumbed your nose a few years ago so you could breath. Took out most of the bends and brakes that you accumulated at Alabama."

"Counselor, I've got another call here. Get back with me."

"Okay, Judge. Let's get together and have a few cold beers. Call me when you get some free time."

"I'll do it. Take care Billy."

Billy clicked on the icon that opened the calendar on his computer to see what he had scheduled for the day. He decided to put everything on hold until he figured out what happened to Terry Jacobs. Terry's mother would be hysterical; Billy doubted if she even knew what had happened. The family is always the last to find out. Mary Jacobs would go through the usual emotions. First, distraught and concerned, then worried and scared, then angry, then demanding justice, then depressed, then resigned to the inevitable price of entering the criminal justice system when the cost of admission is homicide.

Vickie stuck her head in Billy's office. "Mr. Braxton is on the line."

"No. I just talked to him."

"That might be, but he's back on the phone again. Do

you want me to take a number"?

Billy hesitated. "No. I guess I'll talk to him."

"Billy. Sorry to bother you again. But my clerk was out in Frederick this morning, just doing a final record check on the Grey case. I asked him to check the property records for taxes and liens and anything else that may have been recorded since we filed the suit. For some reason, he looked at all the records ... even the documents before we filed." Braxton paused for a moment. "Have you ever heard of Bethesda Equity?"

"Sure. They loaned Seymour some money for an easement."

"Apparently. That's what I understand. But what I don't understand is why we didn't see it when we did the title search the first time for the lawsuit."

"Sometimes you miss those kinds of things. That's why I don't do title work."

"I really don't know how we could have missed it. I looked at the title abstract, and our title clerk records each document, and includes the page, date, and other information. It's almost like Bethesda Equity's lien wasn't in the record book when we did the search. I talked to our title person, and she said that not only did she look at the computer, she physically looked at every page in the lien book. I don't get it. I don't know how we could have missed it."

"You know, I'm just getting in this case, but now that you mention it, I did ask Seymour Grey why Bethesda Equity wasn't a party. For some reason, I didn't think the easement was actually part of the main property, you know, what Federated made the loan on. You sure it's a second mortgage on the main property?"

* * * *

When a bank makes a loan, it usually requires the borrower to sign both a promissory note for the money and a mortgage to secure repayment of the note. The bank files the mortgage in the county court clerk's office where the property is located. Mortgages and other liens that affect property are public records. The idea is to give the rest of the world notice of the debt and if there's a default, the bank or any of the other lien holders can sell the property to pay back their loan.

In a foreclosure, if there is more than one mortgage or lien, repayment from the sale is in the reverse order of when each was filed. There's a saying: "first in time, first in right." Everyone who has filed a mortgage or other lien must be included as a defendant, otherwise the outcome of the foreclosure can be set aside. If there isn't enough money from the sale to repay all of the lien holders, the highest bidder can keep the property and, if there's not enough money to pay the highest bidder, do whatever it can to get paid in full.

However, owning property is rarely a bank's wish. A bank only wants its money, its interest, its penalties, its attorney's fees, its costs, and everything else included in its note and mortgage agreements. A lender doesn't miss a chance to maximize its profit, and that's especially so when there's a default. There's something else a lender doesn't do, a lender never forgets to secure its loan by filing a mortgage. Lawyers orchestrate this whole process. And, of course, it would be an open and shut case of legal malpractice if a lawyer missed any of these basic steps.

* * * *

"What does this mean to your case?"

"I almost hate to think about it, but I suppose I'll have to amend the complaint and include Bethesda Equity. File a motion for leave to amend, get service of process, wait for an answer, and—"

"You know, Mike, this will amount to starting this whole suit again. Like it was never filed."

"I guess you're right. So much for a quick resolution."

141

* * * *

Billy looked up Judge Stewart's telephone number in the Blue Book, a directory for lawyers and judges in the D.C. area. He guessed that Robin Grigsby's number would be the same as the Judges.

"May I speak to Robin Grigsby, please?"

Billy recognized Judge Stewart's secretary's voice. "Who may I say is calling?"

Billy hesitated. "Ah. Billy Tapp."

"Mr. Tapp. How are you? Can I tell her what it's in reference to?"

The question startled Billy. He wasn't prepared to tell Judge Stewart's secretary that he was calling Robin Grigsby with the hopes of getting laid. *Maybe I should say for personal reasons. But, maybe Robin Grigsby was calling for some other reason. For some legal reason.* If he said it was personal, he would sound like an idiot.

"Just tell her. I mean. I'm returning her call. She called me. I'm returning her call."

"Certainly, Mr. Tapp. I'll let her know you're on the line."

After an uncomfortably long wait, Robin Grigsby picked up the phone. "Hello. Is this Billy Tapp?"

"Yeah. How are you? Just returning your call." Billy waited through the terrible silence of his last word.

"Hey. Listen. I'm really sorry about the other night. I had a little too much to drink. And, I got to thinking about it. I ... ah ... got to thinking that I might have made a fool out of myself. I hope you don't think that's the way I am all the time."

"No. No. Don't worry about it. I think you were alright. I don't—"

"Yesterday, I was talking to one of the girls I was with and she said I made a complete fool out of myself. I thought I'd better call and apologize."

"Oh no. Don't worry about it. You were just having a

little fun."

"Well, I'd hate for it to get back to Judge Stewart that one of his law clerks was out drunk trying to pick up a stranger. You know what I mean?"

"Robin, your secret is safe with me."

"God. Thanks. I hope you don't have the wrong idea about me."

Billy got the sinking feeling that Robin Grigsby called to cover her ass. She just wanted to make sure that Billy didn't somehow let slip with Judge Stewart that she was out vamping around in the local bars. There was no law against promiscuity, but judges didn't like their staff doing anything that could either be improper or give the appearance of impropriety. The Code of Judicial Conduct prohibited such shenanigans. But, there was also a canon that said a judge should be patient, dignified, and courteous to lawyers. *How many judges gave that cannon the same deference as the one that said they shouldn't embarrass themselves in public, the one that said they should avoid impropriety?* Without sucking Robin Grigsby into his fleeting concern about judicial conduct, he knew damn well that it wouldn't be good for her career if Judge Stewart knew she was in Clyde's, drunk, and trying to pick up strangers—especially members of the bar who practiced in Judge Stewart's court. He hoped that she called him to continue their discussion from the other night when she announced to her friends that "Billy will take me home." He remembered her invitation when she said, "Call me."

"Do you remember what you said?" Billy asked her.

"Ah ... not really. Did I say anything too bad?"

"Oh no. No. Not really. You don't remember what you said to me?"

"No. Not really. Do I want to know?"

"It wasn't bad."

"What did I say, then."

Billy thought what the hell. *If she's just trying to cover her ass, all she can say is no. It can't hurt to ask. All she can do is say no.* "Well, you told me to call you. You said you'd buy me lunch this week."

There was silence on the other end of the line. Billy waited. He heard what he thought was the sound of Robin Grigsby covering the speaker part of the handset, and then her hand sliding off the telephone.

"Sure. Do you want to do lunch sometime this week? Sure. Did I really ask you that?"

"You offered." Billy waited.

"Sure. That would be great. How about drinks at the Old Ebbitt tomorrow night?"

"What time?"

"How's seven o'clock?"

"Good. I'll see you there."

* * * *

"Vickie. Do you have Seymour's telephone number handy? Could you get him on the telephone for me? I need to ask him something about Bethesda Equity."

After a few minutes, Vickie yelled into Billy's office. "He's on the line. Line two."

"Seymour, do you remember anything about the Bethesda Equity loan? Do you remember if you signed a mortgage, or if you got a copy of a mortgage or anything like that?"

"Counselor. How are you? How was your meeting with Howard Slone? Everything go okay with that? What did you think about him? I have a call here from him but I have not had time to call him back. Thought I would talk to you first. What is going on?"

"Yeah. I met with him. We met at the Willard, and—"

"Great hotel. One of my favorites. Great food. Great rooms. That is about where I would have expected Howard Slone to stay. What did you think of him?"

"Seymour, do you remember who made the loan for you. Who was the lender? Do you remember?"

"Slone. Counselor, it was Howard Slone."

"Well, I know that. But, do you remember what the actual

entity was. The name of the company. Was it South*west* Financial? Or, South*east* Financial. Do you remember any of those details?"

"Not really."

"How would I find out? Is there some quick way I can find out without ... bothering Slone. I ... hate to call him over some detail like this. He might think we don't know what we're doing."

"Of course. All the documents are in your office. Everything should be in the boxes that I brought to your office. Have you looked in those files yet?"

"I've looked at some of them, but not all. But, you're telling me everything that you got from Slone, and whatever entity he was dealing with, is in the boxes that you gave me. Is that right?"

"That is correct. If it is not in those boxes, we did not get it."

"Good. Let me get off the phone and see if I can find what I'm looking for. Are you going to be available for the rest of the day? I may have some questions for you."

"Give me a call counselor. You have all my numbers. I will be available."

* * * *

Vickie took the boxes from the top of refrigerator and put them back on the table in the conference room. There were four banker's boxes with well-organized manila files, each with a label that clearly identified the contents. Advertising, Agendas, Architecture & Engineering, Construction, etc. Despite Seymour's seemingly casual indifference to the details, someone carefully organized the files with all the Frederick Mall development documents and letters.

Billy flipped through the files until he came to a tab named *Financial*. He continued through the subcategories of Financial and, following the divider called *Budgets*, he found several files under the subcategory called *Loan*. The file entitled *Federated Savings and Loan* was by far the biggest. It was three large manila folders numbered *I, II,* and *III,* and contained all the drafts and final documents for the loan agreement, mortgage, and correspondence between Seymour and Federated. Billy also found a file that was originally entitled *Southeast Financial,* but someone crossed through the name and hand wrote the name *Bethesda Equity.*

The loan agreement and the mortgage contained the expected flood of overreaching, one-sided, and painfully verbose boilerplate legalese that characterized every loan transaction that Billy had ever seen. *This is why I don't do real estate law.* There were high powered lawyers who spent thousands of hours and millions of dollars generating such unnecessary legal quagmires. *What does all this amount to? If you borrow money and don't pay it back, the bank can sell your property and keep enough to pay off the loan. Why can't that be said in one paragraph?* Billy rubbed his eyes and leafed through the loan agreement.

There was no amount. The place in the Bethesda Equity loan agreement that should have stated the loan amount was blank. There was a promissory note attached at the back of the loan agreement, it was "Exhibit A." The note amount was also blank, but it contained the following language: "Subject to Lender's sole approval, this note may be increased in amount to Seventy-Five Million Dollars ($75,000,000) ..." The mortgage was in the same folder. It was just like the note and the loan agreement; there was no amount. But, the lender could increase it up to seventy-five million dollars. *These must be drafts of the original documents, and the originals filed somewhere else.* He turned to the signature page, and to his surprise, the loan agreement, the note, and the mortgage were all signed and notarized. He looked for completed documents, but they were not in the folder first called Southeast Financial and then changed to Bethesda Equity.

"Vickie," Billy yelled. "Are there any other boxes or files that Seymour brought by? Is this everything?"

Vickie came into the conference room. "That's all of it."

"You sure? You didn't move any of the files or anything?"

"Nope. I looked at them. I was going to organize the files, but they looked like they were already organized. I just left them alone. Why? Is there something wrong?"

"I don't know. Maybe. None of the Bethesda Equity loan documents have an amount in them. Can't say that I've exactly seen that before."

*   *   *   *

"Mr. Slone. This is Billy Tapp."

"Mr. Tapp. How are you?" There was a long pause. "Is there something I can help you with?"

"Maybe. I was talking to Mike Braxton today, and he told me that apparently his title person missed the Bethesda Equity mortgage."

"Yes." Again, a long pause.

"Did you know that?"

"How would I know that?"

"Well I guess you wouldn't."

"Is that why you called?"

Billy hesitated. "I'd like to get copies of the original documents. Would you have your lawyer fax them over to me?"

"Mr. Tapp."

"Billy. They call me Billy."

"Alright. Billy. I don't have the original documents. Mr. Grey should have copies. Have you asked him?" Howard Slone forced a sarcastic laugh.

"Could you have your lawyers send copies to me?"

Another long pause. "I'm not sure who did this loan for Bet E. I'll check with my office."

"Do you have any idea when I can get them?"

"I'll check with my office."

"When do you think that will be?"

"I can't tell you that. I'll just have to check my office."

"If you want to give me your lawyer's number, I'll call him and you won't have to bother."

The phone line went dead.

"God damn it," Billy said and slammed down the telephone.

Vickie came into his office. "Did you yell at *me*?" Vickie smirked. Here, you left this on my desk, what do you want to do with it?"

"What is it?"

"I don't know. Here, you must have put it on my desk the other day. It looks like a check or something."

It was the envelope that Billy picked up off the floor and put on Vickie's desk. He opened it. Inside there was a cancelled check payable to Seymour Grey, made by Southeast Financial, and drawn on the First National Bank of the Cayman Islands.

CHAPTER FOURTEEN

For the second time in a week, Billy pulled into the parking garage that was located across Canal Street from the Frederick County Courthouse. The courthouse and the parking garage set on the upper bank of Carroll Creek, a small stream that runs through the downtown and had been obsessed over, fastidiously preserved, and renovated far beyond its worth. Carroll Creek was a constant source of historic pride, development aggravation, and flood danger. But, at its best, during the few weeks in the year when the weather isn't too cold or too hot or otherwise too inclement, Carroll Creek is a pleasant green strip of public space that, like so many other ill-conceived public projects, had received far more funding than was actually warranted. Vast underground concrete vaults collected flood water, and a variety of decorative trees and shrubs and flowers flanked its concrete edges, where benches languished in disrepair, trash containers missed lids, and an occasional homeless person smoked cigarette butts and stared at the small stream of water or gazed blankly into the blue sky above.

Billy walked across Canal Street, across the large brick apron in front of the courthouse, and he skipped up the two tiers of steps, walked through the front door and the ubiquitous metal detectors and into the Frederick Circuit

Clerk's office. An overweight boy with bleached blond hair, rimless purple-shaded eyeglasses, and a silver stud in his lower lip looked up from an open file. He peered over the top of his glasses.

"Yessss?"

"I'm looking for the County Court Clerk's office."

"What are you looking for?"

"The County Court Clerk's office."

"I figured that out. That's not what I mean. I mean, what are you looking for? This is the Circuit Clerk's office. Are you looking for court records or what?" The boy cocked his head slightly and smiled.

"Property records. Deeds. Mortgages. Liens."

"That's right. You want the *County Court* Clerk's office. It's on the other side of the elevators. Go out the door and walk around the elevators."

The lady behind the counter in the County Court Clerk's office appeared to be in her mid fifties. She had gray hair pulled back in a ponytail and tied with a bright yellow scarf.

"May I help you?"

"Yes. My name is Billy Tapp; I'm a lawyer from D.C." Billy hesitated and quickly added. "Don't hold that against me." The lady didn't smile.

"If we held that against all the attorneys we deal with, we'd have to close the clerk's office. Just kidding. What can I help you find?"

"I'm looking for a mortgage from a Seymour Grey to a lender called Bethesda Equity . . . I think."

"Okay. Do you know how to look it up?" Without waiting for Billy to reply, she quickly said, "No. Of course not; otherwise you wouldn't have asked me. Right? Here, let me help you. We can start here with the computer. Let's see if it's in the computer. We'll just look in the computer under the name, Seymour . . . . How do you spell that last name? Then we can look at it on the microfilm, and if you want to, we can go to the actual books, and you can look at the document that was recorded. How does that sound?"

"My lord. H . . E . . N . . C . . H. That sounds great. Too good to be true. You know, in D.C. if I asked a clerk to look something up, they'd probably have me arrested. It might be a crime in D.C."

"Not here Mr. Tapp. Seymour Grey. Okeydokey. Let's see here."

The lady pushed her glasses back on her nose and typed something in the computer so fast that it sounded like one keystroke.

"Here it is. I typed in Bethesda Equity too. There are two hits for Grey and one for Bethesda Equity." She grabbed a post-it sticker and wrote three book references. She handed it to Billy. "Two deeds and one mortgage. Do you want to look at the books or the microfilm?"

"I guess I'd like to get copies."

"Okey dokey. It will take me few minutes, I have something else I need to get done right now. Could you come back in, say, thirty minutes or so? Oh. It's also fifty cents a page." She handed him the post-it sticker; it said:

DB 1325, P 18

MB 856, P 91

DB 1325, P 345.

Billy looked at the post-it sticker and Styxed his head. *DB 1325 and MB 856 must refer to the large tract of land, and the second DB reference at page 345 must be for the easement that Bethesda Equity financed, the small piece of land needed for the utility access, which could have been a real problem, the one that Seymour didn't necessarily want Federated or Dozier to know about.*

"I'm going to walk down the street and get some lunch. I'll be back in an hour or so. Is that okay with you?"

"If I'm not here, I'll leave the copies of your documents in an envelope with your name on it. Just ask one of the other clerks how much you need to pay."

* * * *

Billy walked down Patrick Street to North Market Street and

turned left. He headed up North Market, back to Bushweiler's Bar & Grill where he'd had the mediocre tuna salad sandwich and where he'd met the pretty bartender. Unlike the last time, the place was full. There was a hostess at the door and five or six people waiting for seats. He surveyed the room and looked over at the bar where Valerie had waited on him. There was a single empty stool near the wall. He edged over to the young hostess.

"Can I sit at the bar? There's a seat empty."

"Yes sir. The bartender will give you a menu."

Billy twisted past the other people waiting for seats and picked his way around the tables. He sat at the bar and looked for Valerie. A bartender came over and tossed a square cardboard coaster on the bar.

"Yes sir. Can I help you? Want to look at a menu?" The bartender grabbed a menu from behind the bar and handed it to Billy. "I'll give you a minute. Want something to drink?"

"Yeah. Let me have a draft. Whatever domestic beer you have on draft. No. Make that a Heineken. You have that on tap, don't you?"

Billy drank the beer in a few quick gulps. He was sweaty from the walk and still thirsty from his five-mile run earlier that morning. He hadn't taken any time for water and breakfast. He had showered in a hurry, rushed to his office, made a few calls, and jumped in his car for Frederick. He was hot, thirsty, and hungry—and disappointed that the pretty bartender Valerie wasn't waiting on him. He motioned to the bartender for another beer and leaned back in his stool and looked around. Customers were still filing through the door, with the small crowd waiting for seats growing larger.

"Refill? Decided what you want to eat?"

"Yeah. I ran this morning and I'm thirstier than a dolphin in the desert."

"A what?"

"Dolphin in the desert. Don't ask me. It's something my dad used to say. I'll have a cheese burger and fries."

The bartender put another draft in front of Billy and keyed

the order in the computer. The cheeseburger and fries came, and while he ate, Billy read a rumpled newspaper that someone left on the bar. He ordered another beer and finished reading the editorial page of the abandoned *Washington Post.*

"Can I get you anything else? Some dessert? We got some great homemade pies. Cherry. Apple. Banana cream. Interested?"

"Nope. No thanks. I've done enough damage with the cheese, the grease, and the fries ... and the beer. I guess I'll just have the check. Thanks."

Billy folded the newspaper and laid it on the bar next to the wall. As he reached in his pocket for money to pay the check, he felt someone brush against his back and then gently grip his forearm. Valerie stood between him and the wall. She was wearing a short print skirt and a tight white knit shirt that exposed her midsection and displayed a delicate gold ring in her belly button. She smiled and squeezed his arm. She caught Billy off guard. He stared for an uncomfortable moment at the two small erect protrusions in her tight white knit shirt. She looked down and blushed.

"Billy Tapp. Right? You're getting to be a regular in here."

"Yeah. I needed to come back out here on that same case. The shopping center. How have you been? You look great."

"Good. Good. Working. What have you been up to?"

"Same old same old. You know."

"I was going to call you the other day. I thought I had to come into D.C. I was going to take you up on your offer to run the tow path. I need to come into D.C. sometime this week."

"Really. Great. Anytime. In fact ... ah ... you ought to stay and have a drink or dinner. When are you coming in?"

"I don't know yet. Maybe Friday. I need to check with one of my girlfriends. She lets me stay at her place if it gets too late. You say you're still working on that Frederick Mall development. You know ... one of my girlfriends dated a guy whose dad used to own some of that property. His name's Anderson. Did you have anything to do with Anderson? His first name is Tom. I don't know what his dad's name is."

Billy didn't care much about Anderson or his dad. The three beers were sufficient to provide the pleasant numbing buzz that made Valerie's hard nipples the center of his attention. He put his hand on top of her hand and brushed his shoulder lightly against her arm.

"Anderson? No. I don't know any Anderson involved with this project. What'd he have to do with the development?"

"I don't exactly know. Tom told my girlfriend that his dad got into some kind of a fight or something or got mugged in D.C. The next thing you know ... according to my girlfriend ... Tom's dad sells this property that's out near the new mall and then he just sort of leaves town. It was all kinda strange."

"Oh really." Billy smiled at Valerie. "When are you coming to D.C.? Let me know and we'll have a good run and then go to dinner."

Valerie brushed her breasts against Billy's arm and smiled. "Got to get back to work. I'll call you."

* * * *

The lady with the ponytail and the yellow scarf was still in the Clerk's office. She immediately came to the counter and took a manila envelope out of a holding basket and handed it to Billy.

"Here you go. There are two deeds and two mortgages, just like we said. Hope this is what you were looking for."

Billy took the envelope and pulled out the documents. Both mortgages were for the amount of seventy-five million dollars. One had the amount typed in and the other had it written in long hand. He pushed the deeds and mortgages back into the envelope, paid the pleasant lady, and, thinking about Valerie and her hard nipples, walked out the door and up the three flights of stairs in the parking garage to his car.

He looked at the manila envelope lying on the passenger seat and it suddenly sunk in that both mortgages were in the same amount—one typed and one hand written. *When the lady with the yellow scarf looked in the computer, she said there were two deeds and one mortgage.* He tried to open the envelope but the narrow circular exit ramp from the parking garage required all of his concentration. *What the hell? Did those three beers at lunch affect my hearing?* He pulled over next to Carroll Creek and looked in the envelope again. Two deeds and *two* mortgages. He dialed the Frederick County Clerk's office on his cell phone. He recognized the voice of the pleasant lady who had looked up the information on the computer and copied the documents for him.

"This is Billy Tapp. I'm the lawyer who was just in your office."

"Sure. From D.C. How can I help you?"

"Well, I may be losing my mind, but when you looked on the computer, I thought you told me there were two deeds and one mortgage. But what you gave me was two deeds and *two* mortgages."

"Now that I think about it. I do believe you're right. Huh. I wonder what's going on here. Do you want to hold for a minute? Let me go look at the computer."

Two people jogged past where he had pulled off the street, and one of the joggers turned to run backwards and motioned at the shiny Porsche and then, with a big smile, gave Billy the thumbs up sign. The lady came back to the telephone. "You're right; the second mortgage isn't in the computer. I don't know why. Anything else I can help you with?"

Billy pulled his Porsche back out onto the street and a sprinkle of rain hit the windshield. As he maneuvered back toward the freeway, he could see the dark clouds of an approaching storm in the western sky. The Porsche's precision engine spooled up and when the tachometer registered six thousand RPMs, he entered the merge lane on I-270. In an easy motion, he popped the transmission from third gear to fifth gear and made his way back to Georgetown at twenty miles over the speed limit wondering about the second mortgage and thinking about Valerie the bartender.

CHAPTER FIFTEEN

Billy knew that when a developer buys a chunk of property to build a shopping center, he usually tries to borrow enough money to buy the property, pay for the infrastructure— sewers, parking lots, roads, and the like—and also pay for the building construction. If the developer doesn't pay the loan and the project goes into foreclosure, the mortgage permits the lender to foreclose on the property, which includes the buildings and everything else. As far as legal proceedings are concerned, foreclosure is a bland exercise in legal pro forma. File a complaint, serve a summons on the borrower, take a default judgment, have a sale at the courthouse steps, and if no one bids more for the property than the amount of the debt, the lender bids that amount and ends up owning the project.

Commercial lenders prefer that someone else bids the amount of the loan. Banks are in the business of lending money and collecting interest and fees. They aren't particularly good at managing or finishing up partially completed projects. A commercial lender's profitability depends on keeping the ratio of debt to equity in its favor. Billy also knew that if the project goes in the shit-can and is sold at foreclosure, it's best to make sure that there's enough value to entice somebody to pay off the note and take title to the property. Lenders are historically bad developers.

There's one more important thing about mortgages. A mortgage is a lien on the property and liens are enforced in the sequence of when they're filed in the courthouse record. So, if there are three liens, each filed one month apart, and lien holder number two files a foreclosure action, unless lien holder number three or some third party bids the amount of both lien one and lien two, lien holder number three not only loses his lien, he also loses the property that secures his loan. First in time, first in right.

* * * *

The two deeds and two mortgages that the lady with the ponytail copied for Billy were for two separate pieces of property. The first deed and mortgage were for the large tract of land and the infrastructure and buildings for the Frederick Mall. The total amount of the note attached to the mortgage was seventy-five million dollars, payable to Federated Savings and Loan. The second deed and mortgage were for the small tract of land that was necessary for the utility easement. The lender was Bethesda Equity and the amount was seventy-five million, one hundred and ninety-seven thousand dollars. The mortgage for the easement contained the normal boiler plate verbiage, with the added agreement that Seymour assigned all of his interest in the Frederick Mall to Bethesda Equity—cross collateralization. In the blank spaces in the documents that were on Billy's conference room table, the amount of seventy-five million, one hundred and ninety-seven thousand dollars had been hand written in the recorded mortgage and note for the easement.

* * * *

"Do you ever go home?" Jason asked.

"This is home." Billy motioned to Robert Bob. "Bring

this asshole a beer. And, put it on his tab."

"I think that I'm going to the islands this weekend. Want to go?"

"Where?"

"South Andros. It's supposed to be the bone fishing capital of the world. You're the one who told me about it. I think I'm going to fly down this Thursday."

"Bone fishing? Do you have any idea how to bone fish? Do you know what a bone fish is?"

"No. So."

"There'll be a bone involved,' Jason said, "but it won't be fishing. Who you taking with you?"

"Don't know yet." Billy gulped down the beer setting in front of him. "Bring me another one too."

"How long you been here?" Jason asked.

Billy looked at Robert Bob. "Three. Now four beers," Robert Bob said and put two beers on cardboard coasters in front of Jason and Billy.

"What do you know about off-shore banking?" Billy asked Jason.

"What do you want to know?" Jason asked.

"Well, I pretty much know how it works, I guess. But have y'all had any dealings with folks using off-shore accounts?"

"Sure," Jason said.

Robert Bob wiped the bar and asked Billy, "How does that work? That off-shore stuff?"

"It's really pretty simple, or at least it used to be," Billy said. "For example, people take money to the Cayman Islands ... usually ... for two reasons: they can hide it and there's no income tax. Believe it or not, if you ask for it, the Caymanian government will actually agree in writing not to tax your corporation for twenty years.

"First, you set up a Caymanian corporation, which issues what they call bearer stock. The stock certificates don't have your name on them. The person who physically holds the stock is the owner. You contact a firm in Grand Cayman to be your corporate agent. That's required. You sign an agreement that says the agent acts on your behalf and can't tell anybody your name. That's the law. It's a legally privileged communication. Sometimes these agents make you give them a bank reference or a business reference of some kind. But after you sign the agency agreement, you deal only with the agent. Your nominee. Since they have your corporate stock certificate, they're the shareholder for all legal transactions. If you want to open an investment account, they open it for you in their name with you as undisclosed principal. The statements go to them and what they do with them depends on your agreement. If you want to be super-secret, you can have them hold the statements and give them to you in person when you go there to visit your money. Some people open Cayman accounts to invest in securities that aren't legal in the United States. Like some funds operated in China and in the old Soviet Union, some of which have produced huge returns and others, of course, have fizzled out. There are "pink funds" that are partnerships between Communist China and other countries that aren't legal here. Every investment you can make in the United States you can make in the Caymans.

"The United States government tried to get its hands on these off-shore investments. It passed some law that said you're supposed to disclose this stuff to the IRS and tell them how much you deposit into it each year. As long as the money doesn't enter the states, you don't have to pay taxes on it. But if you bring any of it in, you have to pay the taxes you would've owed on the income it produced from the time you socked it away until you bring it back into the U. S. Could be many tax years."

Robert Bob wiped the bar and replaced the cardboard coasters under their beers. "I guess that would be a good place to put your gambling winnings, or the profit from bootleg whiskey."

"Bootleg whiskey. You're talking about my part of the country now," Billy said.

"Yeah. A southern boy. What would your kin-folk say if they knew you were sitting here in public having a beer with me?" Jason asked.

"First of all my 'kin-folk' are probably Nazis. But if they weren't, they'd dismiss it to the liberal Yankee influence of the north."

"Wait a minute. D.C.'s south of the Mason-Dixon Line. Technically it's in the south."

"That being the case, maybe I should ask you to go sit at the back of the bar."

Jason laughed and Robert Bob shook his head.

Jason continued. "Let's guess how many people disclose their off-shore dealings to the IRS. A few years ago, Caymanian banks came up with a wrinkle to skirt that requirement. Your corporation opens a bank account and the bank issues a credit card to you. Not a debit card, but an actual credit card, secured by your bank account. You run up charges in the U.S. and then the bank presents the bill to your agent in Grand Cayman, who pays it with funds from your account in Grand Cayman. The theory is that the debt is owed in Grand Cayman, and therefore the money doesn't enter the U.S. That was such an obvious scam that I think it might be shut down by now."

"Yeah," Billy said. "I thought about doing that when Ann decided that she'd had enough of my charm and wit. Guess I can't say that I blame her. Oh well. What the fuck. I thought about getting an off-shore credit card, but it turned out I didn't need to. She wasn't out for my ass, she just didn't want to be around it anymore."

"That's when I actually gained full respect for her." Jason tipped his beer to Billy. "How's the case with FSLIC going? What's the guy's name?"

"Grey. Seymour Grey. Good. Good. But I saw something interesting at the courthouse in Frederick. There were two deeds and two mortgages, one deed for the main tract of land and the other for a sliver of property that Grey needed to access utilities to the project. Funny thing, the sliver of property had a mortgage for a little more than seventy-five million dollars on it, the mortgage didn't show up in the computer in the Frederick records, and the main tract was included as security for repayment of the loan for the sliver of land."

"How big is the sliver of property?"

"Hell. It can't be more than half an acre."

"More than seventy-five million? What's that all about? Seems a bit excessive. I don't mean to make something out of nothing, but if that easement mortgage is cross collateralized with the main tract, the lender for the main tract might have a bit of a problem with the foreclosure." Jason said.

"Actually, it's the other way around. If the easement mortgage holder doesn't bid the full amount of the main tract mortgage, he'll lose his seventy-five million one hundred and ninety-seven thousand dollars in the sliver of land ... if he actually loaned that amount.

"You're right. He'd have to bid in the seventy-five million, *plus* the amount of his loan on the sliver of property. Then he'd get the whole thing. Or anyone else. Some third person would have to bid seventy-five for the first mortgage to Federated, *plus* another seventy-five million one hundred and ninety-seven dollars for the second. One hundred and fifty million one hundred and ninety-seven dollars. Isn't that twice what the project is worth?" Billy asked.

"Another curious thing about this whole deal is that the Frederick Mall itself looks like it all but done. Some of the tenants are actually moving in right now. It doesn't seem like it ought to be in foreclosure. Seems to me like Federated ... or FSLIC ... would be better served to complete funding the loan and let Seymour finish the deal."

"Have you talked to them about that?" Asked Jason.

"Yeah. I talked to some British prick by the name of Morning or something. He's FSLIC's receiver and he's basically running Federated right now. He was curt but civil when I talked to him, but he's a condescending asshole. He wasn't exactly forthcoming. He seemed awfully evasive. Something just isn't right. I can't put my finger on it yet. But don't you worry Jason my boy, I'll get to the bottom of this little drama."

"I have no doubt."

"Robert Bob, another beer. You ready?"

"No. I need to get back to the office. I'm putting the final touches on a petition for a writ of certiorari to the Supreme Court. Give me a call on Friday." Jason took a ten dollar bill from a gold money clip and placed it on the bar. He patted Billy on the back and nodded to Robert Bob.

"Call me Friday."

"So, I guess there's really a third reason." Said Robert Bob.

"For what?" Billy asked.

"For putting money in the islands. Off-shore."

"Sure. I guess so. What's that?"

"You said it was to hide money and not pay taxes. Seems to me like you forgot to mention illegal dough. If everything you said is actually right ... and I don't doubt it is Billy ... seems like if I was selling drugs, I'd figure out some way to put it in the islands and get me one of them credit cards. Yes sir. That's what I'd do. I could buy stuff in this here United States of America and pay for it with dough in the islands."

"You're a quick study, my man. How about another beer? I'll be right back. Don't let anybody have my seat. I'm going to take a piss."

Several people came in Clyde's while Billy was in the men's room. Three couples went into the back room and a few others took seats at the bar. Among them was an attractive athletic girl who sat at the end of the bar closest to the window. She moved up against the wall and smiled at Robert Bob.

"Could I have a white wine?"

"What kind would you like? We have a variety by the glass. We have—"

"Chardonnay. Whatever your house Chardonnay is."

Billy came back to his seat. Robert Bob brought him his beer and nodded toward the window. "Billy. The cupcakes are on the bar."

"What?"

"The cupcakes are on the bar."

Billy looked past two guys playing liar's poker and a couple holding hands and giggling. She was obscured by the glare from the outside lights and Robert Bob's expansive girth. But when the bartender stepped out of the way ...

Billy walked down to the end of the bar. She was looking at the appetizer menu that set on the bar. She didn't see him at first.

"Valerie." She looked up and smiled.

"Billy. Where did you come from?"

She reached over and hugged him. Pressing her slightly damp spandex running shirt into his ribs. "I was thinking about calling you and seeing if you wanted to meet me for a drink. You saved me the call. Are you sitting at the bar?"

"Yeah. Down at the other end."

"Do you want to come over here and sit with me?"

"Have you eaten yet?"

"No. Not really."

"Let's get a booth. Have you been running?"

"Yes. I'm all sweaty."

"Yeah. I see that," Billy said and lightly placed his hand on her shoulder. Valerie leaned into his touch and smiled. The bartender snapped his towel and asked Billy if he wanted to transfer his tab to a booth.

Billy grinned at him. "What do you think?"

CHAPTER SIXTEEN

The bar was part of the lobby, which was part of the dining room. Cassie Walker ran the place. Everyone called her "Mama." She was a stout round jet black woman whose age could have been anywhere from late thirties to middle fifties. She stood behind the front desk reading a tattered Bible when Billy and Valerie arrived. She told them that they could leave their luggage and equipment on the floor next to the front desk in the lobby and she'd have one of her "little ones" bring it up to their room. She asked them if they wanted a key. Strictly speaking, it wasn't necessary because no one ever locked the doors anyway. On South Andros Island, there was virtually no crime, at least no burglary. Everyone knew everyone else and if something was ever stolen, the thief had nowhere to get rid of it, and if the thief showed up with the stolen item, "Well I guess you know what that would mean, now don't you," Cassie said with a wink. Billy asked for a key anyway and Cassie said that she'd find one and the minute she did, she'd either leave it as the front desk or bring it up to them.

The rooms at the Congo Town Inn were in a separate two story building that was located between the lobby building and the beach and connected by a coral stone walkway. There were eight rooms, five on the bottom floor and three on the second floor. Cassie gave Billy and Valerie a second floor room. It faced the ocean with a small balcony and sliding glass doors.

"De first one at de top 'o de stairs," Cassie said.

The room was clean but sparsely furnished. A king sized bed, two bedside tables, one wicker chair, a desk and chair, two lamps, a tile floor, a bathroom with a separate shower and tub, a small vanity, and a ceiling light that didn't work but a ceiling fan that did. There was no air conditioning, but a small contraption that appeared to be a heater of some kind. The room was closed and stuffy. Billy opened the windows on the island side and slid open the glass doors. Within a matter of seconds, the sea breeze cleared the stuffiness and infused the room with a pleasant warm breeze and the smell of the tropical ocean. After a brief inspection of the room, they took off their shoes and walked down to the beach and let the soft Atlantic Ocean lap at their feet.

They entered the lobby from the ocean side of the building, which lead through the dining room to the lobby itself and the bar on the far side. Cassie sat behind the bar, talking to two old men who were playing checkers. The luggage and diving equipment still lay by the front desk where they'd dropped it some two hours earlier. Mama looked up and smiled.

"Do ya plan on goin' divin' tomorrow?"

"Yep. We do.

"Ya need a boatman, then. Someone to guide ya to de fish. If ya have not hired ya that mon yet, I got just de one fo ya."

"That'd be great. Say. Could we get a beer or something?"

"If ya want a beer, den it's in de cooler dare." Mama pointed to an old Coca Cola cooler behind the bar. "Jes' keep track 'o what ya drink and we settle up when you leave. In de notebook dare."

Billy walked behind the bar and opened the cooler. There were a few dozen or so bottles floating in water with three chunks of ice twice the size of his fist. He fished out two St. Paulie Girls that had skewed paper labels from soaking in the water. He found a bottle opener on the bar and popped the tops. He handed one to Valerie, who had taken one of the four seats at the bar, and took a long pull on his beer. He opened the tattered spiral notebook and wrote his name on the top of the page. Below it he printed St. Paulie Girl and the number 2. Mama explained that she served "de supper" right after the sun went down and tonight they were having johnnie cakes and fish stew. She also explained that the menu for the evening repast frequently depended on the catch of Congo Town Inn's guests. If they caught it, she cooked it. That seemed fair to Billy and he was looking forward to diving the reef and showing his skill with his newly purchased Hawaiian Sling.

Spear guns and scuba gear are outlawed. The Hawaiian Sling is a cross between a sling shot and a bow and arrow. The spear fits in a tube that has heavy rubber bands on each side. You hold the tube with one hand and pull back on the rubber bands with the other. *What could be easier? At least we'll eat well.*

The johnnie cakes and fish stew tasted like a watered down version of bouillabaisse. The johnnie cake was nothing more than simple corn bread. Valerie ate a little bit of the johnnie cake, but couldn't get past the fish head floating in her bowl.

"Don' ya forget now. De generator it goes off at ten o'clock." With Mama's admonition, Billy and Valerie went back to their room and let the soothing Bahamian breeze drift across their naked bodies, locked in a tangle of passion and hidden feelings.

* * * *

South Andros Island is the largest and least inhabited island in the Bahamian Archipelago. It's actually three islands, North Andros, Mangrove Cay, and South Andros, with an untold number of fresh water rivers and creeks and hundreds of acres of virtually unexplored rainforest, mangrove swamps, pine forests and a surprising abundance of wildlife. The first inhabitants of the Andros Islands were the now extinct Arawak Indians. As impossible as it may seem, there's credible evidence that after the Arawaks died off, the earliest settlers on Andros were the Seminole Indians who were believed to have crossed the Florida straits in canoes. Andros is the reputed bone fishing capital of the world and home of the extinct chickcharnie, a two foot tall red-eyed flightless owl that the Indians believed to be bearded elves who lived in the trees. Some of the locals still believe the red-eyed elves live in the primeval rainforest.

The South Andros Island airport, which is really nothing more than an air-strip with a few hangars and a rundown terminal building, is approximately two hundred nautical miles from the Fort Lauderdale International Airport. Flight time in 28 Romeo was less than one hour. Billy and Valerie left the Frederick airport the day before and stopped in Fort Lauderdale before making the short hop to South Andros Island. He'd made reservations at the Congo Town Inn and Beach Resort, the only South Andros Island hotel he found on the internet. He had no idea about the Congo Town Inn or, for that matter, South Andros Island. A few weeks earlier Jason Roberts said that someone told him that they'd just come back from South Andros Island and the skin-diving was superb. That was all Billy needed. He pulled out his cache of flight maps and charts, and planned a long week-end trip to the islands for sun, diving, cold beer, and whatever other hedonistic please he could muster up.

He packed up his diving mask, fins, tanks, and Hawaiian slings and, on Thursday morning, announced to Vickie that he'd see her on Tuesday. He was headed south.

"I'm going to South Andros Island. I'm staying at the Congo Town Beach Resort, and you can't get hold of me. So don't try."

"Where?"

"South Andros Island. In the Bahamas."

"Who's going with you?"

"Vickie! No one."

"Come on. Who's going with you? I know you're not going to the islands by yourself."

"I'm going by myself. A religious retreat."

"Yeah. Oh. By the way. Howard Slone called about twenty minutes ago. He was rude. He's an ass. Said he needed to talk to you right away. I asked him what he wanted … you know … in a nice way, but he said he'd call back. What should I tell him?"

"Tell him I'll be back on Tuesday. I'll call him then. You don't know where I am. Get it?"

Billy hadn't been gone more than five minutes when the phone rang. The caller said, "I'm an associate of Mr. Howard Slone. May I speak with Mr. Tapp?"

"He's out of town. He won't be back until Tuesday."

"It's very important that I talk to him. Do you have a telephone number? A cell phone?"

"No. Ah … I don't."

"Miss. It's really important that I speak to him. Mr. Slone needs to talk with him."

"He went to South Andros Island and you can't reach him. I don't know where he's staying. No. I don't know his flight number. There isn't a flight number. He flew his own airplane. No. I don't know where he's staying."

* * * *

Billy stood beside his airplane, with tail number 5628R—"28 Romeo" as it was called in aviation vernacular—nursing the hangover from too many tepid St. Paulie Girl beers. The door was ajar. Despite his dry mouth and the dull pain in temples, he was certain that he had not only closed the door but locked it as well. He motioned to the line boy skulking in the hangar where he'd been told that 28 Romeo would be parked. When he made eye contact, the boy turned away.

"What the fuck," Billy said. He looked inside the airplane and saw that his flight bag was open and the maps and charts were strewn on the front passenger side seat. He walked into the terminal building.

It was a white one-story block structure with a tower and a beacon on top. Inside the front entrance was a counter with a desk behind it. A middle aged black man in white shorts, a khaki shirt, and aviator sunglasses sat leaned back and dozing in a wooden swivel chair with his feet on the desk. Against the opposite wall, there were two cheap chairs, separated by a plastic table with three old aviation magazines. Mounted on the wall on the far side of the room was a large tattered flight planning chart of the Bahamas Islands. There was a thumb tack stuck in Congo Town with a long string attached to it with a steel washer tied to the loose end. All the windows stood open without screens. The morning breeze wafted through the room carrying the incongruous mix of the fragrant lush foliage and the acrid odor from the nearby salt marsh.

The black man opened his eyes. "Mr. Tapp. Mon. What can I help you with, mon?" A wide grin showed a gold front tooth.

"Say. Andrew. Why's my airplane out on the ramp? I thought you were going to tow it into that hangar over there."

"You see, mon. I thought that hangar it would be open. But it was not. And still not yet. So I could not."

"It's been setting on the ramp then?"

"Yes, mon."

"Well shit. Have you seen ... did you see anybody fooling around with my airplane? The door's unlocked and it looks like someone has gone through my stuff. My flight bag. Do you know anything about that?"

"You say that your airplane's unlocked, mon. Well I can tell you, mon, that you must've left it unlocked."

"I don't think so. But even if I did what about my stuff. My flight bag—"

"The wind, mon. The wind must've blown it about. What other explanation is there? You left the door open, and when my boy Cedric tried to wheel it to de hangar, da wind riled up you papers. What else could it be, mon?"

"Come on, Andrew. I didn't leave my airplane unlocked. And the wind didn't *rile* up my papers. Somebody was in that plane, looking for something." Billy stepped back from the counter and looked out across the salt marsh. "Push it back in the hangar and I'll be back later this afternoon."

"Yessir, mon." Andrew adjusted his sunglasses and sucked air through his front teeth. "Mr. Tapp, mon. It's not a good idea ... here in da islands ... to accuse someone without proof. Be sure to lock your airplane dis time, mon. We'll try to move it back in today when de hangar is opened." Andrew pointed at another airplane on the ramp. "That mon with this airplane over dare is a-leavin' today. I think."

Also on the ramp sat a Lear 55. The auxiliary unit was hooked to the belly of the airplane and powering the jet's air conditioner and other systems. The pilot came into the FBO.

"We're off to Little Cayman. Any word on Mr. ..." He looked at Billy, then Andrew. "... ah Smith?"

"No, mon. No word."

The pilot stepped out the door and pulled a cell phone from his belt. He turned his back to the FBO, bent forward and then nodded his head back in the FBO's direction. He snapped the cell phone shut and walked back to the Lear 55.

* * * *

The road from the airport to the Congo Town Beach Resort runs parallel to the island's eastern shore. The strip of land between the road and the ocean is filled with coconut palms that sway in the morning breeze and lean away from the ocean. The trees were fecund with coconuts in various stages of ripeness. Every so often, a skiff lay upside down on the beach, pulled away from the high tide mark. The islanders use the little boats to fish or dive for Dolphin, Jacks, Wahoo, and Tuna along the Great Barrier Reef that runs the length of the island.

It was about a mile and a half from the Congo Town Beach Resort to the air strip. Billy decided to jog the short distance to check on his airplane to see that it had been moved into a hangar. When he landed the day before, there wasn't any hangar space available. He didn't like to leave his airplane out in the brutal Bahamian sun because with the doors and windows closed, the inside temperature could bake the interior and the avionics. He slipped on his running shoes and the silk shorts that he'd washed and hung out the window last night. Valerie lay naked in the bed half awake.

"What time is it? Are you going to run?"

"It's early. Yeah. I'll be back in an hour or so."

Billy just got into a comfortable pace when a Jeep convertible sped past him, with a passenger in the back seat wearing dark sun glasses sitting beside a diminutive shinny bald head.

"What the fuck," Billy said, and he stopped running and ducked under a palm tree and sat on an overturned skiff. He took his cell phone out of his running belt and dialed Vickie.

"Billy? What time is it?"

"Sorry to call you at home. It's six-thirty. Hope I didn't wake you up."

"No. That's OK. I'm always awake at six-thirty on Sunday morning. What's up?"

"You're going to think I'm crazy, but I think I just saw Howard Slone. Did you tell him where I was?"

"Well. I ah. It just sort of slipped. I'm sorry. I didn't tell him exactly where you were. He called, or someone from his office called, and said it was really important that he get hold of you. I told him you were in South Andros Island. But I didn't tell him where. I'm sorry."

"That's OK. Thanks, Vickie."

Billy jogged back out to the road just in time to hear the roar of the Lear 55 taking off and see it circle to the left and turn to the south. In the direction of Cuba and not Miami or

Washington D.C. or even the United States. He stopped and called Vickie again.

"Yes. The check to Seymour that I found on the floor. The one I put on your desk. Don't you remember?"

"The name of the bank? Let me think. It was something in the Cayman Islands," she said. Billy followed the arc of the Lear 55 and snapped his phone shut.

CHAPTER SEVENTEEN

Death is inevitable. Sooner or later everybody and everything, slows down, quits, stops, and just plain dies. Cats, cucumber plants, elm trees, Christmas cacti, the great society in Pompeii, the Houston Astrodome, the cute little salmonella infested turtles that they used to sell in the pet store, humans, the solar system—the list goes on. In the whole inescapable and inevitable moribund galactic scheme, it's puzzling that such hoopla occurs when people die, and that seems especially true when someone's murdered. Even though most murders are caused by somebody's brain circuits going haywire, a dead person is still just a dead person. But when murder is involved, at least there's someone to blame. Murder is just another way of dying, but it's rarely pleasant, hardly ever forgiven, and it's never forgotten.

Terry Jacobs sat in the Montgomery County Jail charged with murdering a no good scum-bag drug dealing street punk. It was an irony of his situation that, despite the fact that Fatso Boy deserved killing, Terry had a better chance of suicide by holding his breath than making bail.

There are two kinds of incarceration facilities: either city and county jails or state and federal penitentiaries. When someone gets charged with a crime, they start out in the city or county jail; after they're tried and convicted, they go to the state or federal penitentiary. There's a significant difference in how prisoners in local jails and regional penitentiaries are housed. In a local jail, sometimes there are, what's called, hold-over cells, where it wouldn't be unheard of for a murderer to be in the same cell as an otherwise law abiding citizen who refused to pay child support or who was caught driving after drinking three beers at the local pub. That same cell may have sixteen inmates and only twelve beds, in which case inmates are often given hard plastic palates that they call "boats" and a pillow and one blanket and they sleep on the floor. Usually these cells have one toilet with no door and one shower with no curtain. Fights are common and tempers explode with the slightest provocation. It's a predatory environment.

Penitentiaries are more organized and the accommodations are more like a severely restricted dormitory, with everyone having just a little bit of his own space. In either place, if you fuck up, the consequences can be unforgiving.

Terry was probably heading to one or the other for killing Fatso Boy.

* * * *

Fatso Boy sat at his table in the back corner of the Spider Web Bar & Game Room. The Spider Web was on the first floor of a three story brick building in one of the myriad dilapidated and desperately poor sections of our nation's capital. There was a long dark bar on the left and three pool tables across from the bar on the right. Beyond the bar and pool tables there were four booths along the right side wall and five tables in the room that formed the back recesses of the Spider Web. Fatso Boy was at the table farthest from the front door in the back right side corner, giving him a clear view of the entire place. He could see the front door, the bar, the pool tables, the restrooms, the door to the food storage, and the back door. He could see everything and everyone that came in or out of the Spider Web Bar & Game Room.

As far as Terry could tell, Fatso Boy was the only one in the place. No one was playing pool and he didn't see anybody behind the bar. Having just come in from the late morning sunshine, he had a little trouble getting his focus in the dingy room. At first, he wasn't even sure that the fat blob sitting in the back corner was Fatso Boy. He knew from past experience and word on the street that Fatso Boy took his breakfast just before noon at the Spider Web and that he sat in the back corner and didn't like to be interrupted. *Fuck him.* Terry squinted as he came from the sunshine into the dark. He hesitated at the bar and looked around the dank room that smelled of vomit, Lysol, and stale beer. Then he walked back to the corner table.

On the table was a plate with four fried eggs, another plate with a stack of pancakes, another with a rasher of bacon, a soup bowl of grits, and a large plastic glass of milk. Fatso Boy was pouring syrup on the pancakes. He had a large white napkin stuffed in his shirt and a headset covering both ears. His head was bouncing up and down in rhythm to the music and to each pass of syrup over the pancakes. At first he didn't see Terry gawking at the gluttonous spectacle. He cut a triangle of pancakes and stuffed it in his mouth. Syrup squeezed from the corners of his mouth as he looked up. A shadow cast over his face. He pointed at Terry with his fork and flashed a smile that showed a gob of pancakes oozing from his clenched teeth.

"It's the CD faggot. What the fuck you doin' here? This place is off limits to shits like you. Who let your ass in here? Ha. Ha. Ha."

"I come to get my CDs." Terry looked away from Fatso's bloated face and turned his stare to the food on the table.

"You come for CDs or food? Seems to me like you're more interested in the food than CDs. What's wrong? Your momma not feedin' you in the morning? Let me ask you again. What the fuck you doin' here? I thought I told you that you didn't have no CDs."

Terry glanced up at Fatso and look down again. "I come for my CDs. I want my CDs."

"You know, faggot. I thought we settled this once before. I ain't got your CDs. The only CDs I got is mine. The ones you gave me *were* yours, but now they're mine. You understand me? Now, get your ass outta here."

"I ain't leaving until I get my CDs."

Fatso sliced off another triangle of pancakes and smashed them into the yolk of an egg. He stuffed the pancake, syrup, and egg yolk into his mouth and slammed the fork down on the table with enough force to topple the plastic glass of milk. Terry jumped back.

"You son of a bitch rotten punk faggot. If you ain't outta here in ten seconds yer gonna wish you'd never been born." As Fatso yelled, pieces of the pancake spewed from his mouth onto the table.

"Gimme my god damned CDs!" Terry yelled.

"Fuck you!"

Terry reached into the pocket of his tan cargo pants and pulled out a stainless steel Smith & Wesson .357 magnum with a three inch barrel. He pulled back the hammer and pointed it at Fatso's midsection.

"My CDs!" Terry yelled.

Fatso grinned and reached under the table. "You chicken shit asshole. You gonna wish you never in your miserable life ever seen me. You ain't got the balls to use that thing."

"CDs!"

Fatso's hand started to move from under the table. "Go ahead and shoot, you shit eatin' momma's boy." And, in one smooth motion, Fatso pulled the gray .9mm Glock from under the table.

Terry pulled the trigger. The bullet shattered the rasher of bacon and ripped through the table about five inches in front of Fatso Boy. The bullet splintered the table and struck Fatso just above the belly button. The impact knocked him against the wall and the Glock flew from his hand. Fatso looked down at a hole in his stomach that oozed yellow fat and blood.

"Shit! You gonna wish you never seen me! You dead! Yer whore momma's dead! Yer rotten ass brother and sister is dead! Yer cousins dead! Yer *all* dead!"

Terry leaned forward and pulled the trigger again. This time the bullet clipped off the upper half of Fatso's left ear and sent the headset careening into the air and slammed into the plaster wall. Fatso screamed and cupped his hand over his ear. The muzzle was close enough to Fatso's face that it spewed powder burns on his cheek and neck and left eye. Terry cocked the revolver and whispered,

"My CDs."

Fatso's right hand was flailing the air and frantically beating on the splintered table trying to find the Glock and his only hope against this chicken shit momma's boy. "My CDs!" Terry yelled.

"You a dead son-of-a-bitch."

Terry's hand was shaking and he pulled the trigger again. This time, the slug hit Fatso in the left side, just under his armpit. The impact slung him around in his chair. He looked down at his side and the blood on his left hand.

"Fuck you." Fatso screeched.

Terry shot again and missed Fatso altogether. Fatso picked up the plate of pancakes and held it in from of his face as if it would shield him from Terry's rage and the business of the Smith & Wesson .357's revenge, and he motioned with his right hand as if it held the once formidable .9 mm Glock and squeezed his hand in a useless gesture of actually firing the missing gun. Terry's fourth and fifth shot missed. But the last bullet from the revolver shattered the plastic plate and entered Fatso's head just above the right eye tearing off the back of his head and leaving the memory of his crimes, his humiliation from being the fattest kid in school, and his mother's drug use and abandonment splattered against the dirty plaster wall.

The bartender came from the back room of the dingy joint. He stood behind the beaten up Formica bar and flipped a white towel over his shoulder. Terry quickly looked around the room.

"There's no one else in here. We don't open 'til noon."

Terry stuffed the stainless steel gun in his pocket and turned to the bartender.

"Look. I don't know who you are or what your beef with him was. But you need to get your ass outta here. Fatso's got a gang of son-of-bitches that aren't gonna like this one bit. I don't know you. I didn't see you. I was in the back room when all this happened. I came out when I heard the shooting. You better get outta here. I'm gonna call the cops right now. Can't say he didn't get what he deserved. But I ain't the judge of that. Leave that to somebody else. Better get outta here."

Terry turned and ran out the front door.

* * * *

"That's right. There's been another shooting at the Spider Web. This time somebody was shot. Somebody's dead. Yeah. Dead. 'Course I seen it. Young kid. White. About five feet six or so. Cargo pants, tan canvas coat, black sweatshirt, red Nike shoes. Looked like a stainless steel three inch .38 or so. Sure he's got it. He stuck it in his pocket. Dangerous? I don't know what you mean by that, he just shot somebody. Does that make him dangerous?"

* * * *

"You Terry Jacobs?"

Terry opened his eyes at the same time that he felt the impact of a kick on the side of his boat. He'd put his toothbrush and soap in a wash cloth beside his head. The kick sent his toilet articles scattering across the concrete floor. "Hey! What the fuck. Watch out. What's—"

"You Terry Jacobs?"

"Who wants to know?"

Before Terry could sit up, someone kicked the boat again with enough force to send it scooting on the slippery concrete floor and knock the piece of cloth that he had folded over his eyes to block out the light that stayed on day and night. About the only way you could tell the time of day was when the guards turned off the TV, or when day light came through the six inch slits that were the only windows in the cell. The slits were pitch black and everyone was asleep. Before Terry came to his senses, someone put his foot on Terry's head and stuffed a rolled up sock in his mouth. Then he felt a dull blow to the back of his head. He saw what could have been a lightning flash and the night lights went out. When he came to, he lay back in his boat with a lump the size of an orange on the back of his head and a small spot of dried blood in his boat. Two guards stood over him.

"Alright, Jacobs. What happened to you?"

Terry tried to sit up, but the pain from the back of his head made him dizzy and he spun to the side and vomited.

"Aw god damn it, Jacobs. You just puked on my shoe. What's wrong with you?"

"I don't know. Nothing …" His head hurt so bad that at first he didn't feel the burning in his ass.

The other guard saw the blood caked on Terry's underwear. He rolled his eyes and pulled his companion aside.

"We might have a little bit of a problem here. Did you see the back of his underwear? Looks like he might have been up to something last night and it didn't turn out very well for him."

The guards walked back over to Terry who had managed to sit up in the boat. They looked around the cell. "Anybody see what happened here?"

No one said a word and no one returned the guards' look. Two muscular men sat on the metal table that was bolted to the floor under the TV. They sat there with their arms crossed staring at the other inmates. When the guards looked at them they smiled. One had a toothpick in his mouth.

"You know you aren't supposed to have toothpicks in here. Where'd you get that?"

"I don't know. Guess I brought it in last night when one of D.C.'s finest arrested me for public intoxication." He took the toothpick out of his mouth and handed it to the guard. The guard looked away and addressed the cell block again.

"Anybody see anything?" the guards asked again.

No one spoke up. A diminutive red-head serving six months for flagrant non-support sat in the back corner top bunk looking first at Terry and then at the two men sitting on the metal table and then at the floor.

Terry pulled himself up and felt the crusted blood on the seat of his orange jump suit. He shuffled over to the toilet and pulled the make-shift curtain to provide the only privacy in the cell block. He pulled his jump suit back on and looked at the fresh blood on his hand. He pulled the blanket aside and went back to his boat.

"You okay," one of the guards asked.

"Yeah. But I think I need to see a doctor." Terry showed him the blood on his hand.

The guard swallowed hard and led Terry out of the cell. The two men on the metal table grinned at each other, and then one turned toward Terry and winked, showing the small red rose tattoo on his neck.

CHAPTER EIGHTEEN

They left South Andros Island in the morning and after a few diversions for commercial traffic and sequencing for landing, 28 Romeo touched down and taxied to the customs terminal in Fort Lauderdale. After the usual folderol and bureaucratic red tape, Billy, Valerie, and the airplane cleared customs. Because of some bad weather and since the shortest route took them through restricted airspace between Fort Lauderdale and Washington D.C., Billy filed a flight plan and made the four and one-half hour trip back under instrument flight rules.

Billy put on his head-set and pushed the red microphone button on the yoke of his Beechcraft Barron. "Fort Lauderdale clearance delivery, this is Barron 5628 Romeo at terminal India with information delta. IFR to Frederick County, Maryland. Ready to copy."

"Roger 28 Romeo. Cleared as filed direct foxtrot delta kilo. Fly runway heading. Climb maintain two thousand five hundred feet. Expect ten thousand feet ten minutes after departure. Contact departure on 128. Contact ground on 122 for taxi and when in position tower at 118. Good day."

Ground control cleared Billy to runway nine and, with little delay, Billy and Valerie were on their way back to Frederick, where he'd drop her off and fly the twenty-five mile leg from Frederick to the Montgomery County Airport, where he kept his airplane. The departure took him a few miles east of the South Florida coast and his direct flight, slightly west of north, was over the Atlantic Ocean with landfall about at Myrtle Beach, South Carolina. The sun was just coming up on the right side of 28 Romeo and before they reached their final cruising altitude, Valerie had fallen asleep to the constant drone of the engines. They landed in Frederick and after Billy saw Valerie and her backpack into her car, he topped off the tanks with fuel that was twenty cents a gallon cheaper than at Montgomery County Airport, and he flew home at seven hundred fifty feet above the ground. He taxied up to the large hangar, shut down, and went into the FBO terminal.

"Could you put 28 Romeo in the hangar?"

"Sure," the attendant said. "Did you have a good time?"

"Yeah. Ever have a bad time in the islands with a pretty girl?"

"Guess not. Oh. By the way. Did that fella ever get hold of you? He was in here last week. Wanted to know which airplane was yours. Wanted to look at it. Said something about buying in or something."

"Ah … no. No one called me. And, my airplane's not for sale. Must have been a mistake."

"Well, he said your name. Billy Tapp. The lawyer from D.C.. Said he was a friend of yours."

"What was his name?"

"Don't know. Didn't ask. He didn't tell me."

* * * *

As much out of disgust for the heavy handed tactics of the FSLIC receiver as anything else, Dozier Mound called Billy Tapp. He explained to Billy how Federated's profit participation worked and he explained the steps that he and Federated's compliance officer, Joe Franklin, had taken to make sure the profit participation was legal. But, despite that, the FSLIC receiver, Jerome Morning, made the decision that the profit participation agreement between Federated and Seymour Grey violated what he called "applicable banking laws and other related regulations." Morning used that legal violation as justification to foreclose on an otherwise exemplary real estate project.

"First, Morning was wrong and, second, Seymour's shopping center was on schedule and under budget—two facts that weren't always the case in commercial real estate developments. Although the Frederick Mall isn't the biggest or the most significant in terms of size or impact, it may be the best real estate project that Federated had in its portfolio. It was ninety-five percent built and, when Morning took over Federated, only fifty-seven percent funded. Seymour could have finished the project and opened the shopping center in less than six months, with several million left unused in the development loan. It just doesn't make sense to me," Dozier Mound explained to Billy. "Why would Morning foreclose on this project and keep funneling money into some of the other Federated projects that weren't half as financially sound as Seymour's? Have you talked to Morning?" Mound asked.

"Yeah. I called him. About all I could get out of him was a condescending admonition that I didn't fully ... how did he say it ... 'There are more factors that you have not considered.' What the hell is that supposed to mean?"

"I don't know, Mr. Tapp. But what I do know is that there's something going on here and I haven't figured it out yet. I hope you and Seymour don't give up. You need to get to the bottom of this mess. I don't trust Morning. You know, now that I think about it, I never really did."

"Let me change the subject a little," Billy said. "Did you know about the utility easement problem?"

"I didn't know all the details. Joe Franklin told me there was some minor problem with utility access, but he said that Seymour and Morning had apparently worked out the details."

"This the same Morning that's running Federated now?"

"One and the same."

"I understand that he worked for you before he worked for FSLIC?"

"I'm afraid so."

Dozier Mound closed the phone call with more offers of encouragement and a promise to help in any way that he could. He pointed out, however, that FSLIC had stripped him of any authority at Federated and, in point of fact, there really wasn't much he could do. But whatever that was he would do it.

"Thanks," Billy said, "we'll keep you posted."

* * * *

Seymour agreed to meet in Billy's office in the morning. He preferred a languid evening repast at the fetching Madame Claret's La Rouge, but Billy seemed slightly out of sorts and more insistent than usual, so Seymour didn't suggest sweetbreads and French wine. It wasn't that Seymour objected to early morning meetings, in fact, he considered himself a morning person. But, when he was out of town, important matters and critical decisions, good, bad, or otherwise, were best made with a full belly and the analgesic torpor induced by a few bottles of good wine. He arrived at 190 Market Street at 7:45 a.m. and took the elevator up to the fifth floor. Vickie hadn't arrived yet, and Billy sat in the conference room surrounded by the banker's boxes that Seymour had sent a few weeks earlier.

"Good morning, counselor."

"Seymour, I'm having a little trouble understanding where you got which funds for the Frederick Mall. As of right now, I've seen four entities. Tell me if this is right: First you got a loan from Federated for seventy-five million dollars. Then one from Bethesda Equity for forty-seven thousand. Then a check from Southeast Financial for fifty thousand dollars. And, now just a week or so ago, a hundred thousand dollars from Southwest Financial. That sound about right?"

Seymour hesitated. "Yes, counselor. That sounds about right. But I actually forgot about the fifty thousand from … who did you say it was? Bethesda Equity?"

"No. The fifty thousand was from Southeast Financial."

"To be perfectly candid, I do not remember the fifty thousand dollars. Are you sure that is right?"

Billy shuffled a red-well folder from his stack of files and pulled out the blank envelope that contained the check from Southeast Financial that was drawn on the First National Bank of the Cayman Islands. He laid it on the table in front of Seymour.

"Ever see this?"

Seymour picked up the check and flipped it over and looked at the endorsement. "The check is made out to me. I cannot dispute that." He looked closer at the back side. "But that is not my signature on the back. It is not even close."

"Whose is it?"

"I do not know, counselor. But it is not mine."

"Okay. Let me ask you this. Do you have any idea why there are four lenders in this mess and only two mortgages recorded in the Frederick County Courthouse?"

Seymour hesitated again. "I know this is going to sound a bit … ah … unprofessional. But those are details that my accountants and attorneys would have taken care of. My focus was on making sure the construction was within the budget. Making sure we procured quality tenants. And making sure we were on schedule. Counselor, if those three items are in line, the rest of it takes care of itself."

Billy changed directions. "Let me tell you what's going on with the foreclosure. FSLIC isn't foreclosing because of a performance default. According to Jerome Morning, they're foreclosing because the profit participation was illegal. But there's a problem with the foreclosure lawsuit because Michael Braxton, FSLIC's lawyer, hadn't included Bethesda Equity or Southeast Financial or Southwest Financial as defendants. He'll have to amend the court papers and name them as additional defendants.

"The good news is that we've bought some time. The bad news is it doesn't change your legal position. If someone ... other than Slone's bunch ... wants to buy this thing at the courthouse steps, they're going to have to pay Federated and Bethesda Equity and anyone else who has a lien. But, Seymour, just between the two mortgages that I've seen, that amount is a big number. And that has a direct impact on you, too. If you manage to find another lender to replace Federated, they're going to have to pay off all the lien holders—Federated, Bethesda Equity, Southeast Financial, and Southwest Financial. The total amount could be one hundred fifty million, one hundred and ninety-seven thousand dollars. At least according to the county court clerk's record, which, by the way, can't be right. This damn thing's a mess. That's the way this thing looks right now ... according to the court records in Frederick. Is there any way that could be right? This thing could take two years to sort out ... unless—"

"One hundred and fifty million one hundred and ninety-five thousand. How can that be? The whole project budget was seventy-five million, and it looked like we would complete it for just over sixty-eight million, leaving me with seven or so million left over after the rent stabilized. And, like I said the other day, that is tax free money."

"Slone's group, or whatever they are, steps up. The problem is that the mortgage lien for the utility easement is also for seventy-five million plus. It is what it is. It's either what's on the books or what we prove should be on the books. The first will be easy, the second is going to take some time. This damn thing could take a few years to sort out."

"Two years? If this does not get sorted out pretty soon, there is a real chance that I will lose tenants. I do not need to tell you what that will do to the deal."

"Oh. One more thing. What did Morning have to do with the Bethesda Equity's forty-seven thousand dollar loan for the utility easement?"

Seymour thought for a moment. "Now that you mention it counselor, he is the one who told me about Bethesda Equity. We were sitting in his office. He mentioned the name and insisted that we call Bethesda Equity. Before I could say anything, he even made the call for me. We were talking about expanding the seventy-five million dollar loan. He did not like that, so I told him or asked him if he knew where I could get a little loan for a small addition to the project. He said that he did not want to disturb the Federated loan. The next thing I know, someone from Bethesda Equity was on the telephone to me and the deal is done. Tell me this counselor. Is the truth really so complicated?"

"Seymour. The truth is usually pretty simple."

Seymour shrugged his shoulders. Billy looked at the fifty thousand dollar check and then looked back at Seymour.

"One more question, Seymour."

"Yes ... this is your second one more thing, counselor."

"But not the last. How did you get the cancelled check for fifty thousand dollars? Why is it in the stuff that you sent me?"

"Well, counselor, I cannot answer that one. Why did I have it? I do not know. I did not know that I had it."

After Seymour left, Vickie said that Ann had called and wanted to know if Billy intended to pick up the children tonight.

"Call her back for me, will you. Tell her I don't think I'll be able to tonight. I'll call her later today ... this afternoon."

Billy looked at the faded biscuit sign and said to his reflection in the window—*Of course it's per biscuit, you idiot.*

CHAPTER NINETEEN

"It was a complete waste of time. He was down here with some bimbo that he met in Frederick. There wasn't anything in that piece of crap that he flies around, and he apparently didn't have any intention of doing anything but the bimbo. I'll call you when we land," Slone said into his cell phone.

The Learjet 55 is nicknamed the Longhorn. It got that moniker because it was the first general aviation jet to use the winglets that NASA had developed; it looked like a longhorn steer. The Learjet 55 can fly at almost five hundred and fifty miles an hour at fifty-one thousand feet above sea level for more than twenty-five hundred miles. It's fast, sleek, and sexy. The Longhorn requires a flight crew of two and its owners usually equip it with at least one attendant. The Longhorn setting on the ramp on South Andros Island was no exception. The engines had been running at idle and despite the cloudless sky and eighty-nine degree outside temperature, the more than ample air-conditioning held the cabin temperature at precisely seventy-two degrees Fahrenheit.

Howard Slone climbed the retractable flight stairs and settled into a plush, grey leather seat. Sweat lay across his shiny forehead. Before he could ask, a stewardess handed him a chilled damp towel.

"Here you are sir. Would you like this cold towel for your brow?" She gently placed the damp towel on his forehead and laid a dry towel on the armrest of his chair. "Is there anything else I can ... give you? Anything at all." She nudged between his knees and sat softly on his small leg.

Slone came to expect, if not require, such accommodations when he traveled. But he knew that the Lear 55 would be in the Cayman Islands before the Viagra that he kept in his briefcase had time to work, and without it, the pretty stewardess may as well ask him to spin Black's Law Dictionary on a cooked noodle. In his own twisted way, he somehow associated her suggestion with his impotence and it pissed him off.

The door shut and after a brief admonition to fasten his seat belt, the Longhorn charged down the runway and leaped into the air on its way to the Cayman Islands by the most direct route, which took the diminutive Howard Slone and the rest of the crew at five hundred miles an hour right over the midsection of Cuba and the city of Sancti Spiritus.

* * * *

Slone stepped from the black Mercedes limousine and walked up five steps into the plush lobby of an unobtrusive two-story building on East Channel Street that looked like it could have been either a large residence or an office building. There were no signs, only the brass number 1247 attached to the trim above the front door lintel. The room was filled with furniture appropriate for the Cayman Islands, and two intricate oriental rugs covered the polished teak floor. There was no receptionist. A small black sphere about the size of a half grapefruit was attached to the ceiling at the far end of the room. It held a security camera that played to a monitor somewhere behind the two large doors directly beneath it. Before Slone had time to sit, one of the large doors opened and a lithe young woman who appeared to be in her early thirties came into the lobby. She had light strawberry colored hair and wore a yellow print sundress.

"Mr. Slone. How are you today? Mr. Rhodes isn't in yet, but let me take you back to a conference room. Mr. Sanchez is here. He's been expecting you."

She led him down a wide hallway to room with a heavy wooden conference table and six captain's chairs, a couch and two stuffed chairs around a coffee table, and a small wet bar. Miguel Sanchez stood at the bar talking on his cell phone with a glass of rum in his free hand. He held up the rum to Slone and smiled. "*Si. Adios amigo.*" He said and snapped his phone shut. "Technology. Let's hope the amazing communication satellites don't fall out of the sky," he said.

"Howard. How are you, my friend? How was your trip?"

Miguel Sanchez sat a small glass with dark liquor on the bar and embraced Slone with a hug and a kiss on each cheek. Slone stiffened slightly and managed a smile and a half hearted offer to shake hands.

"How ees our good friend Jerome? I trust he's working out well in his new position. It should be a great opportunity for him ... and for us too."

"He is doing just fine." Slone stepped back and adjusted his tie.

"We don't hab such fine rum in Mexico. We hab agave and the West Indies hab the rum. Who es to say which es best? Would you like a drink, my friend?"

"No thank you. I don't much like rum ... or for that matter ... tequila. But maybe I will have a scotch. Is there anything good there? Any single malts?"

"Si. Here es the Glenn Levet. That es a single malt, no?"

"It is. But not much good. If that's all there is, I'll take some. Neat."

There was a knock on the door, and before either could respond, Mr. Andrew Rhodes came into the room. He was tall and slender and surprisingly pale for someone who lives in the islands. He wore a blue seersucker suit with a pink polo shirt and saddle oxford shoes. His hair was thinner, but the same color as the girl in the yellow sundress. He had been Howard Slone's corporate agent in the Cayman Islands for several years, long before he knew or had any association with Miguel Sanchez. He had proven to be reliable and sufficiently impersonal to satisfy Slone's ilk.

"If you would like to review the transactions and balances in the bank records for Bethesda Equity and Southeast Financial and Southwest Financial, you can access each account with the computer terminal that we've placed on the table. I presume you know the passwords. If not, I'll be happy to supply Mr. Slone with them. If you want or need hard copies of any of your records, let me know. You know the laws and regulations for disclosure. If you have any questions, we can find the right answer for you. Just let me know." Mr. Rhodes smiled. He looked at Miguel and then at Slone.

"How was your trip, Mr. Slone?"

"Fine. Thank you."

"Is there anything else I can get you? Is the bar satisfactory? Would you like some snacks or hors d'oeuvres? Anything at all?"

"No. Thank you," Slone said.

"Fine then. I'll leave you two alone. If you need anything, let me know." Mr. Rhodes left as quickly as he came.

"Tell me about the shopping center," Sanchez said.

"We may have a slight delay, but I don't think it is going to be any problem at all. There's some half-assed lawyer involved with Grey. But it looks like he spends a good bit of his time in a local bar, and he seems more interested in booze and broads than this deal. We'll see how it all plays out. I should know something in a few days. I'm going back to Houston and see how the sale is progressing. I don't see any problems that we can't resolve."

"That's good my friend. Bueno. How much ees Federated's loan?

"The commitment for the whole project is seventy-five million. That's what the first mortgage says. But the second mortgage is also seventy-five million or so. So, depending on how this plays out, we could be looking at one hundred and fifty million. At least on the books."

"But Howard, my friend, how much has Federated actually funded under its loan commitment? How much do they need to be paid?"

"I am not exactly sure, but it's less than the total loan commitment. Morning tells me that the project is on schedule and under budget. Don't worry we will take care of that. Our agreement is one-half of net proceeds. There will be a complete accounting. You will be very happy ... as you have always been."

"Amigo, I know. I look forward to that."

"This could be one our best deals yet."

"Fortune ees smiling on us."

"I presume there are sufficient funds available?" Slone looked at his reflection in the mirror behind the wet bar and fiddled with the handkerchief in his blue blazer pocket.

"But of course. Shall we look at the computer?"

"No. That should not be necessary. You and your people have always been good for your word."

"You are a very trusting man, amigo."

Slone smiled. "Well, if there is nothing else, I believe I will be on my way."

"I will see you soon. Have a safe trip."

They shook hands and Slone left Miguel standing in the room. Miguel poured himself another generous rum drink from the cut crystal decanter and downed it with two gulps. He moved to the computer terminal and keyed in a password that had nothing to do with Bethesda Equity, Southeast Financial, or Southwest Financial. The girl in the yellow dress came to the door that Slone left open.

"Oops. Sorry. I thought you were gone. Is there anything I can get you? Is everything alright?"

"No. Gracious. Everything is fine. I'm just leaving."

Slone walked down the street where he met the stewardess from the Learjet 55 at the corner café and escorted her to his beach house. Knowing that the directions on the prescription label cautions against mixing alcohol with the little blue pill, he had taken only one small sip of the single malt scotch.

* * * *

The Learjet 55 touched down at Houston Hobby Airport and taxied to the general aviation ramp. The waiting limousine took him to the museum district and the Four Seasons Hotel. The concierge greeted him by name and asked if Slone needed assistance with his bags.

"No thank you. I'm not staying. I'm just having lunch."

The maitre d' led him to a corner table in the back of the plush Quattro Restaurant.

"On second thought," he said into his cell phone, "it might not be prudent for you to meet me here. I am going back to Hobby after lunch. Meet me at Butler Aviation. I will call you when I get there and tell you which conference room that I'm in."

"Are you staying with us, Mr. Slone?"

"No."

"Would you like a drink before you order?"

"A Citadelle martini. Dry. No olive."

* * * *

"I trust you were discreet. You didn't ask at the desk where meeting room B was?"

"No, sir. Your directions were perfect."

"Good. I believe that we're ready to go on the Frederick, Maryland retail project. Grey has managed to keep all the tenants either in the dark or assured that despite Federated's problem, shall we say, everything is still on schedule. But that's just a temporary situation. We need to get this deal wrapped up. Have you talked with FSLIC's attorneys in D.C.?"

"Yes sir. I guess you know that Grey has hired an attorney who is a bit of a rogue. But I'm assured that he won't be a problem."

"If he becomes a problem, I need to know. We can deal with it. Is there anything else?"

"No sir."

"Wait a few minutes to leave after I am gone. Don't bring attention to yourself." Slone adjusted his cufflinks and left the room.

Five minutes later, Jerome Morning walked out of Butler Aviation and drove back to Joe Franklin's office at Federated Savings and Loan.

CHAPTER TWENTY

"I thought they'd taken him out of general population."

"Apparently they had, after the first incident. But for some reason, they put him back in the main pod. You know Billy, the jail's awfully crowded. Sometimes there's only so much they can do. And let's face it, we don't have Harvard graduates working down there. He's in the hospital. Apparently those fellas who beat him up jammed something in his rectum. It perforated his large intestine. He's not in real good shape. The infection is the main problem. He's had one surgery and it looks like he may need another. Any thoughts, Mr. Bloomberg? Mr. Tapp?" Judge Barr looked over his reading glasses.

"How did they perforate his large intestine?" Billy asked.

"I don't know. You'd be surprised the stuff they can smuggle into the jail."

"I think he's a danger to the people in the hospital. I'm worried that he might do something violent in the hospital." Bloomberg said.

"Has anyone said what kind of surgery they're doing?" Billy asked.

"Your honor. I really think he should be strapped down so he can't hurt anyone in the hospital. I think it's a potentially explosive situation there."

"Good God, Steve. Terry's in the prison ward of the hospital, there are guards everywhere, and he's probably sedated. How's he a threat to anyone?"

"Listen, Tapp. He's killed once. And it wasn't a pretty scene."

"Yeah. Yeah. He did us all a favor. One less drug dealer for you to deal with."

"Alright, gentlemen. That's enough. I've ordered the guards at the hospital to keep me posted on any change in his condition. We'll proceed accordingly. Have y'all talked about a plea in this case? You might want to consider getting him out of the Montgomery County Jail and into the penitentiary. I don't mean to tell y'all your business, but I don't think this little encounter was random. I suspect this kid is in some jeopardy as long as he's here."

"I haven't had time to look at the video tape of Terry's preliminary hearing, and Mr. Bloomberg and I haven't discussed a plea bargain yet," Billy said.

"There wasn't a preliminary hearing. Jacobs didn't have an attorney, so the court appointed the public defender. They waived the preliminary hearing, and the case was sent to the grand jury. So, there aren't any tapes. No hearing."

"Mr. Bloomberg, has your office made an offer ... or do you intend to make a plea offer to Mr. Tapp's client?"

"I don't think that decision has been made. I just got the case a few weeks ago."

"Very well, gentlemen. Let me know what y'all decide. Like I said, I'm worried about this kid."

* * * *

A person charged with murder usually begins his trek through the criminal justice system by getting arrested, then finger-printed, then booked, and then put in jail. He stays in jail until he makes bond or his case is resolved. The first court appearance normally is the arraignment and the next step is a preliminary hearing, where a lower court judge decides if there is probable cause to believe a felony was committed. The preliminary hearing is the first time the defendant or his lawyer hear sworn evidence of the crime. It's not a trial and even if the judge doesn't find enough evidence to think a felony was committed, the state can still pursue the case. It's somewhat of an irony that the evidence at the preliminary hearing—when the strict application of the rules of evidence don't apply—is often the difference between ultimately winning or losing a criminal trial.

If the judge decides that there is probable cause, he sends the case up the ladder to the trial court level and the prosecuting attorney has the choice of tossing it in the trash can or presenting it to a grand jury. However, at this stage of the game, a case, especially murder, rarely goes in the trash can.

The grand jury is a group of regular citizens called together for the purpose of deciding whether there is probable cause that a crime has been committed. On the face of it, the system seems to have at least two levels of review that might safeguard someone from false charges. The true character of the U.S. criminal system, however, is best embodied in the commonly repeated saw amongst criminal lawyers: "You can indict a ham sandwich." For the most part, prosecutors simply take the word of the cops, and the grand jury is a secret closed proceeding where the accused isn't always able to give his side of the story, and even if he does, he can't have his lawyer with him. A commonly known disturbing nuance in this process is that most prosecutors present the facts to the grand jury with the intent of obtaining an indictment. That's why they're called prosecutors.

Billy had had precious few occasions when he'd successfully convinced a prosecutor not to present a case to the grand jury. Or, to present it with the recommendation not to indict. The system just didn't work that way.

After the grand jury returns an indictment, there's another arraignment and another bond hearing in the court with jurisdiction to hear felony cases. That's where Billy and Steve

Bloomberg stood before Judge Barr and debated Terry Jacobs' short-term medical treatment and a possible solution for his long-term fate. The more he learned of the facts, the less optimistic Billy was in a good outcome for young Terry Jacobs. No matter how sympathetic Billy might make Terry, splattering Fatso's brains on the wall was going to be a little difficult to explain. Fatso's virtues were much more compelling in death than they ever could have been in life.

* * * *

Mary Jacobs sat on the green vinyl bench in front of the two swinging doors with bullet proof glass windows. The corridor smelled of ammonia and antiseptic. On the other side of the doors with a night stick in his belt and a glower on his face stood six-foot-six-inch Butch Withrow. Withrow had worked in security in one form or another since his discharge from the army three years earlier. He boasted of combat action and a variety of other heroic episodes, but no one had ever seen actual evidence that his stories were anything more than hyperbole. Withrow was assigned to the prison ward of Mount Sinai Hospital because of what the county jailer called "unsubstantiated allegations of prisoner abuse." Aside from the unsubstantiated allegations, Withrow was dependable, sufficiently obsequious, and certainly imposing enough to get the respect of all but the most psychopathic inmates.

There had been rumors and innuendo against Withrow and questions of his alleged sadistic treatment of prisoners. But why get rid of a perfectly good guard, just because he gets a little carried away every once in a while? Dealing with criminals has a way of affecting even a well adjusted person. And what about the inference of innocence—it should apply to the guards as well as the criminals. Withrow had never been formally charged and, after all, even if he had been, criminals were the ones making the accusations.

"Innocent until proven guilty," the jailer quipped when he told Withrow that they were temporarily transferring him to the prison ward of Mount Sinai Hospital. Withrow had no reaction.

Mary didn't know any of this. She only saw the burly, bald guard as one more obstacle to seeing her son, who she understood to be on the brink of death from poison that leaked into his belly from a hole in his gut caused by the jail's negligence. When she found out about Terry's injury, she called Mr. Tapp. After several hours and a meeting with the judge, Billy had managed to get permission for her to visit Terry. Mary gripped her black patent leather purse in both hands and stood up. She pecked on one of the glass windows. Withrow looked at her and reluctantly moved his ear next to the small crack between the doors.

"Yeah?"

"When can I see Terry?"

"Check at the desk." Withrow pointed at the desk at opposite end of the hallway. The short fat man who was behind the desk when Mary got there an hour and a half ago was gone.

"Do you know when he's coming back?"

Withrow shook his head and moved away from the door. He walked down the hallway and sat in the small chair behind a small desk with a telephone and newspaper and a few magazines. He picked up a magazine and turned his back to Mary. He was too big for the chair, too big for the desk, and too obtuse for the magazine. Despite her emotional roil, Mary thought that Withrow's big body in the small chair behind the small desk looked like a clown in a Shriner's parade or a character in one of the television cartoons that Terry used to watch when he was little. He'd laugh and laugh when he saw a hippo in a tutu. Under different circumstances, it would have made her smile. Mary went back to the bench and took a tissue out of her purse. She dabbed her eyes and blew her nose. The noise echoed down the corridor and she leaned back against the wall and closed her eyes.

The loud crash from a slamming steel door startled Mary.

She opened her eyes to see a short fat man dressed in blue scrubs take a seat at the desk on her side of the bullet proof doors. He was the same person who had been at the desk when she came in more than an hour and one half ago. He didn't look up or even acknowledge Mary. When she stood up and moved toward him, he picked up the black telephone that sat on his desk and pushed one of the buttons. He held the receiver to his ear, but didn't say anything.

"Excuse me," Mary said. "Can you tell me when I'm going to be able to see my son?"

The short fat man held up a finger and then pointed to the telephone receiver. He didn't say anything. Finally he took the receiver away from his ear and held his hand over the mouthpiece.

"Have a seat ma'am. I'll be with you in a moment."

He continued listening, but still was yet to say a word into the telephone. Mary looked at her watch and turned away and started toward the green vinyl bench. Before she was settled, Billy came through the same steel door that the short fat man had entered. He went to the desk and waved for Mary to stay put.

"Good morning. I'm Billy Tapp. I represent Terry Jacobs. That's his mother down there. Here's an order from the court authorizing us to see Terry. What's the drill?" Billy placed a copy of the order on the desk. The short fat man held the receiver away from his ear and pushed the order away.

"Just a moment." He placed the receiver back in the cradle and opened a black notebook. Then he scrolled through a data base on the computer. "Room 712 C." He took out a pad and scribbled something on it. "Here. Show this to the guard." And, he pointed at the bullet-proof double doors.

"Thank you for coming, Mr. Tapp. I've been sitting here for almost two hours and I still haven't seen Terry. He's okay, isn't he? They told me I had to wait. I don't know why."

"We'll see in a minute."

Billy knocked on the bullet-proof doors and held up the piece of paper that the short fat man gave him. Withrow looked over his shoulder and laid the magazine face down on the small desk. He turned in the chair and stared at Billy and the small piece of paper that Billy held against the glass window. He came over to the double doors.

"You got some identification? Driver's license and your bar card."

"You bet'cha."

Billy took his driver's license and bar card out of his wallet and held them up. Withrow looked at them and then unlocked the doors. Mary moved to Billy's side and started through the door.

"Who're you?"

"This is Terry Jacob's mother. We're here to see Terry Jacobs. He's in 712 C." Billy held up the slip of paper.

"His lawyer. Not his mother. Sorry ma'am."

"But ... I ..."

"I have an order for her. Here take a look at it."

Billy handed Withrow a copy of the court's order. Withrow held his hand up and walked back to the small desk. He looked at the order and then dialed a cell phone. Billy was unable to hear what he said, but after a few seconds he snapped the phone shut.

"712 C. Leave your purse here." Withrow took a metal detector out of the desk and scanned Billy and Mary. "Mind if I look in your briefcase?"

"Nope. If you make sure nobody steals it, I'll just leave it hear with you."

Withrow opened it and pushed it back into Billy's hands. He also handed Mary her purse and lead them both down the hallway to room 712. He unlocked the door.

"Knock when you want out."

There were eight beds in room 712, four along each wall. Terry was in the third bed on the left. When Mary saw the tube in his stomach, the needles in his arms, the plastic bags above and below his bed, and the other electronic monitoring equipment connected to Terry's shackled body, she covered her nose with a tattered Kleenex and broke into muffled sobs. His eyes were closed and his breathing was shallow. She bent over and kissed his forehead. He slowly opened his eyes.

"Mom. I knew you'd come to get me. Don't let them hurt me anymore."

"I'm here. I'm here. Close your eyes and go back to sleep."

Billy moved to the end of the room and looked through the bars in the window at the parking lot seven stories below. *He must be dreaming, because that is the only way Terry Jacobs is getting out of bed C in room 712 or, for that matter, where he is headed if he doesn't die first.*

CHAPTER TWENTY-ONE

Federated Savings and Loan is located in a four story Spanish Colonial building with a tan stucco exterior. The doors and windows and much of the exterior resemble the Alamo in San Antonio. Although not an architect, Dozier Mound designed the building, which, with its warm and inviting shape, was slightly anomalous to many of the surrounding monolithic glass structures. The lobby is a three floor atrium, with a ceiling that's crisscrossed by massive wooden beams. The plaster on the ceiling between the beams is festooned with murals depicting various scenes from turn of the century rural Mexico and southwest Texas. The floor is covered with two foot square Saltillo tiles and at the far end, under a balcony that flanks two sides of the lobby, is a row of teller's windows. On the left side of the lobby, a massive rectilinear wooden staircase leads to the balcony. Opposite the staircase is a bank of two elevators.

Three large ceiling fans with ten-foot blades framed in black wrought iron and in-filled, like sails, with white linen are connected by pulleys and a long brown belt. The fans cause a subtle stir, sufficient to barely move the leaves on the several tropical trees and plants that grow in the lobby. Entering the Federated Savings and Loan lobby invokes the feeling of tranquility and trust. It isn't anything like a normal financial institution. That is, until FSLIC took over and inserted Jerome Morning as its representative and removed Dozier Mound from any control or authority.

Morning took Joe Franklin's office, which was on the opposite side of a shared conference room with Dozier Mound. He wanted Mound's office, but since Mound owned the building, Morning's superiors in Washington D.C. felt this may not be a necessary battle to fight, but they left the decision up to him. Despite his mandate from the great pundits at FSLIC in Washington, Dozier Mound was sufficiently intimidating to dissuade Jerome Morning from trying to make a move on Mound's office. Through the capricious tentacles of FSLIC, he'd taken Mound's love, he wasn't sure that he could take Mound's soul. In spite of FSLIC and Jerome Morning, Dozier came to Federated Savings and Loan and his office every day, but he knew that the whole thing was slipping from his grip.

Dozier Mound walked through the conference room between his office and Joe Franklin's office. He pushed open the door to Joe's office. He noticed a recently installed dead-bolt lock that wasn't latched. Jerome Morning sat in Joe's chair with his feet on the desk and Joe's telephone to his ear. Morning jerked around in surprise. He covered the mouthpiece.

"Excuse me! I am on the telephone. You must make an appointment with my secretary." He half turned his back to Dozier.

Dozier moved across the room and sat in one of the captain's chair in front of Joe Franklin's desk. He crossed his legs and stared at Jerome Morning. Morning covered the mouthpiece again.

"Excuse me! I *am on* the telephone." He pointed at the telephone.

"Yes. I see. I'll wait until you're done. I don't mind. Take your time."

"I need to get back to you," Morning said and hung up the telephone. He spun around his chair but avoided looking directly at Dozier. He looked at some papers on Joe's desk and he picked up a leather notebook.

"I am sorry that I do not have time to meet with you at the present. As I said, you can call ... ah ... my secretary and make an appointment. I am sorry, but I have a meeting that I must attend."

Morning stood up and moved toward the door. He was surprised by Dozier's quickness. Dozier leaped from the captains chair and stood between Morning and the door.

"I've been trying to talk with you for weeks and all I've gotten is the run around. We're talking before you leave here. Like it or not."

The blood drained from Morning's face and he swallowed hard. He staggered momentarily and quickly regained his balance. After a long pause, he stepped backwards and looked at Joe's desk.

"Well. What is it that you want to discuss?"

"I want to know about a number of things. First on the list is the Frederick Mall and Seymour Grey. What the hell is going on there?"

"Mr. Grey is in default because of an illegal profit participation and FSLIC is foreclosing on that loan and selling the property to avoid further loss."

"Further loss. What in the hell are you talking about? Do you have the slightest God damn idea about the difference between a good and a bad real estate development? Do you understand the concept of ahead of schedule and under budget? Do you even know what a budget is? Foreclosing on the Frederick Mall is the dumbest God damn thing that I've ever heard of."

"Well ... that may very well be your opinion—"

"Bullshit. That's not my opinion. That's the opinion of anyone who knows anything about commercial retail development. That's the opinion of anyone who knows anything about anything, which you obviously don't."

"Mr. Mound. It is not necessary to attack me personally."

"I'm not attacking you personally. I'm criticizing your

206

knowledge and judgment. Don't you remember? I'm the one who hired you in the first place."

Morning began to regain his composure. He took a half a step forward. "But, of course, you understand that these are my decisions."

"But why the Frederick Mall?"

"Because it was an illegal loan. It was against the law."

"Jerry, you know better than that."

"It is Jerome."

"Alright. Jerome, you know better than that."

"But, I am afraid that I do not."

"Then you're an idiot."

"I would thank you not to call me names. Now. As I said. I have a meeting I must attend."

"You're not going anywhere until you give me a good explanation for what's going on in Frederick."

"Are you standing in my way?"

"I've talked to Seymour Grey and his attorney, Mr. Tapp. Tapp told me that he thinks something's up. He didn't know what it was yet, but he said he was going to get to the bottom of it. And from what I can find out about Billy Tapp, if he says he's going to get to the bottom of something, he will, by God, get to the bottom of it."

"Mr. Mound, are you—"

"You're right. I am standing in your way. Right here, right now, and in Frederick and in any other place where there's a Federated project that you might try to screw up."

"Mr. Mound. Is that a threat?"

"If you want to call getting to the bottom of things a threat. Yes."

"Are we done here?"

"For now we are."

Dozier Mound went over to the conference room door and kicked it shut. "If you're going to install a lock, you ought to have enough sense to lock it."

Jerry Morning hurried out of Joe Franklin's office without closing the door behind him.

* * * *

Billy was sitting at his usual front table by the window next to M Street when Jason arrived. Jason took the chair across from Billy and poured himself a beer from the half empty pitcher. He put his leather Coach briefcase in the chair between them.

"What's up? How was your trip to the islands?"

"Good. Good. A little strange."

"I don't even want to ask you what you mean by a little strange. God knows what that could include."

"Well, the weather and the company were outstanding. But I could have sworn I saw Howard Slone there. I don't have any idea why he'd be on South Andros Island at the same time that I was."

"Who's Howard Slone?"

"You know. He's the little guy I told you about who is involved somehow with Seymour Grey in the Frederick Mall deal. Grey is the guy grappling with FSLIC. The case that you referred to me."

Billy refilled his glass and took a long drink. He belched and wiped his mouth with the back of his hand.

"Tapp. It's always a special treat to be privy to your delicate barroom etiquette."

"Only a select few. And those by invitation and not by chance."

"What does this Slone guy have to do with the FSLIC deal?" Jason asked.

"I'm not completely sure yet. He apparently owns or runs a private financing organization of some kind. When Grey needed a little money to buy a small piece of property for utility easements, Slone made the loan. Compared to the total project, it didn't amount to a piss in the bucket."

"That doesn't seem unusual to me."

"Standing on its own it isn't. But what's got me Styxing my head is the way it was done. Slone took a second mortgage on the twenty-five acre tract where the mall is built plus a mortgage on the utility easement that I told you about the other day."

"Again. Not to sound dense. But that isn't unusual. In fact, it's what you'd expect."

"Not really. Because the second mortgage incorporated the mortgage on the utility easement and it's for seventy-five million dollars plus a hundred ninety-seven thousand dollars. It looks like a first mortgage for seventy-five million and a second mortgage for seventy-five million plus. The loan for the easement was only forty-seven thousand dollars, but the mortgage is for seventy-five million dollars, plus an additional one hundred and ninety-five thousand dollars. And, on top of all that, there's a discrepancy in the Frederick County Court Clerk's record. Some of the documents ... I don't think appear in the record books and some of the documents don't have the totals in them. Some original loan documents have original notarized signatures but no amounts. And, the second loan documents in the Court Clerk's office have the amounts hand written in. I don't think I've ever seen that before."

"Oh. Does your client know this? I presume he must. He must have signed the documents."

"Maybe. He's like every other real estate developer. He sees the big picture and leaves the details to somebody else."

"What impact is this going to have on his case? On the foreclosure," Jason asked.

"Usually commercial loan agreements, and even residential loans, have a clause that says it's a default to permit a lien to be filed on the property. So, I'm willing to bet that Seymour's loan with Federated may technically be in default, simply because he allowed a second mortgage ... which is nothing more than a lien ... to be filed. So, it's an interesting question. It could help him by bollixing up everything and giving Seymour a little more time to work out the problem, or it could fuck him. Plus it might have an impact on the sale at foreclosure," Billy said.

"Sure. You know the drill," Jason said, "it isn't certain, but if the foreclosure runs its normal course, a bidder would have to deal with the second mortgage."

"That's correct, my man. Plus, conceivably, to out-bid Bethesda ... which I'm now more convinced than ever is Slone ... a bidder would have to pay a shit-load more than the shopping center is worth," Billy said.

"That's right," Jason said.

Billy leaned over the table and smiled. "Taken at face value, the seventy-five million-plus-dollar second mortgage accomplishes two things: first, it secures Slone's position, and second, it discourages legitimate buys from getting involved in what appears to be a fucked up mess. Slone wants this project for some other reason than it's a good deal."

"Are you ginning up some conspiracy theory, or are you just being paranoid?" Jason asked in feigned disbelief. "Washington D.C. If it's not a cover-up or a conspiracy, it isn't worth talking about."

"Wait and see," Billy said. "Wait and see."

Billy emptied the pitcher and waved to the bartender for more. The clock behind the bar said 6:45 and the place was starting to fill up. Robin Grigsby and two other young women in dark pant-suits came through the front door and stopped about half way down the bar to look around. Robin caught Billy's eye and offered a discrete wave and a collegial smile. She and her companions moved into the back room. Robin glanced back over her shoulder just before she and her companions disappeared into the back room. A waitress that Billy had never seen brought a full pitcher of beer and sat it in the middle of the table.

"Would you like fresh mugs?"

Billy sloshed full his and Jason's glasses.

"No thanks. Did you see Robin Grigsby just come in?" Billy asked Jason.

"No. But I saw her today at the courthouse and I told her I was meeting the devil for drinks. When I said your name, she chuckled. Did she just come in?"

"Yeah. She was with two other chicks. Dark blue suits. The usual. They went to the back room. She waved ... at me."

"Sure she did. I have to get back to my office. So, what are you thinking about with this FSLIC deal?"

"I don't know yet. But I do know that I don't like Howard Slone, and I don't like that prick Jerry Morning. But I'll tell you this—I'm going to figure out what in the hell's going on ... as long as Mr. Seymour Grey can afford it."

CHAPTER TWENTY-TWO

Ann Rogan grew up in a small farming community about seventy miles south of Chicago. Until leaving for college, Ann helped with the farm chores, just like everyone else in the family. She drove the green John Deere tractors and wheat combine, and she helped put the hay in barn. She was part of the operation. She was born and raised in the same house as her father. Her father and his father and now her brother were the biggest farm land owners in the county and, in addition to a profitable farming operation, due to a large measure on the family's good luck and good sense not to incur unnecessary debt, they also owned the largest insurance agency in a four county area. Her grandfather had been on Northwestern University's board of regents and her father and both she and her brother graduated from Northwestern. Ann's father also received a master's degree in agriculture from Michigan State University and her brother earned an MBA from the University of Chicago. The Rogans were modest, hard working, educated people. They had the unique quality of success without pomp. Billy often told Ann that if her family hadn't been so honest, they could have been successful politicians. "I know," is all she would say.

Washington D.C. was an unlikely choice for Ann. All indications pointed to her staying home, or close to home, and participating somehow in the family businesses. The agribusiness of the farms had become complex to the point that her father could have used some help and there was always something she might have done with the insurance agency. But, her father still ran the farms and her brother ran the insurance agency, and she never got the feeling that they really needed her. Since she was seven years younger than her brother, she suspected that, as a concession, they would find something for her because she was family. So, after graduating from Northwestern with a Bachelor's degree in English and a two year romance that ended a week after graduation, she decided that a change of landscape might be good. On the strength of her family's standing and influence and her excellent academic record, she was offered and she accepted a job with the Smithsonian Institute as secretary to the executive director. The next day, with little fanfare, she packed up her belongings and drove her Volkswagen Jetta to Washington, D.C. and moved into a one room efficiency apartment on the outskirts of Georgetown. For the first six weeks she called her mother every night, who dutifully reminded her to lock her car and set the deadbolt before she went to bed.

In retrospect, her meeting and short engagement to Billy Tapp may have resulted from the loneliness of a stranger in a strange town or because she was on the rebound from her long stable relationship in college or, probably, from both.

* * * *

She hadn't seen Billy sitting on the steps of the Hirshhorn Museum with his briefcase open, eating a sandwich, and reading from an open manila file folder. Just when she stepped past him, a gust of wind snatched a sheet of paper from his file and plastered it against her right thigh. Without looking up, Billy swung his arm around and grabbed both the paper and her thigh hard enough to send her sprawling on the warm stone steps.

"Oh God. I'm so sorry. I didn't mean to knock you down. Are you alright?"

Ann pulled her skirt over Billy's hand and the sheet of paper that he held securely against her leg.

"I think so."

"The wind. Ah. I guess it blew this paper out of my file. I didn't mean to knock you down. You alright?"

Billy jerked his hand off Ann's leg. She reached under her skirt and handed Billy the errant sheet of paper.

"I think I'm okay. Don't feel any broken bones."

Ann sat up and smiled at Billy. She smoothed her skirt and brushed back her hair.

"I'm Billy Tapp." He extended his hand, but quickly withdrew it when Ann didn't take it. "Here. Here's my card. If you're hurt or anything, you can call me at this number."

Ann looked at the card. "Oh. I see you're a lawyer. I guess that doesn't make you too unique in Washington does it?" Ann blushed when she realized that her comment was more caustic than she intended.

"Probably not. But. But, I'm not a government lawyer. I'm in private practice. That sets me apart from that batch of lawyers who work for the Federal Government and all the other agencies."

Ann had been in Washington long enough to understand the differences between the government and the private sector, but this was the first time she'd heard anyone make the distinction with such conviction.

"Oh. I know. I know. My name is Ann. She extended her hand to Billy.

"Nice to meet you," Billy said. "I'm normally not this violent. Are you visiting?"

"No. I moved here about six months ago."

"Really?"

"Really." She reached into her hand bag and handed Billy a card.

"Executive Secretary to the Director. I guess that's not strictly speaking a government job."

"Well, it's not private practice," she said in a slightly sarcastic tone as she stood up.

When Billy stood he saw Ann's lithe figure and pretty face. He gathered his papers and stuffed them back into his briefcase.

"Can I buy you a cup of coffee? I have a little time before I have to be back in court."

Ann was reluctant to take up with a total stranger, even if it was broad daylight and smack dab in the middle of the Federal Mall. She was slightly put off by his distinction between government workers and the private practice. *A hint of elitism, but, what the heck. I haven't talked to a male outside my office since I've been here. How can one cup of coffee in public be a problem?*

There was something about Billy Tapp that she didn't quite like, but there was something else about him that she did.

"Sure. I know just the place," she said.

* * * *

Billy had just gotten settled on Market Street after his debacle at Bracken and Wells and he'd just hired Vickie. Thanks to his law school buddy, Jason Roberts, he had enough work to pay the rent and overhead, and leave enough for the mortgage payment and his measure of alcohol at Clyde's. He had a few contingent fee cases that had the potential of six-figure fees and enough hourly clients to let him sleep at night. Despite Billy's fledgling reputation amongst the D.C. bar as a boozing womanizer, his stint with the Supreme Court stood him in good graces with the local legal intelligentsia. Billy was surprised at the number of single practitioners and small partnerships who were happy to pay him to do their research, and then double the cost to their clients and take credit for it. As long as he got paid, Billy didn't much give a shit. *If they had half a brain, they'd come up with the same legal conclusions that I do.*

Billy followed a half step behind Ann as they wound their way away from the Mall.

"Where exactly are we going? Is there a coffee shop near here?"

"Catch up, Mr. Tapp. We're almost there."

No sooner had Ann spoken, when they arrived at a two-story, little brick building with three tables and a row of four large lead plants forming a wall on the far side from the front door. "The Brewmeister," it said on the window and also across the mocha brown awning.

"Is this coffee or beer?"

Ann ignored Billy's comment and pulled open the front door. The space was about forty feet deep and about half as wide. A bunch of coffee apparatus lined the wall behind the counter at the far end of the shop. There were five tables spaced around the room and a periodical and book rack on the left hand wall. A jolly looking white bearded man stood behind the bar manipulating one of the coffee machines. The chime on the door caused him to look around. He had an apron cinched above his rotund middle and the pocket in his short-sleeved white shirt was stuffed with pens and paper.

"Miss Ann. How nice to see you. What can I get you today?"

"Hello Louis. What's your house brew today?" Ann turned to Billy. "What do you want?"

"Coffee."

"I know that. What kind of coffee. Do you have any preference?"

"Nope. Black."

"Louis, we'll have two large house blends. No room for cream or sugar."

Ann stepped back from the counter and glanced at Billy. When he caught her eye, a barely perceptible flush apppeared on her neck. She quickly stepped back so Billy could pay for the coffee. She suggested that they sit outside under the brown awning. Billy awkwardly maneuvered around the two tables closest to the front door so that he could end up at the far table with his back to the row of lead planters. Ann looked over the top of her sun glasses at Billy's maneuvering and, then, took a chair with her back to the front door.

"Is this table okay?"

"It's fine," Billy said.

"So, you're an attorney and you don't work for the government. What kind of lawyer are you?"

"I'm a great lawyer."

"I'm sure you are."

"Joking aside. I have a general litigation practice. I do some criminal law. Some complex civil litigation. That kind of thing. I was with a big firm, but that didn't work out. I decided to open my own practice. At this stage of the game, most of my practice comes by way of referrals from other lawyers. Lots of times there are conflicts within a firm and they'll send the client over to me. I used to clerk at the Supreme Court, so I managed to get my name around town a little. Plus, I went to law school at Georgetown and that's helped me with contacts."

"I see."

"As I'm sure you know, or you're finding out, Washington is a town of contacts. I'm sure that's the case everywhere, but it's particularly important here."

Ann smiled and turned her face to the early afternoon sun that peeked over the edge of the awning. "Do you come to the Hirshhorn often?"

"Sometimes. It was just such a nice day. The judge recessed early and continued the hearing until tomorrow, so I decided to walk over here and get lunch somewhere. I sort of ended up on the steps reviewing my file for tomorrow. Next thing I know, the wind blows my paper out of the file and I knocked you on your butt. Sorry."

"You really didn't knock me on—"

"Well. You know what I mean."

Billy was in the middle of a suppression hearing in a securities fraud case that a partner at Bracken and Wells had referred. The law firm had represented the defendant before he was charged and the grand jury returned a criminal indictment. When the case made its inevitable transition from a civil violation to a criminal charge, Bracken and Wells politely begged off and, despite having collected more than two hundred thousand dollars in attorneys fees, turned the client over to Billy Tapp. As long as the situation involved "civil matters of legal interpretation" Bracken and Wells was more than willing to play. When the game morphed to unsavory criminal allegations, Bracken and Wells wanted out. You're judged by the company you keep. If Billy could wipe the defendant's slate clean, in due course, Bracken and Wells would, no doubt, welcome the client back into its gentile collective.

"What kind of a hearing were you in?"

"A suppression hearing. It's part of a criminal case. When the cops get evidence illegally, you get to have a hearing and ask the judge to toss out the evidence, so it can't be used in trial. Confessions. Stuff seized without a search warrant."

"Seems to me if someone confesses it should be used at trial."

"Not if the cops beat it out of you."

"But if they don't, then—"

"The Bill of Rights. Remember from social studies or civics or wherever you're supposed to learn it. You have to protect everybody's civil rights ... constitutional rights. That's what the process is supposed to do. Keep the cops at bay, etcetera."

"I learned it," Ann ruffled. "Do you do a lot of criminal law?"

"Some."

"Do you ever represent someone that you know is guilty? How could you do that? I think I might have a problem doing that."

"Sure. But if you're guilty you still get the benefit of your constitutional rights. The constitution wasn't written for just the innocent. It was to protect everybody. Innocent until proven guilty and all that. It outlines the process to determine who's guilty and who's innocent. You can't apply it in retrospect, if you know what I mean."

"Interesting. Guess I hadn't thought of it that way."

The sun had moved below the edge of the awning. Ann looked at her watch. "Well, I've things to do yet today. I enjoyed meeting you."

"Thank you. Would you like to get together, maybe, and have dinner some time? That is if you're not already taken."

"Sure. That would be nice. I'd like to do that." Ann took another card out of her purse and wrote her home number on the back. "Here's my home number."

"Thanks. I'll give you a call."

Billy picked up his coffee and fitted the white cap with the little drinking hole on the tall cardboard cup. He picked up her empty cup and tossed it in the trash container and watched Ann walk away. *She's pretty. I think she's smart. And, I think she likes me. How long will it take me to fuck up this relationship—one that hasn't even started yet.*

CHAPTER TWENTY-THREE

"I just received a large envelope of legal papers from Michael Braxton, FSLIC's attorney in the Grey case. His cover letter says that the documents are from Grey's attorney. They are interrogatories, requests for production of documents, and requests for admissions. Braxton says that we have thirty days to respond. He also says that this attorney, Billy Tapp, has filed a motion asking the court to permit him to file an amended answer to the foreclosure suit. It also looks like he is asking the court to let him bring in other defendants or parties or something. I am not quite sure what it means."

Howard Slone listened. He didn't say anything.

"Are you still there, Mr. Slone?" Jerome Morning asked. "According to Mr. Braxton, we have thirty days to respond."

"I heard you the first time."

"It looks like Tapp is asking about Bethesda Equity and your involvement in the Frederick project. He has asked for all the documents that relate in any way to the entire project, including the utility easement. He has also asked about your involvement in Federated and how you ... here let me read this one."

Interrogatory No. 4. Please describe and explain in detail how Howard Slone or any of his affiliates, including, but not limited to Bethesda Equity, initially established contact with and formulated and entered into a loan agreement, directly or indirectly, with Seymour Grey or any of this affiliated entitles for the real estate development commonly referred to as the Frederick Mall in Frederick Maryland.

After another long silence Slone spoke. "Which other defendants is Tapp asking the court to let him bring in?"

"It doesn't say. It just says that he wants the right to bring in other defendants after he receives responses to these questions."

"Send me a copy. E-mail it to my Fort Lauderdale office right now." Slone closed his cell phone and threw it across the room. It flew into several pieces that scattered down the wall.

"What was that?" The stewardess asked.

Slone walked over to the bed and smiled at her. He bent over and gently gathered her hair in his left hand and lifted her head off the pillow.

"What was that?" He said softly.

Without warning he slapped her across the face with enough force to send her sprawling across the silk sheets. She screamed and covered her face.

"Get your fucking clothes and get the fuck out of here. It's none of your God damn business what the fuck that was. That was for me. Now get the fuck out of here before I break your God damn neck."

* * * *

Basically, there are four stages in most lawsuits: filing the suit, discovery, trial, and appeal. After the lawsuit is filed, the parties go through the discovery process. During the discovery stage, the parties have the right to ask about the evidence they each have, which includes documents, witnesses, looking at property, and seeing other data that ultimately may not even be admissible in the trial or that might lead to evidence that might be used at trial. A bunch of rules concocted by a bunch of legal pundits who suffered from the misguided notion that strict rules would expedite equal justice govern discovery. The extensive explanations for these rules range from getting all the real facts on the table to encouraging negotiated settlements to making sure the parties get a fair trial. In theory the legal scholars were right. But, like any real fight, the rules work best for the lawyer who can effectively manipulate them. There's nothing more effective in trial than popping some undisclosed fact on your opponent that you've legally withheld.

* * * *

"Here's what the son of a bitch is asking for: All documents relating to Bethesda Equity's loan for the Frederick Mall; all correspondence between Bethesda Equity and Grey; all loan documents; ownership of Southeast Financial, Southwest Financial, and Bethesda Equity; my interest in those companies; he wants to know all the banks we deal with, including any off-shore banks; and the God damn list goes on and on. He can't get all of this, can he?"

Dexter Hall looked out of his forty-third floor window at Biscayne Bay and a fleet of small sailboats in their final leg of a bay race, making their downwind run with colorful spinnakers full blown from the hot air coming directly off their sterns. The early evening sun cast the long shadow of his office building across the bay. The sailboats were far enough away that they seemed to move as imperceptibly slow as the minute hand on the large grandfather clock in his office. The ocean view almost looked like a twenty-five dollar Thomas Kinkade couch painting.

"He's entitled to that and probably more."

"Hall, I pay you thousands of dollars and you tell me

'probably more'?"

"Do you want me to lie to you? You pay me for legal advice, not to tell you bullshit. Before I can help you, I need to fully understand what the problem is. The question might be not what he's entitled to, but what he can get. If you know what I mean. Do you want to give me the details?"

"It has to do with a project in Frederick Maryland that we've been working on for a while. It's a project that we are buying out of foreclosure and FSLIC is involved; FSLIC's not the problem. The problem is the developer. I don't want to go into a lot of detail on this telephone on the airplane. I'm almost back to Lauderdale. When I get there I'll give you a call and I'll run down to your office. Does that work?

"Good deal. Just let me know."

Slone's next call was to his office in Fort Lauderdale. "Have Calvin and Thornton meet me at the airport. We should be there in about twenty minutes."

The stewardess looked away when Slone placed the in-flight telephone back in its cradle. She stood against the bulk-head that contained the kitchenette. She had covered the red welt on the side of her face with makeup. This wasn't the first time that Howard Slone hit her. But, it was always followed by an effusive apology and a bonus check that at least doubled the five hundred dollars a day that Slone normally paid her. She hoped that this time wouldn't be any different.

"Are you doing okay, Mr. Slone? Can I get you anything?"

"Just fine. Thank you. Are you alright? I really am sorry about—"

"No. No. I'm just fine. I know you're under a lot of pressure. Business and all that. I'm okay."

"Yes. That's it. Business. Sometimes it's nasty. Sometimes it has to be."

She moved behind his seat and reached over and massaged his shoulders and neck. "How does this feel?"

Slone leaned forward and made a low moan. "You're an angel from heaven."

When the Lear landed, Slone handed the stewardess an envelope with fifteen new one-hundred dollar bills. "Here," he said. "This is for you."

"Thank you Mr. Slone. You have my number."

"Yes dear. I know that I do."

Calvin and Thornton stood at the edge of the huge opening to the hangar. Next to the office sat a black Suburban with tinted windows. Each man wore dark clothes and aviator sunglasses. The jet taxied to within twenty feet of the opening and the men watched passively as the engines shut down. Slone was the first one out of the airplane. The stewardess followed him and she hurried into the office door off the tarmac. Calvin caught Slone's eye and flashed a thumbs up and a wry grin. Slone hurried into the hangar and motioned toward the door that leads into the office from inside the hangar.

"Good job, Mr. Slone."

Slone looked at Calvin and growled. "Fuck that bitch. They're a dime a dozen. You guys meet me in the conference room. I have a little job for you. And wipe that God damn grin off your face."

After Slone dismissed Calvin and Thornton from their brief meeting in the conference room, he went into his large adjoining office. No sooner had he flipped on his computer than there was a knock on the door that led to the main office and the pilot's lounge.

Slone kept the airplane in a private hangar under the aegis of a charter service. The front office was for the pilots and any customer that might hire the service. BlueSky Charters, LLC was the official name of the operation. It employed one full time captain who was on call twenty-four hours a day. Although BlueSky Charters was available for public hire, most of its customers were Howard Slone and his associates.

"Anything else today, Mr. Slone?" the captain asked.

"No. I don't think so. I will let you know if that changes."

Slone looked at his computer monitor. He called up the e-mail with the attachments that he instructed Morning to send to him. His name and Jerome Morning's name appeared in the discovery requests—his thirteen times and Jerome Morning's eight times. It was apparent that the other defendants or other parties that this Billy Tapp wanted to bring into the lawsuit included Jerome Morning and Howard Slone. He called Dexter Hall again.

"The court rules say that Tapp can get discovery on anything that's admissible at trial or that might lead to admissible evidence ... even if it's not admissible. But he can't go on some wild goose chase with questions that are only to annoy or embarrass you or are in bad faith. If we think he's doing that, we can ask the court for a protective order. Send the stuff on for me to look at. After I read it, I'll give Michael Braxton a call and get his take on this thing. This might not be more than some numb-nut lawyer in Washington being a pain in the ass. Let me read the stuff; I'll call Braxton and our office in D.C. and see if they know anything about this Billy Tapp."

"I really don't care what the rules say. I am not going to answer a bunch of personal questions. And it is none of his fucking business what my ownership interest is in anything."

"Well, Howard, it might be. Send me the discovery documents and I'll take a look at it."

"It's not. God damn it."

Slone had no sooner slammed the phone in its cradle when it rang. The LED said that the call was from Jerome Morning in Houston. Slone moaned and picked up the receiver.

"What is it?"

"Right sir. I just received a call from attorney Braxton, he inquired as to how long it would take to answer Grey's legal papers. I told him that I was not sure. I would call him back. Right?"

"Morning. You do your job and we'll do ours."

"Exactly sir. But several of the questions are directed to Federated Savings and Loan and they address my knowledge

of several issues. I suppose that I am looking for your
counsel."

Slone didn't say anything for several seconds. "You don't
say a fucking thing until you talk to me. Do you
understand?"

"Right, sir. Exactly. Not a peep until we talk."

CHAPTER TWENTY-FOUR

Before the urban redevelopment in Baltimore took place, young Thackeray Frederick Johnson stood amongst the train tracks and old buildings. The salty breeze that swept into the city from the harbor whipped the scattered trash between the abandoned railroad cars and the deserted buildings. The wind tossed an empty beer can skidding across the barren concrete, clanking with the hollow sound of no tomorrow. He stood a stone's throw from Baltimore's Inner Harbor and the yet constructed upscale tourist shops and restaurants and the extravagant National Aquarium with tanks full of fish and sea creatures from every corner of the earth. The coming shops and restaurants and angel fish and beluga whales and umpteen species of sharks hadn't yet affected the decay in this nearby part of town. He loitered in a section of Baltimore where some day a few rich men, with the city's blessing and an enormous chunk of taxpayer money, would demolish building after building and construct the grand Camden Yards baseball park for the venerable Baltimore Orioles. He had just turned thirteen years old, and the Camden Yards baseball park was still just an embryonic scheme to nab a gob of downtown property for free and run out the drunks and the winos and the drug dealers—where they'd end up was less concern than getting rid of them.

Urban redevelopment at its best. Take a run-down, crime-ridden area and simply get rid of it.

He looked nervously up and down the railroad tracks and back and forth between the buildings. He waited, like his mother said, for Mr. Smith. She said that Mr. Smith would walk past here in the morning. He always did. She told Thackeray to wait for him. She didn't exactly tell him and he wasn't sure what Mr. Smith looked like. She only said that he knew young Thackeray's daddy. That Smith and Thackeray's daddy had done business together and that they'd played basketball together. She said that Mr. Smith would probably recognize young Thackeray because he looked so much like his daddy. Mr. Smith was a tall handsome man, who had lots of money and a big car. He was rich and he had her medicine.

"You tell him that yo Mama sick. That she need her medicine. That she'll pay him with money if she got it. Or, a favor if she don't. You tell him that. You hurry along now. Yo mama sick. Real sick."

Young Thackeray had rushed out the door and hurried to the railroad yard looking for a man that he'd never seen and, as far as he knew, had never seen him.

Although he didn't know if it was true, his mother repeatedly told him that his daddy was a great basketball player who actually tried out for the Harlem Globetrotters. She told him this between her bouts of spasmodic coughing when she was high on booze or smack. When she was sick because she didn't have her "medicine," she just lay on her side on the floor or the bed with her legs drawn up to her flaccid breasts. Her eyes would water and she'd softly sob.

Thackeray stood between two box cars, knowing that he should be in school and wishing his mother would get better.

As Thackeray was about to leave his spot between the abandoned rail cars, a short fat bald man showed up over next to the loading ramp for one of the old buildings. A few minutes later, two more men appeared. One in expensive clothes and the other dressed, more or less, like a bum.

Almost as soon as he arrived, the bum and the fat man started arguing and waving their arms back and forth and up and down. The fat man pulled something out of his coat and stepped back. Thackeray tried to conceal himself between the railroad cars; he peeked around the edge just in time to see the man in the expensive clothes step up to the fat man and appeared to punch him in the stomach. The fat man fell back against the loading dock. The bum reached into the fat man's pocket and showed something to the man in the expensive clothes. The two then walked off and the fat man toppled to the ground. When the two men were out of sight, Thackeray came from between the cars and trotted over to the fat man. The fat man had managed to right himself and sat on the ground leaning against the loading dock.

"You know my mama? You don't know my daddy do you?" Thackeray asked.

Before Thackeray noticed the growing pool of blood under the fat man and the bubble of red slime forming from the fat man's left nostril, the wail of sirens and the screeching of tires pierced the morning breeze. Four unmarked silver Ford Crown Victorian cop cars converged on Thackeray and the soon to be deceased undercover narcotics DEA officer. The four cars formed a semi-circle around Thackeray and the dying fat man—lights flashing, sirens blasting, and law enforcement officers with guns trained on the thirteen-year-old kid trying to get medicine for his sick mother.

"Don't move," they yelled. "Lay down on the ground with your hands behind your head," and as if it wasn't already apparent, "we have you surrounded."

The most dangerous weapon that they found on Thackeray was his door key to the project housing, turned flop house, where he and his mother lived. He'd seen lots of violence, but he'd never seen anyone killed.

"You have the right to remain silent," they told him, not realizing that he had nothing to say, but even if he did, he was too scared to say it anyway.

The rich man with mama's medicine never came.

Thackeray never saw his mother again and, after being held without bond for almost sixty days in the Baltimore juvenile detention center, he never went back to school. This event was for Thackeray the end of a very difficult life and the beginning of one that was even worse. His future held more time in jail than time on the street.

* * * *

But now, it was time for Thackeray Johnson to decide if he wanted to risk going to trial in Federal District Court. Despite his considerable experience in the criminal justice system, he wasn't able to come up with a plausible answer to the flood of evidence that the U. S. Attorney seemed to have compiled that certainly meant conviction and extended incarceration. His only real hope was to avoid, as much as possible, consecutive jail sentences. Jail time can either run concurrent or it can run consecutive. Conviction on three charges of five years each can either be concurrent—five years total—or consecutive—fifteen years. A big difference. Although, on the bright side of things, as jail time goes, his previous incarcerations in the Federal institutions weren't all that bad.

"Law-yer Tapp. You tell that gov'met law-yer that I still don' know nothin' 'bout no god damn in-surance co-operation. But if he willin' to cut me some slack, I'll save everybody the problem of goin' to trial and maybe him losin' dis case. He don' want to lose dis case."

"Right. He doesn't want to lose your case. But he isn't going to. It looks to me like his case is rock solid. Tell me how you think he's going to lose his case."

"Well sir. You never know what might happen. Fo that matter, the God damn courthouse could burn to the ground. Ever think 'bout that?"

"Yeah. Right. The courthouse burns down, unless you burn down with it, they stick you in jail somewhere until they find a courthouse to finish the trial."

"What if all da evidence burns down wif it too?"

"That isn't going to happen."

"Courthouse burns, evidence burns. That simple. No courthouse. No evidence. No trial. No conviction. That gov'ment law-yer now wonderin' why he don't do ol' Thackeray's deal. Now who da fool?"

"Thackeray, enough of this nonsense."

"What 'chu talkin' 'bout, nonsense? Anything can happen."

"Do you want to take the deal or not?"

"I don' know fo' show'. Let me think on it."

"I need to know by the end of the day. You're scheduled to be back in court in the morning. I need to know today."

Thackeray patted his jumpsuit pockets and stepped closer to the bars. "Say. Mister Tapp. You don' have no cigarettes do you?"

"I don't smoke."

"Good fo' you."

"Now what are we going to do? You plead guilty without a lawyer, and now you want to change your plea. The judge doesn't have to let you do that. You know that don't you?"

Thackeray bent his head forward and looked over the top of his rimless glasses at Billy. "'Course I know that. You think that judge Mitchell would cut me a break ifn' he thought that U.S. law-yer gonna lose his case? How that gonna look? You know, dey not dealin' wif yo average idiot here. I got my GED and twenty-seven hours of college. Dey not dealin' wif yo average foo." Thackeray threw his head back and burst into laughter. "I ain't no *average* foo."

"I'll give you that," Billy said. "What's it going to be?"

"Jail, I 'spect." Thackeray frowned. He stared through Billy. "Plus," he said. "Where'd dey 'spect me to go?" He turned away from Billy.

"What?"

"It's a long time ago. The first time I got busted. Where'd dey 'spect me to go?"

"What?"

"Had no place to go when dey busted me and no place to go when dey let me free. Well, sir. Let me think on it over night. Come by first thing in the morning and I'll let you know. Did I ask you fo a cigarette?"

* * * *

"If you get hooked on drugs, I'll lock you in a cage," Billy's father warned, "and leave it in the middle of the woods until you're cured."

"You'll do no such thing!" Billy's mother shrieked. "Billy doesn't take drugs. And he won't ever take drugs. You don't take drugs, do you? And, you never will, will you?"

"I didn't say he did. I said if he did."

"I know what you said."

Billy looked down at his plate and leaned on his elbows against the table. He held his fork in his left hand and it brushed against the side of his head.

"Billy," his mother said, "take your elbows off the table and don't put your fork in your hair."

Billy's father rolled his eyes and winked at Billy. "I might just get in the cage with you. Give me a little peace and quiet."

Billy smiled back at his father and his mother stormed off to the kitchen, leaving Billy and his father to finish the evening meal.

CHAPTER TWENTY-FIVE

Billy drove south on 14th Street NW past the Thomas Jefferson Memorial and the East Potomac Park and crossed the Potomac River into Virginia on the Memorial Bridge. He followed the George Washington Memorial Parkway to East King Street and the heart of Old Town and the main shopping district. The waterfront lay some five or six blocks to the east along the two mile boundary with the Potomac River. Because he knew that dinner with Seymour Grey would be a protracted affair, he decided to park in one of the many garages and not on the street at a parking meter. He wound his way down toward the waterfront and the Torpedo Factory and a familiar parking garage.

The Torpedo Factory—now the Torpedo Factory Art Gallery—was actually a torpedo factory after World War I and during World War II. It was originally called the U.S. Naval Torpedo Station. After the end of World War II, the building became a storage facility for the Smithsonian and Congress used the expansive building for record storage and German war secrets. In 1969, the City of Alexandria bought the facility and it, more or less, lay fallow until 1974, when truckloads of crap and miscellany were removed and the place began its metamorphosis into the art center that it is today. For a short time after the City of Alexandria bought the building, it wasn't much more than a ramshackle blight and the nightly accommodations for the myriad of bums, hobos, and homeless people who meandered in and out of the nation's capital. Now, arts and crafts sell for as little as five dollars for glass birds that stand next to a glass of water and bob up and down through the heat exchange from vaporization to more than twenty-five thousand dollars for bronze sculptures and oil paintings.

The parking garage was nearly empty. Daytime patrons were gone and scattered to the suburbs, and the evening crowd hadn't arrived yet. Billy turned into the gated ramp and pulled the pink ticket from the steel box that guards the entrance. The box beeped and the black and white gate swung up. Billy made a sharp right turn and drove up one level and parked in a dark corner against the back wall of the garage. He stuck the parking ticket under the window visor, locked the car, and walked to Madame Claret's La Rogue and his meeting with Seymour Grey.

As he walked out of the garage, a few cars passed by. A green Volkswagen convertible, with the top down and four kids giggling and poking each other, and a black Suburban with blacked out windows.

Before the night was over, Seymour buying dinner wouldn't be Billy's only surprise.

* * * *

"Just so we're both on the same page. Let's go over this once more. Let me get this straight. According to your memory, Slone or one of his companies made two loans to you? That right?"

Seymour motioned to the middle aged waiter. "Garcon." The waiter turned and ducked behind the bar and then into the kitchen. Marcel Claret came from behind the small bar and placed her warm hand on Billy's shoulder. She was wearing a sleeveless red satin dress that showed her shapely legs and backside.

"Can I get you something, Billy?"

"We would like another bottle of this excellent Bordeaux," Seymour said.

"But of course." Madame Claret squeezed Billy's shoulder and smiled.

"That is right counselor. One for the utility easement and another one for one hundred thousand dollars. I told you about both of these. Although, I did not know that Slone was behind the utility easement loan until he offered to help out with refinancing after all the crap with FSLIC and that little jackal Morning took over Federated ... or you told me. I do not remember which. Just recently, the one for one hundred thousand dollars. Timing was most auspicious."

"And there was another check for fifty thousand dollars that was made out to you, but you didn't sign. That right?"

"I guess that is right. Madame Claret. She is certainly a breath of fresh air."

The waiter brought another bottle of wine and showed it to Billy. Seymour leaned over to participate in approving the bottle.

"It's good. Open it," Billy said.

The waiter unceremoniously pulled the cork and pointed the bottle at Billy. "Would you like fresh glasses?"

"No. Just pour it," Billy said and pushed his glass over to the side of the table where the waiter stood. The waiter filled Billy's glass to the proper level and prompted by Billy's gesture of disapproval, dumped another inch or so of wine in the glass.

"What about this fifty thousand dollar check? I know you said that you didn't endorse it, but somebody did. Any ideas?"

"None, but it was not me."

"Could it have been someone working for you? Secretary. Bookkeeper ..."

"Counselor, I just cannot imagine anyone who worked for me doing that."

"What about the Cayman Islands? The First National

Bank of the Cayman Islands. Southeast Financial. Ever hear of any of those?"

"Well I guess. Maybe. I was dealing with Howard Slone and I did not pay much attention to the entities ... to the companies. As far as I was concerned, at the end, I was dealing with Slone."

They finished the *confit de canard* and the poached pears filled with raisins, apricots, and cranberries poached in sherry and another bottle of wine and three glasses each of Cockburn's 1970 Vintage Port. The check was over five hundred dollars and, to Billy's surprise, Seymour paid it.

CHAPTER TWENTY-SIX

They'd been at La Rogue for almost three and a half hours. Billy was tired and torpid from the rich sauces and the expensive wine that, much to his surprise, Seymour had paid for. He looked at his watch and decided to swing by Clyde's for a nightcap. It wasn't ten o'clock yet and as best he could remember, there wasn't anything pressing for tomorrow. Plus, maybe he needed something to settle his stomach. As he made his way from La Rogue to the parking garage beside the Torpedo Factory Art Center, a welcome cool, slightly acrid evening breeze wafted up from the Potomac River with just enough strength to cool the uncomfortable dampness caused by too much food and alcohol. He walked past the empty toll booth and the open turn-style, the attendant was either on break or gone home for the night. No one was in sight. Since he had parked one level up, Billy walked up the ramp instead of climbing the stairs that opened at street level on the opposite side of the entry ramp from the toll booth. Billy passed the Volkswagen and noticed that the only other vehicle in the garage was a black Suburban parked around the corner, farther up the ramp. Billy pulled the keys to his Porsche from his pocket and pushed the unlock button. The horn beeped and the lights flashed. That's when he sensed that he wasn't alone.

* * * *

"Hey shyster. I need a word with you. We need to have a little talk."

Billy turned around and faced a large muscular man who was wearing dark pants, a polo shirt with sleeves that fit tightly around the mid-point of his bulging biceps, and dark sunglasses. He held up his right fist and motioned with his index finger for Billy to come to him. He had a slight grin on his face and he looked like he was half kidding—but in a sinister kind of way.

"Ah ... yes."

The man quickly stepped closer, and Billy stumbled into the side of the Porsche. It was becoming clear very quickly that this little talk wasn't going to have a good ending.

"Talk? Talk about what?"

"About this," the man said as he unleashed a left hook that Billy managed to sidestep. The errant punch smashed into the left front driver's side window, leaving a spider web of fractures that were held together by the sandwiched polymer in the safety glass. The flexibility in the safety glass saved the thug's hand from breaking, a fortuity that didn't seem to change his disposition or resolve.

"Fuck!" he yelled and looked at his bleeding knuckles in disbelief. "You shyster asshole." He grabbed Billy by the shirt and slammed him in to the car. He pushed his face so close that Billy could smell his hot bad breath.

"You're gonna pay for that, you fucking prick."

Realizing that running wasn't going to be an option, Billy grabbed the man behind the neck and, with all of his might, lunged forward and bashed his forehead into the man's nose. Blood exploded and the man dropped his grip on Billy's shirt. The man stumbled backward and cupped his bleeding nose with both hands. Without wasting a step, Billy darted toward the stunned assailant and with all his force planted his knee squarely in the man's groin. The man's eyes rolled back and he gasped for air as he stumbled back and fell to the concrete floor curled in the prenatal position holding his crotch and moaning. Billy stepped back to measure the right distance to find the range for a finishing kick to the fallen man's balls when he heard a second voice behind him.

"Jesus Christ. All brawn and no brain," someone said.

Billy felt a dull pain in his right lower back. He saw a flash of bright light and felt a searing pain. Then, he lost the feeling in his right arm and his right leg. Someone spun him around and he stood face to face with another man, this one smaller and holding in one hand what looked like a black sweat sock, which unbeknownst to Billy was filled with number nine lead shot, and in the other a rectangular device with two wires attached to it that were strewn on the floor. The man put the electronic device into the right back pocket of the cargo pants that he wore.

"Mr. Tapp. You need to keep your nose out of things that don't concern you."

Billy's right side was numb and he gasped for breath. "Who are—"

"Doesn't matter who I am. The point is who you are. And, where you're sticking your nose, Mr. Tapp. You're getting in way over your head. Do you understand? I certainly hope you do. I would say this hurts me more than it does you, but that really wouldn't be true, would it?"

Billy mustered all his strength and swung with his left hand at the man's head, but the man stepped back and the punch hit nothing but air. Billy saw the black sweat sock arch through the yellow light in the ceiling and felt it land flush on the side of his head. He crumpled to the floor unconscious.

* * * *

"Hey mister. You okay?" Billy lay on the concrete floor beside his car. He wasn't bleeding and didn't appear to be shot.

"Do you see any blood?" one of the boys asked.

"Nope," one of the girls said. "It looks like he must have hit his head on the window of his car. Maybe he was drunk or something and stumbled into the car."

"Think we ought to call the cops or something? Is he dead?"

"No, he's not dead," the girl with orange hair said.

"How do you know that?" one of the boys asked. "He sure looks dead to me."

"Look, stupid. I'm going to be a nurse. I know these things. Plus, he's breathing. Dead people don't breathe. Maybe we should call somebody. I mean he looks kind of ... well ... rich or something. What if he's somebody important? We wouldn't want to leave him just lying here in this garage."

One of the other boys nudged Billy's shirt sleeve with his foot. "Man. Look at that watch. That's some kind of Rolex or something. That's worth some money."

"How'd you know what somebody's watch is worth?" The other boy asked.

"My old man's got one just like that. I know what it's worth. Thousands. That's what it's worth. Thousands."

"You're right. This guy's not some kind of bum or something. I mean, if he was some bum or homeless person, it might be different."

"Yeah. I don't know too many bums who drive Porches. That's for sure."

"Think we should take it?" the first boy said.

"Maybe. Why not?" the second boy said. "He won't know the difference. Plus, it'll teach him a lesson. Don't get drunk and pass out in a public garage." The kids laughed.

"Yeah, that's right. Plus, if he's dead—"

"Oh my God," the girl who was going to be a nurse said. "Look he's moving!"

The four stepped back and looked at Billy. With difficulty, Billy pulled himself up by the door handle and sat leaning against the car. His right side was still partially numb and his head throbbed. He looked around and saw the four kids looking down at him. No one said anything. He rubbed his head and struggled to his feet. The four kids just looked at him, surprised that the person whose watch they were planning to filch had just come to life. Billy squeezed his eyes shut and shook his head, like a dog waking from sleep.

"Do you want us to call someone for you?" the soon-to-be nurse said.

"Did you see those guys?" Billy asked.

"Are you okay?"

"I think so. Did anybody see those guys?" All four looked at each other and shook their heads.

"What happened? Did you fall and hit your head on the car? Can you drive? Do you want a cab or something?"

"No. I don't need a cab. Ah. Thanks. I think I can drive home."

"Do you think it's a good idea to drive? I mean, don't you think you've had too much to drink."

"Yeah," the boy said who was going to steal Billy's watch, "if you're too drunk to open your car door without smashing your head into the window, do you really think you should drive?"

"Believe me; I didn't smash my head into the window." Billy turned to open the driver's side door and crumpled to the ground.

The next voice Billy heard was that of his mother warning him to put a hat on before he went outside.

"Billy Tapp. It's freezing out there. Don't you dare leave this house without something on your head. Do you hear me?"

Then he heard Judge Poopvitch. "Mister Tapp. Are you going to be on time this time ... or not? Which one is it—on time or not?"

Then he heard his father say, "Leave the boy alone. He doesn't need to be on time to wear something on his head."

Then he heard Judge Barr say, "He'll be okay. Just take him over to the bench and give him some smelling salts. We need him back in the game."

Then he heard someone say, "Yes. We started an I.V. The left side of his head looks like it's swollen. Look's like more than a fall to me."

Billy opened his eyes just long enough to see the reflection of the flashing red lights and to hear the wail of a siren clearing the way for someone racing someone off to somewhere else. Then he heard more voices and saw more faces, and none of it made a bit of sense to him.

CHAPTER TWENTY-SEVEN

When Billy opened his eyes, Ann was sitting beside his bed; she was holding his right hand and looking at her watch. There was a needle stuck in a vein in the back of his left hand and the wires connected to his chest and his head wound their way to a group of monitors and other apparatuses that beeped and flashed.

"You okay?" she asked. "They said that there aren't any broken bones and you should be fine. They just want to keep you in here to make sure that you don't have any permanent damage or something, brain swelling or whatever. They said that you have a concussion, but you should be alright."

"Yeah. I'm fine. A little bit of a headache, though. How'd you get here?"

"They called me. They said you gave them my name and number and asked them to call me. Don't you remember? I was in the car with the kids. It scared them to death. Don't you remember?"

"Not really. Where are the kids?"

"In school."

"Oh. Are they alright?"

"Yes. Why shouldn't they be?"

"Ah ... no reason. Just wondered. How'd you get here? I mean, why are you here? Where exactly am I?"

Ann looked at her watch. "You're in the hospital. They brought you here last night. About two thirty in the morning. Don't you remember?"

"No. Not really. But thanks for coming. Where are the kids?"

"In school. I guess that I should get going now. You going to be alright?"

"Sure."

"Billy, what in the world happened to you?"

"I don't exactly know. We were in Alexandria. I just left a client after dinner and I was going to my car when some big thug grabbed me. I kicked him in the balls, and the next thing I know ... here I am."

"Right. You kicked him in the balls. Well, I called the police, and I think there's someone here to take your statement, or whatever they do. Listen, I need to get going. I have a meeting at noon. Call me later and let me know how you're doing. If you have time, call Lucy. She knows that you're in the hospital, and you know how she worries about everything."

Ann wasn't gone more than two minutes when a police officer came into the room.

"Good morning, Mr. Tapp. My name is Detective Furman. Do you feel up to giving me a statement?"

"Sure."

Billy adjusted himself in the bed, which made the dull throb in his head even worse. A nurse came into the room. She looked at the machines and the needle in the back of his left hand. She thumped one of the machines with her forefinger.

"How you feeling?"

Without waiting for a response, she smiled at Detective Furman and turned and left the room. Detective Furman took a note pad out of his pocket and put one foot on the chair where Ann had been sitting and rested the pad on his leg.

"What happened?"

Billy explained about walking to his car and being accosted by some big guy whom he'd never seen. Billy explained that he bashed the guy in the nose and kicked him in the balls. Then, some little guy zapped him with something and knocked him in the head.

"Yes sir. They told me that the small spots in your back looked like a Taser gun and the blow to your head was probably from a soft blunt instrument. Looks like you have two little holes in your back." Detective Furman made some notes in his pad and looked up. "You know who did this?"

"Yeah. Sure I know who did this." Billy said sarcastically.

"Who?"

"Who? The two guys that kicked the shit out of me. That's who."

"Mr. Tapp. I'm trying to figure out what happened to you. Do you have a name?"

"A name?"

"Yes. A name."

Billy closed his eyes and tried not to focus on the increased throbbing in his head. "No, I don't have a name."

The cop looked up from his note pad. "I have to tell you, Mr. Tapp, without a name, it's going to be difficult to find out who did this to you. We'll use our best efforts. But we've got lots of cases and sometimes these simple assaults get shuffled down."

"Thank you," Billy said. "All I could expect is your best effort."

"Are you missing anything? Money, rings, jewelry.

Billy closed his eyes again and tried to think if he'd forgotten to tell Detective Furman anything. Furman looked at the bedside table where Billy's wallet, his money clip and his car keys were piled. "I see that they didn't take your money or your wallet. Did you have a watch?"

"I did but—"

"It's not with your wallet. Do you have it on?"

Billy rubbed his left wrist. "No. I don't have it on."

Detective Furman closed his pad and thanked Billy. "If

we figure anything out, we'll call."

Billy pushed the nurses call button and dearly hoped that they would give him something stronger than Tylenol to mask the pain that came from being shot with a Taser gun and bashed in the head with a black sweat sock filed with number nine lead bird shot.

* * * *

"What does Howard Slone or Bethesda Equity or Southeast Financial or Southwest Financial have to do with FSLIC or Federated Loan and Thrift?" Michael Braxton asked Billy.

"I don't exactly know. Not yet anyway. But what I do know is that they all keep showing up in this deal, and I've yet to figure out what in the shit's going on."

"I got a call from my client this morning, and he's not willing to get into some wild goose chase over these other folks. FSLIC is hounding me to get this foreclosure over and done with," Braxton said.

"FSLIC? Who in the hell is FSLIC? I'm talking about a bullshit trumped up foreclosure action against a guy whose project is under budget, ahead of schedule, and *not* in default. When you say FSLIC, who exactly do you mean?"

"Billy Tapp, you know my client is FSLIC … as receiver for Federated. Jerome Morning speaks for FSLIC who speaks for Federated. You know that."

"I know all that. So, let's cut out the crap. You're getting your marching orders from Morning."

"Mr. Morning is my client's representative. He speaks for FSLIC. Don't tell me that you don't understand that."

"Morning's an asshole."

"Well, not to put too fine of a point on it, in this line of work, I don't think being an asshole is necessarily disqualifying or, for that matter, even unusual."

"In this case it should be."

"Billy, you're going to have to convince the judge that the information you're looking for is either relevant to this lawsuit or somehow calculated to lead to relevant evidence. Look. I personally don't care. It all pays the same for me. You're just one more of the pile of files in my office."

"Michael. I know the law and I know the rules. But that's all so much bullshit. What I'm talking about here is finding out what the fuck's going on. Don't you wonder about that?"

Michael Braxton hesitated. "Not really. If you want the information that you're asking about, you're going to have to get an order from Poopvitch. Morning has instructed me to object to any question about Slone or Bethesda Equity or Southwest Financial or Southeast Financial. Those are my marching orders. I guess you'll have to file a motion to compel."

Billy rubbed his chin and sensed the eminent force that judicial caprice was about to aggravate his still sore and slightly swollen head. He hadn't yet put it all together, but he suspected that the Honorable Judge Poopvitch was about to administer the next beating he would take in the Seymour Grey Frederick Mall foreclosure case.

* * * *

"Mr. Tapp. Now you're asking the court to make Mr. Braxton answer a number of questions that relate to people and entities that aren't even parties to this lawsuit. Do I understand that correctly?"

"That's right. But they should be, and I'll soon make them parties."

"This looks to me like this is a simple foreclosure action. Your client apparently is in default of the loan and FSLIC wants to foreclose. Isn't that about it?"

"Yes. That's about it, but that's not all of it."

"About it. All of it. What are you talking about, Mr. Tapp?"

"There are a couple of lenders that should be named as defendants in this matter."

"Well, name them then."

"That's why I sent the interrogatories and request for production of documents to FSLIC. Before I file a gob of unnecessary pleadings, I want to find out what these other lenders' interest is in this mess."

"Gob. Mess. What do you say, Mr. Braxton. What does FSLIC have to say about Mr. Tapp's inquires in this lawsuit?"

"FSLIC doesn't think that these questions have anything to do with whether Mr. Grey is in default of his loan."

"They may. That makes the questions relevant. What I already know is that Bethesda Equity is owned or controlled by some guy named Howard Slone. And it looks like this Slone character also has something to do with Southwest Financial and Southeast Financial ... whatever in the world these two entities are," Billy said.

"How do they have anything to do with this foreclosure?" the judge asked.

"Because the loans are secured by liens on the property. Mr. Braxton knows that. I told him."

"But what do they have to do with Mr. Grey?"

"Judge. It's basic real estate law. If FSLIC wants title—"

"Title, Mr. Tapp. Why does FSLIC want title? They want to foreclose. Isn't that what they want?"

Billy looked up at the ceiling and then over at Michael Braxton, who had slouched down in his chair at counsel's table. He sat with both feet flat on the floor and his hands, palm down, on the table. When he caught Billy's eye, he quickly looked down and ever so slightly bowed his head.

"Was the question, why does FSLIC want title? Did I understand that that was the question?"

Judge Poopvitch leaned forward in his chair and nodded his head. "That's right, Mr. Tapp. That was the question."

"Go Poop," Billy said under his breath. A noticeable look of terror flashed across Braxton's face and he recoiled like he'd been zapped by the Taser gun that left its fang marks on Billy's back.

"What was that, Mr. Tapp?"

"I said, Judge Poopvitch ... but I didn't finish my

sentence."

"Well I couldn't really hear what you said, but go on."

"Judge Poop ... vitch. The only way FSLIC can sell the property ... what I should say ... is the only way anybody will buy the property is if FSLIC can deliver a clear title. Which, as you know, means all the lien holders have to be parties to this foreclosure action."

The judge looked at Michael Braxton, who all but leaped to his feet. "That's right, but Mr. Tapp filed a motion to compel FSLIC to answer questions and produce some documents, I don't see what that has to do with adding other parties."

"I'm just trying to kill two birds with one stone. I could have filed a motion to bring in these other folks and had a hearing and then sent the discovery requests and then had another hearing. But wouldn't that have been just more time consuming and we'd end up where we end up anyway? I'm just trying to save time and money ... both my client's and the court's."

"I appreciate your concern, Mr. Tapp, but you worry about your client and I'll worry about the court." Judge Poopvitch smiled.

"Could I make a suggestion?" Billy asked.

"A suggestion? Certainly, Mr. Tapp. What's your suggestion?"

"Let me take Mr. Slone's deposition. I'll agree to continue my motion to compel responses to my discovery requests. And I'll agree that Michael can amend his complaint to include Bethesda Equity, Southwest Financial and Southeast Financial."

"Mr. Braxton, what do you say?" the judge asked.

"If it please the court. Fine by me ... by FSLIC. I actually have the amended complaint here with me in court today. I'll file it right now in open court. If it please the court."

Michael Braxton handed the amended complaint to the bailiff who handed it to the judge, who handed it to his law clerk, who handed it to the court clerk, who stuck it in a file.

"Consider it filed," the judge said. Judge Poopvitch pushed his glasses up on his nose and tapped his pencil on the bench. He leaned back in the leather chair that featured ornate griffin heads carved on either side of the oversized red leather back. He placed the pencil on the legal pad he'd been doodling, put his hand behind his head and squeezed his eyes shut. *Why must I deal with these damn lawyers who keep reciting the most technical points of the law?* "Is there anything else gentlemen? If not, let the court be in recess."

"All rise," the bailiff said, "the court is in recess."

CHAPTER TWENTY-EIGHT

Jerome Morning sat behind Joe Franklin's desk in Joe Franklin's office on the third floor of Dozier Mound's Spanish Colonial Federated Savings and Loan building. Franklin's office door off the balcony was open. Morning watched one of the large ceiling fans making its slow rotation over the lobby below. If he still had anything to do with it, when all is said and done, those ridiculous fans will be the first to go. He'd see that someone replaced them with something a little more appropriate, more in keeping with his image of a proper financial institution. The anecdotal Mexican murals in the ceiling would be the next to go. He didn't think scenes of Mexican peasants chopping on cactus have to do with banking. Or, how a pack-donkey with two brown bags slung over its back was relevant to anything at Federated Savings and Loan. Things would change; it was just a matter of time. He knew that Howard Slone and Miguel Sanchez had plans. He didn't know all the details, but he was reasonably certain they included Federated Savings and Loan and him—Jerome Morning.

"Mr. Morning," the secretary who replaced Franklin's assistant of twelve years said over the intercom. "You have a call on line two."

"Take a message," Morning quickly responded. "I'm right

251

in the middle of something."

After a short pause, the secretary said, "It's Mr. Slone. He said ... he said to tell you ... well ... he didn't care if you were in the middle of something, to tell you to pick up the phone up. Sorry."

"Right. Right. That's fine. You should tell me when it's Mr. Slone. We always take his call."

Morning pushed the flashing button for line two. "Jerome Morning. Hello, Mr. Slone. Hold just a moment and let me close my door." Morning placed the telephone receiver on his desk and dashed to the door and dashed back to Franklin's desk.

"... and, further more, I want to know what the fuck's going on with that ass-hole."

"Who?"

"Who? Haven't you been listening?"

"Oh. Sorry. I put you on hold, or I actually put the phone down so I could close the door to my office. I didn't hear what you were saying."

"I understand from reliable sources that, despite some ... shall we say ... ancillary prompting, this Billy Tapp lawyer is still causing some concern. When was the last time you talked to Michael Braxton? The FSLIC attorney."

"He called yesterday, but I didn't talk to him."

"Didn't talk to him? God damn it, Morning. Call the son-of-a-bitch and call me back. Do it right now!" Slone slammed the telephone down before he heard Morning say, "Yes sir. Right away sir. I will do it right now."

Morning hung up Franklin's telephone and pushed the button for the secretary. No one answered. "Hell," he said and looked at the clock hanging on the wall, which said five minutes before twelve. "Hell," he said again. After a few minutes of fumbling through the electronic card file, he found Michael Braxton's telephone number.

"Yes, Mr. Braxton. Jerome Morning here. Federated Savings and Loan."

"Yep. Good morning, Mr. Morning ... it's still morning,

isn't it? How are you? How can I help you today?

"Right. Checking on the case. The foreclosure. We have some things in the mill. We are wondering what the schedule is, when the Frederick Mall property will come up. We would like to get this one off the books and wrapped up. If you know what I mean."

"I know what you mean. But apparently there are some other liens on the property and we need to amend the complaint in the lawsuit and add a few more parties as defendants. That's going to add a little bit more time to the whole process."

"Do you have any idea of how much more time?"

"Not really. It shouldn't be too much. Maybe four or five months. It all depends on—"

"Five months? This process has been going on for some time now. Is it possible to shorten the five months?"

"Sure. Possible. But the borrower, Seymour Grey, has hired a lawyer named Billy Tapp. He's sort of a wild card. When Tapp is sober and focused, there isn't anybody better. From what Tapp has said to me so far, he thinks that he's about to get his teeth into something ... I don't know what ... but chances are that won't shorten the process. If you know what I mean. Oh. And, by the way, I don't know if he's sober right now, but I'm pretty sure that he's focused."

"I suppose that I know what you mean. But focused? Focused on what?"

"I don't know all the details yet. But apparently Tapp thinks that there's something strange going on with these liens. He called me the other day, but we didn't have time to talk in any great detail. He said something about some off-shore check or account or something. And, something about the mortgage papers not being properly filled out or something. I don't know all the details. We're supposed to get together some time later this week and he's going to show me what he has."

"I know that he has sent some questions for me to answer."

"That's right. I sent them on to you. It's called discovery; they're what we call interrogatories and request for production of documents. We need to get those answered as soon as possible."

"Right. I received your package. I suppose I should get to it."

"The more I think about it, maybe you should wait until I talk to Billy—"

"Billy?" Morning asked.

"Yes. He's filed a motion to bring in three other defendants that he thinks have a stake in this thing. I looked at the motion and can't see any legal reason to oppose it. In fact, if Tapp hadn't filed it, I would have added them as defendants. They're necessary parties. If you know what I mean?

"Who is this Mr. Tapp trying to include?"

"Three lenders. One in Bethesda, one in Florida and one out in the southwest. If you give me a moment or two, I'll pull the motion and read it to you."

"Very good. But I do not think that will be—"

"Ah. Here they are. Wait a minute. I'm sorry. I must be losing my mind. Billy Tapp didn't amend the complaint. I did. I don't know how I could have forgotten that. I guess I have too many cases to keep track. Billy gave me the information, he made copies of the filings in Frederick and I amended the complaint in open court. Open court. Now, how in the world could I have forgotten that? The names of the added defendants are: Bethesda Equity, Southeast Financial, and Southwest Financial. Do you want me to fax them to—"

"Bloody hell." Jerome Morning muttered and hung up the telephone.

* * * *

Miguel Sanchez met Howard Slone in the Round Robin Bar of the Willard Hotel. Slone sat at a table, with a pretty young girl hanging on his diminutive left arm sipping on a Bombay Sapphire martini. She whispered something in Slone's ear and then giggled. Slone looked up from his glass of single malt scotch. The flickering light from the candle on the table top lapped on his shiny bald head. The dim room and candle light accentuated Slone's hawk like nose and his upturned pointed chin. He looked like a five-foot-four-inch tall warlock in a very expensive suit. Sanchez walked over to the table where Slone and the girl sat.

"My friend, Howard. How are you?"

"Miguel. It is good to see you." Slone reached across the table to shake hands with Sanchez. The candle light reflected off his gold cufflinks. "Have a seat. What would you like to drink?"

Howard looked at the girl. "Would you like to finish up here before we talk?"

"Oh, of course. We were just chatting." Slone turned to the girl. "Beat it. I'll call you later."

She stuck out her lower lip and whispered again in Slone's ear. He jerked his head back and handed her a room key under the table. She kissed him on the cheek and gulped the rest of her martini and gathered her purse and sashayed out of the Round Robin Bar, with a final theatrical glance back over her shoulder. Sanchez took the seat that was opposite where the girl had been sitting.

"Howard, my friend. Where ees the Frederick Mall deal? We are ready to go on our side of the deal. What do you think, my friend?"

"We have a couple of minor problems to iron out. Nothing that should take too long. I'm flying out to Houston tomorrow to meet with Jerome Morning. Why don't you come along, if you like."

"That is very generous, my friend, but I must be in Washington for some other business this week. Maybe we could talk later in the week about our next steps. What does our friend Jerome Morning tell us?"

"Good question," Slone said and took a drink of his

scotch. "I talked to him a little while ago. He's called me back a few times, but I haven't talked today. I'll call him back in an hour or so."

"So, my friend. Let's drink to our success." Miguel Sanchez motioned to the waitress who had been talking to the bartender and not paying attention to the two customers sitting at tables.

"Miss. Hey Miss."

Slone motioned with his empty glass. The waitress looked up and Slone motioned for her to come. It was evident that this wasn't Slone's first drink.

"She ees coming, my friend."

"She has two tables to wait on, and she can't even do that."

"Howard, she has other things on her mind. Maybe a boyfriend or a date tonight. Who knows with young people? Especially one so beautiful." Miguel smiled at Slone. "Ees okay."

"Something on her mind? Huh. Yes, and so do I."

* * * *

The ER doctor at the hospital discharged Billy with instructions to call if the pain didn't go away in a few days and to be careful driving or if he felt dizzy or sleepy or confused or if he had memory problems or was nauseous.

"If I call you every time I feel dizzy or nauseous," Billy told the young emergency room doctor, "you wouldn't have time for any other patients."

"A concussion could be serious. Either call me or your family doctor."

Billy called his college friend and former Navy pilot who now practiced family medicine and got the same advice, which Billy gave equal deference.

"Thanks, John," Billy said.

He promised to call if any of his all too familiar hangover symptoms lingered longer than normal or weren't ameliorated by the hair of the dog. The pain in the side of his head was all but gone. Billy decided that a cold beer and a consult with Robert Bob might be a better prescription than the rest and aspirin that both doctors suggested.

"Vickie, any calls?"

"Nothing important. Seymour. Jason. Your latest strumpet from Frederick."

"I beg your pardon. I have only one strumpet from Frederick. So, to be precise, she can't be the latest, and more to the point, she's not a strumpet."

"I know. Just kidding. The only pleasure I get working for you, Mr. Tapp."

"Please …"

"Seriously, though, Seymour Grey is in town; he wants to get together. And Jason called to meet you for a beer at Clyde's. Valerie … I think that's her name—"

"Where did Seymour say he was staying?"

"He didn't say, but he usually stays somewhere downtown, doesn't he? Oh. Wait a minute; he's staying at the Willard. Room 814. He said that he'd call you tomorrow. That he had something to do later tonight."

"Thanks. It's almost five o'clock. You may as well go home. See you tomorrow."

Billy shut his cell phone and told the foreign cab driver to drop him at 3236 M Street in Georgetown. He had dropped his Porsche at the dealership and the service manager told him it would be ready in the morning. When the cab stopped in front of Clyde's, Billy handed the turban-headed driver a twenty dollar bill.

"Thanks. Keep the change."

"Velcome." The cab driver nodded, and with a smile sped off.

Jason sat at Billy's customary table to the right of the door. He was talking on his cell phone and waved to Billy. Robert Bob stood behind the bar and gave Billy the usual exaggerated salute.

"Mr. Tapp, welcome to Clyde's."

"Thank you, sweet bartender. Perhaps a cold beer for the parched rabble."

Billy went over to the table where Jason sat and took a seat with his back to the wall.

"How's your head?"

"No problems."

"Cops have any ideas? You got any ideas?"

"Cops don't have a clue. Me. Here's what I think. I think ... no ... I'm sure that those assholes who bounced my head off the parking garage floor also had something to do with the Frederick Mall foreclosure."

"Why do you say that?"

"Because, it seems like I remember one of them saying something about me getting in over my head or getting into something that I shouldn't be or something. I really can't remember exactly, but that's in the back of my mind somewhere."

"Did you tell that to the police?"

"I don't think so. It just occurred to me. I didn't remember it until about an hour ago when I dropped my car at the shop to have the window fixed."

"How would the Frederick Mall have anything to do with you getting mugged in the parking garage over in Alexandria?"

"Well, I talked to Michael Braxton, you know the assistant U.S. attorney who's handling the foreclosure for FSLIC. I told him that I thought there was something strange going on with the liens filed for the first mortgage and a second mortgage for the shopping center. Some of the documents looked incomplete and were missing some dollar amounts. After I talked to Braxton, Braxton talked to this Jerome Morning, who is FSLIC's guy now in charge of Federated in Houston. Braxton called me back and said that Morning was pissed off and wouldn't cooperate in any way with me or Seymour Grey, and that he just wanted the foreclosure done and over with, and the property sold."

"Just because FSLIC wants to get things wrapped up,

doesn't seem like a motive to beat up the borrower's attorney."

"Normally, I'd say you're right. But this isn't a normal situation. Grey's deal was on time and under budget and not in default. There's more to it than a simple foreclosure."

CHAPTER TWENTY-NINE

Billy's mother, Ruth Tapp, stood in the dining room in front of the large fireplace that took up most of the wall at the far end of the long table. She had put all the dishes that were left in the sink into the dishwasher and wiped clean the red granite countertop and the six-burner commercial gas range. She actually found the mop in the small but surprisingly well organized pantry and wet-mopped the kitchen floor. Lucy sat at the opposite end of the dining room table doing homework. John and Tom were in the library on the second floor watching the television and playing a video game. It wasn't dark yet, and on this rare Thursday evening, Billy left Clyde's before midnight. The pain had returned to the side of his head, and he rode a taxi cab the few blocks from Clyde's to his townhouse in Georgetown.

"Mom. Lucy. What are y'all doing here?"

"Hello, William. We didn't know when to expect you. How are you feeling? Let me see your head."

"Daddy. Hi." Lucy looked up from her homework and gave Billy a quick hug. "Let me see your head too. I can't see anything. Guess you must be okay."

She stepped back and looked at Billy's head again before returning to her books.

These days Ruth Tapp was spending more time in

Washington because Billy's younger brother had been transferred by his small technology company to Chevy Chase. Although Billy enjoyed his brother's company, the transfer to Chevy Chase made it more convenient for his mother's increasingly frequent visits and long stays, which often conflicted with his carousing and the feelings every child is expected to have for a parent.

"I didn't know you were going to be here. How did you get in?"

Lucy looked up from her book and reached into her back pack. She pulled out a keychain with a pink fuzzy animal of some kind and one key. She tapped the key on the dining room table.

"Duh ... Dad. Like ... a key. We used the key that you gave me."

"Oh yeah. That's right. Where are the boys?"

"In the library, thank Gawd," Lucy said. "They're playing one of those stupid video games that you have. They're such dorks."

"Now Lucy. You shouldn't talk about your brothers like that. Someday you'll be glad you have brothers."

"I don't think so, Grandma," Lucy said sarcastically.

"Did you have a late day at the office William?"

"Yeah. But I had a meeting with another lawyer. We were tied up for a while. Jason Robert. You've met him. We were in law school together. Don't you remember?"

"Yes, I remember. Isn't he that well-mannered colored boy you used to have as a friend?"

"Grandma! You mean African-American ... or black ... not *colored!* Jason is dad's best friend. He's not a boy and he's not colored. Pa-lease don't tell me you're prejudice; you're not a bigot, are you Grandma?"

"No, sweetheart, I'm just old and behind the times, I guess. Anyway, what's in a name? I didn't mean to offend you, Lucy."

"You didn't offend me. It's just that ... oh well, never mind."

"All right," Billy said. "Enough. I don't know if Jason is African-American or black or colored or whatever. What I do know is he's a person, and he's my friend. Conversation over."

"Well you don't have to be so snippy," Billy's mother said.

"Oh, I mean, like duh ..." Lucy said and went back to her homework.

"So, Mom, what brings you and the kids here?"

"I was at your brother's house ... he invited me to visit, even though he has less extra room than you do ... since I couldn't get hold of you, I called Ann to see how you were doing. She said that she might have a meeting late tonight and I could take the kids if I wanted to. So I did. We were in Georgetown getting a bite to eat when we decided to come over and see you. We didn't know you wouldn't be here. You don't mind, do you? Have you had anything to eat tonight? Do you want me to fix you something? Do you have anything here?"

"No thanks. I ate at Clyde's with Jason. Lucy, have you eaten yet?" Lucy didn't look up. "Lucy."

"Daaaad. Didn't you hear what Grandma said? We ate before we came here. And that makes me like so not hungry now. Like zero appetite."

Billy walked into the kitchen and took a beer out of the stainless steel double refrigerator. The beer cap fell from his hand and rattled to the tile floor. He took a swig and sat the opened beer on the ledge of the pass-through that doubled as a breakfast counter on the dining room side and provided service from the Pullman kitchen to the dining room. He shuffled through the day's mail that Lucy or someone left on the kitchen counter. His mother came over to the dining room side of the pass-through and sat on one of the three tall stools.

"Don't you think you've had enough to drink?" She scowled at Billy. Lucy looked up from her homework and rolled her eyes at the ceiling, then resumed her studies.

Without saying anything, Billy took a long gulp of the beer

and walked up one flight of stairs to the library. Tom and John were sitting on the blue pleated leather couch watching the television. Billy gave each kid a hug, while they pulled themselves sideways to keep Billy out of their sight-line to the television.

"Am I interrupting anything?" Billy asked jokingly.

"Dad, we're trying to play ... get out of the way," Tom said.

"Sorry."

"Oh, Dad," John said. "Some guy named Sizemore or See ... something called. He said he'd call you back later or in the morning."

"See something?" Billy thought for a moment. "He didn't say Seymour, did he?"

"Yeah. That's it, Seymour. He seemed real nice. He said he was a friend of yours. I think that's what he said.

Shhhhh," Tom said, "I'm trying to get the dragon out of the ..."

The kids spent the night and Billy's mother slept with Lucy. He left early the next day before anyone was out of bed. He left a note on the kitchen counter saying that he'd be back around noon, and they'd all go to lunch together. He told them that he had to go out to the jail and talk with a client.

* * * *

"I'm here to see Thackeray Frederick Johnson. I'm Billy Tapp, his lawyer."

The guard looked up from the paperback book he was reading and then picked up the telephone and pushed a button. He put the paperback book upside down on the desk and leaned back in the wooden chair. After a few minutes and not having said the first word, the guard hung up the telephone and fixed his gaze on Billy.

"You his lawyer?"

"Right. That's what I said. I'm Billy Tapp. I'm his

lawyer."

"Who you here to see?"

"Thackeray Frederick Johnson."

"He expecting you?"

"You'll have to ask him that. I frankly don't know what he's expecting."

"Look here, Billy Tapp, it isn't going to do you much good to get smart with me. I can't let every asshole who walks in here see anybody he wants to."

"First of all, I'm not every asshole. I'm Johnson's attorney." Billy laid his bar identification card in the passage way under the bullet proof glass that separated him from the guard. "And, second I don't want to just see anybody; I want to see Mr. Johnson. Is there a problem with that?"

The guard picked up the telephone again. "Captain, this is the front cage. There's some guy here to see a prisoner. Yeah. Tapp. I don't know, Billy, I think. Johnson. Thackeray Frederick. Yes, sir. Tapp. Yes, sir." The guard hung up the telephone and stood up. "Mr. Tapp, Earl said that they'll bring Johnson up right away. He'll be in the interview cell. That okay with you?"

"It's okay with me ... because I can leave when I'm done."

A few minutes later Earl Sabatini came through the gunmetal grey door at the end of the hallway, walking behind Thackeray Frederick Johnson, who was shackled at the ankles but not handcuffed. Earl and Johnson were both laughing.

"Here he is, Billy. When are you going to get him out of my hair?"

"Listen, boss," Johnson said. "The sooner I gets my po ass outa dis shit hole da happier we both be. Ha. Ha. Ha. I damn sure used to better jailhouse dan dis here in-stitution." Sabatini playfully slapped Johnson on the side of the head and guided him into the interview cell off the lobby.

"Is this private enough for you, Billy?"

"Sure. This okay with you Thackeray?"

"Don' make shit to my po ass."

"You want the door locked?" Sabatini asked Billy.

"Now jus where you motha fuckers think I gonna go, wif dese chain wrapped up on me, like some po field slave. What ya'll talkin' 'bout? Ya'll got me locked fo sho. But you ain't got my soul locked up. That not in chains. You ain't ever gonna get that locked up in no han' cuff or chains. Bet yo ass."

When Billy went into the interview cell after Johnson, Earl Sabatini pushed the door shut but didn't lock it. Earl opened the door and handed Johnson an unopened pack of cigarettes. "Here's your cigarettes. I meant to give them to you earlier. Let me know when you're done."

"Have you had time to think about what you want to do?" Billy asked.

"Yes, sir. Ahs been thinkin."

"You understand what they've offered, don't you?"

"Yep. Day offers me jail or mo jail. Dat's 'bout it."

"You remember what I told you. They offered 151 to 188 months or twelve and a half years to a little more than fifteen years for a guilty plea, but potentially an additional more than nine years if we go to trial and lose. Do you understand all that? I don't see how you can win a trial. They got you dead to rights."

"I understands mo' than you thinks I do."

'I don't think you have a choice—"

"Don' chu kid yo self. I gotta choice. Jes ain't a good choice. I don' guess I need some damn court appointed law-yer tellin' me what my choice is. I know my choices, jes none of dem worf a shit."

"Should I tell them that we'll take the plea offer?"

"Ain't no motha fuckin' we. Way I see it, it's *me*. Not we. I got no choice. I'm gonna die in da jailhouse anyways. What's the difference? Tell da motha fuckers that I'll take it. One more po nigger off to jail. Outta the cotton field into the jailhouse. Every man created equal is just a crock a shit."

* * * *

265

When Billy got back to his townhouse in Georgetown, his mother and the children were gone. Lucy had scribbled on the note he left for them that they were going to look for shoes and if he still wanted to, they could meet him somewhere for lunch. She also said that Seymour had called and wanted Billy to call him back. It was already almost three o'clock and he wondered if his mother and the kids would still be hungry. He called Lucy's cell phone and she answered after the first ring.

"Daddy. Where are you? We're starved."

"Great. Well, not great that you're starved, but great that you haven't eaten yet. I'm at home, where do you want to meet."

"That's easy. We want to go to Clyde's where you go all the time."

"Ah ... Clyde's. Are you sure that—"

"Just kidding. Gawd. Can't you tell when I'm joking? Can you see Grandma in Clyde's?" Lucky asked.

"How do you know what it's like in Clyde's?"

"Don't worry, Daddy, I have my sources."

"Alright, Sherlock Holmes, where do you want me to meet you?"

"The Green Thumb. You know that's my favorite place in all the world."

"The Green Thumb? Do they sell hamburgers there? I can't go someplace where they only serve plant-life. I won't eat anything that didn't walk around before it was killed ... and it had to suffer before it died. Okay."

"Daddy. You are such a bore ... and you're not the least bit funny."

"See you in fifteen minutes. If you beat me there, go ahead and get a table. I'll be there shortly."

At three-thirty in the afternoon, The Green Thumb was all but deserted. The usual gathering of patrons wearing long skirts, flannel shirts, and denim had left. Two of the skeleton wait staff lingered by the kitchen door and looked over the mostly empty dining room, filled with several four-top tables covered with oil-cloth and surrounded by rather substantial looking wooden chairs. Lucy, the boys, and his mother sat at two tables that had been pushed together next to the window.

"Have ya'll ordered yet? Billy asked.

"Nope. We just got here," John said. "What can I have to eat?"

"Whatever you want. What are you having, Mom?" Billy asked.

"I'm not real hungry. I hate to waste food, with people starving all over the world. I don't want to think how much food goes to waste in this place."

"I want a cheeseburger and French fries," Tom said.

"Me too," John said.

"You two are heathens," Lucy said. "I bring you to a restaurant where you can actually get something that's healthy and you want meat and fried potatoes. You'll both die before you graduate from high school, which would be no big loss. You're both too stupid to graduate anyway."

Tom turned from his grandmother and flashed Lucy the bird. She looked at Tom's extended finger then at Billy, then at Tom, then at Billy. She closed her eyes and said, "I hate you, I hate you, I hate you."

"What's that?" Billy's mother asked.

Lucy ignored her grandmother and opened the large menu and placed it, as a screen, between Tom and her.

"Oh nothing, Grandma, just a turd in the punchbowl."

"What did you say?" Billy's mother asked.

"Er ... I said that there's a bird in the lunch bowl." Lucy looked at Billy and he winked. "It's a kind of salad. A The Green Thumb specialty."

"Yeah, right," Tom said.

"Enough. Both of you," Billy said.

"What's in the bird salad? Maybe that's what I'll get," Billy's mother said.

"I don't think you'd like it, Grandma."

"Why is that?"

"Well ... because it has feathers in it ... for decoration," Lucy said. "But—"

"Feathers? You're right. I don't think that I would like that."

"Lucy," Billy said with a slight head shake. "That's enough."

No sooner had the waitress brought Lucy her vegetable medley, Tom and John their cheeseburgers and French fries, Billy's mother a small green salad, and Billy his Hot Brown, when Billy's cell phone rang. Contrary to his custom, although he didn't recognize the number, he answered the call.

"Counselor. Grey here. Do you have a moment to talk?"

CHAPTER THIRTY

Seymour told Billy that if there was any way possible, he wanted to meet right away. He was staying at the Willard hotel—the same place that Slone was staying—a coincidence that concerned Billy.

"I'm having a late lunch with my mother and my kids right now. I need to stop by the shop this afternoon and pick up my car before five o'clock. When do you want to get together?"

"Call me after you get your car. I will meet you at the bar here. I may have some good news."

Billy's mother said, "Ann is coming by to pick up the kids and then I'm going to your brother's house. Ann said that she would take me. I guess you're too busy."

Billy paid the bill and he passed Ann coming in the door on his way out of the restaurant. "I have to pick up my car. They replaced the window."

Ann stopped and looked at Billy's head and waved her hand in a half-hearted gesture of disgust. Without another word, she went over to the table that Billy had just abandoned and took his seat. A cab waited at the curb and Billy gave directions to the Porsche dealership. Thirty minutes later, he was walking into the elaborate lobby of the Willard Hotel. For reasons that he didn't want to explain, instead of going to the bar, he went directly to the front desk.

"I'm here to see Mr. Slone."

The clerk looked up over his reading glasses, but didn't say anything.

"He's expecting me. He said that he'd leave a message for me with the concierge."

The clerk turned to the bank of pigeon holes that corresponded to the rooms at the Willard and then typed something into the computer. "Miguel Sanchez?"

"No. That's not me. John Slone is expecting me. Didn't John leave word?"

"Oh. John Slone. I see. We don't have a John Slone here. I'm sorry, there must be some mistake. We don't have a guest … there's nothing for a John Slone. What did you say your name was?"

Without responding, Billy turned and walked past the elevator bank, the six-foot tall ornate pottery vase and into the Round Robin Bar. Seymour sat by himself at the end of the mahogany bar, sipping from a generously poured glass of red wine.

"Counselor," Seymour said and stood to shake Billy's hand. "Let's sit over there at that table." Seymour waved to the bartender and pointed at the bottle of wine on the bar. "We're moving to a table, could you bring another glass?" Seymour asked with a smile.

"Earlier this week, out of the clear blue sky, I received a call from Howard Slone. It goes without saying that I was slightly taken aback. Although, we have never had cross words, based on recent discussions between you and me, I surmised that there may be some growing … shall we say … animosity." Seymour hesitated for a moment. "Oh. By the by. I meant to ask, how are you feeling? I did not mean to be so rude."

"I'm fine. Just fine."

"So anyway. Slone calls me and … as friendly as he could possibly be … he asks if we can get together and talk about a solution to the Frederick Mall problem. Naturally, I said yes.

I asked him if it would make sense to include you in the discussion, and he was rather insistent that just he and I meet. He said we could always bring in the shysters, as he called them ... his words not mine ... and, of course I agreed to meet. I flew up from Houston yesterday and met with Slone here in the hotel."

Although concerned, but not surprised, Billy said, "You know the foreclosure complaint was amended to add Slone's companies as additional defendants. You know that was just done? You don't suppose that had anything to do with Slone calling you?" Billy asked as he rubbed the side of his head.

"I suppose I knew about the amendments. I did not know when they took effect, or whatever you call it."

"What did Slone have in mind? I can't wait to hear this." Billy took a swallow of the red wine that Seymour had poured in the large round crystal glass that the bartender placed on the table in front of Billy.

"He tells me that he is interested in protecting his investment and ... as if I do not already know it ... if something is not done soon, there is a chance of losing the key tenants. He is right."

"We met here in the hotel, in the Willard Room Restaurant. By the by a fine French cuisine, but not nearly as charming as La Rouge and the beautiful Madame Claret. But then ..." Seymour took another drink of his wine. "What do you think of the wine, Counselor?"

"Ahhh ... it's great. What did Slone have to say?"

"Would you like an appetizer or something to compliment the wine?"

"No. What's the deal with Slone?"

"Yes ... Slone. Well, he wants to make a deal."

"A deal?"

"Yes. A deal," Seymour said with a smile.

"What the fuck does that mean? How can he make a deal?"

Seymour waved at the bartender and discretely motioned for him. The bartender disappeared and a matronly waitress appeared at the table. "Oui m'sieur," she said in a fake French accent, "can I get you something?"

"Yes," Seymour said, "could you bring us an appetizer menu ... or do you have a recommendation? Counselor, do you have a preference?"

"Well, I'd actually like to hear what Slone had to say, but short of that, get whatever you like. I just had a late lunch with the kids and my mother."

"We have zee tuna tar-tar zat ez magnific."

"Perfect. We will take an order. Will that be enough for two?"

"Non. I don' theeenk zo."

"Very well, then. Two orders please."

"Oui."

Billy thumped his wine glass with his index finger and it emitted a delicate ring. "Seymour. What did Slone have to say?"

"Well, he offered to buy in as my partner." Seymour took another drink of his wine. He leaned forward, canted his head and gave Billy what appeared to be a wide-eyed gesture of mild surprise.

"Your partner? What the fuck does that mean? I suspect this is the asshole responsible for damn near bashing my head in and now he wants to be your partner!"

"Let us not jump to conclusions, counselor. He wants me to think about it and then all of us get together and work out the details. He told me that one of his companies has a substantial amount of cash 'on the sideline' as he called it. And, this would be a good time to get in a deal. He said it would be beneficial for both of us."

"Was anyone else with Slone when ya'll talked?"

"No. But some gentleman came over to the table and whispered in Howard's ear."

"Do you know who it was? Did you get a name?"

"No. From his dress and demeanor, he looked to be Latino. Mexican? Howard did not introduce him to me, and I did not ask."

"What did you tell Slone?"

"I did not ask who it was. I did not think it was any of my business."

"Not that. I mean about him being your partner."

"Naturally, I said that I was very interested and looked forward to working out the details. He suggested we do that right away and I agreed."

The table where Seymour and Billy sat allowed a limited view into the lobby. At the same time the tuna tar-tar arrived, Billy saw three men walk past the entrance to the Round Robin Bar. A short bald, well-dressed man, a larger barrel-chested black haired man with a thick mustache, and a man of average stature who looked as fit as an aerobics instructor.

* * * *

Mary Jacobs left a message on Billy's office answering service that the doctors at the hospital were taking Terry back to surgery because his ruptured colon was still leaking and his temperature was over one hundred and ten degrees. She said that she was afraid that he was going to die.

Mary and her children came to D.C. looking for work and leaving her husband, an abusive out of work deep miner, in Grundy, Virginia. Mary found a job at the Washington Dulles International Airport that not only paid a decent wage, but provided health insurance benefits. She worked an eight hour shift and, with her two youngest kids, settled into a small but adequate three bedroom and one bathroom shotgun house near the airport. No sooner were they settled than her husband—without a job and his only source of income a small disability check from a mine injury—straggled his way back into their lives.

Terry's father slept all day and drank all night. With gut-wrenching predictability, the family's living conditions became increasingly tense at the end of each month. That's when Terry's father had drunk his entire disability check and he would either cajole or steal money from Mary that she had fastidiously allocated for food, car payment, utilities, rent, and other minimal living expenses. It was during such a time that Fortuna's capricious wheel brought Mary Jacobs to Billy Tapp.

Mary worked a regular shift at Dulles from eight a.m. to five p.m. in housekeeping. She was dependable, reliable, and never complained—an exception to the rule. One afternoon a bus-boy failed to show up for work at the MetroWind cocktail lounge, which was located at the far end of the main concourse at the Washington Dulles International Airport. Out of frustration more than need, the bar manager drafted Mary to stand in for the missing employee. As luck would have it, on the same day one of the bartenders also failed to show up. The head bartender saw Mary bussing the tables. He asked her if she had ever tended bar, and contrary to her nature and at the expense of not telling the whole truth, Mary seized the opportunity.

"Yes," Mary said.

"Good," the head bartender said, "Here's a shirt. Go in the back room and change into it and I'll show you what you need to do. Think you can handle it?"

"Yes," Mary said.

Mary stumbled through the shift and, at the end of the night, her share of the tips came to slightly more than one hundred and seventy-five dollars. The head bartender came up to her and said, "Would you like a full time job as a bartender?"

"Yes," Mary said. She showed up for work the next morning in housekeeping and told her supervisor what happened the night before and asked if it would be too much of a problem for her to quit housekeeping and take the job as a bartender.

"It will about double my pay," Mary said, "I hope it won't cause you too much trouble. I could use the money. I could work both jobs until you find someone to take my place."

"Lordie, have mercy. Are you a fool or what? Two jobs? Girlfriend, that'd be your death. No, honey. You take that job and God bless."

Despite National Airport, now called Ronald Reagan Washington National Airport, located just across the Potomac in Arlington, Virginia, being measurably more convenient for Billy, he occasionally took commercial flights out of Dulles because of schedule and cost. On one such occasion, while waiting for a nonstop flight to Phoenix, Billy found himself in the MetroWind bar at the end of the main concourse. Mary Jacobs was his bartender.

"You got any kids?" Billy asked.

"Yes. Three. Two boys and one girl. Only two living with me, though," Mary said. "They're a handful. We just moved here, and I think they're having trouble making friends. I got a sister here and my son gets along with his cousins, but still moving is tough on kids."

"I got one girl and two boys. Guess, I should say we've got. Mostly she's got. I'm divorced. Yeah. Sometimes kids don't understand change."

"I'm sorry," Mary said. "I'm not. Not yet anyway. I don't know how to go about it. I guess I need to though."

"Let me have another draft," Billy said.

"You're not driving, are you?"

"Driving? Nope, I'm actually riding, if the airplane ever gets here."

"Can I ask you a question?"

"Sure. Fire away."

"How much trouble is it to get a divorce? Is it expensive?"

"That depends. It's sort of like asking what it costs to buy a car. Some cost a lot and some don't cost much at all. It all depends on the income, the number of kids, the life-style, the amount of property, and all those kinds of things."

"Wow. You sound like you know what you're talking about."

"I should. I'm a lawyer."

"Really?"

"I'm sorry I asked you all those questions. I bet everybody does that. Sorry."

"No problem. I'll be out of town for a few days, here's my card, if you have any more questions, call me. What did you say your name was?"

"Mary. Mary Jacobs. Thank you. I'll call your office next week if you don't mind."

"Not at all, Mary; if I'm not there, schedule an appointment with Vickie, my paralegal. Have a nice night. Let me pay up and go see if American Airlines intends to take me to Arizona."

* * * *

Steve Bloomberg was sitting in the lobby of Judge Barr's chambers when Billy got there. He had an oversized scuffed leather satchel at his side, and he looked like he'd just finished running a marathon. Bloomberg had a way of acting slightly startled when coming face to face with someone. Billy walked through the front door and Bloomberg jumped slightly and pulled his satchel closer to his left calf, as if protecting it from Billy. He adjusted his rimless glasses and scampered to his feet, spilling the folder of paper that he held in his lap. He took one small quick step back, then a small quick step forward, then he adjusted his glasses again and looked away from Billy's surprised stare. When he reached for the scattering papers, he briefly stumbled over the satchel.

"Mr. Tapp."

"Billy," Billy said, extending his hand.

"Billy. Okay. I guess you got the call, too. I was in court and my office called and said that Judge Barr wanted to see us at noon ... if we could make it. I was in court, but I got the message on my cell phone." Bloomberg plucked his cell phone from the holster on his belt and held it up for Billy to see.

Billy pointed at the cell phone and grinned. "Cell phone. Got it."

"Do you know what this meeting is about? Did you call it?"

"Nope," Billy said. "Vickie said something about Judge Barr wanting to dismiss the charges. But ... I couldn't understand the rest of her message. Just that he wanted to see me at noon, if I could make it."

"Who?" Bloomberg asked.

"Vickie."

"What's she charged with?"

"Nothing that I know of," Billy covered his face with his hand and choked back a laugh.

"Who is Vickie? What's her last name? Are you sure she's my case?"

"No, Steve. She's my secretary ... or paralegal ... or whatever you call them these days."

Bloomberg scowled and rubbed his chin. "No, no. That's not what I meant. I didn't mean who called you. I meant who does Judge Barr want to dismiss the charges against?"

"Why, Terry Jacobs. The kid who shot that no good drug dealing Fatso Boy ... the guy you're been trying to arrest for five years."

"What!" Bloomberg all but screamed. "Dismiss charges against—"

Judge Barr's clerk opened the door to his office and asked Billy and Bloomberg to come in. "Thanks for coming on such short notice. The judge will see you now."

Billy politely motioned Steve Bloomberg in first and followed behind, barely able to throttle his amusement at Bloomberg's angst.

"Judge Barr, Your Honor, with all due respect, I have to object. I can't see any rational reason to dismiss any charges. This is a murder case."

Before the judge responded to Bloomberg's protest, Billy said, "Steve, are you asking the court to dismiss the murder charges? That's very generous of you. That'll make a lot of people very happy."

"What! No! You told me that—"

"Gentlemen," Judge Barr said, "have a seat." He smiled at Bloomberg and gave Billy a slightly harsh look. "I knew you were in court today, Steve, and I took a shot at getting Mr. Tapp. We have a little problem here."

"If it please the court, I don't think I can agree to—" Bloomberg blurted.

"Hold on Mr. Bloomberg. I'm not necessarily asking anybody to agree to anything."

"But I thought—"

"Wait a moment and let me explain. According to Earl, down at the jail, Mr. Jacobs ... Terry Jacobs ... just came out of surgery for a perforated bowel that apparently didn't get patched up the first time. Looks kinda grim. Apparently, there's a chance that he isn't going to make it. You know that, Billy?"

"I knew he had to go back into surgery, but that's it. Guess I should call his mother. I'm sure she's a basket case by now."

Bloomberg pulled a prodigious black calendar out of his satchel and flipped through a few pages. "He's scheduled for sentencing or a trial date on this Friday. Can we take a plea in his absence?"

Billy looked at Bloomberg and shook his head. "Damn kid dying and all you think about is putting him in jail. The kid shoots a known drug dealer ... probably in self defense or under extreme mental duress or some kind of temporary insanity ... and now he's about to croak, and you want to put him in jail. You ought to give him a medal."

"Murder is murder is murder—"

"We have some speedy trial issues here. If he dies, of course, that won't be a problem, but if he doesn't, his recovery could be a matter of months. Any ideas?" Judge Barr asked.

"I would like to get permission to sentence him as soon as possible," Bloomberg said.

"I'd like to set him free," Billy said.

"Mr. Tapp," Judge Barr said, "You're not being very helpful. Any thoughts?"

Steve Bloomberg looked at Billy, and Billy raised his

eyebrows and smiled back. Neither lawyer said anything. Billy looked at Judge Barr and shrugged his shoulders.

"I guess we'll have a status hearing on Friday, and decide what to do then," the judge said.

Bloomberg stuffed his calendar back into his satchel. He stood up and said, "May I be excused, Your Honor?"

"Yes, sir," the judge said.

Bloomberg turned to Billy. "If you're planning on an insanity defense ... heaven knows why you would ... don't forget you have to give me notice," he said.

"Thank you," Billy said, "I had completely forgotten." Billy turned and looked at Judge Barr, who was shaking his head.

"Tapp. Can you at least try to get along? You've redefined the meaning of an adversarial legal system. You managed to turn a simple off the record status conference into a major conflict. Get your ass out of here. Call me Friday afternoon; I'll buy you a beer."

CHAPTER THIRTY-ONE

Terry Jacobs was charged with the criminal homicide of Andre Cunningham, a/k/a Fatso Boy. Criminal homicide can be broken down into murder, manslaughter in the first degree, manslaughter in the second degree, or reckless homicide. Murder—the most serious—is a capital crime and the punishment is death or life imprisonment without the possibility of parole. Reckless homicide—the least serious— is what's called a lesser included offense of murder, and it's punishable by up to five years in the penitentiary. Aside from the prosecutor's predilection for justice or revenge, the defendant's intent is the most important factor in determining the level of a homicide offense. Did the defendant intend to commit the criminal act? If Terry had been cleaning his pistol and it accidently fired killing Fatso Boy, the charge against him probably would have been reckless homicide. Terry's version of criminal homicide, however, was murder— as bad as it gets.

You can kill somebody and get away with it if you're crazy. Insanity is a defense because it involves intent. If you don't have the mental capacity either to understand or appreciate that you're doing something that's against the law, you're not responsible for the criminal conduct. Terry was charged with murder, if he wanted to go to trial, some kind of insanity was the only defense Billy could think of.

* * * *

This time Billy passed the guard at the detention section of the hospital without incident, and he walked down to room 712 C. All eight beds in room 712 were still full and Terry lay in the third bed from the door. A nurse stood bent over at his bedside looking over the myriad of tubes and electronic gadgets hooked in one way or the other to Terry. When Billy came closer, the nurse looked up; Terry's eyes were open and he appeared to be awake. Billy was momentarily taken aback by the nurse's red hair and her shapely ass.

"Hello," Billy said, looking into the nurses soft blue eyes—doing his best not to obviously stare at her ass as she remained bent over Terry. "How are you?"

"Are you asking me or Terry?" she said, with a wry smile.

Billy hesitated. "Both of you."

"I'll let Terry speak for himself. Although he's a little hoarse. We just pulled a tube out of his nose, and he's a little sore right now. But he can talk. As for me? I'm fine, thank you. Who are you?"

"I'm Billy. Billy Tapp. I'm Terry's lawyer."

"Really? You're the second person Terry asked about when he came to."

"What can I say?" Billy said with a self-deprecating shrug.

"This is a real sick boy," the nurse said as she pulled the sheet back over Terry's midsection and brushed his hair back from his forehead. She turned to leave the room and discreetly motioned for Billy to follow her into the hallway.

"I probably don't need to tell you this, but that poor kid has some real problems. Somebody did a real number on him in jail. The first surgery patched up the hole in his colon, but he developed an infection. The infection caused the bowel to rupture, and he nearly died from the combination of the infection and his own feces leaking into his gut. One worse than the other. Do you know what a colostomy is?"

281

"Not with all the medical nuances, I'm sure. But I know what the word means."

"Well, that's Terry's condition. What makes his situation more serious is that we don't know how long that he'll have to live with the bag attached to his side."

"You mean while he's in the hospital?"

"No. I mean period. It could be months ... maybe years ... we just don't know right now. Lots of people live relatively normal lives with a colostomy."

"Normal lives. You mean like a permanent condition?"

"Yes. But we haven't told him yet. We don't feel that he's stable enough to process that kind of information."

"How would that work with someone like Terry ... with him being in jail?"

"Frankly, it wouldn't. As you might imagine, there are a number of sanitation and disposal issues that are challenging, to say the least, under the best living conditions. Jail would make the whole process very, very difficult." The nurse noticed Billy's repeated quick glances at her breasts and she momentarily flushed. "Anything else, Mr. Tapp?"

"Can't think of anything. Oh. How much longer will Terry be in the hospital, and is he alert enough for me to talk sensibly to him right now?"

"I can't tell you how much longer he'll be here. You probably ought to talk to his doctor. Terry's awake and alert, more or less. I would prefer that you don't talk about his medical condition. But, as to whether you can talk sensibly, I don't suppose I can answer that one. That's up to you."

"If I have any more questions, can I call you?"

"Sure." The nurse turned and walked away.

"How do I get hold of you?"

"Hold of me? Just call the nurses station and ask for me."

"What's your name?" The nurse kept walking and just before leaving the ward turned and smiled at Billy.

* * * *

The realization that it was Friday and that he would rationalize an early afternoon beer at Clyde's made his weekly 8:30 a.m. status call for Terry Jacobs in Judge Barr's court tolerable. There really wasn't much to report. Terry was still in the hospital, although it looked like he wasn't going to die, the doctors couldn't give an exact date when he'd be released. And, more to the point, they couldn't give an accurate prediction of what his condition would be when he was released. Terry's infection wasn't the ominous MSRA Virus that was killing hospital patients left and right, but the doctors didn't want to take a chance. They thought the sooner they could get Terry out of the hospital the better.

But since he was charged with murder, the question was: Where should he go? Bloomberg wasn't going to agree to Terry going home, but he begrudgingly agreed that it probably wasn't an acceptable alternative for Terry to go back to jail with a bag full of excrement hanging on his side. So, on the doctor's advice, everyone agreed that, for the time being, he'd be better off staying in the hospital until they worked out a more permanent solution to either his plumbing or his accommodations.

"I'm just telling you what they told me. I ain't making this up, Steve."

"If it please the court, your honor," Bloomberg said, "I certainly will not agree to Jacobs going home, and if that's the case and he's not going to enter a plea, I'd like to schedule this case for trial. If he's healthy enough to go home, he certainly can go to trial."

"Well … we haven't decided yet on the plea. Terry's been incapacitated for a while, and I haven't had time to talk with him in any detail about the implications of the plea offer. But under the circumstances, it might make sense to schedule the case for trial, with the understanding that we can have up to thirty days or so before trial to decide on the plea offer. We should set this off a little bit, so we're not back here in a few weeks trying to get a continuance because of Terry's medical condition. That make sense to you, Steve?"

"What do you say, Mr. Bloomberg?" Judge Barr asked.

"This is the second time that I've heard Mr. Tapp allude to Jacobs' capacity. I don't want to prepare for trial without the proper notice of some diminished capacity defense."

"That's why we have rules, Steve," Billy said. "If you don't think I've followed the rules, you can file whatever motion you think is appropriate, and let the judge rule on it."

* * * *

Terry showed up for trial looking like he'd been whipped. He was pale, skinny, disoriented, and he had dark circles the size of ripe bananas under his eyes. As soon as the jailer from the hospital brought him into the courtroom, Mary let out a yelp and a wail that could only come from a broken hearted mother. To Billy's delight, the entire jury panel witnessed this brief episode. Mary sat in the front row and leaned across the rail, attempting to hug her child. A burly bailiff pushed her back while anther bailiff unceremoniously pulled Terry from his mother and pushed him into a seat at counsel's table, where Billy sat watching the prospective jurors' reaction to the drama. The display of unnecessary force and insensitive feeling for a mother's heart break couldn't have been better if Billy had scripted it himself.

Billy almost stood up and cheered when Bloomberg leaned over and said to him, in a voice loud enough for most of the jurors to hear, "Mr. Tapp. Tell Jacobs' mother to stay behind the rail, or I'll ask the judge to remove her from the courtroom."

Choking back his desire to give Bloomberg a big hug, Billy quickly seized the opportunity to prime the jury with the sympathy required for a successful insanity defense, Billy said in a voice loud enough for everyone to hear, addressing the un-sworn jury panel more than Bloomberg.

"Steve. Terry was raped in jail, it almost killed him. Then, when the doctors were patching up the hole in his bowel, Terry almost died in surgery. This is the first time his mother has seen him since surgery. My heavens, she's his mother."

Before the trial, Judge Barr ruled that evidence about Terry's surgery and jailhouse rape were not admissible to show his state of mind when he shot Fatso Boy.

"All that happened after he shot Fatso Boy," the judge said.

During Bloomberg's opening statement, he referred to the shooting victim as Fatso Boy. When he finished, Judge Barr asked both counsel, "Is that what we're calling the victim? Fatso Boy."

"His real name is Andre Cunningham," Bloomberg said. "But either one is okay. We've used the name Fatso Boy all along."

Without saying it, Billy much preferred the more ominous moniker Fatso Boy instead of the demure and less threatening Andre Cunningham. Then turning to the jury, Billy said, "Fatso Boy, it is then. That's what his gang on the street called him."

"I object to Mr. Tapp addressing the jury," Bloomberg said.

"That was his gang name. Mr. Bloomberg told me that. That's what the drug dealers called him."

"Your honor, I object."

Judge Barr looked sternly at both lawyers. "Counsel, approach the bench." Both attorneys walked up to the bench. "Gentlemen. Confine your comments to the court; that's *me*. Mr. Bloomberg would you like me to admonish the jury?"

"Yes, sir. I would like you to admonish them to ignore Mr. Tapp's comment about gang name and drug dealer."

"We're going to prove that, judge. That's part of Terry's defense. That's why he was afraid of Andre. He thought Andre was going to kill him."

Point made.

"Alright, gentlemen. Step back. Ladies and gentlemen of the jury, I'm going to admonish you to ignore, at this time, Mr. Tapp's comment that Fatso Boy was Andre

Cunningham's street name or his gang name. Unless that fact comes into evidence, you are not permitted to consider that comment with your deliberations. Any objections, gentlemen?"

"No sir," Bloomberg said.

"None, except, as you said 'at this time' because we intend to prove that Fatso Boy was Andre Cunningham's street name," Billy said while looking at the jury.

"That's right, ladies and gentlemen. At this time." Judge Barr smiled at the jury and spoke to Billy.

The total jury panel was in the courtroom. From the more than seventy-five prospective jurors, the parties must select twelve jurors and two alternate jurors to hear Terry's murder case. The lawyers proceeded to select the jury through *voir dire* to test the prejudice, competency, and interests of each potential juror. The idea is to give the parties an opportunity to find twelve impartial peers to decide on Terry's guilt or innocence.

Bloomberg started his *voir dire* telling the jury panel: "This case is about the brutal unprovoked and premeditated murder of Andre Cunningham by the defendant Jacobs ..."

Billy started his *voir dire* by telling the jury panel: "This boy sitting before you shot Fatso Boy ... a known drug dealer and gang member ... because Terry thought, with good reason, that Fatso was about to kill him and his entire family. His mother. His sister. And, everyone else."

* * * *

"Mr. Tapp, are you making an opening statement or do you want to reserve it?" Judge Barr asked.

"Your honor, as I told Mr. Bloomberg, we're pleading and will prove extreme emotional disturbance or temporary insanity, so I'd like to reserve my opening statement until Mr. Bloomberg, here, gets done with the stuff he wants the jury to believe."

Bloomberg sprang to his feet. Before he could say

anything, Billy quickly said, "May we approach the bench, your honor?" Judge Barr waved for the lawyers to come forward. Bloomberg stormed to the bench. His face was beet red. Billy casually smiled at the jury and walked nonchalantly up to the bench where Steve Bloomberg stood, fuming and shifting his weight from foot to foot.

"Need to go to the bathroom?" Billy whispered to the prosecutor. Bloomberg slapped his hand down on the rail in from of the judge's bench.

"Did you hear that, your honor? Tapp is making a mockery out of this trial. I want it stopped. Now."

The judge took off his reading glasses and rubbed his eyes. The jury watched the judge. Billy smiled and nodded at Bloomberg and stepped closer to the judge. He turned from the jury and Bloomberg and spoke directly to Judge Barr.

"Would this be a good time for the morning recess?"

Billy looked at Bloomberg and smiled. The judge nodded and looked at the clock at the back of the courtroom.

"I agree. Ladies and gentlemen, this is a good time for the morning recess; we'll reconvene in twenty minutes."

He gave the jury the usual admonition not to talk to anyone about the case, not to read any newspaper account or listen to any news cast, and to report anybody who did.

"I'd like to see the lawyers in chambers during the recess."

As the jury filed out of the courtroom, they couldn't help but see the bailiff escorting the pitiful and frail looking Terry Jacobs back into the holding cell, while his mother sat in the front row dabbing her blood-shot eyes with a tattered Kleenex. After the recess and the jury had returned to the courtroom, Judge Barr smiled at everyone.

"Alright, proceed with your case, Mr. Bloomberg."

The prosecutor spent the first part of the three day trial showing photographs of the dead Fatso Boy and pointing and sneering at the cowering Terry Jacobs.

"And is this … the defendant sitting with Mr. Tapp … the defendant who brutally shot and killed Mr. Cunningham."

To which, without exception, Billy stood and squarely

addressed the jury.

"Your honor, we'll stipulate *again* that Terry shot Fatso Boy. Of course he shot him; he thought Fatso Boy was going to kill him and his family if he didn't."

* * * *

It's always risky to put the defendant on the stand. Despite all the coaching and warning and suggesting, more often than not a defendant is his own worst witness. But if there's any hard and fast rule in a trial, it's that the jury wants to know what happened. It's nearly impossible to convince a jury that a defendant can be scared to the point of killing someone. Bloomberg's final questions gave Billy the entry that he gambled would come. In response to a question on cross examination from Bloomberg, Billy's mother testified that Terry was really sick.

"What do you mean, really sick?" he bellowed. "Not too sick to kill someone."

"No, I mean now. He's really sick now," she said.

Trying to undercut the jury's developing sympathy for Terry, Bloomberg continued his fateful line of questions.

"Dear God," Mary said, "he's in the hospital and he almost died. That thug drug dealer, Andre Cunningham or Fatso Boy or whatever you call him was responsible for Terry getting raped in jail. He's carried out his threat from the grave. Terry's still afraid for his life, and so am I. For my life. For my daughter's life. All of us." And Mary broke down into a heaving sob that everyone in the courtroom knew wasn't an act.

"I object to that testimony and ask that it be stricken from the record," Bloomberg nearly yelled.

Billy slowly stood and looked at the jury. Before he could respond, Judge Barr held up his hand. "Mr. Bloomberg, you asked the question. You opened the door."

"Thank you, your honor," Billy said and sat down.

On redirect examination, Terry told the jury about Fatso

Boy's threats to kill him, his family, and his cousins. He told the jury about the jailhouse rape and his colostomy, and how he almost died in surgery. He cried when he explained his embarrassment at wearing a bag hooked onto his side filled with his own feces. Terry's mother cried on queue and there wasn't a dry eye in the courtroom.

"And ladies and gentlemen," Billy said in his closing argument, "you don't have to be Sigmund Freud to know when someone is scared to death. Scared to the point of not knowing the difference between right and wrong. Scared for his life, scared for the life of his mother, his brother, his sister, and his entire family. This drug dealing scum-bag that the prosecutor wants you to feel sorry for was going to kill Terry. Terry knew it. Everyone on the street knew it. Fatso's gang knew it. How much more proof do you need? Fatso even tried to kill Terry from the grave. Terry's still in danger. And for what? Andre Cunningham, a/k/a Fatso Boy, stole a CD from Terry and threatened to kill Terry when he asked for it back. Who's really the guilty party? Just use your common sense. You can't put someone in jail for trying to protect his family."

CHAPTER THIRTY-TWO

After the lawyers argued about the jury instructions in the judge's chambers, Judge Barr reconvened court and read the instructions to the jury. He dismissed the two alternate jurors and directed the remaining twelve to retire to the jury room for their deliberations. Billy had introduced enough evidence during the trial that—as the law defines it—Terry was temporarily insane when he shot Fatso Boy. Consequently, Judge Barr not only instructed the jury on the offenses of murder, but also on the lesser included offenses of manslaughter in the third degree and on the defenses of insanity and, over Billy's objection, the defense of guilty but mentally ill—GBMI.

Most judges, much less lawyers, can't distinguish the subtle difference between not guilty by reason of insanity and guilty but mentally ill. The problem with guilty but mentally ill is that the jury can decide a defendant is crazy and, therefore, not capable of knowing right from wrong. Then decide that the defendant committed a criminal act and find him guilty—even though to be guilty a person is supposed to possess *mens rea*, or the intent to commit a crime—something a crazy person can't do.

"Guilty but mentally ill cuts the legs out from under an insanity or diminished capacity defense," Billy argued to the judge.

"Oh whoey," Bloomberg said, "It's the law and I'm entitled to the instruction."

The jury hadn't deliberated for more than an hour when a knock came from the inside of the jury room door. The court bailiff who, by court order, kept vigil at the jury room door, guarding against any outside influence opened the door and took a piece of folded paper. He called the judge's chambers.

"Yeah. Tell the judge that the jury has a question."

The judge's law clerk called the lawyers, telling them to meet back in the court room in five minutes. Billy had been sitting in the hallway outside the courtroom, talking on his cell phone. One of the bailiffs called down the hall.

"Mr. Tapp. The jury has a question. The judge will be back in the courtroom in a few minutes. We're bringing Jacobs in right now."

Terry shuffled into the courtroom and stood beside Billy at counsel's table. "All rise," the bailiff said, and the only three people in the court room—who were already standing—looked at each other. The judge came in and took his seat at the bench. "Be seated," the bailiff said, and the three standing people remained standing. Billy leaned over to Terry and whispered, "Sit down, Terry."

"Gentlemen, it looks like the jury has a question." The judge opened the folded paper and read the note. "They want to know the difference between not guilty by reason of insanity and guilty but mentally ill. Any thoughts?"

"The statutes and the instructions are clear. I don't think the jury needs further instruction," Bloomberg said.

"That's nonsense. Insanity means that Terry lacked the capacity to either appreciate the criminality of his act or ... and I say or ... to conform his conduct to the requirements of the law. When Terry shot this known drug dealing scumbag, Terry was so scared for his life and the lives of his mother and sister and brother that he couldn't conform his conduct to the law. That's what our proof was, because that's the truth. Guilty but mentally ill isn't even really a defense.

If the jury finds Terry guilty but mentally ill, Terry gets the same punishment as if they find him guilty. It's a distinction without a difference. Like I said when we argued the instructions, a GBMI instruction is confusing and misleading. If the jury believes that Terry was temporarily insane, they should find that and Terry will get the care he needs, if they don't believe that, they should find him guilty and he'll get the same jail time as if they find him guilty but mentally ill. I knew this would happen."

"You're right, Mr. Tapp. Here's what we're going to do. I'm going to call the jury in and reinstruct them. I'm going to explain the GBMI law, more or less the way Mr. Tapp just said it. Any questions?"

"I object, your honor, for all the reasons that I—"

"Overruled Your objection is noted, Mr. Bloomberg. Bailiff, call the jury in."

* * * *

Seymour Grey was sitting on the leather couch in Billy's office, reading a magazine and rolling an unlit cigar in his mouth. It was after six o'clock when Billy got back; he carried two heavy briefcases, and he was too tired to even act surprised at seeing Seymour. Vickie was gone, but she'd left all the lights on, something she rarely did, and she left a sealed envelope on his desk with his name written in large block letters. Seymour nearly leaped off the couch when Billy walked in. Billy dropped the briefcases on the floor beside his desk and looked over the pile of mail and messages that had accumulated during the last few days of trial. He picked up the envelope with his name on it and absent-mindedly stuffed it in his suit coat pocket.

"Counselor. By God, it is good to see you," Seymour said and extended his hand. It was apparent that he'd been drinking. "I think I have some good news. Looks like you have been up to some serious business."

"Yeah. Got a jury out. Murder case. The longer they're out the better it is ... or at least that's the conventional wisdom."

"What is on your calendar for tomorrow, Counselor? Shall we dash over to La Rouge ... right now ? It is on me. I actually have a driver tonight. The car is just a call away. We can be there in no time flat. Your assistant told me that I could wait in your office. She said she had a class or something. I hope you do not mind me waiting in your office. What do you say about dinner ... on me."

"Sure. What's the good news? Sounds like you got a little head start on celebration."

"I will tell you over a glass of good wine. And you are right. As I think you know, I am staying at the Willard and I sampled some of their excellent, but overpriced, pinot noir. I must say that the second bottle was better than the first. But no mind. It is off to the evening repast."

Seymour dialed his cell phone and by the time they got down to the lobby, a Lincoln Town car sat waiting for the short trip to Alexandria. Seymour ceremoniously lit his cigar and blew the smoke at the sky. Then he opened the car door for Billy and they made for La Rouge. Before they left his office, Billy called Madame Claret and she confirmed that his usual corner table was available. As if on cue, when the black limousine arrived in front of the restaurant, Madame Claret stood at the front door. She pointed at Seymour's cigar and shook her head. He took one last long drag and threw the cigar in the street and Madame Claret walked them to their table. Billy quickly maneuvered to the corner chair and Seymour took the chair next to him, giving Seymour a view of the small bar and the service door to the kitchen.

"Hope you do not mind me sitting next to you. Do not worry, I will not grab your leg. Just like to have a little view of the place."

"No problem," Billy said. "Now what's the good news?"

"Well. Counselor, do you like champagne?" Seymour motioned to a waiter. "Could you send over our waiter, we would like to see the wine list. No rush on the food, though."

The waiter grabbed a wine list from the bar and handed it to Seymour, who opened it and quickly selected a one hundred dollar bottle of Bordeaux. "I think you will like this red wine," he told Billy. "It is reasonably priced too."

"Alright Seymour. What's the good news? Tell me. I've been up to my ass in a losing trial and I could use some good news."

"What kind of case were you trying?"

"Murder."

"Did you win?"

"Don't know. Jury's out."

"Do you think you won?"

"Who in the hell knows? Jury's been out for a while. That's good."

"Did he do it?"

"Yeah. He did it. But he was temporally insane and he killed a known drug dealer. Our defense is insanity. Tough one to sell."

"How long do you think the jury will be out?"

"Who knows. Seymour, God damn it, what's the good news?"

"Well." Seymour looked around the room. "I have settled the Federated case."

"Settled the Federated case? How could you settle the Federated case?" Billy asked at the same time that the waiter arrived at the table with the bottle of wine, which he held for Seymour's approval.

"Excellent," Seymour said. The waiter opened the bottle, placed the cork on the table, and poured a sample in Seymour's glass. Seymour swirled it, smelled it, and tasted it.

"Perfect. Counselor, I think you will like this choice."

"So you've said. Now, what the hell do you mean that you settled your case?"

"Well, sir, I will tell you," Seymour said and took a drink of his wine. "I met with Howard Slone this morning. He is in town. I do not know if you knew that, but he is in town with one of his associates. A Mr. Sanchez. I met him briefly, and I do not even know if he is involved in this at all. But he seemed like a perfectly fine gentleman. He did not say much—"

"The settlement, Seymour. What's the settlement?"

"Patience, counselor, patience. This is a bit complicated."

"Go on."

"As you know ... and not to belabor the point ... the Frederick Mall project was on schedule and under budget. Before FSLIC started the foreclosure, Jerome Morning gave me the option to pay off the loan. I could not do that in the time frame that they allotted, so they filed the foreclosure lawsuit. To back up just a little, you remember that Howard Slone gave me the loan for the utility easement. Forty-seven thousand dollars. Jerome Morning somehow knew Slone ... all this, of course, before FSLIC took over Federated. In any case, Morning referred me to Slone, or Slone to me, I do not exactly remember which. But, suffice it to say, Slone knows Morning. I do not know how or why, but the finance business, as you know, is a small community. And you know that Slone also gave me an interim loan of one hundred thousand dollars after FSLIC filed the foreclosure suit."

"Yeah. I know all that."

Billy impatiently gulped his wine and looked at his watch. It was eight forty-five, and the jury had been deliberating since four-thirty. Four hours and fifteen minutes. That's good. "The longer they're out the better."

"What's that counselor?"

"Oh. Just thinking about my jury. I said the longer the better. Go on. I was listening to your story."

"Yesterday, Howard called me and said that he might have a plan to short circuit the Federated foreclosure suit ... and 'all the stink,' as he called it. He asked me if I could meet him here in D.C. to discuss the case. I told him that I would call you and we could meet. He said that it was not necessary to have you involved yet, plus he said you were in a trial. I do not know how he knew that, but he did. I called your office anyway, and true to his statement, your assistant said that you were in trial. Howard and I met this morning. Actually, Howard and I and Mr. Sanchez. An Hispanic fellow, I think. He did not say much. Howard introduced him as one of his associates."

"So, what's the deal?"

"It was a little bit strange. Right when Howard started talking about the deal, Sanchez interrupted him, and they both left the table. They were gone for a few minutes, and Howard came back ... by himself. I did not see Mr. Sanchez again, and Howard did not offer any explanation."

"What'd this Sanchez guy look like?"

"He was a big man. Big shock of black hair and a big black mustache. Why do you ask?"

"Just curious. So, go on."

Seymour took a long drink of his wine. "Howard comes back alone and sits at the table and says, 'I'm going to propose a win-win deal for you and for me.' I sensed a slight change in his demeanor. But, frankly, I was more interested in what he was about to say than how he was saying it."

"God damn it, Seymour. What's the deal?"

"He said that he had spoken to someone at FSLIC and they agreed that he could buy Federated's loan to me for less than one hundred cents on the dollar. He told me that he would split with me any amount that the project is under budget, which I estimate to be, more or less, seven million dollars, plus he would supply any additional needed capital for the project up to the record debt."

"Additional capital? What's that all about? If the project is under budget, it doesn't need any additional capital."

"What I gather from his explanation is that he will buy the loan from Federated for the discounted amount, and put in whatever additional needed capital."

"Two comments. If he buys Federated's loan for less than the total, plus the foreclosure costs, plus court costs, plus attorney's fees ... there's going to be a deficiency and that you'll have to pay. And if the project is under budget, why would he have to put any more money in the deal? What would your involvement in the project be? Would you still be in the deal?"

"That's right. I would remain in the project, but he did not say exactly how or what my function would be."

"What about any deficiency? What about the dough that you'd owe FSLIC?"

"That is what makes this so interesting. He told me there would not be any deficiency. That was part of the deal he made with FSLIC. He did not go into all the details, but he mentioned that he had spoken with Morning, and it looked like a deal that they would approve."

"Who made the deal at FSLIC? Did he say?"

"No I did not cross examine him. But I gathered that Mr. Morning was the link between FSLIC and Howard's lender."

"Who's Howard's lender?

"I cannot answer that counselor. All I know is that from what I gather Howard is buying the loan at a sizable discount, so someone will have to put enough additional money in the project to complete the construction and the tenant finish. Plus fund the amount that we complete the project under budget."

"Which budget are we talking about? Federated's budget of seventy-five million or the new budget that Slone concocts from the confused recorded mortgage debt?"

"Counselor, you are most suspicious. The project budget is the project budget. Seventy-five million dollars. If we complete it for less, I get one-half of the amount under budget. It is that simple. It is still a loan, and it still comes to me tax free, and the lawsuit is over and we are all on our merry way. What could be simpler?"

"Keep that thought. I need to take a piss. Be right back."

Billy maneuvered into the small men's restroom that was next to the service door to the kitchen. He took off his suit coat and hung it on the hook on the back of the door. After rolling up his sleeves and taking his neck-tie off, he cupped his hands under the faucet and splashed water on his face. When he dried his face and hands he reached for his coat and noticed the envelope that Vickie had left for him. He opened it. There was a copy of the fifty-thousand dollar check with a band of numbers highlighted by yellow marker and a hand-written note that Vickie paper clipped to the check. "Dozier Mound called and said this check was cashed at Federated Savings and Loan in Houston. Don't have a clue what that's supposed to mean, but he said that you'd find it interesting. Have a nice night. V." He stuffed his tie in his suit coat pocket, put the check and note back in the envelope and returned to the table.

"Did you know that the check for fifty thousand dollars was ..." Just then, Billy's cell phone rang. Normally, he wouldn't have it with him, but with a jury out, he either needed to be in the courtroom or be available by telephone. It was nine-thirty. "Tapp," he said. "Sure, in fifteen minutes."

Seymour looked up from the menu that the waiter brought while Billy was in the men's room. "Problems?"

"Don't know. Either another question. They want to go home. They're deadlocked. Or, they have a verdict. In any case, I have to be there." As Billy reached for his tie, his cell phone rang again.

"Billy, Judge Barr here. I have Mr. Bloomberg on the line."

"Good evening, Billy," Bloomberg said.

"Hey, Steve," Billy said.

"Jury wants to go home for the evening. I'd like them to stay and finish, but it's getting a little late and I'm inclined to let them go. We're on the record. If y'all agree, you won't have to come back in tonight. But I need your approval."

"Okay by me," Billy said.

"Mr. Bloomberg?" The judge asked.

"I suppose so. Although, I really don't like to do it."

"It's your call, Steve. Yes or no."

"I suppose so—"

"Is that a yes or a no?"

"Yes."

"Alright, gentlemen. This has been on the record. I'll admonish the jury as usual and send them home for the evening. Be back in court tomorrow at nine-thirty; we'll reconvene then. Any objections?"

"Nope."

"No, Your Honor."

Billy closed his phone. "Well I'll be dammed," he said. "Looks like we can finish the wine."

"What were you saying about the check or something?" Seymour asked.

"Apparently the check was cashed at Federated."

Seymour continued to study the menu. "Huh," he said.

"Yeah, I find that strange too."

"Huh. I am a little surprised to see blue cheese dressing in a French restaurant. Do you find that a little strange?"

"God damn it. I was talking about the—"

"Oh. And Howard agreed to pay the balance of your fee out of the project funds. Which, by the way, I slightly fudged on. Hope you do not mind." Seymour reached in his breast coat pocket and pulled out a check made out to William L. Tapp, PLC in the amount of one hundred thousand dollars. "Here," he said, "paid in full."

CHAPTER THIRTY-THREE

Billy handed the Porsche keys to the valet and headed to the Round Robin Bar at the back of the Willard's elaborate lobby. He passed the concierge desk with a respectful nod from the single attendant at the front desk, and he entered the dim bar, which many think is one of the power booze joints in the United States, if not the world. On the opposite side of the round mahogany bar, through the subdued light and hunter green furnishings, he saw Howard Slone sitting by himself at the same corner table where he had sat when they last met in the plush barroom. Thanks to the venerable Great Compromiser, Henry Clay, the Round Robin featured mint juleps that cost as much as an acceptable bottle of wine where Billy stocked booze for his townhouse in Georgetown. Same table, same oil lamp burning on the table top, same yellow reflection on the diminutive face and same chin, which appeared to point more directly at his beak-like nose than Billy had remembered. Howard Slone sat with his back to the corner and his legs crossed under the table. There was a full drink in front of him and an empty martini glass to his right. When Billy got to the table, Slone motioned to the captain's chair directly across the table. Billy looked at the empty martini glass and paused.

"Oh. Don't worry. She's gone."

Billy extended his hand to Slone. Slone bent slightly forward and shook Billy's hand. "Have a seat, Mr. Tapp."

"Billy."

"Yes. Billy."

"Well, Seymour tells me that you've come to some kind of an agreement to settle this whole thing. All of it ... hide, hair, and bones. That right?"

"Hide, hair, and bones. I suppose that's right. How much did he tell you?"

"Not much, really. He said that you'd made a deal with FSLIC to buy the Frederick Mall loan, that you agreed to provide whatever additional dough that's needed, and you'd give Seymour half of any amount that he finishes under budget. That about it?"

"Yes sir. That's about it?"

"And ... I almost forgot. You paid my fee. Very generous."

"Thank you. Technically, I really didn't pay your fee. The project paid your fee. That money will come from the loan. But that's not really your worry."

"So what do you want me to do?" Billy asked.

"Not much. Just call this Michael Braxton fellow. Explain, generally, what you know and get this foreclosure lawsuit dismissed, so we can get the project back on schedule. We don't want to lose the tenants who have signed leases."

"I'll need to know a few more details. I'm sure Braxton trusts me, but he ain't going to take my word that the horse is back in the barn. If you know what I mean. Do you have a signed agreement with FSLIC? Who are you dealing with there? If they give Braxton the green flag, that might be enough. Wasn't Braxton involved in the settlement?"

"Although it probably isn't necessary for you to know all the details, Bethesda Equity negotiated an agreement with FSLIC to purchase ... as you said ... the project loan from Federated Savings and Loan's inventory of assets at a favorable price."

"How much?"

Slone hesitated and sipped his drink. "Why is that important to you?"

"Just like to understand the deal."

"I'm sure you do. Suffice it to say, the price was favorable, and, let me add, approved by FSLIC. Federated Saving and Loan was in trouble, and ... ah ... should I say ... part of something is better than all of nothing. If Federated is forced to liquidate, fifty cents on the dollar would be a bargain for the Feds."

"But I understand that Seymour's project wasn't even close to going in the shit-can. He was under budget, ahead of schedule, and more than sixty percent pre-leased. For Christ's sake, his deal was worth a hundred and fifty cents on the dollar. How in the hell did you pull this off?"

"Mr. Tapp. Billy. We didn't pull it off. We negotiated an agreement with FSLIC, through Mr. Morning, FSLIC's agent, and came to a mutual agreement."

"*We*, being Bethesda Equity?"

"Correct."

"Who owns Bethesda Equity?"

"It's privately owned."

"By whom?"

"It's private. That information is not public."

"Are you the owner?"

"I'm involved."

"Oh. I'm sure of that."

Slone readjusted his expensive blazer and uncrossed his legs and leaned forward.

"Why is all of this so important to you? We've extricated your client from a foreclosure lawsuit that likely would have taken his project and forced him into bankruptcy; Seymour is still in the deal; the project will be funded; Seymour will pull some tax-free cash out of the deal; and, you've been paid more than you would have billed Seymour if somehow you managed to get the foreclosure lawsuit dismissed. What's the problem?"

"That's the problem."

"Help me with your thinking, Billy."

"I'm not the smartest lawyer in D.C., but I'm not the dumbest one either."

Slone leaned back in his chair. "Tapp, spare me the false modesty. What's your problem?"

"For some strange reason, I've taken a fondness to Seymour. Right now, he's operating in what I call the cut dog mode."

"I'm afraid you will have to explain your bucolic metaphor.

"He'll do anything to get out of the mess he's in. He isn't analyzing all the potential implications and consequences of the deal that you've made with FSLIC. At the expense of being trite, when something looks too good to be true, it usually is. I don't want Seymour to get involved with something that's going to bite him on the ass, somewhere down the road."

"What exactly are you saying, Mr. Tapp?"

"What I'm saying is that I'd like to understand all the details of this agreement, and, maybe most of all, understand who all the players are ... where the money's coming from. If there's something fishy going on, it's better to know it now than after it's too late."

"Fishy. What are you talking about? What could be fishy about a straight forward purchase like this?"

Billy motioned to the bartender and a waitress came over to the table. "I'm sorry, gentlemen, Mr. Slone asked that I not disturb you."

Without saying a word, Slone gestured toward Billy and looked away from the waitress.

"Let me have a Stella," Billy said. "On tap."

"Yes sir. Right back."

"Look, Mr. Slone. I'm just trying to protect Seymour. That's what lawyers do. I wouldn't be doing my job if I didn't ask these questions."

"I'm curious, Billy. Most lawyers would be delighted with this outcome. They'd jump at the opportunity to get their client out of an impossible situation, and get paid for doing it. Don't you agree?"

"I'm not most lawyers."

"I understand that."

The waitress put the beer on a cocktail napkin in front of Billy and picked up the empty martini glass. "Anything for you, Mr. Slone?" Slone shook his head without taking his eyes off Billy.

After a long pause, Howard Slone said, "You've peaked my interest. What do you base your suspicions of a 'fishy' deal on?"

"You really want to know what I think?"

"Humor me."

Billy paused. He wiped the foam off his mouth with the back of his hand.

"First. Bethesda Equity or Southwest Financial or Southeast Financial just happened to show up when Seymour discovered that he needed a small chunk of land to get utilities to the mall. Next thing you know, apparently this Morning guy introduces you to Seymour. The only two people who knew about the easement issue were Seymour and Morning. About the same time, the farmer who owned the piece of property that Seymour needed for utility access gets his ass kicked and then, according to some of the local folks, leaves town with a pocket full of cash.

"Then, lo and behold, a check for fifty thousand dollars is cashed at Federated Savings and Loan. Strange thing about that check. It's made out to Seymour, but he swears it's not his endorsement and that he didn't cash the check and knows nothing about it. The check is drawn on the First National Bank of the Cayman Islands on a Southeast Financial account. Two weeks later, Morning shows up at Federated with a new BMW. Suspicious, don't you think? All this taking place against the backdrop of FSLIC calling Seymour's loan on the advice of Jerome Morning ... the guy with the new BMW. Makes you wonder."

Howard Slone gulped the rest of his drink and motioned

to the bartender. "I'm not sure that I like the implications of your conjecture. But continue. I'm interested in where this is heading."

"So. I'm in the islands with some chick and somebody fucks with my airplane and about the same time, I see a Lear 55 on the ramp. Later, I find out that you scoot around the county in a Lear 55 … at least that's what Seymour tells me. A few days after getting back from the islands, a few goons jump me in Old Town and tell me to keep my nose out of things that aren't my business. Of course, they could be connected to a street gang murder that I'm involved with, but they didn't look like your average street goons. Then Seymour tells me about this Hispanic guy, who I find out is named Sanchez, is all of a sudden involved in the picture."

The waitress brought Slone another drink. "Here you are, sir." She smiled at Billy and placed a bowl of mixed nuts on the table. "Would you like another beer?"

"You bet."

"Go on." Slone said.

"Sometime earlier, I go out to Frederick and find you at the project site negotiating with a tenant, and I go to the courthouse and find the deeds and mortgages seem to be fucked up. Two mortgages, one for seventy-five million dollars and the other for slightly more. Then I find some strange confusion in recording. Makes me suspicious."

"Where exactly is this heading, Mr. Tapp? What exactly do you conclude from these … ah … circumstances?"

"Lots of different thoughts. Maybe nothing. But maybe not. But mostly I'm just worried that Seymour might be getting himself in the middle of a bad situation."

"How much of this have you told to Mr. Grey?"

"Not much. But if he thought about it, he could figure it out for himself. That is, if he wanted to. Which I'm pretty sure he doesn't. You can understand that."

Slone looked at his watch. "What are you worried about? Tell me your worst fears."

Billy hesitated and leaned back in the leather captain's

chair.

"My worst fears?"

"Yes."

"You're in cahoots with Morning to cherry pick Federated's good projects. He does your bidding with FSLIC. Morning cashed the fifty thousand dollar check. You own or control Bethesda Equity, Southwest Financial, and Southeast Financial. You're in business with this Sanchez guy." Billy paused to take a drink of his beer.

"So what? Nothing you've suggested has any bearing on Mr. Grey."

"Except this. What if ... let's say what if. What if the money in Bethesda Equity and Southwest and Southeast Financial was drug money from Mexico. And, what if you were buying ... in this case ... Seymour's project for fifty cents on the dollar, say for thirty-seven million five. Then, let's just say for this discussion, that you fund an additional thirty-seven five to finish the project. The net result could be that you laundered seventy-five million dollars worth of drug money from Mexico. Pretty sweet deal."

Billy drained his beer and motioned to the waitress and continued.

"You end up with a great project that pays debt service of over a half million dollars a year to an entity that's totally funded with tax free drug money. Plus you get the profits from the mall, which could be three times the debt service. And, Seymour is right in the middle of it. Those are my worst fears. I really don't care about you or your dealings. I just don't want Seymour to get hurt."

Howard Slone barely flinched. A small bead of perspiration appeared on his thin upper lip. "You're a smart guy, Billy. Sometimes that can get you in trouble. For everyone's sake, I hope you don't spread this silly speculation around. I would hate to see you bogged down in some kind of defamation dispute ... lawsuit ... or worse."

"I don't have proof of anything. You just asked me my worst fears. Those are my worst fears. I'll probably tell

Seymour, but I can tell you that he'll laugh it off. Why wouldn't he? He can't afford not to."

CHAPTER THIRTY-FOUR

"Well, gentlemen. I was afraid of this. It looks like the jury is hung. They can't reach a verdict. I told them twice to go back and try to reach a verdict, but they can't." Judge Barr looked over his reading glasses at Steve Bloomberg and Billy.

Terry sat at defense counsel's table staring absently at the manacles that were paddle-locked to a chain around his middle that was hooked to another chain that was attached to the manacles on both ankles. Strapped with a colostomy bag and sufficient chains to lift a fallen tree, Terry's chances for escape were about the same as him flying to the South of France on a skate board. He looked around at his mother, who sat in the front row in the courtroom, and he thought about Fatso laughing at him and the awful smell of gun powder and the explosion of blood on the wall.

"It looks like I'll have to declare a mistrial. Any thoughts or comments?" the judge asked the lawyers.

"Nope," Billy said.

Bloomberg looked over at the empty jury box. The jury was still in the jury room; they'd sent their message to Judge Barr on a piece of folded paper handed to the bailiff.

"Your Honor, do we have any idea how they hung?"

"No sir, Mr. Bloomberg. The note just says they can't reach a verdict, and they don't think that there's any chance of reaching a unanimous verdict."

"Steve," Billy said, "you can't ask them how they're divided. That's the *Allen* case. It's error to ask. Might be harmless error ... as far as I'm concerned ... but it's still error."

"That's right." The judge said. "If they tell me that they they're hung, I need to decide if further deliberations might be useful. Then I can tell them four things: first, each juror must agree to the verdict; second, you need to consult with each other to get a verdict; third, each juror has to decide for himself; reexamine your own opinions; and, fourth, don't surrender your honest opinions just to get a verdict. Y'all agree with that? The so-called *Allen* charge. What do you think? Steve."

Bloomberg unbuttoned and re-buttoned his dark blue suit coat and adjusted his glasses. "How can there be any doubt. There isn't any doubt at all. This kid shot ... I don't see what the hang up is. This cold blooded killer is guilty."

"Well," Billy said, "either the jury thought Terry was incapacitated or this scum-bucket Fatso deserved killing."

"Scum-bucket or not, you can't have people going around shooting ... ah ... citizens," bristled Bloomberg.

Terry had been sitting passively at the defendant's table, but he flinched when Bloomberg complained about the jury's indecision.

"That's not the issue," Billy said. "Judge gives the *Allen* charge. Jury comes back still hung. Mistrial. That simple."

* * * *

Judge Barr called the jury back into the courtroom and issued the *Allen* charge. The jury followed the bailiff back to the jury room and fifteen minutes later handed out another note with the following message:

> We cannot reach a unanimous verdict.
> We are split fifty-fifty.

Judge Barr read the note to the attorneys and Terry Jacobs, and then asked the bailiff to bring the jury back into the courtroom to verify the deadlock.

"Are you sure you can't come to a decision if you have a little more time?"

With askance looks, most with a scowl, all but three shook their heads in the negative—the other three actually said, "No."

"I have no choice, then, to declare a mistrial. Ladies and gentlemen of the jury, thank you for your service. You are relieved of further duty in this case. Check with the clerk's office in the morning for further jury duty. You may speak with the lawyers if you like. If you don't want to, however, you don't have to. If you feel like you're being harassed, call my law clerk. Y'all have the number." The judge turned to the lawyers. "Anything else?"

"No sir, Your Honor."

"Nope."

After the jury left the courtroom, Mary rushed from the front row to hug her beleaguered son. The bailiff and deputy jailer intercepted her, but with the consenting nod from the judge, they permitted her to round the bar and flop herself into the chair next to Terry and, in a convulsion of wailing sobs, cradle his head in her heaving breasts.

"My baby. My baby." Terry sat like a pigeon with its wings tied together. Tears ran down his flushed cheeks.

Bloomberg rolled his eyes as the bailiff finally pulled mother and son apart. Mary wiped her eyes and blew her nose, folded her hands in her lap, and watched Terry shuffle out of the courtroom.

"Gentlemen," the judge said to the lawyers after the bailiffs delivered Terry back into custody and the courtroom was cleared. "What are your intentions?"

"Well," Billy said, "I'd think this is the time when Steve would make us an offer that we can live with."

"I haven't decided yet. But, I'm sure we'll want to re-try

the case."

"Then, I guess, we'll make a motion to dismiss."

"On what possible grounds?"

"Don't worry, I'll think of something."

"You don't have a—"

"Alright. It's been a long day. Let's recess until tomorrow morning. Say nine o'clock. We'll decide then. But let me say this to both of you. This case doesn't look like first degree murder, but Mr. Tapp, I'd be surprised if the next jury will let him go on insanity. Having said that, you two can come to some kind of a reasonable resolution in this case." Judge Barr hesitated and looked at both lawyers. "Know what I mean? Any questions?"

CHAPTER THIRTY-FIVE

When the court accepts a guilty plea in a criminal case, the judge goes through a protracted question and answer session with the defendant. The purpose is to make sure that the defendant is competent and not drunk or on drugs and that he understands he's giving up his right to both a trial and an appeal, and, although rarely the case, to inform him that the judge doesn't have to follow the recommendation of the prosecuting attorney. Ostensibly, judges go through this didactic process to make sure the plea is voluntary and considered, but the real reason is to short-circuit appeals and to give the appellate courts a record with sufficient ammunition to summarily deny reversal, despite evidence of prosecutorial over-reaching or proof of innocence. A sad but simple truth. Justitia omnibus.

Judge Mitchell permitted Thackeray Frederick Johnson to withdraw his guilty plea and consult with yet another lawyer and thereby avoid a certain appeal, which would accomplish little more than adding a burden to the Court of Appeals and cause unnecessary work for the Federal District Court Clerk and the contingency of law clerks, paralegals, and secretaries.

The holdover cell in the Federal District Court was located in the marshal's office, off to the right side of the courtroom. Prisoners arrived in the Federal Building through a basement garage and a series of underground tunnels, up a hidden elevator, into the marshal's office, and into the holdover cell, where they await the court's call.

"So. Mr. Billy Tapp. Word come that you hung a jury in a murder case. You da man. What 'chu doin' fo me now?" Thackeray Frederick Johnson rubbed his goatee and through a wide smile showed his five point gold star. "Maybe I be fuckin' nuts, too. Crazy. Dats what did it."

"Temporary insanity," Billy said.

"Temp–or-airy, nuts, crazy. Don' mean shit. What means shit is not havin' yo ass found guilty beyond a reasonable doubt. You get that done fo me, and there be one big ass reward fo you."

"Thackeray, you can't afford to hire an attorney, how are you going to give me one big ass reward?"

"Don' 'chu worry. Get dem ass holes to find me cuckoo and I'll take care o' da rest."

"First of all, you're not insane."

"Day never gave me my rights."

"You signed a Miranda card, which acknowledged that they gave you a Miranda warning."

"Yeah. But I was in-competent at da time."

"Thackeray. Please."

"But if I was cuckoo bird, den deys got to find me not guilty."

"If ... if you feed elephants the right things, they'll shit meat cleavers. You know that don't you?"

"Man, what the fuck you talkin' 'bout? Elephants. Meat cleaver shit. What you talkin' 'bout?"

Johnson turned from Billy and yelled to one of the marshals for a cigarette. The marshal who transported Johnson to the Federal Building came over to the cage and handed Johnson a pack of Kools and then held up a lighted match and handed the pack of matches to the prisoner. After a few deep drags, Johnson looked at Billy.

"You're not insane, and you weren't temporarily insane when you robbed the bank. You know that as well as I do."

"What if day can't prove it was me?"

"You signed a confession."

"What if it was co-erced?"

"You said in your confession that it was voluntary."

"Maybe day beat it outa me."

"The whole thing was videotaped. No one beat you. What about the coat and mask they found in the trunk? In the car with the woman you were living with.

"Maybe she did it. Ever think about that?"

"The video tape in the bank shows a man. Who just happens to be your size and shape? Did you think about that?"

"Whoa, motha-fucker. Whose side you on? You doin' a better job on me than that prosecuting attorney 'bout to do."

"Not true. I'm just pointing out facts. Facts, by the way, that you know. And, if anybody's fucking with anybody, it's you fucking with me and, more importantly with this federal judge and the possibility of you getting at least twelve more years than the AUSA is recommending with a guilty plea."

Johnson turned away and snuffed out his cigarette in the tin ashtray that the marshal gave him when he handed the pack of Kools through the steel bars.

"You're one smart motha-fucker. I see how you hung that jury. Well, let's get this over with so's I can get my po black ass back where I's either been or been headin' all my life. Anything is better than the county hell-hole they call a jail. Get me back to the federal pen as soon as possible."

"So this is what you want to do? This is your decision?"

"It ain' like I'm buyin' no bed in paradise. I jus knows at some point it don' do no damn good to keep ragin' against the storm."

* * * *

"That is right." Seymour said. "I understand from Dozier Mound that apparently Morning cashed the fifty thousand dollar check. As it turns out, the money ended up in an escrow account at Federated. I do not know when or how or any of the details."

"Yeah. But when was the money put in the account? Did you think to ask him that? And by what authority did he endorse your name on the check? Did you give Morning the authority to sign your name?"

"I do not remember if I did or did not give him permission. There was a lot going on back then. When Federated called my loan, I was so surprised that I may have ... not knowing exactly what I was doing." Seymour refilled Billy's glass from the second bottle of expensive pinot noir. "What's done is done. Dozier said that Morning was transferred to another bank and FSLIC had appointed Joe Franklin to act as its representative along with some other young person from D.C. It was good news that Morning was replaced, but Dozier was not optimistic about his retaining ownership of Federated."

"Sweet. Morning steals fifty thousand dollars and God knows what else. Slone steals a first rate real estate development and in the process, coincidently, probably launders seventy-five million dollars ... or more than one hundred and fifty million ... in drug money from Mexico. You lose eighty percent of your shopping center. Dozier Mound gets screwed out of his savings and loan company, which he spent years creating. Some poor shit in Frederick gets his ass kicked just before selling his property to you ... I wonder how voluntary that was? I get beaten up and tasered. I get threatened ... the last time by Slone at the Willard, where, by the way, I saw his accomplice in the drug laundering deal."

"Counselor. I am afraid that you have taken a series of coincidences and woven them into a grand conspiracy."

"You're not stupid, Seymour. Don't you see what's just happened?"

Grey finished the wine in his glass and poured it full again. "Here is the way I see it. Federated got cross-wise with FSLIC, for whatever reason. I am not privy to all those details. But FSLIC then sent a receiver to Houston who assumed operation. Morning referred Mr. Slone to me."

"Right. That rat bastard Jerry Morning, who cherry picked your project and stole fifty thousand dollars. And it looks like he'll get off free as the ... ah ... morning breeze. Don't you wonder why he hasn't been prosecuted? Do you wonder how he just happened to know Slone?"

"None of that is really my problem. I have no control over any of that. I have a great affection for Dozier Mound, but I do not control what the Federal government does. I do not know how he ran his business. Counselor, neither of us is in a position to call that one."

"Don't you have any interest in finding out what really is going on?"

"I know what is really going on."

Seymour waved to the waiter who stood next to the lovely Madame Claret, and he held up his index finger and then pointed at the empty bottle wrapped in a white napkin.

"You know this swill sells for two hundred buck a bottle."

"Do not worry. The tab is on me."

"Thanks."

"My project is out of foreclosure. It looks like I will receive some millions of dollars as a loan that will be taxed from the cash flow generated by the shopping center. My company will probably manage the center for a reasonable fee. You received a very handsome fee. Morning? Dozier? I do not know about them. I do not care one way or the other about Morning. I feel bad for Dozier, but what can I do about that? I am in this business to make money. It is really that simple. Yes, I know what is going on."

The waiter uncorked the third bottle of two hundred dollar wine and sat it on the table.

"Drink up, counselor. I doubt if this would have ended so favorably without your ... shall we say ... involvement."

"Well, maybe. But the whole thing gets up my ass."

"Relax and enjoy. This is about outcome, not justice."

* * * *

"Sorry. I'm a little bit late. But I don't see Bloomberg yet."

"He's already back here in chambers," the judge's secretary said over the intercom. "Come on back."

The door buzzed and the red light over the top flashed. Billy pushed through the door and walked down the long corridor, past the other judges' chambers, which eventually lead to Judge Barr's chambers. Steve Bloomberg was sitting on the blue pleated leather couch just inside the door.

The judge's secretary looked at Billy and then looked at her watch. She shook her head very slightly and smiled. "We've been expecting you."

Bloomberg grabbed his briefcase and almost jumped to his feet. He quickly extended his hand to Billy.

"Good morning, Mr. Tapp."

"Hey Steve. Sorry I'm late. Only five minutes. Couldn't find a place to park. I had to go to the top and back down again in the parking garage. What a pain in the ass."

Judge Barr came out of his office into the reception room. His tie was loosened and the sleeves on his white button-down oxford shirt were rolled to mid forearm.

"Glad you could make it, Mr. Tapp. We've been waiting for you." Everyone laughed—Bloomberg the loudest. "Go on into the conference room; I'll be there in a moment."

The judge went back into his office, and the two lawyers went into the large conference room. Files were stacked around the floor in neat piles and papers were scattered near the far end of the table, which apparently was the judge's work area. Judge Barr sauntered through a connecting door to his office and took his seat at the head of the table. He pushed some of the files aside and placed a legal pad in front of him.

"Do we need this on the record?" The judge looked at Bloomberg.

"Not as far as I'm concerned," Billy said.

"Steve?" the judge asked.

C. W. Arnold

"Well. It's always best to have a record. Just to be—"

"Record? Can't we just put whatever we decide here in an order? We aren't offering any proof. No evidence. This isn't a hearing. It's a conference. An informal conference."

"Does that suit you, Steve?"

"Well. I suppose so."

"Alright. Then we agree not to put this on the record. Have y'all talked about any kind of a plea deal? Have you made any kind of offer to Mr. Tapp?"

"Not yet. As I said in court, my inclination is for a retrial. I don't buy temporary insanity ... or whatever Mr. Tapp is selling. This is cold blooded, premeditated murder."

"Gimme a break, Steve."

"Do I have to put you two in separate rooms?" Judge Barr said. "First of all, I think we'll all agree that we can't put this kid in general population as long as he has that colostomy bag hooked to his gut. Do we agree on that?"

"Yep."

"I don't necessarily agree. Isn't there some way the department of prisons can put him somewhere until that's taken care of."

"Steve. I suggest you offer this kid five to ten years on an amended charge of homicide third degree under diminished capacity, with recommendation of no probation. Mr. Tapp. I suggest you accept. I'll accept the plea and defer sentencing until the kid gets his plumbing reconnected. In the meantime, I'll send him to a secure state medical facility for a physical and mental evaluation. I'll note your objection, Steve. But remember I won't impose final sentence until I find out his real mental and physical condition." Billy nodded and Steve Bloomberg grumbled his acceptance.

318

CHAPTER THIRTY-SIX

Billy waited at his usual table. Robert Bob made a rare service call to the table. Without taking Billy's order, he carried a pitcher of beer and two glasses.

"You read my mind. Thanks Robert Bob. It's been a long week. Profitable, but long." Billy poured a beer and pointed at the full glass. "This is justice. The only place I'm gonna find it."

Without response, Robert Bob returned back behind the bar, at the helm of Clyde's quickly filling barroom. He swiped the bar top with the ubiquitous towel he carried on his right shoulder. Judge Stewart's pretty clerk came through the door, accompanied by two attractive but androgynous females dressed in grey suits. Robin Grigsby surveyed the room and, spotting Billy, came over to his side. She placed her hand on his shoulder.

"I hear you won another murder case. I'm impressed." She extended a collegial hand shake.

"Why, thank you. How in the world did you hear about that?"

"Small world. You can't keep a secret from the judges, and, as you know, I work for a judge. Word gets around."

"It really wasn't a win. Hung jury. Not quite a win, not quite a loss. Somewhere in the middle. Fortunately, I had

Judge Barr. He did the right thing. Too bad there aren't more like him."

"Well, there are some. I work for one."

"Want a beer?"

"Thanks. But I'm with a few friends. We're meeting some new clerks. Maybe when they leave, if you're still here."

When Robin Grigsby joined her friends, Billy's cell phone, which he had placed on the table, vibrated. It was from Ann. A text message. To avoid confrontation, she had, for the most part, stopped calling Billy, resorting instead to texting him—a tactic, Billy told her, that was a communication method best suited for cowards.

"Call it what you want," Ann said. "Lately it's the most reliable way for me to communicate with you."

Billy opened the text message. "Where r u? u're suppost 2 get kids 1 hr ago:("

"Shit," Billy said, and slammed his hand on the table. He rubbed his eyes and leaned back in his chair. When he opened his eyes, Jason was pouring himself a beer.

"Understand you won another murder case."

Billy looked a Jason. "Didn't win. Hung the jury. God damn it. I was supposed to pick up the kids an hour ago. Just got a text message from Ann."

"You're late."

"No shit. I'll be right back. I need to call her."

Billy walked back to the men's room and, on the way, passed Robin Grigsby and her two friends. Robin grabbed his coat sleeve.

"This is Billy Tapp. Billy. Emily. Jami." Both girls smiled at Billy and shook his hand. "Robin was just telling us about you," Emily said.

"Ah ... really? Y'all have to excuse me; I have to make a quick call." Billy smiled at Robin. "Come by the table, Jason Roberts just came in. I'm sure that he'd like to say hey."

"I know that I forgot. I'm sorry," Billy said to Ann's message recorder. "I just got out of court. Would you mind if I pick the kids up tomorrow? Let me know. I'm going to be out of pocket for a bit. Sorry. Let me know."

When Billy got back to the table, Robin and Jason were talking. He took his seat.

"I was just telling Robin that you also resolved a complicated real estate foreclosure case that I referred to you. The case was impossible. I don't know how you pulled that off. At any rate, Seymour called and profusely thanked me for referring him to you."

"Oh well. I didn't do much more than get in the way, and the thing resolved itself."

"Modesty isn't your strong suit, Tapp."

Billy's cell phone vibrated again. Another text message from Ann: "i'll think bout it. call me in am."

"Why don't you and your friends join us?" Billy asked Robin.

"If you're still here when they leave, I will," she said.

Jason smiled at Billy. "You know Billy, you ought to consider getting hooked up with one of the big firms in town. You're squandering your ability."

"You might be right, but it's my ability and I'll squander it any way I want to."

Billy motioned for another pitcher of beer and waved at Robin Grigsby, who had taken a seat at the table with her friends, positioned so she wouldn't have to turn in her chair to see Billy's table.

EPILOGUE

Billy climbed the long stairway, which landed in the hallway leading to the library on the second floor. A dim light that reflected on the wall to his left showed through the double doors that opened onto the balcony off the far side of the library. He tossed his coat on the couch and shuffled into the bar between the library and the living room. He opened a beer and flipped on the CD player. Pink Floyd, in mid-song, boomed over the speakers. He took a swig of the beer and gazed at his reflection in the beveled mirror on the back bar. He grabbed the open bottle of Don Julio Blanco and took a slug of tequila.

"Ariba!," he yelled.

He moved back toward the double doors where the light also played a faint shadow on the floor. As he moved toward the paneled wall, the light grey ghost of his shadow followed him on the floor and then appeared in full on the wall. He stopped and formed a dragon silhouette with both hands.

He snickered and whispered, "Welcome to the machine."

He pulled off his neck tie and shirt and began an unsteady dance with the grey ghost. He took a slow roundhouse swing in the air and began moving in a circle. He punched and punched, dodged and feigned and lunged at the wall. He kicked at the image that parroted his every move. Faster and faster, around and around, back and forth. Unable to slip the ghost that followed every thrust and swing of his assault that, as if mocking his flailing, didn't show the tortured grin that glistened from the sweat that covered his face and stung his bloodshot eyes.

ABOUT THE AUTHOR

Charles W. Arnold is a Lexington, Kentucky, lawyer and member of the Fayette County and Kentucky Bar Associations. He received his B.A. degree in chemistry from the University of Kentucky in 1967 and in 1970, he earned his Juris Doctor degree from the University of Kentucky College of Law.

With nearly fifty years of experience in the practice of law, Mr. Arnold is a partner with Arnold & Miller PLC, a law firm in Lexington. His practice areas include: Aviation, Civil Rights, Construction, Criminal Defense, Family Law, General Litigation, Labor and Employment, Medical Malpractice, Personal Injury and Wrongful termination.

47144906R00194

Made in the USA
Middletown, DE
05 June 2019